P9-DFP-483

THE FINAL
ENCYCLOPEDIA

Volume

> >TWO< <

Tor Books by Gordon R. Dickson

Gordon R. Dickson

THE FINAL ENCYCLOPEDIA

Volume

> >TWO< <

ORB

A Tom Doherty Associates Book
New York

This is a work of fiction. All the characters and events portrayed in this novel are either fictitious or are used fictitiously.

THE FINAL ENCYCLOPEDIA: VOLUME TWO

Copyright © 1984, 1997 by Gordon R. Dickson

All rights reserved, including the right to reproduce this book, or portions thereof, in any form.

This book is printed on acid-free paper.

An Orb Book
Published by Tom Doherty Associates, Inc.
175 Fifth Avenue
New York, NY 10010

Tor Books on the World Wide Web:
http://www.tor.com

Design by Basha Durand

Library of Congress Cataloging-in-Publication Data

Dickson, Gordon R.
        The final encyclopedia / Gordon R. Dickson.
        p.   cm.
        "A Tom Doherty Associates book."
        ISBN 0-312-86188-5 (v. 2)
        1. Dorsai (Imaginary place)—Fiction.   I. Title.
PS3554.I328F56   1997
813'.54—54—dc20   96-29217
                                                            CIP

First Orb Edition: February 1997

Printed in the United States of America

0 9 8 7 6 5 4 3 2 1

The **Final Encyclope**dia, *and the Childe Cycle of books of which it is a part, are dedicated to my mother, Maude Ford Dickson, who in her own way in ninety-five years has achieved far greater things.*

The Worlds of
The Childe Cycle

- **●** Planet
- **O** STAR
- **− − −** *Distance from Sol in light years (not to scale)*

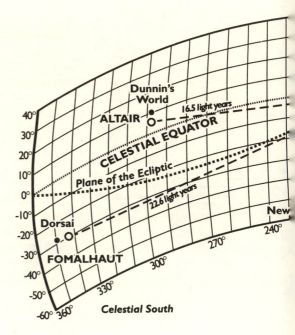

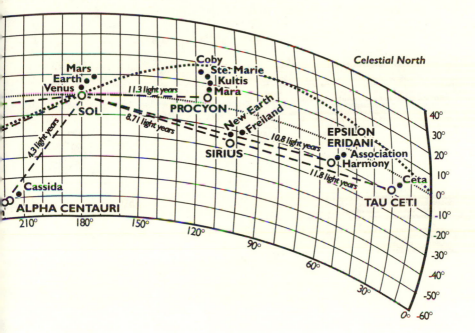

THE FINAL
ENCYCLOPEDIA

Volume

> >TWO< <

Chapter

> > **38** < <

Hal lay, his long body clad in a yellow Exotic robe, listening to the interweaving of the melody of birdsongs with the sound of a fountain beyond a screen of three-meter-tall, willow-like trees, to the left of the small, depressed sitting area, like a conversation pit, in which he was resting. The harmony that existed in all surroundings created by Exotic minds was soothing to the remnants of a tension that still lived deep inside him. Above, either blue sky or that same sky with a weather screen between himself and it, flooded everything about him with the distant, clear light of Procyon A. That sun shared its energy not only with this world of Mara, but with its twin Exotic planet of Kultis, as well as with the smaller inhabited worlds of Sainte Marie, half again the distance of Mara out from that sun, and Coby.

He had been reading, but the capsule had dropped from his fingers into his lap, and the words printed on the air before him had vanished. He felt soaked through by that dreamy lethargy that continues to stain for days human bodies recovering from severe illness or great and prolonged physical effort; and his present surroundings, one of those Exotic homes in which it was often uncertain as to whether he was indoors or out, lent itself to a feeling that all eternity was available in which to do anything that needed to be done. At the same time, with the recovering of his strength, a note of urgency, that had kindled in him in the Militia cell, had been growing in insistence.

Something in him had sharpened. He had aged swiftly, these last few weeks. He was not likely now to imagine—as he might have, six months earlier—that the Exotics had smuggled him off Harmony to Mara, here, merely out of kindness or because of a private concern on Amid's part. In principle, the Exotics were kind; but, above all, they were practical. There would be further developments resulting from all this care and service; and, in fact, he welcomed them, for he, himself, had things to talk to his hosts about.

He had not seen Amid except for a few brief visits since he had arrived here, at Amid's home. Before that, from the moment in which he started off-Harmony, his contact had been almost solely with a woman named Nerallee, OutBond to Consulate Services on Harmony. She had been his companion and nurse on the voyage here. Lately now, as he had grown stronger, Nerallee had been less and less in evidence. He felt the sadness of a loss, realizing that she must, of course, soon be returning to her duties on that Friendly World; and that there was little likelihood that he and she would ever meet again.

He lay now, reconstructing the ways by which he had got here. When the door of the Exotic Consulate in Ahruma had opened for him, those within had simply led him to a room and let him sleep for a while. His memory recalled no drugs given to him; but then, while the Exotics had no objection in principle to using pharmacological substances, they preferred to do so only as a last resort. More to the point, he could remember no specific treatment or manipulation of mind or body. Only, the bed surface beneath him had been exactly of the proper texture and firmness, the temperature had been exactly as he would have wished, and the gently moving air about him had been infinitely warm, soft, and enfolding.

He had woken, feeling some return of strength. Staff members of the Consulate had given him quantities of different, pleasant liquids to drink, then padded and dressed him to resemble the tall, portly Exotic who had greeted him at the door.

Nerallee had been involved with him from the first moment; and it was Nerallee who had finally accompanied him out of the Consulate to a closed, official vehicle. This had then delivered them through special diplomatic channels past the usual customs and passport checks, directly to an Exotic-owned ship in the fitting yards, where Nerallee and the supposedly ill Consulate member she had in charge were ushered aboard.

Hal could not remember the ship lifting from Harmony's surface. He did recall the first few ship-days of the trip, but only as long periods of sleep, interrupted only briefly by moments in which Nerallee was always with him and encouraging him to eat. He recovered enough, finally, to realize that she had never left him, ship's-night and ship's-day, from the beginning; and that whenever he had woken he had found her in the bed beside him. So, simply and easily, without consciously thinking about it, he had fallen halfway in love with her.

It was a small, wistful, transitory love, which both understood could not last beyond the short time they would have together. Clearly Nerallee was a Healer, in the Exotic tradition, and making herself totally available to him was part of her work. Clearly, also, she had fallen in love with him in return, finding something in him beyond what she had discovered in any other of those before who had needed her ability to repair their bodies, minds and souls—he read this in her even before she told him that it was so.

But, even with her experience and training, she found herself incapable of telling him what it was about him that was different, although they talked in depth about this, as well as many other things. It was part of the requirements of what she did, to open herself to those she ministered to as fully as she attempted to bring them to open themselves to her. One of the things she did tell Hal was that, like all those in her work, she grew—and expected to grow—within herself, with each new person she helped; and that if ever she should become unable to do this, she would have to give up what she did.

Even lying here, listening to fountain and birdsong after several weeks of almost constant association with her, Hal had trouble summoning up in his mind's eye a clear image of her face. Following nearly three hundred years of concern with genetics, there was no such thing as an Exotic who was not physically attractive in the sense of possessing a healthy, regular-featured face and body. But for what Nerallee looked like beyond that, Hal's physical perception had become too buried under his other knowledges of her to tell. She had seemed to him unremarkable, at first, almost ordinary-looking in fact, during their first few days together, but after that from time to time she had appeared to have worn so many different faces that he had lost count. Those faces had ranged from the most dramatic of beauties to a gentle, loved familiarity that washed all ordinary notions of beauty away—the familiarity that finds the faces of parents responded to so strongly by their very young children, or the appearance of a partner who has been close for so long that there is no single memory-picture possible and the person is simply recollected in totality.

But she had been able to do for him what he had so badly needed without having realized that he needed it—absorb his attentions so wholly that she could give him rest. A rest of the sort that he had not known since the death of his tutors. It had been what he had required at the time. But, with his strength now recovered, he was no longer in desperate need of it; and, therefore, Nerallee would be going elsewhere, to others who needed her.

He lay listening to the bird voices and the tinkle of splashing water.

After a while there was the faint scuff of foot-coverings on the floor above the conversation pit, behind him. He turned his head to see Amid coming down the three steps into the pit, to take a seat facing him, in what appeared to be a rock carved armchair-fashion. Hal sat up on the couch on which he had been lying.

"So, we're going to have a chance to talk, finally?" Hal said.

Amid smiled and folded the rust-colored robe he was wearing around his legs. On each of the half-dozen earlier occasions that he had appeared, the former OutBond had spent only a few minutes with Hal before leaving, on the excuse that he had a great deal to do.

"The business I've been occupied with," the small, wrinkle-faced old man said, "is pretty well taken care of now. Yes, we can talk as long as you like."

"Your business wouldn't have been caused by my visit here?" Hal smiled back at him.

Amid laughed out loud. In accordance with his age, the sound resembled a dry chuckle, rather than a laugh; but it was a friendly sound.

"You could hardly come to Mara," he said, "without involving us with the Others, even if indirectly."

"Indirectly?" Hal echoed.

"Indirectly, to begin with," said Amid. His face sobered. "I'm afraid you're right. For some days now it's been directly. Bleys knows you're here."

"Here? At this place of yours?"

"Only that you're on—possibly in this hemisphere of Mara," said Amid. "Your exact location on this world is something he'd have no way of finding out."

"But I take it he's putting on pressure to get all of you to give me up to him?" Hal said.

"Yes." Amid nodded. "He's putting on pressure; and I'm afraid we'd have to give in to him, if we kept you here long enough. But we don't necessarily have to react right away. For one thing, it'd be rather beneath the dignity of one of our worlds to give in at once to a demand like that, in any case."

"I'm glad to hear that," said Hal.

"But not particularly surprised, I take it," said Amid soberly. "I gather you realize we've got a particular interest in you, and things to discuss because of it?"

Hal nodded.

"I suppose you've connected me with the calculations Walter the In-Teacher had run on me when he first became one of my tutors?" he said.

"That," said Amid, "of course. Your records were flagged at that time as someone who might be of force historically. Consequently, a record was kept on you that went without interruption until the deaths of your tutors and your entrance into the Final Encyclopedia—"

"Kept with Walter's help?" Hal said.

Amid gazed at him for a moment.

"With Walter's help, of course," Amid answered calmly. "After his death and your entrance into the Final Encyclopedia, we lost you; and only traced you to Coby after Bleys' interest pointed you out to us, again. The fact that you've been able to keep out of his hands is, to say the least, remarkable; and it's that, primarily, that's raised our interest in you. Generally speaking, you're someone we've all been keeping an eye out for, lately. When it became obvious Bleys was making a serious effort to flush you out on Coby, we arranged for one of us to be on each of the ships available to you then for off-world escape. I was lucky enough to be on the one you took."

"Yes," said Hal. "I see. You're interested in me because Bleys is."

"Not because—for the same reason—Bleys is," said Amid. "We assume he wants you neutralized, or on his side. We want you made effective in opposition to him. But not just because he's interested in you. We're interested—we've always been interested—in you, simply because our ontogenetic calculations recommend an interest."

"A little more than recommend, don't they?" Hal asked.

Amid tilted his head a little to one side like a bird, gazing at him.

"I don't believe I follow you," he said.

Hal breathed slowly before answering. The lethargy was all gone out of him now. Instead there was a sort of sadness, a gray feeling.

"Bleys threatens the very existence of your Culture," he answered. "I suppose I ought to say that it's the Others who threaten its very existence. Under those conditions, don't your calculations do more than just recommend an interest in me? Or—let me put it a little differently. Is there anyone else they recommend an equal interest in, in that respect?"

Amid sat in the sunlight, looking at him.

"No," he said, at last.

"Well, then," said Hal.

"Yes," said Amid, still watching him. "Apparently you understand the situation better than we thought you did. You're barely into your twenties, aren't you?"

"Yes," Hal said.

"You sound much older."

"Right now," said Hal, "I feel older. It's a feeling that came on me rather recently."

"While you were on Harmony?"

"No. Since then—since I've had time to think. You talked about my staying out of Bleys' hands. I haven't been able to do that, you realize? He had me in a cell of the Militia Headquarters in Ahruma."

"Yes," said Amid. "But you escaped. I take it you've talked face-to-face with him, then, since the moment of your tutors' deaths?"

"I didn't talk to him at the time of my tutors' deaths," said Hal. "But, yes, a day or two before I got away he came to my cell and we talked."

"Can I ask about what?"

"He seems to think I'm an Other," Hal said. "He told me some of the reasons why he expects me to come over to their side in the end. Mainly, they add up to the fact that there's no other position that'll be endurable for me."

"And I take it you disagreed with him?"

"So far."

Amid looked at him curiously.

"You're not completely sure he isn't right?"

"I can't afford to be sure of anything—isn't that the principle you've always held to, yourselves, here on the Exotics?"

Amid nodded again.

"Yes," he said, "you're older than anyone would have thought—in some ways. But you did mail your papers to me. You did come to us for help."

"To the best of my knowledge I'm on the opposite side of Bleys and the Others," Hal said. "It's only sense to make common cause with those who're also opposed. I had a long time to think in that cell, under conditions where my thinking was unusually concentrated."

"I can imagine," said Amid. "You seem to have gone through a sort of a rite of passage, according to Nerallee."

"How much did she tell you?" Hal asked.

"That was all—essentially," said Amid. "She's got her personal responsibilities as a Healer; and, in any case, we'd rather hear what you wished to tell us about such things, in your own words."

"At least at first?" said Hal. "No, I've no objection to your knowing. When I talked to her, I assumed what I said was going to be made available to the rest of you, if you thought you needed to know it. Actually, what I went through isn't the important point. What's important is I came out of it with a clearer picture of the situation than—possibly—even you here on the Exotics."

Amid smiled a little. Then the smile went away.

"Anything's possible," he said slowly.

"Yes," said Hal.

"Then, tell me," said Amid. The old eyes, set deep in their wrinkles, were steady on him. "What do you think is going to happen?"

"Armageddon. A final war—with a final conclusion. A quiet war that, when it's over, is going to leave the Others completely in control; with the Exotics gone, with the Dorsai gone, with what was the Friendly Culture gone, and all progress stopped. The fourteen worlds as a large estate with the Others as landlords and no change permitted."

Amid nodded slowly.

"Possibly," he said, "if the Others have their way."

"Do you know any means of stopping them?" said Hal. "And if you do, why be interested in me?"

"You might be that means, or part of it," said Amid, "since nothing in history is simple. Briefly, the weapons we've developed here on Mara and Kultis are useless against the Others. Only one Splinter Culture's got the means to be effective against them."

"The Dorsai," said Hal.

"Yes." Amid's face became so devoid of life and motion for a second that it was more like a living mask than a face. "The Dorsai are going to have to fight them."

"Physically?"

Amid's eyes held his.

"Physically," he agreed.

"And you thought," said Hal, "that being raised as I've been—so that effectively I'm part Exotic and part Dorsai, as well as being part Friendly— I might be the one you'd want to carry that message to them."

"Yes," said Amid, "but not just that. Our calculations on you show you as a very unusual individual in your own right—it may be that you're particularly fitted to lead in this area, at this time. That would make you much more than just an effective messenger. You must understand how high some of us calculate your potential to be—"

"Thanks," said Hal. "But I think you're dealing in too small terms. You seem to be thinking of someone who can lead, but only under your direction. I can't believe that the Exotics, of all people, don't have a clearer picture of the situation than that."

"In what way?" Amid's voice was suddenly incisive.

"I mean," said Hal, slowly, "I can't believe you, of all people, have any illusions. There's no way what you've built here and on Kultis can survive in the form you know it. Any more than the Dorsai or the Friendly Culture can survive as they now are; whether the Others are stopped, or not. The only hope at all is to try to win survival for the whole race at whatever necessary cost, because the only alternative is death for the whole race—because that's what's going to happen if the Others win. It'll take them some generations, maybe, but if they win, in the end their way will end the human race."

"And?" The word was close to being a challenge from the small man.

"And so the only way to survive means facing all possible sacrifice," said Hal. "What is it you and your fellow Exotics would be willing to give up everything else to preserve—when it comes down to that?"

Amid looked at him, nakedly.

"The idea of human evolution," he said. "That, above all, mustn't die. Even if we and all our work in the past four centuries has to be lost."

"That, yes. I think ideas can be saved," said Hal, "if the race is going to be saved as a whole. All right, then. I imagine you've got a number of people you want me to meet?"

He stood up. Amid rose also.

"I believe," he said, "we've underestimated you."

"Perhaps not." Hal smiled at him. "I think I'll change clothes first. Will you wait a minute?"

"Of course."

Hal went back to his sleeping quarters. Among the clothing suspended there, cleaned and waiting for him, were the clothes he had been wearing on Harmony when he had knocked at the door of the Exotic Consulate. He exchanged them for the green robe he had been wearing and went back to Amid in the conversation pit.

"Yes, we did indeed underestimate you," the old man said, looking at the clothes when Hal returned. "You're much, much older than when I met you aboard the ship to Harmony."

Chapter

> > **39** < <

"*As it happens,*" said Amid, leading Hal through the pleasant maze of rooms and intervening areas that made up his home, "the people who want to talk to you are already here. While you were dressing, I called around and they were all available."

"Good," said Hal.

He strode along beside the much smaller man, holding his pace down to the one that age dictated for Amid. The self-restraint reminded him, suddenly, of how frail the other actually was. Amid must be far up in years, considering the state of Exotic medical science; nowhere near as old as Tam Olyn, of course, but old in any ordinary human terms.

"I've no idea," Amid said, "where your knowledge of our ways stops. But I suppose you know that, like the Dorsai, for all effective purposes we don't have governing bodies on Mara or Kultis. Decisions affecting us all become the concern of those in whose field they most clearly lie; and the rest of us, in practice, accept the decision those experienced minds come up with for the situation—though anyone who wants to can object."

"But they generally don't?" Hal said.

"No." Amid smiled up at him. "At any rate, the point is that the four people you're to talk to aren't political heads of areas or groups, but people whose fields of study best equip them to evaluate and interpret your capabilities. For example, my own study of the Friendly Worlds makes me particularly fitted to understand what you did, and what the results may be from what you did, on Harmony. The others are comparable experts."

"All in fields as applied to ontogenetics?"

"Ontogenetics underlies nearly everything we do—" Amid broke off. They had reached the entrance to what seemed to be less a room than a porch, or balcony, projecting out from a wall of the general house. Beyond the graceful, short pillars of a balustrade there was nothing visible but sky and the distant tops of some deciduous trees. Some empty chair-floats, but nothing else, were visible on the balcony. Amid turned to Hal.

"We're early," he said, "and that gives us a moment. Step across the hall with me."

He turned and led the way into a room with its entrance opposite that of the balcony. Hal followed, frowning a little. The neatness of the opportunity to tell him something was almost suspect. It could be sheer accident, as Amid had implied; or it could be that what the other was about to tell him was something that the Exotics had wanted him to know before they spoke with him, but something they had not wanted him to have too much time to think over beforehand.

"I should explain this, so you aren't puzzled by the fact that some of those you'll be talking to may seem to doubt you unreasonably." Amid closed the door behind them and stood looking up into Hal's face. "Walter the InTeacher taught you at least the elements of ontogenetics, I think you said?"

Hal hesitated. At fifteen, he would have answered without hesitation that he understood a great deal more than just the elements of ontogenetics. But now, standing at his mature height, after five years of life experience with a number of people on two strange worlds, standing face-to-face with a born Exotic, on Mara, he found a certain restraint in him.

"The elements, yes," he answered.

"You're aware, then, that ontogenetics is basically the study of individuals, in their impacts on current and past history, the aim being to identify patterns of action that can help us to evolve an improved form of human?"

Hal nodded.

"And you know," said Amid, walking over to a small, square table with a bare top, apparently carved of some light-colored stone, "that beyond its statistical base and its biological understandings, the work's always been highly theoretical. We observe, and try to apply the results of our observation, hoping that the more knowledge we can pile up the more clues we'll find, until eventually, we'll be able to see a clear pattern leading to the evolved form of humanity."

He paused, now standing beside the tabletop, and looked up at Hal again.

"I suppose you know it was our interest in that sort of piling up of knowledge that led us to supply most of the funds that made the building of the Final Encyclopedia possible; first as an institution in the city of St. Louis, on Earth, then as it is now, in orbit around that world. Though, as you also must know, neither the Exotics nor anyone else owns the Final Encyclopedia, now."

"I know," said Hal.

"Well, the point I wanted to make is that there're innumerable ways to graph individual potential."

Amid drew the tip of his forefinger from right to left on the tabletop beside him; and a black line sprang into existence in the light, stony material of the surface, following his touch. He crossed the line he had drawn with a vertical one at right angles to it.

"One of the simplest ways to graph ungauged genetic potential for the race at any given moment"—he drew another, horizontal line lifting at a small angle from the base line of the graph—"gives us what seems to be a slowly ascending curve. Actually, however, this line is only an average derived from a number of points scattered both above and below the base line, where the points above the line refer to historical developments clearly traceable to the action or actions of some individuals—"

"Like Donal Graeme and the fact he made a single legal and economic whole of the fourteen worlds?" said Hal.

"Yes." Amid looked at him for a moment, then went on. "But the points can also refer to much smaller historical developments than that; even to single actions by obscure individuals whom it's taken us several centuries to identify. However—below the baseline the points refer to individual actions that can only probably be linked in a cause-and-effect pattern, with the historical developments that concern us. . . ."

He paused and looked at Hal.

"You follow me?"

Hal nodded.

"As it happens," Amid turned back to his graph, "inevitably, when this sort of charting is done, we end up with certain individuals being represented by points both above and below the line. Individuals of developing historic effect will often be represented by points below the line before their effect emerges above the line, where their points show a clear relation between their actions and certain historical results. Points below the line, unfortunately, don't necessarily indicate the eventual emergence of points above, for any individual. In fact, points below the line are often achieved by individuals who never show any effect above the line at all."

He paused again, and looked at Hal.

"Now, all of this may mean anything or nothing," he said after the pause. "All work like this, as I said, is theoretical. The results we get this way may have nothing whatever to do with the actual process of racial evolution. However, it's only right that you know this sort of figuring, projected forward, is one of the ways we use to try and estimate the ontogenetic value of any given individual, and the probability of that person having an ability to influence current history."

"I see," said Hal, "and I take it that as of the present moment I'm one of those who charts out with points below the line but none above?"

"That's right," said Amid. "Of course, you're young. There's plenty of time for you to show direct influences on the present history. And your effects below the line so far are impressive. But the fact remains, that until you show some direct evidence above the line, your potential to do so remains only that, and estimates of what you may be able to perform in your lifetime are a matter of individual opinion, only."

He hesitated.

"I follow you," said Hal.

"I'd expect you to," said Amid, almost grimly. "Now I, myself, speaking from knowledge of my own particular specialty and seeing what you did in the short time you were on Harmony, estimate you as someone I expect to be highly effective—effective on a scale that can only be compared to that of Donal Graeme in his time. But this is only my opinion. I believe you'll find that some of those you're about to talk to may regard your potential as no more than possible, on the basis of the same calculations that cause me to think the way I do."

He stopped. For a moment, Hal ignored him, caught up by his own thoughts.

"Well, thanks," he said at last, rousing himself. "It's good of you to warn me."

"There's more," Amid said. "I mentioned earlier that you seemed a great deal older than I remembered you on ship to Harmony. As a matter of fact, this is something more than a subjective opinion on my part. Our recent tests of you show certain results that we've never found before, except in rather mature individuals—those middle-aged, at least. I was simply confirming this from my own feelings. But if you really are unusually mature, for some reason we can't yet understand, this could be something that might incline some who presently doubt to favor the opinion of someone like myself about your potential effectiveness, provided we can find an explanation for it. Can you think of anything to explain it?"

"When were these tests made?" Hal looked into the eyes of the small man.

"Recently," said Amid. His returning gaze was perfectly steady. "In the last few weeks."

"Nerallee?"

"It's part of her work," said Amid.

"Without mentioning to the person she's taking care of that she's making such tests?"

"You have to understand," said Amid, "a great deal may be at stake here. Also, as a matter of fact, knowledge that the tests are being made on the part of the subject could affect the results of the test."

"What else did she find out about me?"

"Nothing," said Amid, "that you don't already know about yourself. But I asked you if you had an explanation of these indications of an unusual maturity."

"I'm afraid not," said Hal, "unless being raised by three men all over eighty years old had something to do with it."

"Not in any way we can understand." Amid was thoughtful for a moment. An abrupt sweep of his hand above the table-surface erased the lines on it. "If you do think of any explanation while we're talking this afternoon, though, I suggest you mention it. It would, I think, be to your advantage."

"In what way?" said Hal.

Amid turned from the table and went toward the door of the room. Hal went with him.

"We'd be more inclined to trust you—and therefore to help you—with whatever you've got in mind," said the small man. "As I keep pointing out, there's something of a division of opinion among those of us who're responsible for making a decision on you. If you seem to be someone on whom we actually can pin our hopes of the future, that could be tremendously useful to you. On the other hand, if—as some of us think—the correct reading on you shows you as at best only a wildly-random factor in the present historic pattern, then our two worlds are going to be very reluctant to put ourselves at dependence on your possible actions."

He led the way through the doorway into the hall; and paused.

"Think about it," he said, and turned once more toward the door to the balcony. "The others are probably there by now. Come along."

Hal followed him. They went out of the room they had been in, crossed the hall and stepped onto the balcony, which now had two men and two women seated on it, in a semicircle facing the entrance. One of the men, wearing a sky-blue robe, was obviously very old; the other was a reserved-looking, thin man in a gray robe. Of the two women, one was small and black-haired, wearing green, while the other was taller and ageless, with bronze skin, curly brown hair, and an umber-colored robe. Two floats had been left vacant with their backs to the door, completing the circle; and it was to these that Amid led Hal.

"Let me introduce you," said Amid, as they sat down. "From left to right, you're meeting Nonne, Recordist for Mara—"

Nonne was the small, black-haired woman in green. She looked to be about in her mid-thirties, her face a little sharp-boned, and her eyes very steady on him.

"Honored," said Hal to her. She nodded.

"Alhonan of Kultis. Alhonan, Hal, is a specialist in Cultural interfacing."

"Honored."

"Very glad to meet you, Hal," said Alhonan, a narrow man, with a voice as dry and reserved as his appearance.

"Padma, the InBond."

"Honored," said Hal. He had not appreciated at first glance how old indeed the one called Padma was, but now he remembered Ajela's mention of this man. The Exotic face he looked at now was still relatively unwrinkled, the hands holding the ends of the armrests of his float were not extravagantly shrunken of skin or swollen of vein; but the utter stillness of the body, the unchanging eyes, and other signals too subtle to be consciously cataloged, radiated an impression of almost unnatural age. Here now, indeed, was a man to rival Tam Olyn in antiquity. And the title he bore was a puzzle. Hal had never heard of an InBond among the Exotics. Any one of them might be OutBond—assigned, that was—to some specific place or duty. But InBond . . . and to what?

"Welcome," said Padma; and his voice, neither unusually hoarse nor deep nor faint, seemed somehow to come from a little distance off.

"And Chavis, whose speciality is a little hard to describe to you," Amid was saying at his shoulder. "Call her a specialist in historical crises."

Hal had to tear his eyes away from the gaze of Padma to look at the woman in the umber robe with black markings of random shapes.

"Honored," he said to Chavis.

"I take that as a compliment," she said, and smiled. Her age could be anything between late twenties and early sixties; but her voice was young. "Time may show that it's you who're honoring us."

"Sit down," said Amid.

"That'd take some doing," Hal answered Chavis, as he took his seat. "I don't think I'm likely to find four Exotics like yourselves brought together on my account, except under very unusual conditions."

"But it's unusual conditions we've met to talk about here, isn't it?" said the voice of Amid from the float to Hal's left. The two of them sat facing the half-circle of the others. Still, the feeling was plain in the atmosphere of the balcony that Amid was not with Hal, but with those who confronted him.

It was a feeling that triggered another touch of sadness in Hal. With the memory of Walter the InTeacher still strong within him, of all the three Cultures with which he had grown up believing he had a strong kinship, the Exotics had been those from whom he had expected the most in the way of sensitivity and understanding. But he sat now, intellectually almost at swords-points with those before him. He could feel their concern, first for the survival of their own way of life; and only secondarily with his own interest in the race as a whole. The thought came instinctively to him that it was a rarefied sort of selfishness they were displaying—a selfishness, not for their personal sakes, but for the sake of the principle to which they and their Culture had always dedicated their people. It was a selfishness he would have to bring them to see beyond, if there was to be any hope of racial survival.

Looking at the faces around him, Hal's innate confidence in his cause sagged. It might be true, as Amid had said, that tests had shown him to have unusual qualities of maturity. But at the present moment he sat facing a total of several centuries of living and training in those facing him. To deal with all that, all he had to show were twenty years of life-experience, and perhaps sixty hours of intense thought under conditions of exhaustion and high fever.

"How much do you know about the history of the crossbreeds in general?" Nonne's voice roused him from his emotions. Her voice was a very clear contralto. "I'm speaking specifically, of course, of crossbreeds from the Dorsai, Friendly and Exotic Cultures."

He turned to face her.

"I know they started to be noticed as appearing more frequently about sixty to seventy years ago—" he answered. "I know very little attention was paid to them as a group until about fifteen or twenty years ago, when they began to call themselves the Other People, show this charismatic skill of theirs, and put together their organization."

"Actually," said Nonne, "their organization began as a mutual-help agreement between two who were both Dorsai-Exotic crosses—a man named Daniel Spence and a woman named merely Deborah, after our own Exotic fashion—who were living together on Ceta, forty-two standard years ago."

"They were the first to call themselves 'Others,' " put in Alhonan.

Nonne glanced at him briefly. "Like most close partnerships among the crossbreeds," she went on, "the physical association didn't last; but the agreement did, and it grew rapidly over the next five years until there were over three thousand individuals involved—an estimated seventy-nine per cent of all crossbreeds from the three major Splinter Cultures who were in existence at that time. Both Spence and Deborah are now dead; and the current top leader of the organization for the past twelve years has been a man named Dahno, who led the meeting of Other leaders at your home, the time your tutors were killed."

"I saw him then, through a window," said Hal. "A big, heavy-bodied man—not fat, but heavy-bodied—with black, curly hair."

"That's Dahno," said Alhonan, in a precise, remote voice.

"We've been told that he was the son of Daniel Spence and Deborah," said Nonne. "And that Bleys was taken in by their family as a boy of about eleven, a bit younger than Dahno. Further evidence indicates he may have been a nephew of Daniel Spence, left with relatives on another world—possibly Harmony—to raise."

"Do you believe this?" said Hal.

"There may be more to it than that," Nonne said. "Frankly, there are reasons to suspect that some false information has been planted in the records on various worlds. And it's even possible that Bleys himself doesn't know the full truth about his past—many of these crossbreed families have been very unstable."

"In any case," Alhonan said, "Bleys is a powerful leader. Clearly more brilliant than Dahno; he seems to prefer that Dahno wear the mantle of supreme leadership. You've met Bleys."

"Yes," said Hal. "Three times, now; and I talked to him this last time, when I was in that prison cell on Harmony. Dahno, I saw only once, that first time; but my own feeling is that you're right. Bleys is more capable, and more intelligent—both."

"Yes," said Chavis, softly. "In fact, we've wondered exactly why he seemed content with second place. My own guess has been that he simply doesn't have any great desire to lead."

"Perhaps," said Hal. "Or he could be biding his time." Like the dark shadow of a cloud, sweeping briefly over his mind, the feverish memory returned of Bleys, seeming to tower enormously above him as he had lain on the cot in the Militia prison. "But if he's better than Dahno, he'll have to lead, in the end. He won't have any choice."

There was a moment of silence from those around him that stretched out noticeably before Nonne broke it.

"So, you think," she said, "that it'll be Bleys we'll be dealing with in the long run?"

"Yes," said Hal. A wing of the dark cloud still shadowed his mind. "Even if he has to remove Dahno himself."

"Well," said Nonne. There was a dry briskness in her voice; and he roused himself to give her his full attention, putting the shadow from him. "In any case, we've ended up facing something we're not equipped to handle. There was a time when to any of us here the thought of any socio-logical development arising that we couldn't control would have been unthinkable. We know better now. If we'd moved to control the cross-breeds even two decades ago, we might have succeeded. But some of us were blinded by the attractive hope that they might be the first wave of that evolutionary development of the race we've looked and worked for so hard, during the past four centuries."

She gazed at Hal grimly.

"I was one of the blind," she said.

"We all were," the distant voice of Padma broke in.

Again, there was a silence that lasted a fraction of a second longer than Hal felt was normal.

"However, the end result's been the emergence of a historical force, in the shape of the Others, for which our current interstellar civilization's got no counter and no control," Nonne went on. "Organized interplanetary crime was always something that the sheer physical difficulties and expense of interplanetary travel made impractical. It'd still be impractical for the Others, except for the fact that some of them have developed this charismatic skill—"

"If only some can manage it, it needs to be called an ability rather than a skill, doesn't it?" Hal asked, suddenly remembering once more Bleys looming over him in the cell. . . .

"Perhaps," said Nonne. "However—skill or ability, it's what makes the organization of the Others effective. With it, even the relative handful of them can manipulate key figures in governments and planets. This gives them political power and financial reserves we can't match. It isn't even necessary for more than a large minority of those in their organization to have this charismatic ability, although they seem to be able to teach it to each other, and even to some of their followers—which, come to think of it, answers your question about why we call it a skill rather than an ability—"

"I take it, then, that you haven't been able to duplicate it among your own people here on Mara and Kultis?" Hal interrupted.

Nonne stared at him, her lips closed in a straight line.

"The apparent techniques involved are all Exotic ones," she answered. "It's simply that the Others seem to be able to use them with increased effectiveness."

"The point I'm making—" said Hal, "is that they can do something that you here on the Exotics can't seem to duplicate. Doesn't that sound like something based on a particular ability?"

"Perhaps." Nonne's stare was immovable.

"I say that because I think I may be able to tell you why they can," Hal said. "I'm beginning to believe that behind their use of those techniques you mention there's a force in operation that's been cultivated only in the Friendly Culture—the drive to preach, to proselyte. Take a look at those followers you mention who've been able to pick up and use some of what you see a minority of Others using. I'll bet you don't find one of them who wasn't either a product of the Friendly Culture to begin with, or the child of at least one parent who was."

There was another fractionally too long silence.

"An interesting point," said Nonne. "We'll look into it. However—"

"If I could get a native of Harmony or Association to come to you for training," persisted Hal, "would you be willing to see if you could develop that person into a charismatic of the Other level?"

Nonne and the others traded glances.

"Of course," said Padma. "Of course."

"We'd be glad to," said Nonne. "You mustn't think that we're indifferent to what you may be able to suggest to us, Hal. It's simply that time's a factor. We're under strong pressure from Bleys to give you up; and we're either going to have to do that or get you off the Exotics very shortly. In that short time we've got things to talk to you about; and it's to all our advantages if we stick to the point."

"I think what I've been trying to get at is at least involved in the point," answered Hal. "But go on."

"What I'm trying to do here," Nonne said, "is lay out the situation and its history. That, and make sure you understand what our basis for concern is, and what we'd like to do about the situation."

"Go on," said Hal.

"Thank you. Wherever the charismatic skill or ability comes from, the fact remains, it's the key to the Others' success. They can't use it, of course, to control us—or the Dorsai people, or at least some of the Friendlies. In addition, a certain percentage of people everywhere seem to be resistant; particularly most of those on Old Earth, for reasons we haven't identified. But if they can use it to control a majority of the race, that's all they need to do. As I started out by saying, our present civilization on the fourteen worlds hasn't any counter to that ability. The result is, the Others have grown in power and wealth to the point where they can win, economically, even against us. They've simply got too many chips to play with. Our two worlds alone can't match their resources in the interplanetary marketplace. As a result, Mara and Kultis are slowly becoming economic captives of theirs, even though they've made no direct move to dominate us—yet."

Nonne paused. Hal nodded.

"Yes," he said. "Go on."

"The point I keep making is," Nonne said, "we can't do anything to stop them. The worlds they already control obviously aren't going to stop them. Old Earth's people have never all gotten together on anything in their history; and, since they're largely immune to the charismatic influence, themselves, they'll probably simply continue to ignore the Others until they wake up one day to find themselves surrounded by thirteen other worlds, all under crossbreed control, and with no choice but submission. The Friendlies are already half-conquered; and it's only a matter of time until the natives the Others control on Harmony and Association dominate those two worlds completely. That leaves the Dorsai."

Once more Nonne paused.

"As you say," said Hal, soberly, "it leaves the Dorsai, which is slowly being starved to death for lack of off-planet work opportunities for its people."

"Yes," said Alhonan, "but—forgive me, Nonne, but this is my department—such starvation takes time; and that's one world the Others aren't at any time going to try to take over by force. They might be able to do it in the long run, but the cost wouldn't be worth it. In fact, if the Dorsai would be willing to settle temporarily for being a backward planet, lacking the technological and other advantages that dealing with the other settled worlds would give them, they could settle down to a meager but independent existence for a century or more, living on what the oceans and the small land surfaces of their world could provide them. And they're just stubborn enough to do that."

"In other words," said Nonne, swiftly, "for the Dorsai there's still time to act, and that's important; because of all the Splinter Cultures, they alone still have the capability to stop the Others. In fact, they've got the ability to remove the threat of the Others, completely."

She stopped speaking. Hal stared at her; and the longest of any pause that had occurred so far held the balcony.

"What you're suggesting," he said at last, "is unbelievable."

Nonne looked back at him without answering. Glancing around the circle, Hal saw the others all similarly sitting, waiting. "What you're suggesting is a Dorsai campaign of assassination," Hal said. "That's what you mean, isn't it? That the Dorsai eliminate the Others by sending individuals out to murder them? They'd never do that. They're warriors, not assassins."

Chapter

> > **40** < <

Chavis, *after a* long moment, was the one who spoke.

"We're prepared," she said, softly, "to do anything in our power—to give them anything they need or want that we have to give, without reservation, including our lives. If we'll do that much to stop the Others, surely they can put principle aside this once, for this great need?"

Hal looked at her. Slowly, he shook his head.

"You don't understand," he said. "It's the one thing they'd never do, just as you'd never give up your faith in human evolution."

"They might," it was the voice of Padma, speaking across the great reach of years to him, "if you convinced them to do it."

"I convince them—?" Hal looked at them all.

"Can you think of any other way to stop the Others?" Nonne asked.

"No! But there has to be another!" Hal said to her, violently. "And what makes you think I could convince them to do anything like that?"

"You're unique," she said. "Because of your upbringing. In effect, you can speak the emotional languages of all three of our largest Splinter Cultures—"

Hal shook his head.

"Yes," said Nonne. "You can. You proved that on Harmony, when you fitted in with one of the resistance groups there. Do you really think the native Friendlies in Rukh Tamani's Command would have taken you in, or kept you for more than a day or two, unless they felt, instinctively, that at least part of you was capable of thinking and feeling as they did?"

"I wasn't that accepted by them," said Hal.

"Are you so sure?" put in Amid beside him. "When I talked to you aboard the ship going to Harmony, you could have convinced me you were a Friendly, for all that you knew less about their history and society than I did. There's a particular feel to Friendlies, just as people of other Cultures tell us there is to Exotics, and as everyone knows there is to the Dorsai. Recognition of that Friendly feel is something I've spent a lifetime acquiring, and I don't make mistakes now. You felt to me like a Friendly."

"You also," said Alhonan, "feel to all of us like an Exotic. And to the extent of my specialty, you also feel to me like a Dorsai."

Hal shook his head.

"No," he said. "I'm none of these, none of you. The fact is, I don't be-long anywhere."

"Do you remember," said Amid, against his ear, "a moment ago, when you first understood what Nonne was suggesting the Dorsai do about the Others? You answered right away that the Dorsai wouldn't do it. Where did you get the certainty you felt in telling us that? Unless you, yourself trust yourself to think like a Dorsai?"

The words rang with uncomfortable persistence in Hal's mind. They also, without warning, touched off a sudden, inexplicable, deep sadness inside him; so that it was a moment before he got control of his feelings enough to go on. He made an effort to think calmly.

"It doesn't matter," he said, finally. "The idea of Dorsai individuals as-sassinating the Others, one by one, aside from anything moral or ethical about it, is too simplistic a solution. I can't believe I'm listening to Ex-otics—"

"Yes, you can," interrupted Amid. "Check the Exotic part of yourself."

Hal went on talking, refusing to look at the small man.

"—Whatever else the Others are, they've emerged as a result of nat-ural forces within the human race," he went on. "Attempted genocide's no answer to them, any more than it ever was for any situation like this, as long as historic records've run. Besides, it ignores what's really going on. Those same forces that produced them have been building to this mo-ment of confrontation for hundreds of years."

He paused, looking at them all, wondering how much of what he now felt and realized could be made clear to them.

"When I was in that cell on Harmony," he went on, "I had a chance to think intensively under some unusual conditions; and I'm convinced I ended up with a clearer picture of what's going on historically, right now, than a great many people have. The Others pose a question, a question we've got to answer. It's not going to work just to try to erase that ques-tion and pretend it was never asked. It's our own race that produced the crossbreeds—and their Other organization. Why? That's what we've got to find out—"

"There's no time left for that sort of general investigation, now," said Nonne. "You, of all people, ought to know that."

"What I know," said Hal, "is that there has to be time. Not time to burn, perhaps, but time enough if it's used right. If we can just find out why the Others came to be what they are, then we'll be able to see what the answer is to them; and there's got to be an answer, because they're as human as we are, and the instincts of a race don't lead it to produce a species that could destroy it—without some strong reason or purpose. I tell you, the Others were developed to test something, to resolve something; and that means there has to be an answer to them, a solution, a resolution that'll end up doing much more than just taking off our backs what looks now like a threat to our survival. If we can only find that answer, I'm sure it'll turn out to mean more to the whole race than we, here, can begin to imagine."

He felt his words dying out against the silence that answered him, as calls for help might die against a wall too thick for sound to penetrate. He stopped talking.

"As Amid's pointed out," said Nonne after a moment, "you react in part like an Exotic. Ask the Exotic part of yourself, then, which of two answers is most likely to be right—the conclusions you've come to on your own? Or the unanimous conclusion of the best minds of our two worlds, on which the best minds have been sought out and encouraged for nearly four hundred years?"

Hal sat, silent.

"We could, however, ask Hal what alternative he sees," said Padma.

For the first time Nonne turned directly to face the very old man.

"Is there any real point to it?" she asked.

"I think so," said Padma; and in the pause following those three words of his the silence seemed to gather in on itself and acquire an intensity it had not had until this moment. "You talked about being one of those who were seduced and blinded by the hope that the crossbreeds were what we had looked for, these hundreds of years. Your fault in that was much less than mine, who'd watched them for more years than any of you, and was in even a better position than anyone else to see the truth. I, for one, can't risk being seduced a second time, and blinded by our own desire for a quick and certain solution—a solution which Hal has properly called simplistic."

"I think—" began Nonne, and then fell quiet again as Padma raised his hand briefly from his lap.

"Not only did I make the mistake of assuming the crossbreeds were something they weren't," he said, "unlike the rest of you, I made another mistake, one that still haunts me. We Exotics had the chance, and closed our eyes to it, to find out if Donal Graeme was a real example of evolutionary development. Now, too late, I'm convinced he was. But he was never checked; and we could have had that done at any time in the last five years of his life. If we had only done that much, we'd have been able to read him positively, one way or another. But we failed; and the result was that the chance he might have offered us, eighty standard years ago, was lost forever when he was. I don't want to make another mistake like that."

The other Exotics looked at each other.

"Padma," said Chavis, "what's your personal opinion of Hal's potential, then?"

The intensity that had come into the room a moment before when Padma had spoken was still there.

"I think he may be another like Donal Graeme," he said. "If he is—we can't afford to lose him; and in any case, the least we can do is listen to him, now."

The eyes of the other four robed individuals consulted once more.

"We should, of course, then," said Nonne.

"Then—?" Chavis glanced around at the others, all of whom nodded. "Go ahead, Hal. That is, if you've got something specifically to suggest that's a workable alternative to our ideas."

Hal shook his head.

"I don't have any answers," he said. "I just believe they can be found. No, I know they can be found."

"We haven't found any," said Alhonan. "But you think you can?"

"Yes."

"Then," said Alhonan, "isn't what you're asking just this—that our two worlds should trust you blindly; and blindly take on all the risks a trust like that implies?"

Hal took a deep breath.

"If you want to put it in those terms," he said.

"I don't know what other terms to put it in," replied Alhonan. "But you do think you, alone, can solve this; and we should simply follow you wherever you want to take us?"

"I've got nothing else to think." Hal looked at him squarely. "Yes."

"All right," said Chavis, "then tell us—what would you do?"

"What I decided to do in that cell on Harmony," said Hal. "Learn what's involved for the race in this situation, decide what's to be done, then try to do it."

"Calling on us for whatever help you need," said Alhonan.

"If necessary—and I'd say it will be," Hal said. "You, and any others who also want a solution."

The four before him looked at each other.

"You'll have to give us a specific reason," said Chavis, gently. "You must have a basis for this belief of yours. Even if there's something there for you to find, What is the reason why you should be the one to find it, when we haven't been able to?"

He gazed at her, then at Padma, and finally at Nonne and Alhonan.

"The fact is," he said, slowly at first but gaining speed and emphasis as he spoke, "I don't understand why you, with your ontogenetic calculations, don't see it for yourselves. How is it you can't recognize what's under your noses? All that's needed is to look—to stand back for a moment and look at the last five hundred years, the last thousand years, as a whole. It's people building forward—always forward—that makes history. The interaction of their individual forces—conflicting, opposing, mingling and finding compromise vectors for their impinging forces; like an orchestra with millions of instruments, each trying to play a part and each trying to be heard in its own part. If the brass section sounded as if it was dominating the rest of your orchestra, would your solution be no more than eliminating the brass section?"

He paused, but none of them answered.

"That's exactly what you're suggesting, with your idea of setting the Dorsai to destroy the Others," he said. "And it's wrong! The orchestra as a whole's got a purpose. What has to be done is find why the brass section's too prominent; and from that knowledge learn to use the whole orchestra better. Because it's not happening by accident—what you hear. It's a result, an end product of things done earlier, things done with a purpose that you haven't yet understood, that the individual players even in the brass section don't themselves understand. It's happening for a reason that has to be found; and it won't be found by anyone looking for it who doesn't believe it's there. So I suppose that's why it has to be me who goes looking for it—not you; and that's why you'll have to trust me until I do find it, then listen when I tell you what needs to be done."

He stopped at last. The three other faces before him turned to Padma. But Padma sat without saying anything, with no expression on his calm face that would indicate his opinion.

"I think," Chavis said, carefully, "that at this point we might do better to talk this over by ourselves, if Hal doesn't mind leaving us."

Beside Hal, Amid was getting to his feet. Hal also rose, and Amid led him from the balcony. They went left along the hall to a down-sloping ramp, that let them out into a garden which plainly lay below the balcony where the others still sat. A tall hedge enclosed a small pool and fountain, surrounded by deeply-hollowed blocks of stone, obviously designed as seats.

"If you don't mind waiting alone," Amid said, "I'm one of them, and I ought to be up there with them. I'll be back, shortly."

"That's fine," said Hal, seating himself in one of the stone chairs with its back to the balcony. Amid left him.

The gentle sound of splashing water amid the otherwise silence of the garden enclosed him gently. Looking back over his shoulder and up, he could see the balustrade of the balcony: but the angle of his view was too steep for him to see even the tops of the heads of those still there. By some no-doubt-intentional trick of acoustics, he could hear nothing of their voices.

He looked away from it, back to the leaping water, a jet rising from the center of the pool some fifteen feet in the air before curving over and breaking into feathery spray. Curiously, a feeling of defeat and depression lay like a special darkness upon him.

His thoughts went back to the moment in his cell when he had suddenly broken through to an understanding of all things racial, enclosing him in that moment of his comprehension. The complete picture had been too immense for him to grasp all at once, then; and he still could not do it. During the past weeks he had explored the entity of that understanding section by section, as he might have explored some enormous picture inlaid upon a horizontal area too large to be seen from any one point on it. As he had explored, he had grown taller in knowledge; so that he could see more and more of it from a single point. But, even now, he could not begin to grasp the shape of it as a whole.

However, he could feel it as a whole. He was aware of its totality, the living moment of the great human creation he was now carefully examining, bit by bit.

Already, it had become almost incredible to him that the existence of something he could be so aware of, in its immensity, should not equally, overwhelmingly, be apparent to everyone else; above all, to seekers after understanding like Amid and the other four upstairs. How was it that the Exotics, all through the centuries of their existence, had never developed a special study of this great, massive forward progress of the race, that was the result of the interaction of every human individual with its fellows, along the endless road of time?

But they had, of course, he told himself. That was what ontogenetics had been intended to become. Only, apparently it had failed in its purpose. Why?

Because—the answer grew in him slowly out of his new awareness of what he now searched, and tried to understand—ontogenetics had been crippled from the start by an assumption that its final answer would be what the Exotics desired as an ultimate goal.

A feeling of depression, a sensation and an emotion such as he had encountered before, was born in him and grew, slowly, undramatically but undeniably. The one people he had counted on had been the Exotics, clothed in the colors of perceptivity and understanding he had found in Walter the InTeacher. Now, at last, he had been brought to doubt those qualities in them; and, doubting them for the first time, he came at last to doubt himself. Who was he to think that worlds of men and women should listen to him? The task on which he had so confidently launched himself from the cell loomed too great for any single human, even with all things made easy for him. He had little more than twenty years of life's experience to draw on. He was alone—even Amid stood on the other side of the barrier that separated him from all others.

The depression he felt spread to fill him and settle itself in the place of the certainty that had been so much a part of his nature until now. At its base was the dark logic of Bleys, now reinforced by the deaf ears to which he had just been speaking. He lost himself in wrestling with this new enemy and the fountain played. Time passed; and it was with a small shock that he was aware of Amid, once more at his elbow.

Hal got to his feet.

"No," said Amid, "no need to go back up. I can tell you what's been decided."

Hal looked at him closely for a second.

"Yes?" he said.

"I'm afraid we can't go along with you, blindly," Amid said. "I don't believe there's any reason not to tell you, though, that I argued for you as much as I could—as did Padma. And Chavis."

"That's three out of five," said Hal. "A majority in my favor?"

"Something more than a simple majority's needed in a situation like this," said Amid. "An element of doubt exists, and eventually we all had to fact that."

"In short, you all ended by deciding against me?"

"Padma took himself out of the decision." Amid looked up at him; and there was no apology on the small man's face. "I'm sorry you have to be disappointed."

"I'm not," said Hal, wearily. "I think I expected it."

"It's still open to you if you want," said Amid, "to be our representa-tive to the Dorsai. To go to them with our message to them as it was ex-plained to you. Perhaps you should take the opportunity, even if you don't agree with it. At least you'll be doing something toward dealing with the Others."

"Oh, I'll do it," said Hal. "I'll go."

Amid looked at him a little strangely.

"I didn't expect you'd agree so easily," he said.

"As you say," Hal answered, "I'll be dealing with the problem of the Others, even if not the way I'd planned to."

He was suddenly aware that he was smiling tightly. With an effort, he stopped.

"I'm surprised," murmured Amid. His eyes had never left Hal's face. "Just like that?"

"Perhaps with one condition," said Hal. "After I'm gone, will you remind Nonne and the rest that it was their own assessment that the forces at work right now aren't something I could control, and that they themselves told me time is limited?"

"All right," said Amid. He seemed to be on the edge of saying something more, when he apparently changed his mind and turned about.

"Come along," he said. "I'll help get you prepared and started on your way."

Chapter

> >41< <

A *brisk chime* commanded Hal's attention to the communications screen in one wall of his stateroom. The screen stayed blank, but an equally brisk feminine voice spoke from it.

"Give me your attention, please. Take your place in the fixed armchair by the bed and activate the restraining field. Control is the red stud on the right armrest of the chair."

He obeyed, a little surprised, aware that activating the field would register on a telltale in the control room, forward. But the order had caught him deep in his own thoughts and for the moment, automatically, he returned to them.

A corner, at least, of that dark shadow of defeat and depression, which had come to touch him in the garden below the balcony at Amid's home on Mara, had stayed with him through these five standard days of ship's time it had taken for his journey to the Dorsai. He had not met the woman who was evidently the pilot of this small courier-class vessel, on which he seemed to be the only passenger; and she had not come back from the restricted control area forward to make any sort of self-introduction. As a result, he had been free to think, uninterrupted, and there had been a great deal to think about.

Now, however, when they must be almost upon the Dorsai . . . he found those thoughts interrupted by the unusual demand that he put his body under control of a restraining field, something ordinarily requested of passengers only when their vessel was docking in space, as the jitney had been when it brought him to and into the Final Encyclopedia.

But this Dorsai light transport was no spaceliner, of course, and the commanders of Dorsai vessels had their own way of doing things, as all the fourteen worlds knew. He reached out and flicked on his room screen to see how close they actually were to going into a parking orbit.

What he saw made him sit up suddenly. They were indeed close enough to go into parking orbit. Blue and white, the orb of the Dorsai loomed large on his stateroom screen, the edge between night and day of the dawn terminator sharp below them. But, far from parking, the ship was still phase-shifting inward toward the surface of the world below. Even fifty years before, the psychic shock of a rapid series of shifts such as these would have required him to medicate himself in advance. But research at the Final Encyclopedia itself had found a way to shield from that shock. So there had been no warning.

It was a second before Hal recalled that the Dorsai—unlike pilots from other planets—had a habit of trusting themselves to shift safely right down into the atmosphere of any world on which they had good data; in fact, to within a few thousand meters of its surface. It was a skill developed in them as part of their normal training in ship-handling, as a practical matter of cutting jitney and shuttle costs on their far-from-wealthy world. The protective restraint was merely a routine precaution against some passenger panicking under such unusual approach maneuvers and getting hurt as a result. In fact, a moment later they came out of a series of very rapid, successive shifts with a jerk that would have thrown him from the chair, if the protective field had not held him anchored.

They were now no more than a thousand meters up, at most, and beginning to descend on atmosphere drive toward a spaceport misted with early morning rain under gray skies; a spaceport larger in area than the small city to which it was adjacent. Clearly, they were about to land at what Amid had earlier told Hal was the intended destination of the ship—the closest thing to a capital city that the Dorsai possessed. This was the city of Omalu, which housed the central administrative offices of the United Cantons, the districts into which the Dorsai had come to be organized for purposes of local self-government.

Actually, however, as Hal knew as well as the Exotics who had sent him here, these offices formed no more than a library and storage center for contractual records; and a contact point for discussion of matters that could not conveniently be discussed and settled locally in or between the cantons concerned. The Dorsai had even less than the Exotic Worlds in the way of a central government.

In theory, the cantonal officers had authority over the individuals and families living within the boundaries of the individual canton; but in actuality even this authority was more a matter of expressing local public opinion than otherwise.

Neighborliness—a word that held a special meaning on the Dorsai—was what made a social unit of this world. The cantons, even in theory, had only a courtesy relationship to the central administrative offices of each island on this world of islands, large and small. And the island offices did no more than communicate with the United Cantonal Offices here in Omalu. It was the only way a world could operate on which families, and individuals in those families, were constantly dealing on a direct and independent basis with off-planet governments and individuals scattered over all the other thirteen worlds.

Ironically, Hal had been sent out at Exotic expense to speak to representatives of a world which had no representatives, at least officially. It was ironic because the Exotics, who trusted nothing they could not test and identify, had in this case simply trusted the people of the Dorsai world to bring Hal somehow to those to whom he should speak.

But the spacecraft was now landing at the port, almost as precipitously and economically as it had phase-shifted to within a breath of ground level. As it settled down and became still, the sign winked out over the door. Hal shut off the restraining field. He got to his feet and collected a shoulder bag supplied and filled by Amid, and containing necessary personal clothes and equipment. Amid had reminded him—unnecessarily—that the Dorsai was one world where it was not always possible to buy suddenly-needed clothes and other personal necessities conveniently close at hand.

Leaving his stateroom, he had to squeeze his way past crates of Exotic medical machines of various sizes and complexity, stacked even in the central corridor of the craft. A majority of these were new, replacements for worn-out units in Dorsai hospitals; but a fair number were older machines which had been taken back to their designers on Mara for repair or the additions of improvements beyond the training of the local Dorsai technicians doing ordinary maintenance on them. There were even more of these filling the vessel than Hal remembered encountering when he had come aboard. It had been remarkable that a craft this small could lift from the surface, packed with this much cargo.

Finding his way out of the entry port at last, Hal stepped into the cloudy morning and the gusting rain above the landing pad. Descending the ramp to the pad, Hal found at the foot of it a tall, lean, middle-aged woman in gray coveralls, in brisk conversation with a lean-faced, older man riding a small hovertruck.

"—You'll need bodies!" she was saying. "The way that equipment's packed in there, you're not going to get it out alone, even with handlifters. Even the two of us can't do it. We're going to have to lift three things to get one clear enough for you to carry it off."

"All right," said the man. "Back in five minutes."

He turned his truck and slid off swiftly across the pad toward a blurred line of gray buildings in the distance. The woman turned and saw Hal. Saw him, and stared at him for a long moment.

"Are you Dorsai?" she said, at last.

"No," said Hal.

"I was about twenty meters away from you, over by the truck, unloading, when they took you on board," she said. "You moved like a Dorsai. I thought you were."

Hal shook his head.

"One of the people who raised me was Dorsai," he said.

"Yes." She stared at him for a moment more. "So, then, you've never had ship-handling. There ought to have been two of us on a trip like this, and I wondered why you didn't come up front and offer to give me a hand. But I had my own hands full; and when you didn't, I took it there was some reason you wanted privacy."

"In a way," said Hal, "I did."

"Good enough. If you couldn't help, you did just what you should have by staying out of my way. All right, no harm done. I made it here well enough by myself, and you're where you wanted to go."

"Not exactly," said Hal. "Foralie's where I wanted to go."

"Foralie? On Caerlon Island?" She frowned. "Those Exotics told me Omalu."

"They were assuming something," said Hal. "I'll be coming back to Omalu here, eventually. But for now, I want to go to Foralie."

"Hmm." The pilot glanced over at the buildings. "Babrak'll be back in a moment. He can give you a ride to the terminal and they can tell you there how you might get to Foralie. You'll probably have to change boats several times—"

"I was hoping to fly straight there," said Hal. "I've got the interstellar credit to pay for it."

"Oh." She smiled a little grimly. "Interstellar credit's one thing we can always use these days. I should have guessed you'd have some, since you came aboard on one of the Exotics. Well, as I say, Babrak'll be back shortly. Let's get in out of this weather; and meanwhile, how about giving me a hand clearing enough space just inside the entry port for him to get started?"

Less than two hours later, Hal was airborne in the smallest jitney-type space and atmosphere craft in which he had ever ridden. He sat side by side with the driver before the control panel; there were two more empty seats behind them, and beyond that only a small cargo space.

"It's about a third of a circumference," said the pilot, a thin, brisk, black-haired man of about thirty in a fur-collared jacket and slacks. "Take us something over an hour. You're not Dorsai, are you?"

"No," said Hal.

"Thought for a moment you were. Hold on." The jitney went straight up toward the upper edge of the atmosphere. The pilot checked his controls and looked over at Hal, again.

"Foralie Town, isn't it?" he said. "You know someone there?"

"No," answered Hal. "I've just always wanted to see Foralie. I mean, Foralie itself. Graemehouse."

"Foralie's the property. Graemehouse's the name of the house on it. Which is it, the property or the house you want to see?"

"All of it," said Hal.

"Ah."

The driver watched him briefly for a moment longer before returning his gaze to the stars visible above the far, curved horizon of the daylit surface below. The brilliant white pinpoint of the local sun, Fomalhaut, which had been before them during liftoff, began to rise in the windshield. "You didn't happen to have a relative who was a Graeme?"

"Not as far as I know," said Hal.

The dry tone in which he had unthinkingly answered had its effect. The driver asked no more questions and Hal was left in the dimness of the jitney's interior to his own thoughts once more. He sat back in his seat and closed his eyes. When he had been very young, one of his fanciful dreams had indeed been that his parents might have been related to the Foralie Graemes. But that sort of wishful thinking was long past now. The pilot's question had still managed to touch an old sensitivity.

However, now that he was actually headed toward Foralie, he found himself strangely uneasy with his decision to go there first, before doing anything else on the Dorsai. He had no sensible reason for making this trip now—only his early fascination with the history of the Graemes and the stories Malachi had told him of Ian and Kensie, Donal, and the others.

No, it had simply been that, darkened by the shadow which had come over him in the garden on Mara, he had felt a reluctance to move too swiftly here on the Dorsai—in his execution of the commission that Nonne and the other Exotics had asked him to undertake, or anything else; and in the face of that feeling, on the trip here, he had decided to do what he had always wanted to do since he had been a child, and that was see the Foralie which Malachi had so many times mentioned to him.

The deeper reason was less clear, but more powerful. It was that of all his dreams and fever-visions during the period in the cell, the one that still clung in his mind and moved him most strongly was the dream of the burial. Its events were solid and real in his mind even now—the tearing sorrow and the commitment. He did not need to hunt out points of evidence within that dream to know that it had been about some place and people on the Dorsai. To someone raised as he had been, the fact was self-evident—the very color and feel of what he had dreamed was Dorsai. So powerful had been its effect on him that he felt it like an omen— to be disregarded at his peril; and since Malachi had been the last of his own family, there was no place on that world to which Hal could relate strongly but the household of the legendary Graemes of which he had heard so much in his younger years.

It was true, he had always wanted to see the birthplace of the Graemes. But something more than that was at work in him, now—something beyond his present understanding of that vision of death and commitment—that was still hidden from his conscious mind and which drew him instinctively toward some place or time strongly Dorsai, for a fuller understanding.

Besides, it was curiously apt that he should go there now. Malachi, or the shade of Malachi which he had conjured up with those of Walter and Obadiah four years past at the Final Encyclopedia, had told him that there would be no reason for him to go to the Dorsai until he was ready to fight the Others. Well, he was at last ready to fight them; and it had been from the starting point of Foralie that Donal Graeme had gone in his time to gain leadership of the whole fourteen worlds. An almost mystic sense of purpose seemed to beckon Hal to the same place of beginning.

Also, he was in a mood that needed support, even mystic support. He had failed dismally to get the Exotics to listen to him or help him. There was no reason to expect the Dorsai to do more. In fact, considering the independence of its people on that harsh world, there was less reason. What had happened to him in Amid's garden as he had waited for their decision had been something outside his experience until that moment. A certain belief in himself with which he had emerged from the Militia cell on Harmony, and which he had then thought impregnable, had been struck and weakened by the blindness of the Exotic attitude.

It had not been merely the fact that they had not listened. That had been only the final assault that had breached the inner fortress of his spirit. But the breach had been made only after a number of recent blows that had already cracked and weakened what he had always thought was unbreakable in him. Where he had once taken for granted that whatever he defended was unconquerable, he now could see defeat as a real possibility.

Granted, there were excuses. The emotional pain of having to trick and abandon his friends in the Command, his illness at the time, his driving of his body far beyond its physical limits and, finally, his rite-of-passage—as Amid had referred to it—alone in the Militia cell, had all had their effect. Even the arguments of Bleys, which, even denied, had weakened him in preparation for this final blow that was the Exotic refusal to hear what he had to say. Of all peoples, he had expected the men and women of Mara and Kultis to understand, to recognize something once it was pointed out to them.

But knowing these things did not help. The grayness, the feeling of defeat remained. He looked at his life and could not see that from the start he had achieved anything. His early dreams, put to the test out on the worlds, had vanished like pricked soap bubbles.

Who was he to think that he was anything but a minor annoyance to the Others—a mouse dodging about under the feet of giants who would sooner or later crush him? He was nothing; not Friendly, not Exotic, not Dorsai. He had no reason even to believe that he had any claim to belong to Earth. That ship in which he had been found could have been coming from anywhere; and been headed to anywhere. What was this present trip to Foralie, but a clutching at a straw floated to the surface of his mind by a dream? He had no real proof that he was not, indeed, a crossbreed, as Bleys had said. He had no identity, no home, no people. He was a stranger in every house, a foreigner on every world, his only known family three old men who had been no actual relations; and even they had only been with him for the first, early years of his life.

He had wanted to stay at the Final Encyclopedia, and his feeling that he must strike back at the Others had driven him from it. He had found a way of life as a miner; then, to save his life, had been forced to run and leave that way of life behind. He had found friends, almost a family, in Rukh's Command; and he had deliberately made the choice to abandon them. The Exotics had had no place or use for him except as a messenger; and there was no hearth waiting for him here on the Dorsai, where there were not even relatives of Malachi's to sit with for a moment and tell about Malachi's death. To have found even one other person who could have shared his grief over the loss of Malachi and the others, would have strengthened him to bear the dry emptiness of his solitary position in the universe.

He drew a deep, slow breath. Long ago, Walter the InTeacher had told him how to deal with psychic pain like this; and he had remembered dutifully, if without great interest, seeing that the technique was for something that he could not imagine happening to him. Walter's instruction had been not to fight the depression and the self-condemnation, but to go with them and try to understand them. In the end, Walter had said, understanding could drain the destructive emotion from any situation.

He made an effort to do this now; and his mind slid off into a strange area, without symbols, where he seemed to feel himself tossed about by the vectors of powerful forces he could not see—like someone swept overboard from a ship in a hurricane. It went against his instincts not to fight these pressures; but Walter had emphasized the absence of resistance. Sitting in the thrumming near-silence of the jitney, hurling itself through the space where air and void meet, he forced himself into passivity, searching and feeling for some pattern to the situation that held him. . . .

"Going down now," said the voice of the pilot, and Hal opened his eyes.

They were back into the atmosphere, descending fast over what seemed open ocean. Then a point of darkness near the horizon became apparent, enlarging as the jitney fell in a long curve toward it, until it was clearly visible as land. A few moments later they were low above mountain meadows and stony peaks; and shortly thereafter they dropped vertically to earth, on a concrete pad at the edge of what had seemed to be a small village beside a river.

"Here you are," said the driver. He punched a control on the panel before him and the entry to the jitney swung open, steps sliding down and out to the pad surface. "Just head up that road there. Center of Foralie Town's beyond the trees and the housetops, there."

"Thanks," said Hal. He reached for his case of credit papers, then remembered he had paid for this trip before leaving Omalu. He got up, taking his shoulder bag with him. "Is there a central office or—"

"Town Hall," said the driver. "It's always in the center of town. Just follow that road in. You can't miss it and it'll have a sign out front. If you do get lost, ask anyone."

"Thanks again," said Hal, and left the jitney, which took off before he had covered half the width of the pad to the road the driver had indicated.

They had flown forward into mid-afternoon. No breeze stirred. The trees that the jitney driver had mentioned were variform maples, and the color on them spoke of autumn. But it hardly needed that to tell Hal of the time of the year in this part of the Dorsai; for the clear, clean light of fall spoke of the season in every quarter. Under an almost cloudless sky, the still air was scentless, cool in the shadow but hot in the sun. The shadows of the trees and, after a bit, the shadows of the wooden buildings when he had passed through the trees and found himself in the streets of Foralie Town itself, seemed hard-edged, they lay so crisply where the brilliant sunlight was interrupted. The colors of the houses glowed, clean and bright, as if all structures there had just been freshly washed and painted against the oncoming winter.

But the town itself was still and quiet, and the relative silence of it touched Hal strangely. He felt an emotion toward its houses and its streets that was an unusual thing to feel to a place never seen before. No one was in the streets through which he walked, although occasionally he heard voices through the open windows he passed. He came after a few moments to a central square; and facing him at the far end was a white building of two stories, its lower level half-sunken into the ground. There were two doors visible; one at the top of a flight of six steps to the upper story, the other preceded by a shorter flight, down to the floor below.

The white building plainly showed its difference in design from the obvious homes that fronted on the other three sides of the square. Hal went to it; and as he got close, he saw the word *Library* above the door to the semi-basement entrance. He went up the stairs to the higher door and touched its latch panel. It swung open and he entered.

Inside was a space about ten meters square, divided by a room-wide counter with a gate that marked off the back half of the space into an area with three desks and some office equipment. A thin, handsome boy about ten or twelve years old got up from one of the desks and came to his side of the counter as Hal walked up to the front of it. He stared at Hal for a moment, then visibly pulled himself out of his first reaction.

"I'm sorry," he said, "my aunt's the Mayor and she's out in the hills at the moment. I'm Alaef Tormai—"

He broke off, gazing at Hal penetratingly once more.

"You're not even Dorsai," he said.

"No," said Hal. "My name's Hal Mayne."

"Honored," said the boy. "I'm sorry. Forgive me. I thought—I thought you were."

"It's all right," said Hal. For a moment, a sort of bitter curiosity moved in him. "Tell me what made you think so?"

"I—" The boy hesitated. "I don't know. You just do. Only something's different."

He looked embarrassed.

"I'm afraid I'm not too good an observer. After I get through my training—"

"It's not you," said Hal. "A couple of adult Dorsai have already had to look twice at me to see what I was. What I'm hoping is to get up in the hills myself and take a look at Foralie. Not for any particular purpose. I've just always wanted to see it."

"There's no one there now," said Alaef Tormai.

"Oh?" Hal said.

"I mean, all the Graemes are off-world right now. I don't think any of them are due back for a standard year or so."

"Is there any reason I can't go up and look around, anyway?"

"Oh, no!" said Alaef, uncomfortably. "But there'll be no one home. . . ."

"I see." Hal thought carefully for a second about how to phrase his next question so as not to hurt the other's feelings. "Isn't there someone close to the Graemes I could talk to? Someone who might be able to show me around?"

"Oh, of course!" Alaef smiled. "You can go talk to Amanda. Amanda Morgan, I mean. She's their next-door neighbor. Fal Morgan's her homestead—do you want me to show you how to get there?"

"Thanks," said Hal. "I'll have to rent a vehicle."

"I'm afraid there's nothing in town here you could rent," said Alaef, frowning. "But that's all right. I can slide you up there on our skimmer. Just a minute, I'll call Amanda and tell her we're coming."

He turned to a screen on one of the desks and punched out call numbers on its deck of keys. A line of printing flooded across the screen in capital letters. Hal could read it from where he stood.

"GONE TO BRING IN THE BRUMBIES."

"She's gone after wild horses?" Hal asked.

"Not wild." Alaef turned back to him from the screen and looked embarrassed again. "Just the stock she's had running loose for the summer in the high pastures. That's what we mean when we say brumbies, here. It's time to bring them in to shelter for the winter. It's all right. We can go ahead. She's got to be back before dark; and she'll probably be home by the time we get there."

He started out the gate to Hal's side of the counter.

"What about the office?" Hal asked.

"Oh, that's all right," Alaef said. "This late in the day, no one's likely to come by. I'll leave word with my aunt on the way out of town, though."

Hal followed him out, and five minutes later found himself a passenger in an antique-looking ducted-fan skimmer being piloted up one of the slopes enclosing the valley that held Foralie Town, headed toward the high country beyond.

The sun was reaching down toward the mountaintops and a time of sunset, when they came at last over a little rise and Hal saw before them a high, open spot surrounded in front and on both sides by wooded gullies like the one from which they had just emerged; and, beyond that, having a small open field that lifted at the far end to a treed slope, enclosed by the omnipresent mountainsides. In the center of the open area stood a large, square two-story building with walls of light gray stone, accompanied by what seemed to be a long stable, some outbuildings and a corral, all of log construction.

"I guess she isn't back yet, after all," said Alaef, as he brought the skimmer up close to the house. "She's left her kitchen door ajar, though, to let people know she'll be right back."

The skimmer's fans died and the vehicle settled to the grassy earth outside the partly open door with a sigh.

"Do you mind if I just leave you here, then?" said Alaef, looking at Hal a little anxiously. "It's hardly polite, I know, but I told my aunt I'd be home in time for dinner. Amanda's got to get those brumbies in corral before sundown, so she'll be along at any minute; but if I wait with you I'll be late. You can just go in and make yourself comfortable."

"Thanks," said Hal, standing up from his seat in the open skimmer and stepping down onto the earth. "I think I'd just as soon stand out here and watch the sunset. You get on back; and thanks for bringing me up here."

"Oh, that's just neighborliness. Honored to have made your acquaintance, Hal Mayne."

"Honored to have made yours, Alaef Tormai."

Alaef started up the fans, lifted the skimmer on them, spun it about, waved and slid off. Hal watched him until the vehicle and youngster dipped into a gully and were lost from sight. He turned back to look at the sun.

It was touching the tops of the mountain range with its lower edge and the light was red and full. For a moment the color of it brought back a memory of another sunset with the red light upon the water of the private lake of the estate on which he had been brought up; a sunset-time in which he had been racing the edge of moving sun-shadow across the water and Malachi and Walter had been standing on the terrace of the house. . . .

He shivered, slightly. There was something stark and real about this Dorsai landscape that let the mind and the emotions run full out in any direction that beckoned them. He looked about once more at the edges of the tabletop of land on which he stood, alone with the Morgan house and outbuildings. If this Amanda was indeed sure to be in before dark, she would have to be putting in an appearance very shortly.

Barely a couple of seconds later, his ear caught a sound of distant whooping, followed by an increasing noise of hoofbeats and torn brush; and, as he watched, horses boiled up over the edge of one of the gullies, flanked by a blue-capped rider who passed them up and raced flat out before them toward Hal and the clump of buildings.

By this time, somewhere between a dozen and fifteen loose horses were up on the flat, being chivvied forward by two other riders, who looked to be no older than Alaef. Meanwhile, the one in advance had galloped to the corral and was unlatching and swinging open its gate, throwing one quick glance at Hal as she passed.

This, he thought, had to be the Amanda Morgan he was here to see, although she did not look much older than her two assistants. She was tall, with the breasts and body of a grown woman, in spite of her slimness; but an amazing litheness and an indefinable general impression of youthfulness made it hard for him to believe that she was much beyond her middle teens.

She swung the gate wide. The other two riders were already driving the loose horses toward the corral. These thundered past Hal at less than ten meters of distance. One gray horse with a white splash on its face balked at the gate, dodged and spun about, bolting toward Hal, the house and freedom beyond. Hal ran forward, waving his arms at full length on either side of him and shouting. The gray checked, reared, and dodged aside again only to find its way barred by one of the young riders, who turned it finally back into the corral.

They were all in, and the sun's upper edge disappeared as the gate was swung to and locked. Suddenly shadow and a breath of coolness flooded over all the level land. Amanda Morgan said something Hal could not quite catch to the two younger riders. They waved, swinging their mounts around, heading off at a canter in the direction from which they had come.

Hal, fascinated, watched them down into the gully and out of sight. He looked back, finally, to find Amanda dismounting in front of him. For the first time he got a good look at her. She was as square-shouldered as she was slim, dressed in tan riding pants, heavy black-and-white checkered shirt and leather jacket, with a blue, wide-billed cap pulled low over her eyes as if to still shade them against the direct sunset light that had now left them. Twilight filled the area below the surrounding mountains.

She took off the cap and he saw that her barely shoulder-length hair, gathered and tied behind her, was white-blond; her face was slim-boned and regular with a beauty that he had not expected.

"I'm Amanda Morgan," she said, smiling. "Who're you, and when did you get here?"

"Just now," he answered automatically. "A boy called Alaef Tormai from the Foralie Town Hall office brought me up on a skimmer. Oh, I'm Hal Mayne."

"Honored," she said. "You've got business with me, I take it?"

"Well, yes. . . ."

"Never mind," she said. "We can talk about it in a moment. I've got to put Barney here into the stable. Why don't you go into the living room and make yourself comfortable? I'll be with you in twenty minutes."

"I—thank you," he said. "All right, I will."

He turned and went in, as she led the horse off by its reins toward the long, dark shape of the stable.

Through the door, the interior air of the house was still, and warmer than the first night-coolness outside. The lights in the ceiling came on automatically and he saw he had stepped into a large kitchen. He turned right from it down a short corridor that had a large painting on one wall, apparently of the woman he had just met—no, he corrected his thought on stopping to examine it more closely, the woman pictured was at least in her thirties, but so alike to the Amanda Morgan he had met outside that they could have been sisters, if not twins. He went on into another room furnished with large couches, overstuffed chairs and occasional tables, all of them articles of solid furniture, with nothing of float construction visible.

At his left as he entered was a wide fireplace, the mantelpiece above it filled with small, apparently homemade bits of handicraft, ranging in artistry from obviously childmade objects such as a long-skirted woman's figure made of dried grass stems tied and glued into shape, to the bust of a horse, its head and arched neck only, carved in a soft reddish stone. The lifelikeness of the horse was breathtaking. Hal was reminded of some early Eskimo carvings he had seen in the Denver museum on Earth, in which an already wave-formed rock had been barely touched by the carver's tool, to transform it into the figure of a seal, or that of a sleeping man. The same kind of creative magic had been at work here, even to the red graininess of the rock evoking the texture and skin-coloring of a roan horse.

In a multitude of small ways, he thought as he took one of the comfortable chairs, it was the kind of room he had not seen since he left his own home on Earth. Not just the noticeable lack of modern technologies created this feeling. There had been none at all to be seen in the farmhouses that had put him up, together with the other Command members, on Harmony. But there was something different, here. A deliberately archaic feel lived within the walls surrounding him—as if it had been a quality consciously sought for and incorporated by the builders and owners of this place. The same sort of feel had been evident to an extent in Foralie Town also, and might be typical of the Dorsai in general for all he knew; but here, it amounted almost to a fineness, like the warm sheen upon cherished woodwork, lovingly nurtured and cared for over the years.

Whatever it was, like Foralie Town itself, it touched and comforted him like a home long familiar to which he was just now returning. The emotion it raised in him relieved some of the depression he had been feeling ever since the garden on Mara. Sitting in the armchair, he let his thoughts drift; and they slid, almost in reflex, back into a maze of memories from his own early days, memories that for a change were happy ones, of the years before Bleys had appeared.

So caught up in these memories was he that he only woke from them with the entrance of Amanda into the room, her cap and jacket removed, carrying a tray with cups, glasses, a coffeepot and a decanter on it that she set down on a square, squat table between his chair and the one facing it.

"Coffee or whisky?" she said, sitting down facing him on the other side of the table.

Hal thought of getting used to one more taste-variety of coffee.

"Whisky," he said.

"It's Dorsai whisky," she said.

"I've tasted it," he said. "Malachi—one of my tutors—let me taste some one Christmas when I was eleven."

He saw her raised eyebrows.

"His full name was Malachi Nasuno," he added.

"It's a Dorsai name," said Amanda, tipping some of the dark liquor into a short, heavily-walled glass, and handing it to him. Her eyes studied him with an intensity that tightened the little muscles in the nape of his neck. Her gaze reminded him of the way young Alaef Tormai had stared in the first moment of their meeting at the Town Hall. Then she bent the silver crown of her head and poured coffee for herself, breaking the moment of her glance.

"I had three tutors," said Hal, almost to himself. He tasted the whisky, and its fierce burn brought back more memories. "They were my guardians, as well. I was an orphan and they raised me. That was on Earth."

"Earth—so that's how you know about horses. That—and being raised by a Dorsai, explains it," she said, looking up and meeting his eyes again. He noticed the color of hers, now. Under the indoor lighting they were a clear, penetrating bluish green, like deep sea waters. "I took you for one of us at first glance."

"So have a number of other people since Omalu," said Hal. He saw her glance was questioning. "I landed there from Mara, just a few hours back."

"I see." She sat back in her chair with the coffee cup, and the color of her eyes seemed to darken as they met his now in the last of the twilight that was flooding the room through its wide windows. "What can I do for you, Hal Mayne?"

"I wanted to see Foralie," he said. "Alaef said none of the Graemes were home, but you were their closest neighbor; and I could talk to you about looking at the place."

"Graemehouse's locked up now; but I can let you in, of course," she answered. "But you won't want to go tonight. Aside from anything else, you'd see a lot more in daylight."

"Tomorrow?"

"Tomorrow, by all means," she said. "I've got an errand to run, but I can leave you there on the way over and collect you on the way back."

"That's good of you." He swallowed the rest of the whisky in his glass, breathed deeply a moment to get his voice back, and stood up. "Alaef ran me up here, but he had to be back in time for dinner. I don't want to impose on you but do you know anyone I can call for transportation back to Foralie Town?"

She was smiling at him.

"Why? Where do you think you're going?"

"Back to town, as I said," he answered a little stiffly. "I've got to arrange for a place to stay."

"Sit down," Amanda said. "Omalu has a hotel or two, but out here we don't run to such things. If you'd stayed in town, the Tormai or one of the other families there would have put you up. Since you're out here, you're my guest. Didn't your Malachi Nasuno teach you how we do things, here on the Dorsai?"

He looked at her. She was still smiling at him. He realized suddenly that, as they had talked, he had completely lost his earlier image of her as a barely-grown young woman. For the first time he began to consider the possibility that her chronological age might be even greater than his own.

Chapter

> > **42** < <

He sat at a table in the large kitchen of Fal Morgan while Amanda fixed dinner. It was a square, high-ceilinged room paneled in some pale wood gone honey-colored with time, which reflected the house lights that had seemed to strengthen as the outside twilight faded. It had two entrances; the one to the hall by which he had gone to the living room and by which they had come back in, and one to a presently-unlighted dining room in which Hal could dimly see dark paneling, straight-backed chairs, and part of a long, dark table. In the kitchen the cooking surfaces, the food storage cupboards, and the phone screen hanging high on one wall were modern and technological. Everything else was home-built and simple. Amanda moved about with an accustomed dexterity and speed. His own hands were idle.

"I could give you something to make it look like you're helping," she had told him as they had come in, "but there's no point to it. There's nothing you can do here that I can't do faster and better myself. So just sit back out of my way, and we'll talk as I go. More whisky?"

"Thank you," he had said. Sitting with a glass in his hand at least gave him the appearance of a reason for sitting still while she worked.

He had expected to feel self-conscious sitting there, nonetheless; but the essential magic of the house, the warmth of the kitchen with her movement about in it, made all things right. Only, for a second, and reasonlessly, watching her now, he felt an unusually sharp stab of that loneliness that had been always part of him these last four years. Then he put that aside too, and merely sat, sipping the dark, fierce whisky, wrapped in the comfort of the moment.

"What do you like—mutton or fish?" she asked. "That's our choice, here."

"Either is fine," he said. "I don't eat much."

Strangely, this had been true since his time in the cell on Harmony. His familiar, oversize appetite had been lost somewhere. On the trip from Harmony to Mara, he had eaten only when meals were pushed upon him; and on Mara itself the indifference had continued. It was not that food did not taste good to him once he began to eat—it was just that hunger and appetite had somehow lately become strangers to him. He did not think of eating until he had been some time without food; and then just enough to take the edge off his immediate need was all he would find himself wanting.

He became aware that Amanda had paused at his answer, and was looking back intently across the room at him from the food-storage cupboard she had just unsealed.

"I see," she said after a second. She went back to taking things from the cupboard. "In that case, why don't we have both? And you can tell me which you like best."

Hal watched her as she worked. It seemed that Dorsai cookery had something in common with that on Harmony. Here, as there, a little meat was made to go a long way by adding a lot of vegetables. Fish, however, was used somewhat more freely. There appeared to be a fair amount of preparation to all the dishes Amanda made; but each came together and went onto the cooking surface with surprising speed.

"Well, tell me," she said, after a few minutes, "why do you want to see Foralie?"

The memory of the burial dream floated unbidden to the surface of his mind. He pushed it back down, out of consciousness.

"Malachi, the tutor I mentioned," he said, "told me a lot about it—about Donal and the other Graemes."

"So you came to see for yourself?"

He caught the unspoken question behind the one uttered out loud.

"I had to come to the Dorsai anyway," he told her. A desire to be open with her, more than he had intended, stirred in him for a second; but he repressed it. "Only, when I got here, I found I wasn't ready to get down right away to what I'd come for. So I thought I'd take a day or two and come here first."

"Because of the stories Malachi Nasuno told you?"

"Stories mean a lot when you're young," he answered.

She sat down at the table opposite him with a cutting board and began to chop up what looked like variforms of celery, green pepper and chives. Her glance came across the table at him. In the warm illumination of the lights off the golden paneling, her eyes flashed like sunlight on turquoise water.

"I know," she said.

They sat in silence as the bright blade of her knife rocked up and down on the board, dividing the vegetables.

"What was it you wanted to see there?" she asked, after a bit, sweeping the chopped vegetables into a pile together and getting up to carry the board with them back across the room.

"The house, mainly, I suppose," he smiled to himself, talking to her slim, erect back, "I'd heard so much about it, I think I might even be able to find my way around it blindfolded."

"Your Malachi may have been one of the officers the Graeme family used to use a lot on their contracts," she said, almost to herself. She turned back to face him again. "I've got to visit one of my sisters tomorrow morning. I'll give you a horse—you can ride, I suppose, from what I saw earlier?"

He nodded.

"I can take you to Graemehouse, let you in, go on to make my visit and come back afterward. Then after I'm back, if you like, we can go around the house and its land, together."

"Thanks," he said. "That's good of you."

Without warning, she grinned at him.

"You haven't been here long enough for people to tell you that neighborliness doesn't require thanks?"

He grinned back.

"Malachi told me about neighborliness on the Dorsai," he said. "No one since I landed has had time to go into the details for me, though."

"One of the ways we survive here is by being neighborly," Amanda said, sobering, "and we Morgans have survived here since the first Amanda, a good number of years before Graemehouse was even built."

"The first Amanda?" he echoed.

"The first Amanda Morgan—who built this house of Fal Morgan and brought our name to this part of the Dorsai, nearly two hundred and fifty standard years ago. That's her picture in the hall."

"It is?"

He watched her, fascinated.

"How many Amandas have there been?" he asked.

"Three," she said.

"Only three?"

She laughed.

"The first Amanda was touchy about her name being pinned on someone who couldn't live up to it—she was a person. No one in the family named a girl-child Amanda until I came along."

"But you said there were three. If you're the second—"

"I'm the third. The second Amanda was actually named Elaine. But by the time she was old enough to run about, everybody was starting to

call her Amanda, because she was so much like the first. Elaine-Amanda
was my great-grandaunt. She died just four years ago last month; and she'd
grown up with Kensie and Ian, the twin uncles of Donal. In fact, they
were both in love with her."

"Which one got her?"

Amanda shook her head.

"Neither. Kensie died on Sainte Marie. Ian married Leah; and it was
his children who carried on the Graeme family line, since Kensie died
unmarried, and neither Donal nor his brother Mor lived to have any children. But after his sons were all grown and Leah had died—in her sixties—Ian used to be over here at Fal Morgan all the time. I remember
when I was very young, I thought that he was just another Morgan. He
died fourteen years ago."

"Fourteen years ago?" Hal said, automatically calculating in his head
from what he knew of the chronology of the Graeme family. "He lived a
long time. How old was your great-grandaunt when she died?"

"A hundred and six." Amanda finished putting the last dish on the
cooking surface; and came back to sit down with a cup of tea at the table.
"We live a long time, we Morgans. She was the Dorsai's primary authority on contracts, right up to the day she died."

"Contracts?" Hal asked.

"Contracts with whoever on other worlds wanted Dorsai to work or
fight for them," said Amanda. "Families and individuals here have always
made their own agreements with governments and people on the other
worlds; but as the paperwork got more complicated, an expert eye to check
it over became useful."

"I'd have thought all the contract experts would be in Omalu," said
Hal. The purpose of his being on this world stirred in the back of his mind.
"Who's the leading expert on contracts on the Dorsai, now?"

"I am," said Amanda.

He looked at her.

"Oh," he said.

"It's all right to be surprised," Amanda told him. "We Morgans not only
put in long lives, we tend not to look our age. I'm not as young as I might
seem; and the second Amanda saw to it I cut my teeth on contracts. I
was reading them when I was four—not that I understood what I read
until a few years later. The Second Amanda's also the one who saw to it
my parents named their oldest daughter Amanda; and she took me over
almost as soon as I was born. In a way, I was always more hers than
theirs."

"If she hadn't pushed it, they wouldn't have given you that name?"

She grinned again.

"Otherwise no member of this family would've risked giving a child that name."

A timer chimed from the cooking surface and she got up to take care of something.

"Everything's ready," she said.

Hal got to his feet, turning toward the dining table in the still-unlit room.

"No," she said, glancing back over her shoulder at him at the scrape of his chair legs on the floor. "We'll eat in here, since there's just the two of us. Sit down. I'll bring things."

He sat down again, pleased. The kitchen was more attractive to him at this moment than the dim room with the long dining surface that must have been capable of feeding a dozen people or more.

"That's quite a table in there," he said.

"Wait until you see the one at Graemehouse," she said, carrying dishes to the table. She got the food brought and arranged and sat down herself. "I'll fill a plate for you to start you out since you won't know any of these dishes. Eat what tastes good, and tell me what you think. As far as the size of the table goes, when there's a contract to be estimated, even tables like that can be all too small."

She passed the laden plate to him, and started to fill one for herself from the dishes between them.

"You don't understand?" she said.

"Contract estimating takes space?" said Hal.

"It takes space to work with the subcontractors," she answered. "A large military contract could take a week and more to put together; and during that time everyone's living with it around the clock. Try some of the red sauce on the fish, there."

Hal did.

"Suppose," she said, resting her elbows on the table, "someone like Donal Graeme had been asked by a local government on Ceta if he'd put together a force to take military control of some territory that's currently under dispute; and hold it while its true ownership is negotiated between that government and the other claimants. He'd first sit down and make a general plan of how the job might be done and what he would need to do it—troops, transport, housing, weapons, medical, supply units . . . and so forth."

Hal nodded.

"I see," he said.

"Do you? Well, having made his own preliminary, general estimate, he'd then call other individuals, or even families, from around the Dorsai, with whom he may have worked in the past, and whose work he'd liked; and ask each of them if they'd consider working under him on the contract on which he was currently putting together a bid. Those who did would come to Foralie and they'd all sit down together, take his general plan and break it down into particulars. On the Dorsai, every officer is a specialist. We Morgans, for example, tend to be primarily field officers with infantry experience. One or more of us, for example, might take the part of Donal's plan that called for infantry in the field and look at it from the standpoint of what they'd need to do that part of the overall job. They'd tell Donal what they thought would work and what wouldn't, in that area, and how much it would require and cost to do that part successfully. Meanwhile, the other specialists would be working with other parts of the plan . . . and so it'd eventually all be put together; and Donal'd have the hard figures of what it would cost him to fulfill the contract."

"Not simple," said Hal.

The food—everything he tasted—was very good. He found himself eating steadily and hungrily as he listened.

"Not even as simple as I make it sound, actually," said Amanda. "The fact is, that whole process I just told you about would have to be gone through twice, at least. Because the first figures they'd come up with would have been arrived at according to orthodox military practices; and what that would give them would only be what any responsible mercenary commander would have to charge as a bottom figure—just to break even. But then, once they had that—the competition price—they'd sit down and begin to come up with unorthodox ways of cutting the expenses they'd just figured, or ways of achieving their objective faster, until they'd end with a total that would both underbid any competitor and allow them a profit that made it worth their while to take the contract. It'd take a week or more with the pressure on each specialist there to pull rabbits out of his or her hat; and each bright new idea that was produced could force everyone else to adjust and refigure."

"I see," said Hal, "and all this took place on the dining table?"

"Ninety per cent of it," said Amanda. "The table'd be piled halfway to the ceiling with maps, schematics, sketches, models, gadgets, notes . . . and, occasionally, food—when they'd call a break long enough to eat. And all that's only the business use for a large dining room table. It's also the place where the whole family gets together, and family decisions are made. But that's enough talk of tables. What's your preference at this one? The fish, or the mutton?"

"I can't tell you. Both." Hal came very close to answering with his mouth full.

"That's good," said Amanda. "Just help yourself, then."

"Thank you. You're really a remarkable cook."

"Growing up in a house with a lot of people to feed every day, anyone gets good at cooking."

"I suppose . . ." Hal thought for a second of his own solitary childhood. "You said the Morgans were here even before the Graemes? How did the Morgans happen to come to the Dorsai?"

"The first Amanda," this Amanda said. "She's the answer to most questions about the family. She came from Earth in the early days when emigration to the newer worlds first became practical; and when everyone was leaving, or thinking of leaving, to make a new society somewhere."

"What made her come to the Dorsai?"

"She didn't, at first. Her husband died shortly after they were married. His parents had power and credit; and by pulling legal strings they got her young son away from her. She stole him back, and left Earth so that they couldn't get him again. She emigrated to Newton and married a second time. When her second husband died, Jimmy—the boy—was half-grown. She took him and came to the Dorsai. She was one of the first permanent settlers on this world—the very first in this area. When she came, Foralie Town was only a sort of transitory tent-city headquarters for the out-of-work mercenaries who were camping out in the hills around here, until they could get taken on by some outfit. . . ."

Hal ate and listened, only occasionally asking questions. It was a strange, dark unrolling of the years that she described for him; the hard times and the hard world gradually producing a people to whom honor and courage were as necessary tools for the making of their living as plow and pump might be to settlers elsewhere—a people shaped by their own history, until it finally began to be said of them, over a hundred years ago, that if they chose to fight as a unit, not all the military forces of the other worlds combined could stand against them.

It was a flamboyant statement, Hal thought now with a part of his mind, listening to Amanda. In the end, numbers and resources could not be withstood in the real universe; and against the military strengths of all the other settled worlds, combined, those of the Dorsai would not be able to win—or even hold out very long. But an odd, small truth within the statement remained. Given that the Dorsai could not win in such a confrontation, it might still be correct to say that the worlds combined would always be slow to test their strength against them. For though the fact that the Dorsai could not win or survive such a test was undeniable, the fact that they would fight against any odds, if attacked, was certain.

Gradually the history of the Morgans, which was also in a sense the history of the Dorsai itself, began to take shape for Hal. The Morgans and the Graemes had lived side by side for generations, had been born together, grew up together, and fought together, with the special effectiveness that such special closeness made possible. They were separate families, but a common people; and, as he touched the life of the Morgans from their beginnings now, in this particularly living way through the voice of Amanda, he found himself brought closer than he had ever been before to the life of Donal, to the lives of Donal's uncles, Kensie and Ian Graeme, to that of Eachan Khan Graeme—Donal's father—even to the life of Cletus Grahame, the ancestor of all of them, who had written the great multi-volume military work on strategy and tactics which had made the effectiveness of the specially-trained Dorsai soldier possible.

"—Now, is there anything else I can offer you?" The voice of Amanda, interrupting herself, brought Hal's mind back from the place into which it had wandered and almost gotten lost.

"I beg your pardon?" said Hal, then realized she was speaking about food. "How could I eat any more?"

"Well, that's a question, of course," said Amanda.

He stared at her, then saw the smile quirking the corners of her mouth, and woke to the fact that every serving dish on the table was empty.

"Did I eat all that?" he said.

"You did," Amanda told him. "How about coffee and after-dinner drinks, if you want them, in the living room?"

"I . . . thank you." He got to his feet and looked uncertainly at the empty dishes on the table.

"Don't worry about that now," said Amanda. "I'll clean up later."

She got up, herself, put coffee, cups, glasses and whisky once more on the tray she had carried back from the living room earlier. They went out of the kitchen and down the hall.

The lights in the kitchen went out, and those in the living room went on, softly, as sensors picked up the traces of bodies leaving and entering. Amanda put the tray on a low table before the fireplace and picked up a torch-staff that was leaning against the stonework there. She held it to the kindling and logs already placed. A little flame reached out from the tip of the staff and licked against the shavings under the kindling. The shavings caught. Fire ran among the kindling and along the underside of the laid logs, then blossomed up between them. Amanda leaned the staff back against the stonework.

The new light of the flames had picked out four lines of words carved into the polished edge of the thick slab of the granite mantelpiece. Hal leaned forward to read them. They were cut so deeply into the stone that shadow hid from him the actual depth of their incision.

" 'The Song of the House of Fal Morgan,' " said Amanda, looking over his shoulder. "The first verse. It's a tribute to the first Amanda. Jimmy, her son, wrote it, when he was a good-aged man."

"It's part of a song?" Hal looked at her.

"It is," she said.

Unexpectedly, softly, she sang the words cut in the stone. Her voice was lower-pitched than he would have thought, but it was a fine, true voice which loved singing, with strength behind the music of it.

"Stone are my walls, and my roof is of timber,
But the hands of my builder are stronger by far.
My roof may be burnt and my stones may be scattered,
Never her light be defeated in war."

The words, sung as she had chosen to sing them, triggered off a sudden emotion in Hal so powerful that it approached pain. To cover his reaction, he turned back abruptly to the tray on the table and made a little ceremony of pouring some of the whisky into a glass and sitting down in an armchair at one side of the fire. Amanda gave herself coffee and sat down in an identical chair facing him on the fire's other side.

"Is that all of the song?" Hal asked.

"No," said Amanda. Self-consciously, he was aware of her watching him again, closely—and he thought—strangely. "There're more verses."

"Sometime," he said quickly, suddenly afraid that she might sing more, and wake again whatever had momentarily touched him so deeply, "I've got to hear those, too. But tell me—where are all the Morgans and Graemes, now? Graemehouse is empty and you're—"

"And I'm alone here," Amanda finished the sentence for him. "Times have changed. For the Dorsai people, life's not easy now."

"I know," Hal said. "I know the Others are working to keep you from getting contracts."

"They can't keep us from all of them," said Amanda. "There aren't enough of them to interfere with all the contracts we sign. But they can stop most of the big ones, the top ten per cent that brings in nearly sixty per cent of our interstellar credit. So, since times are difficult, most of us of working age are either out on the fisheries or at some other job on the Dorsai that ties in with surviving on our own resources. Others have gone off-world. A number of individuals, and even families, have emigrated."

"Left the Dorsai?"

"Some think they don't have any choice. Others of us, of course, would never leave. But this world's always been one where any adult's free to make his own decisions, without advice or comment unless she or he asks for it."

"Of course . . . ," said Hal, hardly knowing what he was saying.

He was caught up entirely in what he had just heard. Since the hours in the cell on Harmony he had known that the time of the Splinter Cultures was over. But for the first time, with what Amanda had just told him, the knowledge hit deeply within him. The Dorsai world without the Dorsai people was somehow more unthinkable than the same thing on any of the other Younger Worlds. All at once, his mind's eye saw it deserted; its homes empty and decaying, its level lands, oceans and high mountains without the sound of human voices. His whole being tried to push the image from him; and still, in the back of his mind, the certainty of it sat like a certainty of the end of the universe. This, too, had to end; and the concept that had been built here with such labor must finally vanish with it, not to come again.

He roused himself from the feeling that had suddenly crushed him like the grip of some giant's icy hand, into a perfect silence. Across the table with the tray holding glasses, cups, coffee dispenser and whisky decanter, Amanda still sat watching him almost oddly, as she had watched him in that first moment of their meeting.

He was conscious of something, some current of feeling that seemed to wash back and forth between them, virtually unknown to each other as they were.

"Are you all right?" he heard her ask, calmly.

"I'd kill time if I could!" He heard the words break from him without warning, shocking him with their intensity. "I'd kill death. I'd kill anything that killed anything!"

"But you can't," she answered, softly.

"No." He pulled himself back to something like normal self-possession. The whisky, he told himself—but he had drunk very little and alcohol had always had only small power to touch him. Something else had driven him—was still driving him to speak as he just had. "You're right. Everyone's got a right to his own decisions; and that's what creates history—decisions. The decisions are changing and the times are changing.

What we were all used to is going to be put aside; and something new is going to be taking its place. I tried to tell that to some Exotics before I came here; and I thought if anyone would listen, they would."

"But they didn't?"

"No," he said, harshly. "It's the one thing they can't face, time running out. It sets a limit to their search—it means that now they'll never find what they've been looking for, all this time since they called themselves the Chantry Guild, back on Earth. Strange . . ."

"What's strange?" he heard her ask, when he did not go on.

He was staring into the dark, firelit pool of whisky in his glass, kneading it between his hands again. He looked up from the glass at her.

"Those who ought to see what's happening—the people who could do something—refusing to see. While everyone who can't do anything about it seems to know it's there. They seem to feel it, the way animals feel a thunderstorm coming."

"You feel it yourself, do you?" she asked. Her eyes, darker now in the firelight, still watched him, and drew him. He talked on.

"Of course. But I'm of those caught up in it," he said. "I've had to face up to what's happening, and will happen."

"Tell me, then," said Amanda's voice softly. "What is it that's happening? And what is it that's going to happen?"

He pressed the hard shape of the whisky glass between his hands, staring now into the flames of the fireplace.

"We're headed toward the last battle," he said. "That's what's happening. No, call it a last conflict, because most of it won't be a battle in the dictionary sense. But, depending on how it comes out, the race is either going to have to die or grow. I know—that sounds like something too large to believe. But we've made it that big ourselves, over the centuries. Only, those in the best position to understand how it could happen, wouldn't ever look squarely at the situation. I couldn't see it myself until my nose was rubbed in it. But if you look back at what's been happening in just the last twenty or thirty standard years, you see the evidence all over the place. The Others appearing . . ."

He talked on, almost in spite of himself. The words ran from him like dogs unleashed, and he found himself telling her about everything that he had come to understand in the cell on Harmony.

She sat quietly, asking a brief question now and then, watching him. He felt a tremendous relief in being able to uncap the pressure of that explosion of understanding. It was a pressure that had been growing steadily in him lately, as his mind developed and extended its first discoveries. His original impulse had been to do no more than sketch the situation for her; but he found himself being drawn, by the way she listened, from that to the people and things that had led him to understanding. He felt captured by her attention; and he heard his own voice going on and on as if it had developed an independent life of its own.

Once, it crossed his mind again to wonder if the Dorsai whisky had something to do with it. But once more he rejected the idea. It had been in his first year on Coby that he had found that alcohol did not affect him in the same measure as it seemed to affect the other miners. When they had finally drunk themselves into silence and even slumber, he would be still awake and restless, so restless he had been driven to those long, solitary walks of his down the endless stone corridors. It had been as if a part of his mind had withdrawn a little farther with each step his body took toward intoxication; until he had existed apart from the moment, wrapped in a sadness and a sense of isolation that would drive him eventually out, away from the unconscious others to walk those lonely distances.

But what he was feeling now, with her, was, if anything, the opposite of that sense of isolation; and, in any case, there was a reasonable limit to the strength of alcoholic liquors made for the pleasure of drinking. Beyond a certain proof they were uncomfortable to the palate and throat; and that point the Dorsai whisky, though strong, had not exceeded. Nor was the amount he had drunk at all great, measured by the meterstick of his experience. . . .

He found himself telling the third Amanda about Child-of-God, and the effect of Child's death upon his own understanding.

". . . When I first met him," he was saying, "I thought he was another Obadiah—I told you about my other two tutors, didn't I? Then, as I got to know him, I began to have less and less and less use for him. He seemed to be a fanatic and nothing more—not able to care or feel, not interested in anything but the rules of that religion of his. But then, he was the one who spoke up when the local people wanted the Command to send me away; and for the first time I began to see a pattern to what he was; and it was larger—much larger—than I'd thought."

"You were still young," said Amanda.

"Yes," he said. "I was young. We're always young, no matter how old we are. And then, when he insisted on staying behind to slow down the Militia; and I couldn't stay with him—knew that it wasn't for me to stay with him—and that he understood that, this man I'd thought had no sensitivity, no understanding beyond the church rules he lived by, then it all opened up for me. I knew the difference between someone like him, then, and someone like Barbage, who was my jailer in that Militia cell, the man whose life I'd saved in the mountain pass. . . ."

The lights of the living room blinked once.

"Curfew," murmured Amanda. "We save power, nowadays, for those who most need it."

She got to her feet. The hard fabric of her riding pants whispered lightly, leg against leg, as she stepped to the fireplace once more; and the firelight, reflecting from the polished apron of black stone before it, sent glitters of light into the small wave of her bright hair, where it clung close against the tanned skin of her neck. She lit the stubs of two large candles that stood on supports on either side of it. They looked from their thickness to have been as long as her forearm to begin with; and the stands they rested on were tall, lifting the candle flames even now above Hal's eye-level as he sat in his armchair. The candles themselves seemed to be made of grayish-green, waxy-looking seeds, pressed together into sticks. As the generous flames rose from their wicks, the built-in lighting of the room dimmed itself gradually into extinction. Shadow moved in from the corners of the room, until Hal and Amanda were in a little illuminated space constructed by candlelight and firelight alone. A faint, piny odor reached Hal's nostrils.

Amanda sat down again. Even as close as she was to him, her outdoor clothing was lost in the shadows of her chair, so that the whiteness of her face seemed to float in a friendly gloom, watching him.

"You were telling me about someone whose life you saved in a mountain pass," she said.

"Yes," he said. "Barbage's life. I didn't understand then the sort of things the Militia did to anyone from the Commands that they got their hands on; and what Barbage himself must have done to prisoners from the Commands, while he was working his way up through the ranks to Captain. And still, there wasn't anything false about him, either. He was—he is wrong. I think I know why now—but he was what he was. That's why the other Militia officers were afraid of him. I saw him face down another Militia Captain, the one time I managed to get close to their camp. . . ."

He talked on. The candles burned lower; and, imperceptibly, he found he had drifted from telling her about those he had met to telling her about himself. Something within him, some small alarm sensor, was trying to catch his attention, but the force pushing him to talk was too great to be denied. Amanda hardly needed to ask questions, now; and in the end he found himself telling her about what it had been like for him when he was very young.

". . . But what was it, specifically," she asked, finally, "that made you identify so with the Graemes?"

"Oh, well," he said, staring into the fire, his mind adrift in the flame-lit darkness and carried on by the force within him, "you've got to remember I'm an orphan. I've always been . . . isolated. I suppose I identified with Donal's isolation. You remember how when he was at the Academy, they used to speak of him as an odd boy, different from anyone else—"

—Something happened in the room. He looked up swiftly.

"I'm sorry—" He gazed at Amanda but she was exactly as she had been a moment before. The small alarm sensor was now obvious within him. Deliberately, he forced it from his consciousness. "Did you say something?"

"No," she answered. Her eyes were steady on his in the dimness of the room. "Nothing."

He tried to pick up the thread of what he had been saying.

"You see he had always been alone inside, always . . ." His voice ran down. He put his hand to his forehead, felt dampness, and took it away again. "What was I saying?"

"You're probably tired," Amanda leaned forward in her chair. "You were saying Donal was always alone. But he wasn't. He married Anea of Kultis."

"Yes, but that was his mistake. You see, he was hoping then that, after all, he could still live an ordinary life. But he couldn't. He'd been committed so early . . . it was something like the mistake Cletus made with Melissa Khan; although that was different, because all Cletus had to do was finish his book. . . ."

His thoughts slipped away from him once more. He wiped his forehead with his hand and felt the cool dampness of perspiration.

"I guess you're right," he said. "I guess I am tired—it's been a large day. . . ."

He was, he realized suddenly, exhausted, sodden with fatigue.

"Of course it has," said Amanda, gently. "I'll show you how to get to your room."

She rose, taking one of the candles from its stand, and led the way into a corridor beyond a farther doorway in the wall to the left of the fireplace. He lifted himself woodenly to his feet and walked after her.

Chapter

> > **43** < <

His sleep was a dead sleep, so heavy as almost to be exhausting in its own right. He roused once during the night, for only a moment, and lay there in the darkness in an unfamiliar bed, wondering where he was. Remembering, he dropped like a stone back into sleep again.

When he woke again, the bedroom in which he lay was bright with morning sunlight diffused through thin white drapes. He vaguely remembered Amanda as she had turned, candle in hand, to go back down the hall, telling him that there were two sets of window drapes to pull, the light and the heavy. Clearly, he had forgotten to pull the heavy, outer set.

But it did not matter. He sat up, swinging his naked legs over the edge of the bed. He was now up for the day; and he felt fine—except for a mild fuzziness in the head that made his surroundings seem at one remove from him. The room he was in had no lavatory facilities. He remembered something else Amanda had said, put on his pants and found his way down the hall to another door which let him into a lavatory.

Fifteen minutes later, cleaned, shaved and dressed, he walked into the kitchen of Fal Morgan. Amanda was there, seated at the round table, talking on the phone with her sister. Hal took a chair at the table to wait for the end of the conversation. The sister, seen in the screen high on the wall, was more round of face and yellow, rather than white-blond, of hair, but unmistakably a sibling. Like Amanda, she was beautiful, but the intensity Hal had noticed so clearly in Amanda was missing in this other Morgan—or, he thought, perhaps it just did not come through as well on a phone screen.

But his inner senses rejected the latter explanation. The intensity of Amanda was a unique quality, something he had felt in no other human being until now. It was beyond reason to suppose that her whole family shared it.

Amanda had been explaining that she had to take Hal to Graemehouse first before arriving as promised. Now she ended the talk, shut off the phone and looked across the table at him.

"I was just about to wake you," she said. "We should be going as soon as you're fed. Do you feel like having breakfast?"

Hal grinned.

"As much as it turned out I felt like having dinner," he said. His appetite was back to normal.

"All right," said Amanda, getting to her feet. "Sit tight. It'll be ready in a minute."

Fed and mounted, they started off in the morning light of Fomalhaut, a brilliant pinpoint now in the eastern sky, making the snowfields of the mountains just below it glitter like mirrors. It was a cool, clear, still morning with only an occasional cloud in view. The horses fought their bits and waltzed sideways until they were let run to the edge of the tableland on which Fal Morgan stood. At the edge of that flat stretch, however, Amanda pulled the gray under her back to a walk and Hal followed her example.

They plunged over the edge onto a steep downslope thick with variform conifers and native bush forms. The clear ground between the growths was stony and only sparsely covered with small vegetation. They rode through such gullies and alternating stretches of open mountainside for perhaps ten minutes before they came out into an area of high rolling hills covered with the brown, drying grass of late fall. Tucked back up on a high point above these hills, so that it was not visible until they came up over the crest of the slope below it, was a shelf of long, narrow land on which Graemehouse stood.

It was a house of dark timber, two-storied, but low-looking in relation to its length, that seemed to hug the slight curve of the earth on which it and its outbuildings stood. Barely a dozen meters behind it, the ground lifted suddenly in a bare, steep slope toward the mountainside above. They climbed their horses onto the shelf and approached the homestead from the side. The morning sun was ahead of them as they rode toward the buildings; and Graemehouse itself sat at an angle to their line of approach, facing south and downslope toward the lower hill area from which they had just come.

"Not as sheltered as Fal Morgan," said Hal, almost absentmindedly, looking at it. Amanda glanced over at him.

"It's got other advantages," she said. "Look here—"

She reined to her right and led the way to the edge of the shelf. Hal halted with her. From the edge they could see clear down to the river below and Foralie Town.

"With a scope up on the roof of that house," Amanda said, "you can keep a watch on half the local area. And that rise behind cuts off most of the snow and wind that would ordinarily bury a homestead this high up and exposed, when winter comes. Cletus Grahame knew what he was doing when he built it—for all that he called himself a scholar instead of a soldier."

She turned away from the rim and walked her horse toward the house. Hal rode with her. At the front entrance, they dismounted and dropped their reins. The horses lowered their heads to nibble at the grass of the front lawn.

Amanda led the way to the front entrance, and put her thumb into its lock sensor. The wide, heavy, dark door there swung open. She led the way into a square entry hall with pegs on the walls, from some of which sweaters and jackets still hung. Straight ahead was an open archway into what seemed a lounge—or, as Amanda had called the equivalent space at Fal Morgan, a living room.

The atmosphere in the house was still and empty, without being life-less. Amanda turned to Hal.

"I'll leave you now," she said. "I'll be back either right around noon, or shortly after. In the meantime, if I get delayed and you want something to eat or drink, the kitchen and storage rooms are at the west end of the house, to your left. Help yourself to whatever's there—that's how we do things here. I don't suppose I need to tell you to clean up after yourself."

"No," said Hal. "But I'll probably just wait to eat with you."

"Don't hold back out of politeness," she said. "The food and drink are there to be used by whomever in this house needs them. You'll also find phones in most of the rooms. My sister's married name is Debigné. Just code for the directory and call me if you need to."

"Thanks again," said Hal. A certain awkwardness of feeling came over him. "I appreciate your trusting me this way, leaving me here alone."

Her curiously-intent gaze held him. Once more, he felt the strange wash of feeling between them.

"I think the house'll be safe enough," she said; and turned toward the door. "I'll be back in a few hours."

"All right," said Hal.

She went out.

He was left alone in the crystalline stillness of the untenanted home. After a moment, he went into the living room.

It was a large, dark-paneled room, larger than its equivalent at Fal Morgan. The long shape of the house required it to be rectangular rather than square; and there was probably comfortable seating space in it for as many as thirty people. Up to fifty could probably be gathered here, if necessary. Its north wall was nothing but windows, the room-wide drapes upon them drawn back now to the daylight, giving a view of the steep slope behind the house. There would be sensors, he thought, to pull these drapes back each morning, part of the automatic machinery that would manage the purely physical establishment through daylight and dark, summer heat and winter cold, in the absence of its people.

The east wall, to his right, was pierced by a single entrance to what appeared to be a long hallway. The wall itself had only one object on its sober paneling. A full-length, life-size portrait of a man standing, dressed in an old-fashioned military uniform that could have been worn only on Earth, two hundred or more standard years ago. The man was very erect, tall, slim and middle-aged. He wore a gray mustache, sharply waxed to points, which ruled out the possibility that it was a picture of Cletus Grahame. Of course, thought Hal, it would not be Cletus. It was a picture of Eachan Khan, the father of Melissa Khan, who had been the wife of Cletus; and from what he remembered about the family, Cletus himself had done the painting. The archaic uniform would be the one Eachan Khan had worn as a general officer in the Afghanistani forces, before he and Melissa had emigrated from Earth.

The south wall, behind Hal, showed nothing but its paneling, with the entrance from the entry hall in the center of it. The west wall, on his left, had entrances at each end of it. The nearest of these opened on stairs rising to the floor above, with beyond them a hallway which must lead to the kitchen Amanda had mentioned; and the farther entrance, lit by the sunlight from the windows in the adjacent north wall, was obviously the entrance to the dining room. He could even see a corner of the dining table Amanda had spoken of, when he had commented on the size of the one at Fal Morgan.

The shortened wallspace between these two entrances was almost entirely occupied by a wide and deep fireplace built of a gray-black granite, including the long and heavy mantelpiece over it; carved into the thick edge of the mantelpiece where the verse had been cut at Fal Morgan was a shield shape, showing three scallop shells upon it. Above the mantelpiece hung a sword in a silver-metal scabbard, as antique as the uniform in the picture on the wall across from it, and plainly also an original possession of Eachan Khan.

Hal sat down in one of the large overstuffed armchairs. The silence of the house around him pressed in on him. He had come here, he had told himself, because he had felt himself unready to speak to the representatives of the Dorsai. Not unready to deliver the message the Exotics had sent with him, but unready to give the Dorsai people his own words, in terms that would make them listen and understand.

How much of this was simple lack of confidence after his failure on Mara, he did not know. He had gone into the meeting with Nonne,

Padma and the rest taking it for granted that they must understand him. He had never felt that sureness where the Dorsai were concerned; and Foralie had drawn him aside from his earlier planned destination like the magnetic North of Earth swinging about to itself the point of a compass needle. The decision to come here first had been born from the moment he had seen this blue and white, ocean-girt world mirrored in the vision screen of his stateroom aboard ship.

Sitting now in the silent living room, it seemed to him as if he could feel the house speaking to him. There was something here that picked him up, body, mind and soul, and held him in a way that was very nearly eerie. As he sat, he could feel the short hairs on the back of his neck lifting and an electric chill starting at the base of his skull and spreading downward, along his spine and across his shoulders. The house pulled at some ancient strings anchored deep within him. A soundless voice called him; and he rose slowly in answer from his chair, and turned to the corridor leading back to the kitchen.

He went down the corridor. It took six paces to traverse, and it was clear within him that he had known it would take that many and no more. It was a little more than twelve meters in length. There were no openings off it until he stepped from its farther end into the kitchen. Like the kitchen at Fal Morgan, it was large, perhaps even larger than Amanda's. Like that one, also, another doorway in the wall to his right led into the dining room, giving a glimpse of its end, opposite the one he had seen from the living room.

The corridor he had just come down had parallelled the dining room's length.

In the kitchen here as well, the paneling was dark, unlike that at Fal Morgan, and the kitchen table was not round but octagonal. It was also larger than the one he and Amanda had sat at that morning. But in all important ways, it was a room like its counterpart at Fal Morgan.

He stood for a moment. There was nothing in particular to see, but the intense, high-altitude sunlight beat through the windows to his left and the dark wood of the walls drank up the illumination. There was nothing to hear; but to his imagination it seemed he could almost hear a hum of voices that had soaked, like time, into the panelling, and were now sounding just below his auditory threshold. The unheard sound brought back to him a feeling of the people, now dead and gone, who had sat here living and told each other of their doings and their thoughts.

He stood, feeling the minutes slip past him like stealthy sentinels returning to their posts, until with an effort he broke free and moved across the room to a door let into the west wall of the kitchen. The door opened

at a touch and he stepped into the daylight of the morning and the back-
yard of Graemehouse. Around him and off to his left were the outbuildings that had been hidden by the bulk of the house on his approach, the
stable, the stores buildings, the barn and—closest of all—that building
that on the Dorsai he knew was customarily called the fieldhouse.

He walked across the short distance of stony and sunlit earth. The field-
house was unlocked and he let himself in. It was an unpartitioned building as wide as Graemehouse and almost as long. Its height was greater.
Above its walls, the roof arched to a full two stories over the pounded
earth of the floor. There were no windows in the walls, but skylights in
the arched roof let sunlight down to fill the air of the interior with danc-
ing motes of dust. It was a place for winter exercise; and as Hal knew, it
could be heated, but barely to above the freezing point.

Now, it was not yet the season for artificial heat. The sunlight stream-
ing down from the skylights warmed the interior air to a summer temperature; and Hal felt himself touched once more by the ghosts of sounds.
To this building Donal Graeme would have come as soon as his infant
legs could carry him, following the older members of the family. He would
have tottered his unsteady way along the temporary winter passageways
set up between the house and the outbuildings to give a weather-protected
route. To the young child this building would at first have seemed enormous; and the activities of his elders here magical and frustrating, involving elements of balance, strength and speed that his very young body
was not mature enough to imitate.

But he would have tried to imitate, regardless. He would have tried to
turn in swift, flowing movement, as his elders turned, to run as they ran,
and to struggle in the fashion they struggled with each other in their unarmed practice bouts; and he would have demanded also that they pretend to go through the motions of these activities with him, as they did
with each other. By the time he had been five years old, his movements
would have begun to resemble theirs, even if more slowly and clumsily.

The memory of that young bright time, in which he had been an instinctive part of his people and thought of himself as no different from
them, would have been something Donal would have looked back on
often from the standpoint of his later years. . . . Hal turned suddenly, and
walked on through the fieldhouse, to let himself out by a farther door.

Outside, he paused for a second, then turned to go through the other
outbuildings, which were also not locked. The interiors of these revealed
themselves as clean, neat, and in most cases still stored and fitted with
what they would have contained if the house was occupied; but while
there was an echo from them of lives lived down the generations, they

did not produce the strong effect on him that the house and the field-house had. He was of half a mind to turn back again to the house itself, when he saw a final building that was the stables, with a stand of willows beyond, all but hidden by the stables' bulk. He went forward, stepped through the door into the half-gloom within, and all that he had felt before came back.

Once again, something closed about him and the hair on the back of his neck stood up. The stalls on either side of the central aisle before him were empty. He looked down to bales of hay, neatly stacked at the far end, and that which he had come here to meet stood at last face-to-face with him.

For a long moment he stood, breathing the dusty, clean-stable odor of the structure; and then he turned and went once more out the door. He turned right and went down along the farther length of the stables' outside wall, turned the corner at the end and saw, under the long, gently downreaching limbs of the willows, the white-painted picket fence that enclosed the private graves of those who had lived here.

For a moment he stopped, only looking at it; and then he went forward to it.

There was a small gate in the fence. He opened it, went through and closed it softly behind him. Each grave had an upright headstone of gray rock the color of the mountains looking down on him. On and between the grave plots the grass was neatly cut. There was space to walk between the graves and the headstones all faced to his left, six across in orderly ranks. He turned to his right and went to the head of the graveyard, where the older plots were.

There he paused, looking down at the names cut in the upright stones. Eachan Murad Khan . . . Melissa Gray Khan Grahame . . . Cletus James Grahame . . . he moved down the ranks . . . Kamal Simon Graeme . . . Anna OutBond Graeme. On his right, Mary Kenwick Graeme and Eachan Khan Graeme, with a single headstone for their graves that lay side by side with no space separating them.

His step faltered. Then he took one more stride forward and looked down. On his right again, Ian Ten Graeme . . . Leah Sary Graeme . . . and Kensie Alan Graeme. Farthest from him, Kensie's grave lay against the far line of the picket fence, so close to the willows there that the branches had grown down until they lightly swept the grassy surface of his grave with their tips, like fingers gently stroking in the little air that stirred about Hal as he stood watching. And in the next rank beyond the graves of Ian and Leah and Kensie were three more identically-cut gravestones. His step hesitated again.

Then he stepped forward, turned and looked down. Under the willows beyond Kensie's grave, but untouched by them as Kensie's had been touched, was a plot with the name of Donal Evan Graeme upon it. Next to it was the grave of Mor Kamal Graeme. And next to Hal, himself, so close that the toes of his boots almost touched the edge of it, was a stone with the name upon it of James William Graeme. . . .

He could not weep. In the cell, pared thin by fever, exhaustion and the struggle to breathe, he had wept. But here, nearly a century later and in a grown body, he could not. Only his throat clenched painfully and a coldness began to grow in him—not the electric coldness now of the back of the neck and shoulders, but the different, indestructible, unyielding coldness deep in the center of him, spreading out to stain his whole body within. In his mind he felt the powerful arms of his uncle around him once more, heard the voice of Kensie calling on him to come back, come back. . . .

He came back. The coldness went and he turned away from the graves. He went out by the little gate in the picket fence, closing it quietly behind him, and started back up to the house.

He reentered the kitchen door through which he had emerged. It latched softly and he looked at his chronometer. Time had passed. The figures on it now showed less than an hour to noon, the time at which Amanda was due to return.

He went back down the corridor from the kitchen to the living room. Now that he had entered the house for the second time, he felt a difference in his response to it. It was no longer a place in which he was a stranger; and every part of it seemed to have a latent power to kindle emotions in him. The sights and echoes of it were familiar, and the living room, when he came to it, enclosed him like a place well remembered.

He turned his attention to the rest of the building. The stairs off the living room led to bedrooms upstairs, but the bedroom toward which he now felt impelled was down on this level. The corridor opposite the one to the kitchen and leading toward the east end of the house went only a short distance before making a forty-five degree turn to the left for an even shorter distance, then turned back again to its original direction, to run approximately down the centerline of the house.

In the left-hand wall of the small cross-corridor there was a doorway into a room which was adjacent to the living room he had just left. Hal stepped through the doorway into a library, almost as long and wide as the living room itself. A large writing table of very dark, polished wood stood in one corner near the far windows. As with the living room, the north wall was almost all glass, and the outside daylight lit the shelves of reading cubes and old-fashioned volumes. Low on one shelf near the windows was a long row of tall books, bound in a dark brown leather. Hal walked across to them and saw that they were bound manuscript copies of the volumes of Cletus Grahame's work on Strategy and Tactics. He ran his finger along their spines, but did not disturb them from their quiet order.

He turned and left the room.

Interior lighting went on, down the long leg of the corridor beyond, as he moved through the remaining downstairs part of the house. This section was nearly half of the total building; and the first doors he passed opened on bedrooms to his left, and workrooms like offices to his right. Then the workrooms ended, giving way to bedrooms on both sides. He counted six bedrooms and four offices before the corridor ended at last at a combined master bedroom and office, that took up the full width of that end of the house.

Coming back from the master bedroom, he found the room that would have been Donal's. Biographies written after Donal's death had identified it as the second back from the master bedroom. Of course, Hal thought, it would be this far back, and this small. The youngest of the family and those ill almost always had the rooms closest to the master bedroom; they would be moved farther from it as the larger, double bedrooms became vacant closer to the living room, through the death or departure of their occupants. Donal had been the youngest in the household at the time he had left home to go out on his first contract; and he had never returned.

It was a very small room, a closet-like space for a single occupant, in contrast to the bedrooms closer to the living room, which were usually occupied by married members of the family. Many other young Graemes would have owned this room since Donal. Neither the furniture nor any object within it could be counted on to have been in his possession during the years of his growing-up.

Nonetheless, Hal stood, gazing about, and the lighter, earlier chill took him again, spreading from neck to shoulders. The walls here were the walls remembered; and the view through these windows of the steep slope guarding the back of Graemehouse was as it had been.

He put out one hand to touch the wood-paneled wall, worn by the cleanings of years to a silky smoothness; and stood, fingertips against the vertical surface, gazing out at the slope seen so many times in the years of Donal's growing up, reaching . . . reaching. For a long moment he stayed as he was; and a fragment of the poem he had written in the Final Encyclopedia came without warning, to him. . . .

"Within the ruined chapel, the full knight
Woke from the coffin of his last-night's bed;
And clashing mailed feet on the broken stones—
Strode to the shattered lintel and looked out . . ."

Then it was as if a wind that was purely of the mind blew through the room and he was suddenly made part of a whole—himself, the wall, and the slope outside, all welded together—caught up in one moment of experience no different from another such moment known many times by the one to whom he reached.

I am here, he thought.

The chill grew, spreading out to take over his whole body. The hair rose again on the back of his neck; and a soundless shrilling, as if the very temporal structure of the moment was in vibration, commenced and mounted swiftly, in and about him, as his identity with the man who had lived here came finally, fully into existence in his mind. He stood—as Donal—in the room; and he looked out—as Donal—on the scene beyond the bedroom window.

Chapter

> > **44** < <

As *abruptly as* it had arrived, the moment was gone, leaving him unsure that it had ever been. His hand dropped from the wall; and a moment later, when he lifted it to his forehead, he felt the skin there chilled and damp, as if half the strength in him had just been drained away by a massive effort.

For a moment he continued to stand in the room. Then he turned and went back out into the corridor; and turned again toward the living room. Going up the corridor, the drained feeling was strong within him and he recognized its kinship, much greater, but like, to the emptiness and fatigue that had always followed upon the making of a poem that had come suddenly and unexpectedly to life within him, a reaction to the violence of a massive inner effort that had left him forever changed.

But with a poem, he told himself, he had always been left with something accomplished, something solid to hold that he had not had before. While in this case . . . but, even as he thought this, he realized that something had also been accomplished here. A change had taken place in him, so that now he was seeing the house about him with a difference.

Now, as he looked about him, there was a quality of familiarity that lay like a patina on everything at which he looked. As he stepped into the living room, the face of Eachan Khan in the portrait had become one he knew intimately, in all details. With the sword above the fireplace, his fingers and palm seemed to recall the grasp of its hilt, and his mind's eye saw the sudden flash and glitter of its blade, as it was drawn from its scabbard. All about him the rest of the room echoed and reechoed a similar sense of recognition.

He sank into the chair in which he had seated himself when he had first arrived; and sat there, feeling his strength slowly returning to refill the emptiness left by his last coldness at the graveside. All around him, now, the house vibrated with the silent noises of its past. He sat listening to them; and after a while an impulse brought him up out of the chair to his feet. He walked to the corner of the room where the last panel of the east wall touched the windowed north wall. The wood surface was a polished blank before him; but an impulse moved him to put the palm of his right hand flat upon it; and it moved easily, sliding to the right to open a tall, narrow entrance directly from the living room into the library.

He stood, gazing into the opening. He remembered now, hearing it spoken of by Malachi in the stories the old man had told him of Graemehouse. There had been talk of this doorway—and something special about it. For a moment he could not recall just what that was, and then it came back to him. This was the place in which the young Graemes had measured their height as they were growing up.

He looked at the left post of the doorway, from which the panel had slid back. Plain there, now that he gave his attention to it, were thin, neat, dark lines with initials and dates beside them. Looking down, he found Donal's initials, close to the floor, but none any higher than would indicate a measurement had been taken after he had been about five years of age.

Donal had been the smallest among the adult male Graemes of his time. Once he had become conscious of this, it would not have been surprising if the boy had avoided further measurement. Hal looked at the doorway. The patina of recognition lay heavily upon it also, and he remembered something more, how Malachi had told him that in all their generations, none of the Graeme family had ever filled that doorway from top to bottom and side to side, except the twins—Donal's uncles, Ian and Kensie. Hal stared at the doorway with its years of markings; and an emotion compounded of something like fear, mixed with a strange, strong longing moved in him. Ian and Kensie had been outsize, even for Dorsai—and it was Ian he imagined now, dark and massive, standing in the doorway, filling it.

It was foolish to think of measuring himself against the marks here, even in the privacy of this moment that no one else need know about. But the desire grew in him as he stood, until it was undeniable.

The logical front of his mind tried to push the notion aside. There was no real purpose to it. In any case, size alone meant nothing. On the fourteen worlds there must be no end of individuals not only big enough to fill the doorway, but too large to fit themselves into it. But the logical arguments had no strength. It was not a question of his size that was pulling him forward to measure himself, it was part of that same search for identity with those who had lived here, that had drawn him to reach for Donal in the small bedroom.

He shook off the last objection. What summoned him was only a part of what he had come to Foralie to do. He stepped into the doorway and stood erect there.

With a sudden, cold shock, he felt the underside of the frame's top rail come hard against the top of his head. He stayed as he was, unmoving. For a second his mind denied the implication of that contact with his scalp. He had been aware for years that his eventual height would be far above ordinary. He had even come to take for granted in recent years his looking down at other people. But still, inside him, he shrank from a reality in which his height was also the height of Ian Graeme. The Ian of his imagination had for so long towered like a giant above all others, that for a moment he would not accept what the doorway told him.

Slowly, acceptance came; and only after it had, did he realize that, while he had felt the top rail with his head, he had felt no corresponding touch of the vertical members of the frame against his shoulders. Looking right and left, now, he saw that four to six centimeters of space showed between the shoulder welts of his jacket and the stiles of the doorframe on either side of him. Granted that he still might grow and put on weight, it was hardly likely he could make up that much difference in shoulder width. Ridiculously, a feeling of pure relief woke in him. He was not ready—not yet—to try to be an Ian.

He stepped back out of the doorway. As if its sensors had been only waiting for his leaving, the door slid closed and the wall was whole once more. He turned back to the living room. With the moment of his identification with Donal in the bedroom, his awareness had heightened. But now with his measurement of himself in the doorway, that awareness had been raised near to a point of pain.

The scent of the air in his nostrils, the colors, the shapes, the sounds and echoes of the house as he had moved about it—the light from the windows and the interior lights of the long corridor past the offices and bedrooms—all these had finally built a connection between him and those who also once moved about here; and he finally now felt that, like them, he belonged to the house.

There was no miracle to it. He knew that all he had achieved here so far was humanly quite possible. His re-creation of Donal and the others to the point where he literally felt their presence about him was within what he knew of the capability of the human mind and imagination. But nonetheless it felt as if he teetered on the border of something far more awesome; a step beyond the possible into some area where no one had gone before.

He shivered. With the heightened sensitivity had come a clarity of mind that also was close to painful; and with that clarity in him he now identified the one part of the house he had been unconsciously avoiding all this time. The dining room, Amanda had told him, was the area of a Dorsai house where decisions were made; not merely business decisions, but family ones as well. Remembering this, his mind turned him at last toward the dining room, knowing that, if anywhere, he would find there the greatest locus of Donal's being and purpose.

He took a step toward it. But a fear stopped him. He checked himself and sat down in one of the living room's chairs. Sitting, he gazed at the entrance before him, trying to understand the faceless, but very real, terror that had flared at the instant of his decision to go in.

He reached out to grapple with it, as Walter had taught him. Consciously, he made the almost physical effort needed to put emotion apart from him. In his mind he made himself visualize what he feared, as a formless shape standing a little distance from him. Having given it form, he considered it. In itself, it was not important. It was only its effect on him that was important. But to understand that effect, he must understand what it was; and what was it?

It was not the room, itself, nor the thought of what he might find there. It was that irrevocable thing that the finding of it might do to him, that he feared. To enter the dining room in his present state of sensitivity could be finally to discover what part of him was himself and what was Donal. And if he should come to know what he feared to know . . .

. . . He might find himself committed to something from which there would be no drawing back. Perhaps, before him was that boundary of which all men and women were instinctively afraid—the boundary between the possible and the impossible; and if so, once into the impossible he might belong to it forever.

It was an old fear, he understood suddenly; one not merely old to him, but old in humankind. It was the fear of leaving the safeness of the known to cross into the darkness of the unknown, with all the unimaginable dangers that might wait there. And there was, he realized now, only one counter to it—equally old. The great urge to continue, no matter what, to grow and adventure, to discover and learn.

Understanding this at last, he understood for the first time that the commitment he had feared just now was one that he had already made for himself, long since. Faced with the choice of entering the unknown, he was one who would always go forward. Like a messenger, a few lines from a poem by Robert Browning returned to him, out of the depths of memory:

". . . they stood, ranged along the hillsides, met
To view the last of me, a living frame
For one more picture! In a sheet of flame

I saw them and I knew them all. And yet
Dauntless the slug-horn to my lips I set,
And blew."
"Childe Roland to the Dark Tower Came."

The path he had chosen for himself had led him to the cell on Harmony. And the path he had chosen for himself there had led to this house, this room and this moment. He got to his feet and walked into the dining room.

Within, the long, silent chamber was in dimness. Here, unlike in those other rooms he had entered, automatic sensors had not pulled the drapes back from the windows. Nor did the drapes pull back as he entered now. They were of heavy but soft cloth, a light brown in color, and the white daylight of Fomalhaut did not so much shine through them as make them glow softly, so that the room seemed caught in a luminous, amber twilight.

In that twilight the long, empty slab of the table and the upright, carved chairs ranked on both sides, with one only at the top end by the kitchen entrance, gleamed in a wood so dark a brown as to be almost black. The ceiling was lower than that of the living room, and beamed, so that the very air of the place, enclosed and populated by stillness, seemed even more hushed and timeless than that in the rest of the house.

On the long wall opposite the windows was the only active color in the dining room. Spaced along it at regular intervals were six small, archaic two-dimensional pictures in narrow frames, showing outdoor scenes; and offset behind the single chair at the head of the table, to Hal's left as he looked at them, was the entrance from the kitchen.

The light and stillness of the place seemed to flow about Hal, enclosing him from the rest of the house. *All else may alter,* the dining room seemed to say, *I have not changed in two hundred years.* He stepped forward and walked slowly down the wall side of the table, pausing to look at the small framed pictures as he passed.

They were scenes variously showing mountain, lake, glen and seashore, in reproductions which must be as old as Eachan Khan's memory of such places. And they were of Earth. The colors of land and sky, the relationships of slope and level were of the kind that was to be found nowhere else. A thousand tiny, subtle details authenticated the origin of what each represented. For a moment they recalled memories of Hal's that had not come to his mind for a long time; and he felt a sudden, intense homesickness for the Rocky Mountains he remembered from his own youth.

But then the feeling was gone, washed away by the power of the emotion that came from all that surrounded him. It was an emotion stained into walls and floor, chairs and table, and most of all into those pictures on the wall—the emotion of a family that had lived and died according to its own private code for more than two hundred years. There had been a saying that Malachi had quoted to Hal once when he had been very young—that the Dorsai, more than any other world, was its people. Not its wealth, or its power, or its reputation—but its people. Here, in this long, silent room, that saying stood forward from his memory to confront him.

As those of this family would have stood. Hal walked slowly to the head of the table and stood a little back from the corner of it, there, looking down its length. They had all sat here, at one time or another, since these walls had first been raised. Those whose names he had seen on the gravestones—Eachan Khan, Melissa and Cletus Grahame, Kamal Graeme; Eachan, who had been the father of Donal, Mor—Donal's brother; James, Kensie and Ian—his uncles; Leah—Ian's wife; Simon, Kamal and James—Ian's sons . . . and others.

Including Donal.

Donal would have sat here often before the night of his graduation from the Academy, the night before he was to leave under his first contract. But that one night, after dinner, for the first time, he would have joined those others in the family who had already made their outgoing; those who had left the planet of their birth under contract to fight for other people they did not know. For the first time, then, he would have felt himself one with these older relatives who had already achieved what he had privately feared was beyond any strength and skill he would ever manage. That evening, for the first time, the door to the fourteen worlds would have seemed to stand open to him; and he would have looked through it, and on those beside him, with new eyes.

Hal moved slowly up past the pictures to the head of the table and stood behind the single chair there, looking back down the room. The night before Donal's leaving, who would have been here at Foralie of those who had gone out to the other worlds?

Kamal Khan Graeme—but he would not have been with the rest at the table. By the time of Donal's outgoing, he was confined to his bed. Eachan, of course, who had been home since his right leg had been so badly wounded that field command was no longer practical for him. Hal tried to remember who else might have been here; and, slowly as if of their own accord, the names swam up to the surface of his memory. Ian and

Kensie had been home then. And Mor, Donal's oldest brother, had been home on leave from the Friendlies. James had died at Donneswort seven years before.

So . . . there had been five of them at the table after dinner that night. The unchanging twilight of the room about Hal seemed to thicken. Eachan would have been here, at the head of the table—in the chair before Hal. Ian and Kensie, as the two next senior, would normally each have taken the first chair on either side, at Eachan's elbows. But the twins always sat side by side—this night they had sat on Eachan's left, out of the habit of years, with a wall at their backs and both entrances in view. At Eachan's right, then, would have been Mor; and in the chair next to Mor, then . . .

Hal left his station at the head of the table and moved down to stand behind the second chair on Eachan's right, the one Donal would have occupied.

He focused mind and eyes together, rebuilding the scene in his mind. Gazing at the empty chairs, he filled them with the images of the men whose pictures he had seen in the books about Donal. Eachan, tall and gaunt, now that he could not be as physically active as he had been—so that his shoulders looked abnormally wide above the rest of his body, and below the dark, lean face. The face with the deep parentheses around the mouth and the frown-line born of chronic, unmentioned pain deep between his black, level brows.

Ian and Kensie, alike as mirror images—but unmistakably different, with the inner characters that altered their whole appearance. Kensie bright, and Ian dark; both of them taller even than Eachan and Mor and with the massiveness of working muscle that Eachan had lost. Mor, leaner than both his uncles, smooth-faced and younger, but with something lonely and hungry in his dark eyes.

And Donal . . . half a head shorter than Mor, and even slimmer, with the double difference of greater youth and smaller boning, so that he looked like a boy among men at this table.

Eachan, leaning with his forearms on the table, Ian upright and grim, Kensie laughing easily as he always laughed. Mor leaning forward, eager to speak. And Donal . . . listening to them all.

The talk would have been of business, of working conditions for professional soldiers on the worlds they had last left to come home. Ordinary shoptalk, but with an ear to Donal, so that they could inform him without seeming to directly give him advice . . .

The sound of their voices had run and echoed off the beams overhead, fast and slow. Statement and response. Pause and speak again.

". . . The lusts are vampires," Eachan had said. "Soldiering is a pure art. . . ."

". . . Would you have stayed home, Eachan," Mor had asked his father, "when you were young and had two good legs?"

"Eachan's right." It was Ian speaking. "They still dream of squeezing our free people up into one lump and then negotiating with that lump for the force to get the whip hand on all the other worlds. That's the danger. . . ."

"As long as the cantons remain independent of the Council . . .," said Eachan.

"Nothing stands still," said Kensie.

And with those last three words the whisky they had been drinking had seemed to go to Donal's head in a rush; and to him it seemed that the table and the dark, harsh-boned faces he watched seemed to swim in the dimness of the dining room and Kensie's voice came roaring at him from a great distance.

About Hal the room was filling with others, other Graemes from before and since, taking the other chairs at the table, joining in the talk, so that the voices rose and mingled, the atmosphere of the room thickened . . . and then, abruptly, the after-dinner gathering was over. They were all standing up, to go to their beds ready for an early start in the morning. The room was full of tall bodies and deep voices; and his head spun.

He had to get out, himself. He was very close to something that had now picked him up and was carrying him away, faster and faster, so that soon he would be beyond the power of his strength to get free. He turned toward what he thought was the living-room entrance to the dining room, but which he could no longer see for the shapes all around him. He pushed his way between them, stumbling, feeling his strength go. But he could not see the entrance and he did not have the strength to turn and go back the other way—

Strong arms caught him, held him and steered him, on unsteady feet through a mist of wraiths. Suddenly there was fresh air on his face, a breeze blowing against him. His right foot tripped on a downstep and dropped to a yielding surface, and the arms holding him brought him to a halt.

"Breathe deeply," commanded a voice. "Now—again!"

He obeyed; and slowly his vision cleared to show him earth and mountains and sky. He was standing on the grass, just outside the front door of Graemehouse; and it was Amanda who was upholding him.

Chapter

> > **45** < <

"*I'd better get* you home," Amanda had said.

Dazed and numbed, he had not objected. The sensation had lasted through most of their ride back to Fal Morgan, so that he remembered little of it. Only when they were nearly to Fal Morgan did his head clear and he became conscious of the fact that he felt hollowly weak; drained as if by some emergency physical effort that had taken all his strength.

"I'm sorry," he said to Amanda, when he had stumbled at last into the living room of Fal Morgan, "I didn't mean to be a problem. I just seem to be knocked out. . . ."

"I know," she said. Her eyes were steady on him, almost grim, and un-fathomable. "Now, you need rest."

She turned him about like a child and steered him down the hall, into the room he had used the night before and to a seat on the edge of the bed. He was vaguely aware of his boots being pulled off; he did not see her signal the sensors, but the drapes came together over the windows and the room dropped into semi-darkness.

"Sleep now," said Amanda's voice clearly out of the gloom.

He heard the door close. He was still sitting on the edge of the bed, but now he fell back. Chilled, he turned on his side and reached out to pull over him the heavy quilt that topped the bedding, then fell instantly asleep.

He did not wake until the following morning. Pulling himself out of bed, he dressed and went in search of Amanda. He found her in an of-fice off the living room, at a desk stacked with what appeared to be bound printouts of contracts. She was gazing at a screen inset in the desk surface, stylus in hand, apparently making corrections on what was being shown her on the screen. She lifted her head as he looked in.

"Come along," she said; and he came in. "How do you feel?"

"Wobbly," he said. In fact, he felt as if he had hardly slept at all since dismounting from his horse after the ride back from Foralie.

"Sit down, then," she said; and herself laid down the stylus she had been holding.

He dropped gratefully into an overstuffed chair. She eyed him keenly.

"You'll have to be quiet for a few days," she said. "What can I do for you?"

"Tell me how to arrange for some transportation back to Omalu," he said. "I've imposed on you long enough, here."

"I'll tell you when you've imposed," Amanda said. "As far as Omalu goes, you're in no shape to go anywhere."

"I've got to go," he said. "I've things to do there. I've got to go about seeing whoever it is that represents the Dorsai."

"You want the Grey Captains."

He stared at her.

"Who?"

She smiled.

"It's an old term," she said. "Grey spelled with an 'e,' incidentally. I don't think anyone knows where it came from, originally. It was back in Cletus' day we stopped using the term Captain as a military rank anywhere but on spaceships. What the name's come to mean here is someone who's a leader, confirmed and accepted, a woman or man other people trust— and trust to make decisions. The first and second Amanda were Grey Captains."

"And the third?" He looked at her.

"Yes. The third, too," she said, unsmiling. "The point is, though, that it's the Grey Captains you want to talk to; and they aren't usually in Omalu. They're wherever they live on the Dorsai."

"Then I've got to go talk to them individually and get them to agree to get together so I can talk to them all at once."

She watched him for several seconds without speaking.

"If you were in shape," she said at last, slowly, "which you're not, that'd still be the wrong way to go about it. As it is, right now you're not up to talking to anyone. The first thing you do is get your feet back under you— and that means about a week."

He shook his head.

"Not that long," he said.

"That long."

"In any case," he put his arms on the arms of the chair, ready to get up, "this can't wait—"

"Yes, it can."

"You don't understand." His hands fell away from the arms of the chair. "To begin with, I've got an important message for the Dorsai people generally, from the Exotics. But, even more important, I've got to talk to these Captains, myself. There's something I've got to make them understand— that what we're headed into may destroy everything the Dorsai's stood

for, and most of everything else. . . . I don't know how to make you understand—"

"You already have," she said.

He stared at her with the uneasy feeling that matters were being rushed
upon him.

"The first night you were here." She watched him, unwaveringly, and
there was no end to the turquoise depths of her eyes. "You told me all
about it."

"All about it?" he said. "All?"

"I think, all," she said. There was that several second pause, again, as
her eyes watched him. "I know what you need done; and I know—which
you don't—the way to do it. Before you can meet with the Grey Captains, they're all going to have to come together at some place. That place
might as well be Foralie."

"Foralie?" He stared at her.

"Why not?" she said. "It's got the space to handle a meeting that size,
and it's not being used right now."

She stopped speaking and sat watching him. He did not say anything
for a moment, himself. There was a cold feeling inside him at the thought
of his speaking to these people in Graemehouse and for a moment he almost forgot she was there. Then his mind and his eyes came back to her,
to find her still watching.

"I can call the Captains for you; and get some help from around the
district, here," she said, "if it's needed to take care of the situation. It
shouldn't take more than a day, unless some of them need to stay
overnight before starting home."

He hesitated.

"You could suggest they come?" he said. "And you think they'd come?"

"Yes." It was a blunt statement. "They'll come."

"I can't—" Words failed him.

"Can't what? Can't impose?" She smiled a little. "It's for our benefit,
isn't it?"

"It is . . . ," he said. "Of course. Still . . ."

"Then it's settled," she said. "I'll send the word out to the ones who
should be here. Meanwhile, you can get rested up. You need a week."

"How long does it take to get them together?" he asked, still with the
uneasy feeling that matters were being rushed upon him.

"Six hours in an emergency." She looked at him almost coldly. "In the
case of something like this where there's no emergency, at the very least
a week to find a time when most of them can get together. In a week you
ought to be able to talk to at least two-thirds of them."

"Only two-thirds?" he said. "Is two-thirds enough?"

"If you can convince most of the two-thirds," she answered, "you'll have no trouble carrying most of the full number in the long run. Each one is going to make up his own mind; but they're all sensible people. If they hear sense most of them will listen to it and pass it on to their own people."

"Yes," he said. He was still unsure about all that she had said; but this talk, mild as it had been, had exhausted him.

"Then I'll take care of it." She looked keenly at him. "Can you fix yourself something to eat? I've got my hands full at the moment."

"Of course," he said.

She smiled for a second and her face transformed. Then she was level-mouthed, level-eyed, all business again.

"All right, then," she said, picking up her stylus again, and turning her attention back to the screen in her desk. "Don't hesitate to call if you need me."

He stood looking at her for a second more. There was something odd, here. When he had first come, she had been a friendly stranger, polite but open. Now, she was at once much closer and at the same time walled off from him—encased in some armor of her own. He turned and went off to the kitchen, conscious of the rubberiness of his legs and the labor of moving his body along the passageway with them.

He ate and immediately was avaricious for sleep again. He went back to his bedroom and fell on the bed, rousing later, briefly, to eat and sleep once more.

Amanda had been right. It was almost a full three days before he began to feel like himself again. It began to look as if the week until the Grey Captains could be gathered together would be welcome to him after all.

It was a different weakness that had gripped him, this time. Undoubtedly, the remnants of the physical attrition he had endured on Harmony were still with him. Nonetheless, the essential nature of his exhaustion right now did not seem merely physical, but something more—something he considered labelling with the word psychic, then drew back from the term.

What was undeniable was that what had done this to him was the purely non-physical experience in Graemehouse; and his mind, which could never leave anything alone, but was forever digging at things and taking them apart to find out how they worked, would not get off the subject of what had happened to him in the dining room.

There were all sorts of possible explanations.

One that stood up to examination was that he had found exactly what he had gone looking for—an understanding of the Graemes in general, and Donal in particular, so intense that for a moment he had been able, subjectively, at least, to relive an episode out of Donal's life. But there was another one that brought back the chill and the lifted hairs on the back of his neck. He shied away from it, turning back defensively to the first explanation.

Given his training in concentration, and the creative instinct that had led him into poetry, the moments in which he had become Donal, in the bedroom and in the dining room, were not impossible. But still . . . he found he could start comfortably down the route of a sensible explanation—adding together his mental techniques, his young desire to identify with Donal, his hangover of physical exhaustion from Harmony, and the emotional effect of his disappointment on Mara—but in the end he came to a gap, a quantum jump, in which something unknown, something not explainable, had to have happened in addition, to produce what he had experienced.

Something above and beyond knowledge—something almost like magic—had been at work there. And yet, was there not something very much like that sort of quantum jump, or magic, involved in the creation of any piece of art? You could follow down the line of craft and skill only so far—and then something would happen which not even the best craftsman could identify or explain; and the result was art.

In the same way, he had come to a quantum jump-point—first, in his dream of James' burial, back on Harmony, and again in Donal's bedroom, but much more so than either earlier instance, in the dining room— which was unidentifiable and unexplainable. It was easy to tell himself that it had all been the result of a sort of self-hypnosis, a self-created illusion. But deep within himself he did not believe it.

Deeply within himself, he knew better. He knew it the way he knew beyond a shadow of a doubt, sometimes, that the lines of poetry he had just put on paper said something more than the total of their individual words could explain. The poem that worked, that involved the quantum jump, opened a doorway on another universe, which could be felt—as he had felt himself to be Donal.

In the same sense there had been more to the moment in the Graeme-house dining room than all the unconscious memories of what he had heard about the Graemes could account for. Deep within him, too deep for any denial, he knew—as he knew that he lived—that what he had experienced in the dining room was not what could have happened the night of Donal's graduation from the Academy, but what had happened.

In the day or two that followed, as he began to shed his drained feeling, as the inner reservoir of physical and psychic energy began to be replaced, he began to turn more of his attention to Amanda. She was up before dawn, taking care of the house, the stable and everything else around the place. By ten in the morning she would be at work in her office with contracts; and outside of ordinary interruptions in the way of phone calls, meals and other duties around the house, or occasional necessary trips outside it, she worked steadily through until late at night.

Her efficiency was unbelievable. Clearly, she had developed the most economical technique possible for each thing she had to do; and when the time came, she did it swiftly and surely. But none of the things she did were done with the sort of habitual, machine-like response that such a conscious approach often produced. On the contrary, her executions were as easy as breathing, with the unconscious grace of an accomplished artist in the practice of her art.

On the morning of the second day, however, because his conscience bothered him, he cornered her as she started out to the stable.

"Can I help?" he asked.

"I'll tell you if you can," she said; then, watching him, her voice and expression softened. "Fal Morgan is mine. You understand?"

"Yes," he said; and stood aside to let her go.

By the third day his normal energy and strength had largely returned. He had spent most of the time sitting around, reading and thinking; but by that evening a physical restlessness began to build up inside him like water building up behind a dam. After dinner, Amanda went as usual back to her office and he tried again to read; but his thoughts wandered. The teeth of unanswered questions gnawed at him. As the days passed, he had felt something inside himself reaching out to her more and more; and his instinctive perceptions of her had sent back the message that she responded to this reaching out. But if anything, since the day at Foralie, she had drawn more and more back behind the brisk armor of her duties—and the reason for this eluded him.

Also, whatever else had taken place there, he had gone to Foralie with the purpose of finding the truth in his dream; and he had found it, only to realize that it concerned Donal Graeme—and that Donal had been an untypical Dorsai—as Cletus had been before him—and the experience in Graemehouse had been no help in bringing him to feel that he could make himself understood to the Grey Captains.

After nearly three days of circular thinking on these topics, the protest of his body at the long stretch of inactivity that had held him lately rose to an uncontrollable pitch. He put the cube he had been reading after dinner abruptly aside, and went to look through the half-open door of Amanda's office, to see if she was still at work.

She was. He left the office door and went to the closet by the back door of Fal Morgan, where an assortment of work clothing, sweaters and jackets occupied pegs on a wall-long rack. There was no jacket there quite big enough for him, but one of the sweaters, a loosely-knit bulky affair, was ample in size. He put it on, and stepped out into the night.

His intention had been only to go for a walk in the immediate vicinity of the house. But the Dorsai's single moon was nearly full and high in the sky, and the landscape around him showed clear and bright with moonlight. He walked to the edge of the open area in which Fal Morgan sat and looked down into the gully below him. Its tangle of light and dark, and the rocky upslopes beyond, attracted him; and he went down into it.

He had no real fear of getting lost. The surrounding mountain peaks were visible from any position below them; and they made excellent fixed reference points, particularly to someone raised in such territory. He crossed the gully he had chosen and continued up the slope beyond into a bare rock area of small cliffs and passes.

He lost himself in roaming the rocky area. After several days of walking only between rooms, to move freely in the open air was a relief. He had forgotten—even on Harmony when they went through the mountains, he had forgotten—how he had felt as a boy in the Rockies. Now that feeling came back. The peaks above him were not ominous and unknown shapes brooding upon the moonlit horizon; but, as they had been on Earth, sheltering giants within whose shadow he felt a freedom not to be found anywhere else. His stride lengthened, the breath in him came from the depths of his lungs, and from far inside him came a longing to cut loose from all larger duties and purposes and simply work to live, in such a place as this.

He woke, finally, to the fact that he had been walking for at least a couple of hours. Unnoticed until now, the night had chilled; and he had chilled, even with his exercise and clad in the heavy sweater. Also, now that he came down from the feeling that had uplifted him among the mountain peaks, he became conscious of the physical weariness in his not-yet-recovered body. He turned back to Fal Morgan.

As he approached the house, he carried the mountains still with him in his mind; and as he laid his hand upon the back door of Fal Morgan to open it, he discovered himself nursing a small, irrational resentment that, self-barricaded from him as she now was, Amanda had become someone he could not tell of his walk and how it had made him feel. He laughed softly and wryly to himself at the disappointment in him at that discovery, quietly opened the door and went in.

The house held the stillness of the hours toward midnight. He thought suddenly to look at his chronometer, and was startled to see that he had been outside almost three hours. Amanda would certainly have finished work by this time and be in bed.

Although there was no danger of her hearing him from the other end of the house, he went softly, out of a touch of conscience, through the kitchen and into the corridor to the living room. As he entered it, he realized that there was still light in the living room—and he hesitated. Then he realized, from the waxing and waning of its illumination, that it must be the light of the fire, still burning in the fireplace; though it was not like Amanda, in her automatic housekeeping, to go to bed with the fire still burning.

She might have left it burning for him; or she might still be up. He went forward quietly, on the chance that the second possibility was correct; and before he was halfway down the corridor he heard the sound of her voice, singing very softly, as if to herself, in the firelit room.

He was suddenly unsure; and he stopped. Then he took off his boots and went forward; not merely quietly, but with the utter silence of his early training in movement. He reached the corner of the entrance to the living room and looked cautiously around it toward the fireplace.

The fire had burned low; but flames still flickered along the dark lengths of the heavy back logs, painting the near floor of the room with ruddy color. Amanda, a half-empty cup beside her which must have originally been full of tea, for it had a milky color and she drank her coffee black, sat cross-legged on the dark red, rectangular carpet directly before the fireplace, gazing into it, her wrists on her knees and her hands relaxed, palm-upwards.

She sat like a slim, erect shadow against the light of the fire. He looked at her almost from the side, but slightly ahead. She was wearing the dark brown work pants and the soft yellow shirt she had had on earlier at dinner; but her shirt had been opened at the neck, and the wings of the collar lay out on her shoulders. Her hair was untied from its earlier, workaday restriction and lay loosely on her neck. Her face was tilted slightly toward the fire, and pensive. Close as he was now, in the silence of the house, he could hear the clear magic of her voice, in spite of its softness, plainly singing:

"*. . . green flows the water by my love's bright fancy.*
Green are the pools at the foot of the falls,

Dark under willow—and past is the sleeping.
Light in the morning, a little bird calls. . . ."

He drew back abruptly into darkness, closing his ears to the rest of the song. It was as if he had come upon her naked and sleeping. Silently, he retraced his steps to the kitchen; and stood, uncertain.

From the living room, the murmur of her singing ended. He took a deep breath, stopped to put his boots back on, then stepped back without a sound and reached for the door by which he had entered earlier. He opened it silently, closed it noisily, and walked forward without carefulness through the passage and into the living room.

She was standing by the fire as he entered, looking in his direction as he came through the entrance into the room. Her eyes focused on the sweater he wore and widened a little. He stopped, facing her with a little distance between them.

"I went for a walk," he said. "I grabbed this off one of the pegs to wear. I hope that was all right?"

"Of course," she said. There was a second's hesitation. "It was Ian Graeme's."

"Oh, it was?"

"Yes. One he knitted for himself, one winter." She smiled just a little. "We tend to keep our hands busy in the winter here, when we're snowed in."

There was another brief pause.

"You're feeling more lively, then?" Her eyes, darkened in the firelit room, watched him.

"I was. I'm ready for sleep now." He smiled back at her. Their eyes met for a second, then glanced aside.

"Goodnight," he said, and went on into the corridor leading to his bedroom, hearing her answer "goodnight" behind him, and leaving the large room, the firelight and her, behind him.

He reached his own room, went in, and closed the door. He was conscious of the weight of the sweater, still upon him. He took it off and proceeded to undress, then lay down on his back on the bed. A wave of his hand over the night table signalled the sensor there to turn off the lighting; and the bedroom around him was plunged in darkness.

He lay there. After a while the sound of her steps came down the hall, passed his bedroom and went on to her own. Silence claimed the house. He continued to lie, awake, staring into the darkness, his heart torn by a sorrow and longing he did not dare to investigate too closely.

Chapter

> > 46 < <

The following day was Sunday, according to the weekly calendar on the Dorsai. Amanda took Hal with her to visit several of the neighboring homesteads, where there were individuals who had offered to help at Foralie during his meeting with the Grey Captains.

One of these was the Debigné household; and Hal had his suspicions confirmed that the intensity of Amanda was not something shared by her younger sister. What was necessary was for someone to be in residence at Foralie from the day before to the day after the meeting; and for others to help with meals and maintenance from the time the first of the Captains arrived—as much as an estimated twenty-four hours ahead of the meeting time until the last of them left—as much as twenty-four hours after.

On the way back to Fal Morgan after lunch, Amanda took Hal by a route somewhat out of their way to an observation point even higher up than Foralie. It was a patch of grass on a flat ledge hardly large enough to have supported Fal Morgan. They dismounted; and Amanda took a scope out of one of her saddle bags.

"Sit down," she said to Hal, dropping down herself, cross-legged upon the grass. He settled beside her and she gave him the scope.

"Look there," she said, pointing. She was directing his attention beyond and below Graemehouse, the roof of which, with the roofs of its outbuildings, was visible perhaps a kilometer below and to the left of them.

Hal put the scope to his eyes and located the spot she had indicated. It was a green patch surrounded by trees somewhat less than eight hundred meters below the house.

"I see it," he said. "What is it?"

"The site of the original Foralie—the house," she said. "Foralie was built by Eachan Khan, in the first place. When Cletus married his daughter, Melissa, he built Graemehouse on Foralie land where you see it now. After Cletus defeated Dow deCastries in his attempt to control all the Younger Worlds with the power of Old Earth, and Melissa went with Cletus to Graemehouse, Eachan Khan began to show his age—he hadn't much before—and Melissa talked him into joining her and Cletus at Graemehouse. He did, and Foralie was left empty—but with everything still in it for a year or two. Eachan didn't seem to be able to make up his mind what to do with it. Then, one night, it caught fire and burned down. Since then Graemehouse has been Foralie."

"I see," said Hal. The green space below him was certainly a pleasant place to have put a house, much more sheltered among the trees than Graemehouse on its high perch. He lowered the scope and looked at Amanda.

"We could have ridden down there," said Amanda, "but there's nothing much to see when you get there; and actually from here you get a better picture of how it was."

"Yes," he said; and passed the scope back to her.

"No. Hang on to it for a bit," she said. "You can also see Fal Morgan down there—or at least part of its roofs. The trees get in the way, a bit. But you may remember you couldn't see it at all from Graemehouse, for the trees."

"You're right." He put the scope to his eyes again and looked. Then lowered it once more to look at her. All this about the original Foralie, and the rest of it, was certainly the sort of thing she might expect him to be interested in; but he could not help feeling that there was a reason behind her obvious one for telling him about this, and showing the original Foralie to him, from this vantage point.

"It was Foralie, the original house, that Cletus came back to after Dow deCastries had moved in with his troops to take over the Dorsai, when all her fighting men were gone," she said. "You know about that?"

Hal nodded.

"That was in the early days, wasn't it?" he said. "Nearly two hundred years ago, when the Earth was split between the Alliance and the Coalition? And Dow was a Coalition man who got the two governments to combine their forces, under him, so he could take over the newer worlds? I know about it. Cletus Grahame opposed Dow, Dow arranged contracts to drain all the trained soldiers off Dorsai, then moved in here to take the planet over; and those who were left here, the grandparents, the children and the mothers, stopped him."

He grinned.

"There're still historians who think Dow must have cut his own throat; because noncombatants can't defeat elite troops."

"Did you ever think that?" Amanda asked.

"No." He sobered. "But I heard about it first from Malachi when I was very young. It seemed perfectly natural to me, then, that they could do it, being Dorsai."

"Nothing happens by reputation alone," she said. "Each district—we didn't have cantons in those days—had to decide how to defend itself. Cletus left only Arvid Johnson and Bill Athyer, with six trained men, to organize the defense. . . ."

She fell silent, her eyes gazing down upon the slopes below. He watched her, still trying to understand what she was aiming at. Even seated, her body had an erectness that no man could have possessed without stiffness; and her face had the quality of a profile stamped on a silver coin.

"Amanda . . . ," he said, gently.

She did not seem to have heard him; and he felt a clumsiness in himself that made him unsure of prodding her further. Beside her, in his much taller, larger-framed but gaunt—thinned down by the experiences of recent months—body, he felt like some dark bird of earthbound flesh and bone, bending above an entity of pure spirit. But as he waited, her eyes lost their abstraction and she turned to him.

"What is it?" she said.

It crossed his mind to wonder if perhaps he should avoid further mention of the Defense of the Dorsai—as it was called in the histories.

"I was just thinking how much you look like that painting in your hall—was it of the first Amanda? It could be a picture of you."

"Both the second Amanda and I look like her," she answered. "It happens."

"Does it just happen that she had her picture painted at the same age you are now?"

"No." She shook her head and smiled, almost mischievously. "It wasn't."

"It wasn't?" He gazed at her.

"No," Amanda laughed. "That picture in our hall was made when she was a good deal older than I am now."

He frowned.

"It's true," she said. "We age very slowly, we Morgans. And she was something special."

"Not as special as you," he said. "She couldn't be. You're end-result Dorsai. She lived before people like you had been born."

"That's not true," Amanda said swiftly. "She was Dorsai before there was a Dorsai world. What she was, was the material out of which our people and our Culture's been made."

"How can you be so sure of what she was—nearly two centuries ago?"

"How can I?" She turned her head to face him and looked at him strangely. "Because in many ways I am her."

The last few words came out without any particular emphasis; but they seemed to ring in his ears with an unusual distinctness. He sat as he was, careful not to move or change his expression, but his inner awareness had just been alerted.

"A reincarnation?" he said, lightly, after a moment.

"No, not really," she answered. "But something more . . . as if time didn't matter. As if it's all the same thing; her, there in the beginning of this world of ours; and I, here. . . ."

And now the feeling came clearly to him that her reason was out in the open, that she had told him—warned him, perhaps—of what she had brought him here to be warned about.

"Here at the end of it, you mean?" he challenged her.

"No." Her turquoise eyes had taken on a gray shade. "The end won't be until the last Dorsai is dead, and wherever that Dorsai dies. In fact, not even then. The end is only going to be when the last human is dead—because what makes us Dorsai is something that's a part of all humans; that part the first Amanda had when she was born, back on Earth."

Something—a fragment of cloud across the white dot of the sun, perhaps—shuttered the sunlight from his eyes for a split second. There was some connection between all this she was presently speaking of, the lost house of Foralie, the Defense of the Dorsai and herself, that was still eluding him.

"You think so much of her," he said thoughtfully. "But it's the Cletus Grahames and the Donal Graemes that the rest of the worlds think of when they talk about this world."

"We've had Graemes as our next neighbors since Cletus," she replied. "What's thought of them, they earned. But the first Amanda was here before either of them. She founded our family. She cleared the out-of-work mercenaries from these mountains before Cletus came; and it was when she was ninety-three that she held Foralie District against Dow deCastries' troops, who'd landed here, thinking they'd have no trouble with the children and women, the sick and the old, who were all that was left."

"So, she was given charge of Foralie District?" he said. "Why her? Had she been a soldier once?"

"No," she answered. "But, as I said, During the Outlaw Years here, she'd led the way in clearing out the lawless mercenaries. After she did that, and other things, with just the noncombatants to help her, the rest of the districts followed her example; and law came to the Dorsai. She led when Dow came because she was the one best fit to command in this district, in spite of her age."

"How did she do it?"

"Clean out the outlaws, or defeat deCastries?"

"Not the outlaws—though I'd like to hear about that sometime, too," he said. "No, how did she defeat deCastries when all the experts then and now claim there was no way a gaggle of housewives, children and old people could possibly have done it?"

Amanda's gaze went a long way past him.

"In a way you could say the troops did defeat themselves. Did you ever read Cletus' *Tactics of Mistake?*"

"Yes," he said. "But when I was too young to understand it well."

"What we did was in there—it was a matter of making them make the mistakes, putting our strength against the weaknesses of the invaders."

"Weaknesses? In first-line troops?"

She looked at him again with the gray tint to her eyes.

"They weren't as willing to die as we were."

"Willing to die?" He studied her. "Old people? Mothers—"

"And children. Yes."

The armor of sunlight around her seemed to invest her words with a quality of truth greater than he had ever known from anyone else.

"The Dorsai," she said, "was formed by people who were willing to pay with their lives in others' battles, in order to buy freedom for their homes. It wasn't only in the men who went off to fight. Those at home had that same image of freedom, and were willing to die for it."

"But simply being willing to die—"

"You don't understand, not being born here," she said. "It was a matter of our being able to make harder choices than the soldiers sent in to occupy us. Amanda and the others in the district who were best qualified to decide sat down before the invasion and considered a number of plans. All of the plans meant casualties—and the casualties could include the people who were considering the plans. They chose the one that gave the district its greatest effectiveness against the enemy for the least number of deaths; and, having chosen it, the ones who had done the choosing were ready to be among those who would have to pay for its success. The invading soldiers had no such plan—and no such will."

He shook his head.

"I don't understand," he said. "I suppose it's because I'm not a Dorsai."

She looked at him for a moment, like someone who considers saying something, then thinks better of it.

"Then you don't understand the first Amanda?" she said. "I think you'll need to if you're going to talk to the Grey Captains."

He nodded, soberly.

"How did it happen?" he asked. "How did she—how did they do it? I have to know."

"All right," she said, "I'll tell you."

And she did. Sitting there in the sunlight, listening to her talk of a past as if it was something she herself had lived through, he thought again of what she had said about the first Amanda and herself being the same person. The story was a simple one. Dow's troops had come in and bivouacked just beyond Foralie Town. The first Amanda had gotten their commander's permission to continue with a manufacturing process in town that was necessary to the district's economy; and the process, according to plan, had flooded the atmosphere of the town and its vicinity with vaporized nickel carbonyl. One part in a million of those vapors was enough to cause allergic dermatitis and an edema of the lungs that was irreversible. In short—a sure death.

What had lulled the suspicions of the invaders until too late had been that there were inhabitants of Foralie Town also getting sick and dying, just as the soldiers were. Even when at last they understood, it had been unbelievable to Dow's military that townspeople could choose to stay where they were and die, just to make sure that the invaders died with them.

At the last, there had been a situation in which Dow had held Cletus as a captive at Foralie, with healthy troops on guard. An assortment of the older children, armed, plus the eight professionals Cletus had left to organize defenses, and Amanda, had reversed the situation. Amanda, in her ninety-third year, had finally captured the soldiers guarding Foralie by threatening to blow them and herself up together.

Compelling as the story was, it was not so much that which caught at Hal's attention. It was Amanda's way of telling it, as if she herself had been there. More strongly than ever came the impression that there was something she was trying to tell him under the screen of words which he was failing to understand. An anger stirred in him that he should be so unperceptive. But there was nothing to be done but wait and hope for some word that would wake him suddenly to her meaning.

So, he sat with her in the bright sunlight, hearing not merely the story of the defense of Foralie District, but of Kensie's death on Sainte Marie; and about how the second Amanda, who had loved both Kensie and Ian (but Ian more) had decided at last to marry no one. But even when they remounted their horses, he still did not know what it was she wanted him to understand. The afternoon had moved in upon them as she had talked; and Fomalhaut was halfway down the sky by the time they rode once more into the yard of Fal Morgan.

". . . And I," she said again at the end of the story, "am the first and second Amandas over again."

They did not get the chance to talk again at any length until after the meeting. The next day, Monday, Amanda was gone on a business trip; and on Tuesday she was busy away from Fal Morgan, directing and helping with the preparing of Graemehouse for the meeting. Hal stayed where he was at Fal Morgan, puzzling over her as much as over what he would say to convince the Grey Captains. There was something in him like a superstition—which, strangely, Amanda seemed to understand—that made him unwilling to return to Foralie until the actual meeting time should arrive.

The Captains from farthest away began to arrive late Tuesday; and were welcomed at Graemehouse by Amanda and the neighbors who were helping. She did not get back to Fal Morgan until late evening; and after a quick meal she sat with Hal over a drink in the living room for only a few minutes before going to bed.

"What was it you said—that I'd need to convince most of those that come?" he asked her as they sat before the fire. "What percentage is 'most'?"

She raised her gaze from the flames, which she had been watching; and smiled a little. "If you can get through to seventy per cent of those who come, you'll be a success," she said. "Those who don't get here will eventually react in pretty much the same proportions, after talking to those who did."

"Seventy per cent," he echoed, turning the short, heavy glass slowly in his hands and looking at the firelight through the brown liquid he had barely tasted.

"Don't expect miracles," her voice said; and he looked up to see her watching him. "No one, except Cletus, or maybe Donal, in his lifetime, could carry them all. Seventy per cent will give you what you want. Be very happy with that. As I told you—everyone makes up his own mind here, and the Grey Captains more than most."

He nodded.

"Do you know what you're going to say?" she asked after a moment.

"Part of it. The part that's the Exotic message," he answered, nursing the whisky glass between his palms. "For the rest—it doesn't seem to plan."

"If you tell them what you told me, your first night here," she said, "you'll be all right."

He looked at her, startled.

"You think so?"

"I know so," she said.

He continued to look at her, searchingly, trying to remember all of what he had said that first night.

"I'm not sure I remember exactly what that was," he said, slowly.

"It'll come to you," she told him. The words lingered on his ears. She got to her feet, carrying her half-empty glass.

"Well, I need sleep," she said; and watched him for a second. "Possibly you do, too."

"Yes," he said. "But I think I'll sit here just a little while longer, though. I'll take care of the fire."

"Just be sure the screen's in place. . . ."

She went off. He sat alone for another twenty minutes before he sighed, reached out to wave his hand over the screen sensor, and stood up. The screen slid tightly across the front of the fireplace, and the last of the flames, cut off from fresh oxygen, began almost immediately to dwindle and die. He drained his glass, took it to the kitchen, and went to bed.

The meeting was not to be held until an hour after lunchtime at Foralie. Half an hour before then, Hal and Amanda saddled up and rode from Fal Morgan.

He did not feel like talking, and Amanda seemed content to leave him in his silence. He had expected his mind to be buzzing with possible arguments he could use. Instead, it had retreated into a calmness, utterly remote from the situation into which he was heading.

He was wise enough to let it be. He sat back in the saddle and let his senses be occupied by the sound, scent and vision of the ride.

When they reached the mounded level of the area on which Graeme-house was built, they found a couple of dozen air-space jitneys parked before the main building; and as they dismounted at the corral by the stable, the sound of internal activity reached out to them, through an opened kitchen window. They removed saddles and bridles from their horses, turned them loose in the corral, and went in through the front entrance.

In the living room, they found only two people, seated talking in an adjoining pair of the overstuffed chairs. One was a square, black woman with a hooked nose in a stern face, and the other a pink-faced, small man, both at least in their sixties.

"Miriam Songhai," said Amanda, "this is Hal Mayne. Rourke di Facino, Hal Mayne."

"Honored," they all murmured to each other.

"I'll go round up people," added di Facino, getting to his feet, and went off toward the office and bedroom end of the house. Amanda stayed with Hal.

"So you're the lad," said Miriam, in a voice that had a tendency to boom.

"Yes," said Hal.

"Sit down," she said. "It'll be a while before they're all together. Where do you spring from originally?"

"Earth—Old Earth," said Hal, taking the chair di Facino had vacated.

"When did you leave? Tell me about yourself," she said; and Hal began to give her something of his personal history.

But they were interrupted by others entering the room in ones and twos, and the necessity of introductions. Shortly, the conversation with Miriam Songhai was lost completely and Hal found himself standing in a room full almost to overcrowding.

"Everybody's here, aren't they?" said a tall, cadaverous man in at least his eighties. He had a bass voice that was remarkable. "Why don't we move in and get settled?"

There was a general movement toward the dining room and Hal found himself carried along by it. At the entrance to the dining room, for a second only, a small hesitation took him; and then it was gone. The long room before him was no longer dim and filled with amber light in which ghosts might walk. The drapes had at last been drawn and the fierce white illumination of Fomalhaut reflected off the gray-white surface of the steep slope behind the house and sent hard light through the windows, to carve everything animate and inanimate within to an unsparing three-dimensional solidity. Hal went on, saw Amanda standing beside the single chair at the table's head beckoning to him, and walked forward.

He sat down. Amanda went to seat herself, several chairs from him on his right. The room had filled behind them and empty chairs were rapidly being occupied. In a minute, they had all been filled; and he found himself looking along the polished tabletop, above which thirty-odd faces looked back and waited for him to speak.

Chapter

> > **47** < <

As they all sat watching him and waiting, an awareness he had never felt before woke suddenly in him.

Later, he was to become familiar with it, but this was his first experience; and it came on him with a shock that there could be a moment in which the universe seemed to stand still, like a ballet dancer poised on one toe; and for a fraction of a second all possibilities were equal. In that moment, he found, a form of double vision occurred. He saw the surrounding scene simultaneously from two viewpoints—both directly, and at one remove. So that he was at the same time both observer and observed; and he became aware of himself, for the first time, as part of something separate and remote. In that transient moment, for a split second, his detachment was perfect; and his remote, viewing mind was able to weigh all things dispassionately, itself included.

Caught so, he understood for the first time now how those who knew they would be staying in Foralie Town under the vapors of the nickel carbonyl could have made the decision to use it. For at the core of such a moment was a perception tuned too sharply in self-honesty for fear or selfishness to affect decision.

Caught up in wonder at this new perception, Hal did not react for a long moment to the waiting faces as he ordinarily would have; and Rourke di Facino, far down the table on Hal's left, spoke instead to Amanda.

"Well, Amanda? You hinted at some strong reasons for our coming to this meeting. We're here."

Hal had not realized the quality of the acoustics in the dining room. Di Facino had spoken in no more than a soft conversational tone, but his words had sounded clearly across the length of the space between himself and Hal.

"I said there might be strong reasons for listening to Hal Mayne, Rourke," answered Amanda, "and I think there are. One, at least, is the one I told you about—that he's been sent here from Mara by the Exotics, to give us a message. And we could have other reasons for listening to him, as well."

"All right," said di Facino. "I only mention it because—no offense in-

tended, of course—the ap Morgans have been reported before this as seeing things that aren't there, on occasion."

"Or perhaps," said Amanda, "they merely saw things other people were
too blind to see. No offense intended, of course."

They smiled at each other like friendly old enemies across half the
length of the dining room. Still caught in his moment, watching them
all, Hal found Amanda standing out among the others as one very bright
beacon might stand out in a bank of duller ones. The average age of the
Grey Captains was at least in the fifties; and she, in her apparent youthfulness, looked almost like a young girl who has slyly slipped into a solemn
gathering of family elders and waits to see how long she can hold her place
before being discovered.

"In any case," the booming voice of Miriam Songhai reached them all,
"we've no prejudice on the Dorsai against people being sensitive, simply
because what they're sensitive to isn't easily measured, weighed or
tagged—I hope."

She turned to Hal.

"What's this message from the Exotics?" she demanded.

Hal looked at the waiting faces. There was a quality of difference in
those here, compared to the five he had faced on Mara. It was a difference in quietness. The Exotics had not fidgeted physically; but he had
been conscious of conflict and uncertainty within each of them. Those
sitting at this table with him now radiated no such impression of inner
concerns. They were at home here, he was a stranger, and it was their job
to decide whatever needed decision. In the hard daylight, here and now,
there was no room for the ghosts and the memories he had found in the
dining room earlier. He felt isolated, helpless to reach them and convince
them.

"I was on my way to the Dorsai, in any case," he said. "But as it happened, I got to Mara first; and so it was the Exotics I talked to—"

"Just a minute." It was a heavy-bodied man in his fifties with a brush
of stiff, gray hair; the one person there with oriental features. Hal rum-
maged in his memory for the name he had heard when Amanda had introduced them. Ke Gok, or K'Gok, was what he remembered hearing her
say. "Why did they pick you to carry their message instead of sending one
of their own people?"

"I can tell you what they told me," Hal said. "Amanda may have explained to you how I was raised by three tutors, one of them a Dorsai—"

"By the way, does anyone here know of a family named Nasuno?"
Amanda's clear voice cut in on him. "They should have a homestead on
Skalland."

There was a moment's silence, then the cadaverous man—whose name, in spite of the mnemonics of Hal's early training, had freakishly been lost—spoke, thoughtfully.

"Skalland's one of the islands in my area, of course. I know you asked me about that when you called, Amanda. But in the time I had I couldn't seem to turn up any such family. Which doesn't mean they aren't there— or weren't there—a generation ago."

"It's hardly likely someone could pose as a Dorsai for a dozen years, even on Earth, and get away with it," said Ke Gok. "But what I'm still waiting to hear is why the Exotics thought someone tutored by a Dorsai should be particularly qualified to talk to us for them."

"I was also tutored by a Maran—and by a Harmonyite," said Hal. "They seemed to feel the fact I'd been brought up by people from both their culture and yours might make me better able to communicate with you, than one of them could."

"Still strange," said Ke Gok. "Two worlds full of trained people and they pick someone from Earth?"

"They'd also run calculations on me," said Hal, "which seemed to show I might be historically useful at this time."

He had been dreading having to mention this; and he had chosen the mildest words in which to put the information, fearing the prejudice of practical people against anything as theoretical and long-range as Exotic calculations in ontogenetics. But none of those before him reacted antagonistically, and Ke Gok said no more.

"In what way," said a slim, good-looking woman named Lee, with large, intent brown eyes and gray-black hair, "did they think you could be historically useful?"

"Useful in dealing with the present historical situation—particularly with the situation created by the Others," he answered. "It's that same situation I'm concerned with, myself; and that I'd like to talk to you about, after I've given you the Exotic message—"

"I think we'll want to hear anything you've got to tell us—Exotic message and whatever else you want to talk to us about," said Lee, "but some of us have questions of our own, first."

"Of course," said Hal.

"Do I understand you right, then?" said Lee. "The Exotics are concerned about the Others; and they sent you to us because they thought you could do a better job of convincing us to think their way than any one of their own people could?"

Hal breathed deeply.

"Effectively," he said, "yes."

Lee sat back in her chair, her face thoughtful.

"How about you, Amanda?" di Facino said. "Are you part of this effort to bring us around to an Exotic way of thinking?"

"Rourke," said Amanda, "you know that's nonsense."

He grinned.

"Just asking."

"Don't," said Amanda, "and save us time, all around."

She looked about at the others. No one else said anything. She looked up at Hal.

"Go ahead," she said.

Hal looked around at them. There was nothing to be read from their faces. He plunged in.

"I assume there's no point in my wasting your time by telling you what you already know," he said. "The interstellar situation's now almost completely under the control of the Others; and what they're after in the long run is no secret. They want total control; and to have that, they've got to get rid of those who'll never work with them—some of the people on the Friendlies, essentially all of the Exotics, and the Dorsai people. The point the Exotics make is that the Others have to be stopped now, while there's still time. They think that, of all those opposed to the Others, the Dorsai are the one people who can do that; and they sent me with word that they'll give you anything they have to give, back you in any way they can, if you'll do it."

He stopped.

The faces around the table looked back at him as if they had expected him to continue.

"That's it?" said Ke Gok. "How do they think we can stop the Others? Don't they think we'd have done it before this, if we knew how?"

There was a moment of silence around the table. Hal thought of speaking and changed his mind.

"Just a minute," said the cadaverous old man. "They can't be thinking—this isn't that old suggestion we go out and play assassins?"

It was as if a whip cracked soundlessly in the room. Hal looked down the room at the hard faces.

"I'm sorry," he said. "I was obligated to bring you the message. I told them you'd never do it."

The silence continued for a second.

"And why were you obligated?" said Miriam Songhai.

"I was obligated," said Hal, patiently, "by the fact that delivering the message gave me the chance to speak to you all about what I, myself, believe is the only way to deal with the Others."

Another tiny silence.

"Perhaps," said di Facino—very softly, but the words carried through the dining room, nonetheless—"they don't realize how they insult us."

"Probably they don't—in the emotional sense," said Hal. "But even if they did, it wouldn't matter. They'd have to ask you anyway, because they don't see any other way out."

"What he's telling you," said Amanda, "is that the Exotics feel helpless; and people who feel helpless will try anything."

"I think you can tell them for us," said the cadaverous man, "that the day they give up the principles they've lived by for three hundred years, they can ask us again. But our answer will still be that we don't give up our principles."

He looked around the room.

"What would we have left, if we did something like that to save our necks? What would the point have been of living honestly, all these centuries? If we'd do assassin's work now, we'd not only not be Dorsai any longer; we'd never have been Dorsai!"

No one nodded or spoke, but a unanimity of approval showed clearly on the faces around the table.

"All right," said Hal. "I'll tell them that. But now can I ask, since I've got you all here, what you do intend to do about the Others, before they starve you to death?"

Hal looked at Amanda. But she was still merely sitting, a little back from the table, watching. It was Miriam Songhai who spoke.

"Of course we've no plans," she said. "You evidently do. Tell us."

Hal took a breath and looked at them all.

"I don't have a specific plan, either," he said. "But I believe I've got the material out of which a plan can be made. What it's based on, what it has to be based on, is an understanding of the historical situation that's resulted in the Others being so successful. Basically, what we're involved in now is the last act of an era in human development; and the Others are there to threaten us because they stand for one attitude that exists in the race as a whole; and we—you Dorsai, the Exotics, the true Faithholders on the Friendlies and some others scattered around all the other worlds—stand for the attitude opposed to it. Natural historical forces in human development are what are pushing this conflict to a showdown. We're looking not merely at the ambitions of the Others, but at an Armageddon. . . ."

He talked on. They listened. The light lancing in through the windows made the long, smooth surface of the table glisten like wind-polished ice; and the Grey Captains sat listening in utter stillness, as if they had been carved in place as they sat, to last forever. Hal heard his voice continuing, saying the same things he had said to Exotic ears; and much of what he must have said to Amanda, that first night here. But there was no sign or signal from this audience to tell him if he was reaching them. Deep within himself, the fear grew that he was not. His words seemed to go out from him, only to die in the silence, against minds that had already shut them out.

He glanced fleetingly at Amanda, hoping for some signal that might give him reassurance; and found none. She did not shake her head, even imperceptibly; but the unchanging gaze she returned to him conveyed the same message. Internally, Hal yielded. There was no point in simply continuing to hold them hostage with words, if the words were not being heard and considered by them. He brought what he had been saying to a close.

There was a moment without anyone speaking. The Captains stirred slightly, as people will who have sat for some time in one position. Throats were cleared, here and there. Hands were placed on the table.

"Hal Mayne," said Miriam Songhai, finally. "Just what plan do you have for yourself? I mean, what do you, yourself, plan to do next?"

"I'll be going from here to the Final Encyclopedia," he said. "There's where most of the information is, that I still need, for an effective understanding of the situation. Once I've got a complete picture, I can give you a specific plan of action."

"And meanwhile?" said Ke Gok, ironically. "You're merely asking us to hold ourselves in readiness for your orders?"

Hal felt a despair. He had failed, once more; and there was no magic, no ghosts were here, to save the day. This was reality; the incomprehension of those who saw the universe limited to what they already knew. Unexpectedly, an exasperation erupted in him; and it was as if something put a powerful hand on his shoulder and shoved him forward.

"I'm suggesting that you hold yourself in readiness for orders from someone," he heard himself answer, dryly.

There was a shock in hearing it. The voice was his own, the words were words he knew, but the choice and delivery of them was coming from somewhere deep within him; as far back as the ghosts he had heard speaking at this table. He felt a strength move in him.

"If I'm fortunate enough to be the one who first gets on top of the situation," he went on in the same unsparing voice, "they could indeed come from me."

"No offense, Hal Mayne," said di Facino, "but may I ask how old you are?"

"Twenty-one, standard," said Hal.

"Doesn't it seem, even to you," went on di Facino, "that it's asking a lot of people like ourselves, who've known responsibility on a large scale for twice or three times your lifetime, to take you and what you suggest completely on faith? Not only that, but that we should mobilize a planetful of people in accordance with that faith? You come to us here with no credentials whatsoever, except a high rating according to some Exotic theory—and this world is not one of the Exotics."

"Credentials," said Hal, still dryly, "mean nothing and will never mean anything in this matter. If I find the answers I'm looking for, my credentials are going to be obvious to you, and to everyone else as well. If I don't, then either someone else is going to find the answers, or no one will. In either case, any credentials I have will be very much beside the point. The Exotics knew this."

"Did they?" said di Facino. "Did they tell you so?"

"They showed me so," said Hal. The strange sense of strength in him carried him forward irresistibly. It was as if someone else spoke through him to them; and the exasperation within him had given way now to a diamond-hard sense of logic. "Sending me here with their message, which they had little hope you'd agree to, guaranteed I'd have a chance to give you my side of things, without their having in any way endorsed it. If it turned out you accepted me, they'd have no choice but to accept me, too, in the long run. If you didn't, they had no responsibility for what I said to you on my own."

"But," said Ke Gok, "we haven't accepted you."

"You'll have to accept someone, if you're going to deal with the situation," Hal said. "You were the one who just said a few moments ago that you'd have stopped the Others before this if you'd known how. The plain fact is you don't know how. I do—perhaps. And there's no time to wait around for other solutions. This late in the day, even all the strength that can be joined against the Others may not be enough. You and the Exotics are in the same camp whether you like it or not—if you don't face that, you and they are going to perish singly, as you're both on the road to perishing now. Only unlike the Exotics, you Dorsai are a people of action. You can't close your eyes to the need for it, when that need crops up. Therefore, the only hope for you and them is that someone will come along who can lead you both, together—and no one has, but me."

"The necessity to accept someone," said the cadaverous man, "hasn't been proven, yet."

"Certainly it has." Hal looked directly into the almost-black pupils of the other's eyes. "The Dorsai is already beginning to starve. Slowly . . .

but it's beginning. And you all know that starvation is being caused deliberately by the Others, who are also doing other things to other people. Clearly, this is no problem that can be kept contained between you and the Others, only. It's a case of one part of the human race, spread over many worlds, against the other part. You don't need me to tell you that, you can see it for yourself."

"But," said Lee, softly, "there's no guarantee it has to explode into Armageddon, with what that would mean for all our people—who are the fighters."

"Take another look if you believe it doesn't have to," said Hal. "The situation's been developing for over thirty years. As it develops, it grows exponentially, both in numbers of peoples involved and in complexity. How else can it end except in Armageddon? Unless you and the Exotics and those like you are willing to abandon everything you've believed in, to suit the Others; because that's the only thing the Others'll settle for, in the end."

"How can you be sure of that?" said Lee. "Why shouldn't the Others stop before they push it that far?"

"Because if they do, they'll be the ones to be wiped out in a generation; and they know it," said Hal. "They're riding a tiger and don't dare get off. There're too few of them. The only way to make life safe for themselves, as individuals, is to make the worlds—note, I said worlds, all the worlds—safe for all of them together. That means changing the very face of human society. It means the Others as masters and the rest of humanity as subordinates. They know that. For everything you love, you have to know it, too."

There was a long moment of silence in the room. Hal sat waiting, still strangely gripped by the clarity and fierceness of thought that had come on him.

"It's still only a theory of yours—this idea of historical confrontation between two halves of the human race," said Miriam Songhai, heavily. "How do you expect us to trust something like this, that no one ever proposed before?"

"Check it out for yourselves," said Hal. "It doesn't take Exotic calculations to see when and how the Others started, how they've progressed, and where they must be headed. You know better than I how the credit and other reserves of your society are dwindling. The time's coming when the Others'll own the souls of everyone who might hire you, off-world. What happens to the Dorsai, then?"

"But this idea of them as a historical force, with all the dice loaded in their favor against us," the cadaverous man said, shaking his head, "that's leaving common sense for fantasy."

"Would you call it a fantasy, what's already happened on all the worlds but Old Earth? And it hasn't happened there only because the Others have to get the other worlds under control first," Hal answered. "The Others' specialty is to attack where there's no counter. There's no present defense against them. How else could they explode the way they have, into a position of interstellar power in just thirty standard years?"

He paused and looked deliberately around the table at all the faces there. There was a strange brightness, almost a light of triumph in Amanda's eyes.

"Against their charisma, and the pattern of their organization," he went on, "none of our present Cultures have any natural defense. If you could put all of the Others on trial in an interplanetary court right now, I'd be willing to bet you couldn't find legal cause to indict one of them. Most of the time they don't even have to suggest what they want done. They bind to them people with exactly the characters they want, put each in the specific situation each one is best suited for, and each one does exactly what the Others want, on his or her own initiative."

Hal turned to speak to the table as a whole.

"Look at the large picture, for your own sakes," he said. "Think. The Exotics could have handled in its beginning any ordinary economic attempt to dominate all the worlds. You could have handled early any purely military threat. But against the Others you've both been helpless; because they haven't attacked in those forms. They've attacked in a new way, one never anticipated; and they're winning. Because the pattern of human society is changing, as it's always done; and the old, as always, can't resist the new."

He paused.

"Face that," he said. "You, the Exotics, the Friendlies, everyone else who lives by an older pattern, can't resist the Others as you've resisted other enemies until now. If you try going that way, you'll lose—inevitably—and the Others will win. But the possibility is there for you to resist them successfully, and win, if you let yourself become part of the new historical patterns that are shaping up into existence right now."

He paused again; and this time he waited for comment or objection, a response of any kind. But none came. They sat silent, watching him.

"The Others aren't aliens," he said. "They're us, with a difference. But that difference can be enough to give them control as things stand. Again, as I say, it's simply one more instance of the old giving way to the new; only the problem in this case is that the new way the Others want to bring in is a blind alley for the race. Humanity as a whole can't survive in stasis, with one Master to millions of slaves. If it's made to go that way, it'll die."

He paused. None of them made the slightest movement or sound. They only continued to watch him.

"We can't allow that," he went on, "but not allowing it doesn't mean we can keep things as they are. That would also mean stasis—and a race death. So, we have to acknowledge simply what is. Once more, the face of human society is changing, as it's always done; and as always we'll have to change with it or go by the boards. Here on the Dorsai you're going to have to be prepared to let go of many things, because you're a Splinter Culture that always held to tradition and custom. But that adaptation will have to be made, for the sake of your children's children. Because, I tell you again, what's at stake isn't the hard-won ways of the Dorsai, or those of the Friendlies or the Exotics, but the survival of the whole human race."

Chapter

> > 48 < <

Hal stopped talking at last, and waited for a response. But this time, the silence from his listeners continued. They were looking now at the table-top before them, at the wall or window opposite them, in any direction, in fact, but at him or at each other.

"That's all I have to say," he told them, finally.

Their eyes went to him, then. Miriam Songhai sighed.

"It's not an easy picture to look at, the one you've just painted," she said. "I believe I need to think this over."

There was a mutter of agreement around the table. But the cadaverous man got to his feet.

"I don't need to think it over," he said, looking directly at Hal. "You've answered every question I could have asked. You've convinced me. But the only answer you have isn't for me."

He looked for a moment around the table.

"You know me," he said. "I'll do anything necessary for my people. But the Dorsai as it is now is what I've lived and fought for all my life. I can't change now. I won't have any hand in making it and its people change. The rest of you can travel this new road we've just been hearing all about, but you'll do it without me."

He turned toward the door. Two other men and one woman pushed their chairs back also and got up. Ke Gok started to rise, then sat down again, heavily. In the doorway, the cadaverous man stopped and turned back for a moment.

"I'm sorry," he said to Hal.

Then he was gone and the three others followed him out.

"I gather," said Hal, in the following hush, "that most of you, like Miriam Songhai, want to think about what I've said. I can wait on Dorsai up to another week, if any of you want to talk to me further. Then, as I said, I'll be leaving for the Final Encyclopedia."

"He'll be at Fal Morgan," said Amanda.

The meeting broke up.

Hal had assumed that he also would now be heading back to Fal Morgan. Instead, he found the living room half-filled with fifteen of the Grey

Captains who wanted to talk to him further about the situation as he saw it. Ke Gok, surprisingly, was one of them.

They were, Hal learned from what they had to say, those who had already brought themselves to a belief in the historical situation as Hal had explained it—though not necessarily in him or whatever plan he might develop for dealing with it. He found discussing matters with them to be a clean mental pleasure after the uncertainties and secrecies of the Exotics. They were people who were used to taking problems apart and dealing with them either in section or in whole; and clearly they had accepted him as one who worked in the same manner.

At the same time he was uneasy, conscious of a difference as he talked to them informally in the big living room. For a little while in the dining room he had found himself wearing a cloak of certainty so strong that he had not even needed to think of the words to use. What he had wanted to say had simply come to him out of the obviousness of what they needed to understand. Now, in the living room, with an audience already half-convinced, that diamond-brilliant clarity and conviction was gone once more. His own, usual abilities of expression were still more than adequate to the occasion; but the difference in that from what he had tapped for a short while in the dining room was jolting; and he made himself a promise to find out what it had been that had so touched him then, as soon as he had time to examine his memory of it.

In the end it was five hours later when he and Amanda rode back through the early evening to Fal Morgan.

"What were these strong reasons you hinted at, according to Rourke di Facino?" he asked her, when they and their horses were lost to sight from Graemehouse.

"I told them I was convinced you had greater ties with the Dorsai than it might seem in this situation."

He considered that answer for a few seconds as their horses walked, side by side.

"And what did you say to the ones who asked you what those ties were?"

"I told them it was a perception of mine, that they were there." She turned her head as she rode and looked at him squarely. "I said they could take my word and come, or doubt it and stay away."

"And most came. . . ." He gazed at her. "I owe a lot to you. But I'd like to know more about this perception of yours, since it's about me. Can you tell me about it?"

She looked away again, back out over the ears of her horse.

"I can," she said. "But, in this case, I don't think I will."

They rode on in silence for a few seconds more.

"Of course," he said. "Forgive me."

She reined her horse to a standstill so sharply it tossed its head against the pressure of the bit. He pulled up also and turned to see her almost glaring at him.

"Why do you ask me?" she said. "You know what happened to you at Graemehouse!"

He studied her for a second.

"Yes," he said, finally. "I know. But how could you?"

"I found you there," she said, "and I knew something like it was likely to happen."

"Why?" he said. "Why would you expect anything to happen to me at Graemehouse?"

"Because of what I saw in you, your first night here." Her voice was challenging. "You don't remember, do you? Do you at least remember telling me that you felt an identity with Donal—because he'd always been considered such an odd boy by his family and his teachers at the Academy?"

The echo of his own words sounded in his memory.

"I guess I did," he said.

"How did you know that about him?"

"Malachi, I guess," he said. "Malachi must have told me. You said yourself he'd probably been involved in contracts taken by the Graemes."

"Malachi Nasuno," she said, "would never have known. The Graemes never talked about each other to people outside the family. They didn't even talk about each other to Morgans. And no teacher at the Academy would discuss a student with anyone but another teacher, or the student's parents."

Hal sat his horse, saying nothing. There was nothing in him to say.

"Well," she demanded, at last. "What made you think Donal was isolated? Where did you get the idea that his teachers referred to him as an odd boy? Are you going to tell me you made it up?"

Still, he could find no response in him. She started walking her horse again. Automatically, he put his in motion to follow her; and they rode on again, side by side.

After a while, he spoke; not so much to her as to the universe in general, staring forward meanwhile at the route they followed together.

"No," he said, somberly, "whatever else may be, I didn't make it up."

They rode on. His mind was suddenly so full it blinded him, and Amanda did not intrude upon his thoughts. When they reached the stable door at Fal Morgan and dismounted, she took the reins from his hand.

"I'll take care of the horses," she said. "Go and think things out by your-self for a bit."

He went into the house. But instead of continuing on down the cor-ridor to the privacy of his bedroom, he found himself turning into the living room. The lights there went on automatically as he entered, and the brightness blinded him for a second. With a wave of his hand at the nearest sensor, he turned them off. The living room was left dimly lit by only the light from the corridor to the kitchen down which he had just come. The gloom was comforting. He walked in and dropped into a chair before the unlit fireplace, staring sightlessly at the kindling and logs laid waiting there.

There was a strange mixture of emotion in him. Part of it was a large feeling of relief and triumph; but another part was a dark sadness he had never experienced before. Once again, he was conscious of his own iso-lation from everyone else. The memory of the cadaverous man turning in the doorway to say he was sorry would not leave him. He was in-escapably aware of all that the other man had to lose. In fact, he was aware of how they all would lose, if they followed him into the struggle against the Others. But they would lose even more if they did not join him. Still, with him, they would lose much; and he could not turn away from the fact there was no way to temper what would be, just to protect them from their pain.

He heard, with the corners of his consciousness, the kitchen door open and close and the sound of Amanda's footfalls come down the corridor to the living room, enter, and stop suddenly.

"Hal?" Her different, unsure voice erected the hairs on the back of his neck. "Is that you—Hal?"

He was on his feet, turned about and standing over her, where she had backed against the wall next to the entrance, before he realized he had moved.

He towered over her. He had never before been this aware of his size, in relation to hers; and it seemed to him she had grown smaller, shrunk back against the wall as she was. But he could see nothing to terrify her. They were alone. Their faces stared at each other in the half-light, across a few inches of distance; and his soul turned over in him to see her so frightened.

Gently, he took hold of her shoulders; and was shocked to discover how small the bones and flesh of them felt, wrapped and enclosed by his own large hands. Gently, still holding her, sliding his hands about her shoul-ders, he stepped aside and behind her, urging her from the wall to one of the chairs facing the unlit fireplace.

"No," she said, closing her eyes as she reached the chair, pulling away from him and seating herself. He sank down into a chair half-facing hers, and stared at her. His own eyes, adjusted to the dimness, saw the paleness of her face.

"It's all right . . . ," she said, after a long moment, in a hushed, breathless voice. She opened her eyes and went on, a little numbly. "It was just for a moment there. I'd thought you'd naturally go to your room to think. He got thin in the last years, but his hair stayed black—like yours. He . . . sometimes forgot to light the fire; and he used to sit like that, stooped a bit. It was a shock, that's all."

He stared at her.

"Ian," he said. "You mean . . . Ian."

Out of all his feeling for her came a sudden understanding.

"You were in love with him." He could not have pulled his gaze from her face with all the willpower he possessed. "At his age?"

"At any age," she said. "Every woman loved Ian."

A dull knife slowly cut and churned him up inside. The reciprocal feeling for him that he believed he had sensed in her—everything he thought he had understood—all wrong. He had been only a surrogate for a man dead for years, a man old enough to be her great-grandfather.

"I was sixteen when he died," she said.

—And then he understood. To love and not be able to have, as she was growing up, would have been bad enough. To love and watch the dying would have been beyond bearing. The terrible fire of loss within him was flooded out by love for her and the urge to comfort her. He reached out, to her, starting to get up.

"No," she said, quickly. "No. No."

He dropped his arm back, the pain returning. Of course she would not want to be touched by him—particularly now. He should have known that.

They sat in silence for several minutes, he not looking at her. Then he got up, almost mechanically, and lit the fire. As the warmth and the light of the little red flames, moving out and multiplying among the pieces of firewood, began to take over and change the room, he ventured to look at her again. He saw that the color had begun to come back to her face, but the face itself still showed a rigidity from the lingering effects of her shock. She sat with her arms upon the arms of the chair, her back straight against its back.

"You did well, today," she said.

"Better than I'd hoped," he answered.

"Not just that. You did well, very, very well," she said. "I told you, carrying anything over seventy per cent of them would be a victory. You only lost four out of thirty-one people; and you didn't even really lose them. You convinced them too thoroughly, that's why they left."

"I suppose," he said. A little of the earlier feeling of relief and triumph returned for a brief second. "But I was losing them to begin with, there. And then Rourke di Facino asked that one question and it seemed to trigger off just what I wanted to tell them. Did you notice?"

"I noticed," she said.

Her brief reply did not encourage him to talk further about the explosion of competence that had come so unexpectedly upon him at the meeting. He turned away to poke the fire; and when he looked at her again, she had gotten to her feet.

"I'd better get us something to eat," she said; and waved him back as he started to get up. "No. Stay there. I'll bring it in here."

She crossed the room quickly to the table with the drinks on it, poured some of the dark whisky into a glass and brought it back to him.

"Sit and relax," she said. "Everything's fine. I'll call Omalu and find out the situation on a ship that can get you out toward the Final Encyclopedia."

He took the glass, smiled; and drank a little from it. She smiled back, turned, and left the room. He put the glass down on the table beside him.

He had no desire for it, now. But she would notice if he did not drink at least some of it. He set himself to get it down, gradually; and had almost succeeded by the time she came in with two covered hot-dishes on a tray, which she set down on a small table between his chair and the one she had occupied earlier. The tray divided to become two trays; and she passed one over to him, with tableware and a covered dish on it.

"Thanks," he said, uncovering the dish. "It smells good."

"There's a question you're going to have to think about," she said, uncovering her own dish. "I called the spaceport at Omalu. A ship's leaving for Freiland, from which you can transfer to one headed for Earth. It leaves tomorrow at midday. If you don't take that, the next might be in three weeks—or more. They're not certain. But it'll be at least three weeks. Do you still want to give them a week here?"

"I see," he said, laying his fork down. She was looking at him with a face on which he could read only the concerned interest of a householder with a guest. "You're right. Perhaps I'd better be on that one, tomorrow."

"It's too bad," she said. "If you could have stayed a week, some of those you met yesterday would've had a chance to talk to you again. There was a time when finding passage out of Omalu to any of the other thirteen worlds was something you could do almost overnight. But not now."

"It's too bad, as you say," he said. "But I'd better take the ship I know is leaving."

"Yes. You're probably right." She lowered her gaze to her plate and became busy eating. "You've got interstellar credit enough for passage, of course?"

"Oh, yes," he said to her forehead. "There's no problem there. . . ."

They ate. In spite of the newly-empty feeling inside him, his appetite did not let him down; and the soporific effect of the good-sized meal on top of the tensions of the day dulled his emotions and made him realize how tired he was. They talked for a little while about the next day's plans.

"I think some of those who were there today may want to have a last word with you," she said. "I'll phone around and see. We could get to the spaceport early and talk in the restaurant, there; if you don't have any objection."

"No objection, of course," he said. "But maybe I should be the one to call them?"

"No," she said. "Get some sleep. I'll be up for a few hours yet, anyway, with things I've got to do."

"All right," he said. "Thank you."

"It's no trouble."

Shortly, he went to bed; and in the darkness of his room escaped at last into the cave of sleep.

He slept heavily. He was roused by Amanda calling him on the house phone circuit; and he looked up from his pillow to see her face in the screen.

"Breakfast in twenty minutes," she said. "We've both slept late enough."

"Right," he said, half-awake.

The kitchen was bright as he came into it and took a seat at the table. Thick soup and chunks of brown bread were already waiting for him. She sat down with him.

"How do you want to make the trip to Omalu?" she asked.

He swallowed some bread.

"Is there a choice?"

"There's two ways," she told him. "We can hitch a ride, if someone from the area happens to be flying into Omalu today; or, if no one is, which is most likely, we can call for transportation for you from Omalu. In either case, you'll have to pay your way to whoever we ride with. I won't. Of course, I can take you. Because of the work I do, I've got my own jitney."

He frowned. What she had just said had somehow seemed to end hanging in the air.

"In which case I wouldn't have to pay," he said, slowly. "But the Dorsai can use any interstellar credits it can get from me; isn't that right?"

"That's right," she said. "If you can afford them."

"Of course," he said. "Just let me know how much I ought to pay you for the ride."

"We'll go by the fuel used." She got to her feet. "I'll go roll the jitney out now. You finish here and collect anything you've got to take with you. Then come down beyond the stable and you'll find me."

There was nothing that he particularly needed to bring beyond what he had carried in when he had come. What he was carrying away that was important, from the Dorsai and particularly from Fal Morgan and Foralie, was immaterial and interior. They lifted off into the same almost-cloudless sky that had graced all the days he had been there.

—And they descended into an unbroken layer of clouds a little more than an hour later, over Omalu.

Below the clouds it was raining; not heavily, but steadily. They landed on the planetary pad, on the other side of the terminal from the pad for deep-space ships; and ran together through the rain to the side door of the terminal.

When they got to the restaurant on the building's second level, the list on the reservation screen showed the Grey Captains in Cubicle Four. Amanda led Hal through the open central dining area to the private rooms beyond. Cubicle Four turned out to be a room more than adequate to hold the nearly forty people already seated at square green tables there. Three sides of the room were white-dyed concrete walls, with the fourth side all window, giving on the downpour over the planetary pad. Remnants of early breakfasts were scattered around a number of the tables.

"You've got nearly two hours," said Amanda. "Come along. There's at least a dozen people here you haven't met yet."

She took him off to be introduced. It developed that two of those who had walked out the day before, one woman and one man, had returned, and with them were Grey Captains who had not chosen, or had not been able, to make the first meeting. After Hal had been introduced he took a chair facing a semicircle of others drawn from the tables and began to answer questions. After a little more than an hour, however, he called a halt.

"I don't think we're making much progress this way," he told them. "Basically what you're all asking me for are specific answers. This is the very thing I don't have to give you, simply because I haven't got them myself yet. I don't have a specific plan, as I've already told you, several times. That's what I'm going to the Final Encyclopedia to work out. All I can do for you now is what I've done; point out the situation and leave you to look at it for yourselves until I've got more information."

"No offense intended, Hal Mayne," said Rourke di Facino. He was sitting in the center of the semicircle, looking small and dandified, with the large, padded collar of his travelling jacket thrown open to the warmth of the cubicle. "But you've raised a demon among us; and now you seem to be refusing to lend a hand in laying it."

For a moment it seemed to Hal that the certainty that had visited him in the dining room stirred and threatened to take him over again. Then it subsided; and he kept a firm grip on his patience.

"I'll repeat what I've said before," he said. "I've only pointed out to you the situation as it exists; and that was something you actually already knew. You've all made it plain that you won't promise to do anything more than consider what I've told you. On my side, I can't promise anything more than I have, either."

"At least," said Ke Gok, "give us some idea of what to expect, some idea of what direction you're heading in. Give us something we can tie to."

"All right," said Hal. "Let me put it this way, then. Would you all be willing to move against the Others if the chance could be offered in the form of ordinary military action?"

There was a general chorus of assent.

"All right," said Hal, wearily. "As far as I know now, that's what I'll be trying to find for you. It's your strength; and it's only sensible to work with it."

"And on that note," said Amanda, getting to her feet. "I'm going to take Hal Mayne away. He'll be going directly to his ship. Those of you who want to say goodbye, say it now."

To Hal's surprise, they all crowded around him. It was not until Amanda had finally extricated him and they were going down a flight of old-fashioned stairs to the ground level, that he thought to look at his chronometer.

"We've got a good ten minutes yet before I'd have had to go," he said.

"I wanted to talk to you alone," said Amanda. "Here, this way."

She led him off from the foot of the stairs to a small waiting room with a door in its far wall. She led him to the door, opened it and they stepped out onto the spaceship pad.

The door sucked shut behind them under the differential in air pressure between Pad and Terminal. Weather control had been turned on over the Pad, now that liftoff was close. The clouds lay thick above, appearing to be humped up into a dome over the Pad by the action of the control; and gray, wavering curtains of rain edged the three open sides of the pad. Out here, the air felt damp and thick, with that peculiar stillness found in atmosphere artificially held. The increased pressure and the stillness, together, gave the impression that they were suspended in a bubble outside of ordinary time and space. Eighty meters distant, out on the Pad, the spaceship for Freiland lay, lengthwise, enormous and mirror-bright, with her polished skin holding the images of the Terminal, the clouds and the rain nearby, fuming off the last of the decontaminant gas from her loaded cargo holds.

Amanda turned and began to walk eastward along the blank lower face of the Terminal, pierced only by glassless, self-sealing doors like the one that had let them onto the pad. Hal fell in beside her.

"You realize," she said, "you've only been here eight days." She was walking along with her eyes fixed on the rain curtain at the Pad edge, two hundred meters ahead of them.

"Yes," he said. "It hasn't been long."

"It's not easy to get to understand someone else in eight days—or eight weeks or eight months, for that matter," she said. She glanced sideways at him, briefly; then turned her attention once more to the rain at the edge of the Pad. "If two people come from different Cultures, they can use the same words and mean two different things; and if their reasons for doing what they do aren't understood, then without planning to, either one of them can completely mislead the other."

"Yes," he said. "I know."

"I know you were raised by a Dorsai," she said. "But that's not the same as being born here. Even born here, you could be wrong about someone from another household. You don't know—and in eight days you couldn't learn to know—the Morgans. Or the Amandas. Or me."

"It's all right," he said. "I think I know what you're trying to tell me. I understand. I simply look like Ian."

She stopped, turned and stared at him. Necessarily, he also stopped, and they stood, face-to-face.

"Ian?" she said.

"That's what I found out last night, wasn't it?" he said. "That he looked in his old age something like me; and you'd been . . . fond of him."

"Oh!" she said, and looked away from him, back at the rain. "Not that, too!"

"Too?" He stared at her.

"Of course I loved Ian," she said. "I couldn't help loving him. But after he died, I grew up."

She broke off. Then began again.

"I tried to help you understand," she said. "Weren't you listening when I talked to you about the first Amanda, and the second? Couldn't you hear what I was telling you?"

"No," he said, "now that you ask, I guess I didn't. I didn't realize you were trying to tell me something."

She made a small, harsh sound in her throat and walked for a few seconds toward the rain without saying anything more. He went in silence beside her.

"I'm sorry," she said, after a minute, more gently. "It's my fault. I was the one trying to explain. If you didn't understand, then it's my responsibility. I told you about the other two Amandas hoping you'd understand about me."

"What was it I should have understood?" he asked.

"What I am—what all three of us are. The first Amanda had three husbands; but really—even including Jimmy, her first son, who was a special case—what she lived for was her family and people in general. She was a galloping protector." Amanda breathed deeply, going ahead with her eyes still fixed on the rain curtains at the edge of the pad. "The second Amanda understood herself. That's why she wouldn't marry Kensie or Ian—particularly Ian, whom she loved best. She gave them both up because sooner or later she knew a choice would come for her, between the one she'd chosen and her duty to everyone else; and she knew that when that happened it wouldn't be him, but everyone else she'd choose."

She walked a few more paces.

"And I'm an Amanda, too," she said. "So, I'm going to be just as wise as the second Amanda; and save myself and other people heartache."

They walked on.

"I see," said Hal, at last.

"I'm glad you see," said Amanda. She did not look at him.

"Well," said Hal, after a moment. He felt numb; and in the domed space created around them by the weather control, everything appeared artificial and unreal. He looked at the spaceship. "Perhaps I ought to be getting on board."

She stopped, and he stopped with her. She turned to him and held out her hand. He hesitated for a fraction of a second, then took it.

"I'll be back," he told her.

"Be careful," she said. Their hands still clasped tightly together. "The Others aren't going to like what you're doing. The easiest way for them to stop it, is to stop you."

"I'm used to that." He stood, looking into her eyes. "I've been running from them for over five standard years, remember?"

He smiled at her. She smiled back; and with an effort they both let go.
"I'll be back," he said again.

"Oh, come back!" she told him. "Come back safely!"

"I will."

He turned and ran for the spaceship. When he reached the top of the
landing ladder and paused to turn his papers and certificate of passage over
to the ship's officer, just inside the airlock, he looked back and saw her,
made very small by the distance, still standing a little beyond the east end
of the terminal building, and looking in his direction, with the curtains
of the rain distant behind her, still coming down.

Chapter

> > **49** < <

"Tell them," *said* Hal, "that I don't have a pass. But ask them to contact Ajela and tell her there's a message from Hal Mayne."

He stood in the debarkation lounge of the spaceship that had brought him from Freiland to Earth orbit, and which now lay holding its distance at ten kilometers from the Final Encyclopedia. He was talking to the debarkation officer, a slim, gray-haired man who did not seem disconcerted by Hal's use of a name different from that on his travel documents. The two of them were alone in the lounge, now that most of the hundred and fifty-three other passengers had left for Earth's surface.

At the farther ends of the long lounge, the lights had already automatically dimmed themselves to a level of standby illumination; and there was a coolness in the air; because for the few minutes yet the lounge would remain open, it was not economical for the heating elements to remedy the drop in room temperature caused by the sudden absence of the large crowd of warm bodies who had abruptly and noisily left it for the landing jitney. The slight chill wrapped around Hal, bringing back to his mind once more the dream from which he had woken in the mountains on Harmony, to find himself trying to strangle Jason Rowe. The dream had come again, ten hours ago, his last night here on shipboard. Again, he had taken leave of those with him, had dismounted and started off alone across the rubbled plain toward the distant tower; only, this time, he had penetrated farther into the plain than ever before, and discovered the deception of its appearance.

From its edge it had appeared level and smooth, all the way to the tower. But as he went, he found that the scant grass and hard, pebbled earth of the surface on which he had started had gradually begun to show a change. For one thing, the slope of the ground was deceptive. The fact emerged that the plain actually rose as it approached the tower; and only some trick of perspective had made it seem level, seen from far off.

But, more important, the farther he had penetrated across its bare openness, the more the apparent flatness and smoothness of it had revealed itself to be an illusion. The ground gradually became seamed with cracks enlarging to gullies, the pebbles were superseded by rocks, and the rocks by boulders; and what had been stony soil became only stone; so that his toilsome progress toward the tower had been hindered and slowed to the rate of a man climbing a cliff. . . .

But now, as he stood chilled and separate from the officer who was talking on his behalf with the Final Encyclopedia, it was not his recollection of the struggle across the rocky land, his turnings and backtrackings between the great rocks barring his way, that had been brought back to mind. It was something remembered from very early in the dream and very simple. It had been the creak of his saddle leathers as he had swung down to the ground, the decisive abandonment of the warmth and strength of the horse-body between his knees, the overall feel of leave-taking from all who were familiar, in order to take up the unmarked path of a pilgrimage to some hidden but powerfully-attractive goal. Something about this moment and this waiting for entrance this second time to the Final Encyclopedia had brought it back to him. . . .

But the ship's officer had finally gotten into talk with someone at the Encyclopedia who could undertake the conveyance of the message Hal had asked sent to Ajela.

"Stand by," said the male voice of whomever was at the far end.

Silence fell on the speaker grilles by the phone.

"Who's this Ajela, then?" the officer asked.

"The personal assistant to Tam Olyn," said Hal.

"Oh." The officer looked down and became busy with a stylus on the desktop screen under his fingers. Hal waited. But in less than a minute, the voice came again.

"No need to pass that request on," it said. "I thought I'd seen the name before, so I just checked. Hal Mayne's on the permanent pass list."

"Thanks," said the officer into the phone. "All right. We'll have him straight over to you."

He cut connection and turned to Hal.

"You didn't know you had a permanent pass?"

Hal shook his head, smiling a little.

"No."

"All right," said the officer, into the phone. "Launch Deck—is the repair boat ready yet?"

"Already on its way."

"Thank you."

In fact, the officer had hardly cut connection for a second time before the warning chime from the airlock announced that a boat had docked at it and was unsealing. Hal turned and went to the lock, and the officer came along behind him.

They waited, listening to the sounds of the unsealing process, that carried through the closed inner airlock door. Finally, it swung open; and Hal could look through the matched airlocks to the repair boat's interior, cluttered with machine-shop equipment.

"Have a good trip, sir," said the officer.

"Thanks," said Hal.

Carrying his small satchel of personal possessions, he ducked through the matched locks, feeling the brief but sudden deeper chill from the cold metal of the lock interiors, and stepped into the repair boat.

"This way, sir," said a middle-aged, muscular shipwoman in white coveralls. "You'll have to thread your way through the equipment, I'm afraid."

"That's all right," Hal said, following her along a complicated route, around and between the hard-edged pieces of equipment, toward the control cabin in the bow of the boat.

"It's just that the regular ship-to-surface passenger jitney is too big for the entry lock at the Encyclopedia," she went on over her shoulder. "That jit is built to carry up to two hundred passengers and crew."

"They explained that," said Hal.

"Just so you don't feel snubbed." She laughed. "In here, now. . . ."

They entered the cabin and Hal found himself in a room full of control consoles and screens, with three operations chairs up ahead, facing a segmented vision screen. The chair on the far left was already occupied by a shipman, sitting idle.

"Take the seat in the middle, if you don't mind," said the shipwoman.

Hal obeyed. She seated herself to his right and laid her hands on the console before her. Behind them, there was the sound of their airlock resealing and a brief jolt. Then all feeling of motion ceased.

"That's it, up ahead," offered the shipman. He was a wiry man in his forties, smaller than his partner.

Hal looked into the large screen. Its segments at the moment were combined to show a single wide image that spread itself out before them. It was an image of star-filled space; and in the center of it, in full sunlight, floated the small, misty globe of their destination.

The Final Encyclopedia hung there—as they also seemed to hang still, facing it—like a ball small enough for the hand of a young child to hold comfortably. But as Hal watched, it began to enlarge. It swelled and grew before him until it had filled the screen and began to loom, smoke-gray and enormous, over their repair boat, shutting out their view of half the universe.

An opening of bright, yellow light appeared before them as an iris dilated; and they rode through into the same noisy metal cavern that Hal remembered from his first visit, five years before.

The shipwoman got up with him, and steered him back through the equipment in the main cabin of the repair boat and out through the airlock that was already standing open.

He walked down the sloping ramp, his ears assaulted by the clangor of machines moving about on bare metal decking. Ahead of him was the faintly-hazy circle that was the entrance to the interior of the Final Encyclopedia; as he stepped through it, the sound behind him was cut off. He stood, and let the moving corridor onto which he had just stepped carry him forward toward a vision screen on the wall to his right, ahead. The screen had been blank, but just before he came level, it illuminated, and the face of Ajela looked out.

"Hal? Take the first door on your right," her voice told him.

He rode along for another ten meters, saw the door and went through it into another, shorter corridor without a moving walkway. At the end of this was a second door. He pushed it open when he reached it, and went in.

As it sucked shut softly behind him, he saw that he had come into a room half office, half lounge. The farthest wall, almost a copy of what he remembered seeing in Tam Olyn's suite, appeared to give on a stream winding through a summer forest; but here the light was like the sunlight of early morning. Ajela was already rising from behind a large desk. Her pink gown rippled as she ran to him, kissed him, then stood back to stare.

"Look at you!" she said.

He had, in fact, been looking at her. After Amanda, and other women he had met on the Dorsai, she gave an appearance of being tiny and fragile—not merely small in stature, by comparison, but more delicate in bone and feature. And yet, he knew that in comparison to the general run of humanity she would not be considered so.

"Look at me?" he answered, triggered by her warm smile to smiling back at her, for no other reason than that she was radiating such happiness. "Why?"

"You're a monster. A giant!" she told him. "Twice the size you were when I saw you last, and savage-looking enough to scare people."

He laughed at that.

"Savage-looking?" he said.

"See for yourself." She turned him toward the wall at his left, and must have signalled some sensor; for the misty blueness of the wall changed to a mirror surface that gave him back his own image and that of the room around him.

He gazed, startled in spite of himself. He was used to seeing himself every morning as he wiped off the stubble of his beard; and from time to time otherwise, he had caught glimpses of himself in reflecting surfaces like this one. But he had not viewed himself as he now did, with Ajela beside him and in sudden empathy with how she must see him.

The sudden stranger he now saw in the mirror towered above the slim, blond-haired young woman at his elbow. The man's body was lean, broadening from a slender waist to a wide chest, and shoulders broad enough above the narrowness of waist and hips to make him look almost top-heavy. The face above the shoulders was strong-boned, the mouth level, the nose straight; and the eyes, dark gray with a slight difference in color between them, looked out under straight black brows and a wide forehead topped by straight, almost coarse, black hair. But even these features, in total, could not by themselves make for the overall impression that had caused Ajela to call him savage-looking. There was something else, an impression about the figure he stared at which might have been called one of controlled violence, if it had not been for a somber thoughtfulness of eyes, that seemed to overwhelm the general impression of face and body, alike.

He turned from the screen to Ajela.

"Well," she said. "You're back to stay? Or is it only a visit?"

He hesitated.

"Both," he said. "I'll have to explain what I mean by that—"

"Yes, you will," she said; and suddenly hugged him again. "Oh, Tam's going to be so happy!"

She took his hand, towed him toward her desk and pushed him into a padded float beside it.

"How are you?" she said. "Are you hungry? Can I get you anything?"

He laughed.

"I've still got a pretty good appetite," he said. "But let's just talk for the moment. You sit down."

She perched on the edge of her desk, facing him.

"Let me explain what I meant, just now," he said; and hesitated, again.

"Go on," said Ajela.

"I've been thinking about how to explain this to you," he said slowly. "I was going to ask you to believe me when I said there's nothing I could imagine myself wanting to do more, than take Tam up now on his offer to work here at the Encyclopedia. . . ."

"And then you realized it wasn't true," said Ajela, quietly watching him. "Is that it?"

"Yes and no." He frowned at her. "The Encyclopedia pulls me like a moon pulls the tides. I've got things to do here. In the real meaning of the words, it's a tool I've wanted all my life. I know there're things I can do with it, if I had time, that haven't even been dreamed of by anyone else, yet. When I was here before, I really wanted to stay. But you remember I found out I couldn't. There were other things that had to be done. Well, I've still got most of them to do."

"That's the whole reason that's holding you back from staying with us?" She was watching him closely.

He smiled a bit ruefully.

"That's the immediate reason," he said. "But, you're right, to be honest, it isn't all of it. You see, these last few years I've been out among people—"

He hesitated, then went on.

"It's not that easy to explain," he said. "Put it that I've found I've got things I have to do with people, too; and in any case, right now, there's something more immediate and important. I'd like to talk to you and Tam together, about it. Is that possible?"

"Of course," she said. "I haven't told him you're here yet; simply because I wanted a minute or two with you myself, first. The fact is, he's sleeping right now; but he'll be upset if I wait until he wakes up to tell him you're back. Just a second. I'll call him—"

She swung around and reached back over her desk.

"No. Wait," said Hal. "Let me give you a general idea of what I'm talking about, first. Let him sleep. There're things with me now, I want you to understand, and it'll take me a few hours just to bring you up to date."

"All right," Ajela drew her arm back and turned to face him, smiling again. "Now, are you sure you don't feel like having something to eat?"

Hal laughed.

"Well, maybe . . . ," he said.

They went to eat at a table in one of the dining rooms; and Ajela, touching the table's sensor controls, enclosed them this time in something new to him, the privacy of four illusory stone walls.

"Could we have the stars, instead?" Hal asked. "All around us the way I can have them in a carrel?"

She smiled, moved her fingers over the control pad on the white cloth surface of the table, and abruptly they seemed to float in space, with the large, blue-white circle of Earth appearing to hang only a small distance off to their side, and Earth's moon just beginning to emerge from behind it.

In all other directions were the lights and distances of the universe. Hal looked about and overhead and down below his feet at them, picking out Earth's sister worlds of Mars and Venus; and gazing toward the other suns of the race—Sirius, Alpha Centauri, Tau Ceti, Procyon, Epsilon Eridani, Fomalhaut, Altair. In his mind's eye he saw beneath them what his physical eyes could not, humanity's other thirteen planetary homes—Freiland and New Earth, Newton and Cassida, Ceta, Coby, Sainte Marie, Mara and Kultis, Dorsai, Harmony and Association, Dunnin's World.

Imaginatively, he saw not only them but the people upon them; and for a second he breathed deeply, the emptiness he had felt earlier at the thought of their numbers returned.

"What is it?" Ajela asked, her voice suddenly more soft, her summer-green eyes deeply watching him now.

"Too much to tell at once, probably," he said, recovering. He smiled to reassure her. "Anyway, let's have that food, and I'll tell you what's been happening to me."

They sat among the stars, eating; and he talked. He told her of the mines on Coby, and of Sost, Tonina and John; and of Jason, Rukh and James Child-of-God on Harmony; and of his own solitary breakthrough in the cell on that world, with everything that had happened since.

"But what is it you think you can find here, to deal with the Others?" she asked, when he was done.

"To deal with the problem of present history, you mean," he said. "I'm not sure. But the answer's either here or nowhere. It's not just that I've got to find a way to stop the Others. What I have to find is a way that'll be both obvious and convincing to the Exotics, the Dorsai and anyone else who's needed to fight them."

"And you really think what you're looking for is here?"

"It has to be here," he said. "Didn't Mark Torre originally say that the Final Encyclopedia eventually had to be something more than just a storehouse of knowledge? Hasn't Tam guarded it all these years so that a way might be finally found to do something larger with it than anyone's ever conceived of, yet? If it was my idea alone, I might doubt. But we all can't have been wrong. Three of us—all three—coming to the same conclusion about it, each on his own."

"But if it's really true that the ultimate use of the Encyclopedia has always been something more—" She broke off, suddenly thoughtful.

"That's right," he said. "If it's true, then a lot of things begin to make sense. The historical equation balances, then. Otherwise, the dice have been loaded too overwhelmingly by the race-animal in favor of the Others; and that makes no sense. Because the race-animal isn't out to choose one favorite out of the factions within it to win—it's out to get answers on how to survive. The root causes behind the emergence of the Others go back and back in history; and so do the causes leading to the building of the Final Encyclopedia."

"How sure can you be of that, though?" she asked.

He gazed at her across the table.

"Did you ever hear of Guido Camillo Delminio, or the Theater of Memory?" he asked her.

"The Theater of Memory?" She frowned. "I think I have heard that mentioned, or read about it someplace. . . ."

"Mark Torre mentions it in his *Memoirs of Construction*," Hal answered. "That's where I ran across it, myself, when I was young, in the library of my home. It was a great library; and back when I was young enough, anything I read about, that sounded interesting, I wanted. So when I read the *Memoirs* and saw the words 'Theater of Memory' the first thing I thought of was that I wanted to build one. I went to Walter the InTeacher to show me the way to find out how, and he helped me research the actual, historical article."

Ajela frowned at him.

"There actually was something built that was called a Theater of Memory?"

"Partially built, at least, first in Bologna, and later in Paris with the help of funds from Francis I of France. The Guido Camillo Delminio I mentioned conceived of it and spent his life trying to turn it into a reality. That was in the sixteenth century, and his aim was to build a theater where anyone could stand on a stage and look out at art objects ranked on rising levels and put in a certain order, and give speeches calling on all the knowledge in the world, which would be cued by the sight of the art objects before him as he spoke."

She stared at him.

"Where did he get the idea for something like that?" she said. "The sixteenth century . . . " Her voice trailed off, thoughtfully.

"He was born about 1480," said Hal. "He had a professorship at Bologna, but he was always hard up for funds to build with—that's how he and the Theater came to be connected with Francis I. There was a strong desire in Renaissance times to unify all knowledge and that way see through it to the very essence of creativity. The idea of objects as mnemonic cues goes back into classical Greece, at least. The early churchmen and scholastics made it a moral practice, and later on Renaissance mysticism saw it as a framework for esoteric enlightenment. It produces Guido's Theater in the sixteenth century, in the thirteenth century it had already produced Ramon Lull's combination-of-wheels device—and that was nothing less than a sort of primitive computer. The same idea affected people from Bacon to Leibniz, who in the seventeenth century actually did invent calculus. In effect, the Theater of Memory was one of the root causes of later technology and of this Encyclopedia, itself."

"I see," she said.

"I thought you would," he said. "The point is, the whole chain of effort from the Theater to the Final Encyclopedia represents a struggle, an effort by the race-animal to discover greater possibilities in itself. This is the important truth that underlies the struggle between the Others and everyone else—that's where the real battlefield is and is going to be for a while. So that's where I'll have to be for a time, yet."

"I see," she said, again. "All right. I understand, then."

She nodded slowly, her eyes abstracted.

"Yes," she said. "Yes, I think, after all, the sooner you talk to Tam, the better. If you're through eating, I'll call him and we'll go now."

"Even if I wasn't through." He smiled. "But as it happens, I am."

They went.

To Hal's eye, it was as if Tam Olyn had not altered in appearance or moved since he had seen the very old man last. Tam's suite, with its illusion of a forest and stream, and all its float furniture—chairs, desk, and everything else—seemed not to have been shifted a millimeter out of place, in the intervening years. Above all, the expression of Tam's face was the same.

But his voice was different.

"Hello, Hal Mayne," he said; and let Hal come to him to grip hands. The difference was not great; but Hal's ear registered the barely diminished volume, the slightly-greater threadiness of breath behind the words and the infinitesimally-increased length of the pauses between them as Tam spoke.

"Sit down here, Hal," said Ajela, leading him to a cushioned float at no more than arm's length from the chair in which Tam was sitting and pulling one up alongside his for herself.

"You've come back," said Tam.

"Yes," Hal said. "But I've come back with something I've got to do that involves not only the Encyclopedia but everything else, as well. What that's going to mean, though, is that I think the Encyclopedia is going to be put to use the way it ought to be, at last."

"Is it?" said Tam. "Tell me about it."

"You were right when you talked to me about Armageddon, when I was here before," Hal said. "I've taken nearly six years coming to understand what you meant. When I left here to go to the mines on Coby, I didn't know what I was doing; only that I was running, both because I had to find someplace safe for me and because there were things I had to do. What, I didn't know then. I do now."

"Yes," said Tam. The deep hoarseness of age with which he spoke seemed to make his words walk under Hal's like those of a ghost speaking from a crypt at their feet. "You had to find yourself. I knew that, even then."

"I didn't understand people," said Hal. "I'd been brought up under glass. That was why my tutors wanted me to go to Coby. On Coby I began to wake up. . . ."

He told Tam about Walter, Malachi and Obadiah, about Coby, Harmony, and his hours in the Militia cell; with all he had come to understand there and all that had followed from that until now. Tam sat and listened with the motionlessness of face and body that time had brought to him. When Hal finally stopped talking, he did not speak for a long moment.

"And it ends with you back here," he said at last.

"That much of it ends," said Hal.

Tam sat looking at him. A younger individual would have frowned, questioningly. But Tam no longer needed gross facial movements to signal his reactions.

"That much was only the beginning," he went on. "I can understand the situation, now, I can look beyond the Others and know that they're only a part of the real problem; a symptom, not a cause. The real problem's that we've all of us finally come to the point where there's no longer a choice. Now we've got to take charge—consciously—of what's going to happen to us; instead of going on blundering forward instinctively, the way we've always done ever since we first began to look beyond the next meal, or the next dry place to sleep. And the one tool that can let us do that is here. The Final Encyclopedia's the only thing we've managed to show for all those long centuries of savagery and the short centuries of civilization; that so far've only brought us to the point where a handful of us can kill off everyone else."

"Yes," said Tam. For a moment he did not say anything more. His gaze went past Hal and Ajela alike; and when he spoke again, it was clearly to himself as well as them.

"Do you know what it means to try to control history?" he said. He looked back to Hal. "Do you know the mass and momentum of those forces you're talking about laying your hands on? I tried something like that—and I had power. I raised a social tidal wave against a whole people. A tidal wave that ought to have drowned the Friendlies, forever. And all it took to stop me was Jamethon Black, one man of faith who wouldn't move out of my path. On him all that great force I'd built up broke; and it drained away, in a million little streams, in a million directions, doing nothing, harming no one."

Ajela leaned forward and put one of her hands over one of his, where it lay on the padded arm of his float. Hal looked at the warm, white young hand over the dark, gnarled one of age.

"For nearly ninety years you've been making up for that," she said, softly.

"I? All I've done is watch the hearth, keep the candle lit. . . ." His head shook on his shoulders, slightly, from side to side. "But I know the strength of history when it moves."

He looked back at Hal.

"And it's what you're talking about working with," he said. "Even if you're right about using the Encyclopedia, even if everything you hope for gathers behind what you know needs to be done, you'll still be an ant trying to direct a hurricane. You know that?"

"I think so," said Hal, soberly.

"God knows," said Tam, "I want to see you try. God knows it'd justify me, make me of some worth after all these years to the people I'd have destroyed if I could; and also it'd justify Mark Torre and everyone who's come to work here, after him. But think—you could just as easily close your eyes to where it's all going. You could use your mind and your strength to make a comfortable safe niche out of the storm for yourself and any you might love—for the few years your body still has to give you—just by closing your eyes to what's going to happen eventually to people who'll never really know who you were or what it costs you to try what you want to try. You can still turn back."

"No," said Hal. "Not anymore. Not for a longer time than you might think."

Tam breathed in deeply and pushed himself more upright in his float.

"All right, then," he said. "Then you ought to know that you've already got most of the Younger Worlds set in motion against what you want. Bleys Ahrens has put in motion a plan for the mobilization of the credit and the force to take over everything the Others don't already control, by military means if necesary."

There was a moment's silence among the three of them.

"Bleys?" said Hal. "What about Dahno?"

"We've gotten several reports that Dahno died, unexpectedly but conveniently, four standard months ago," said Tam. "Of course, we've been given false trails before. But in any case, it's definite that Bleys controls the Others now. In fact, he may have already for some time now; and plainly he's come to feel he can't risk waiting any longer to act."

Hal watched the old man, fascinated.

"How do you know that?" he asked. "How do you know about this plan, this mobilization?"

"It's reflected in hundreds of thousands of ordinary news items," said Tam. "All I needed, to pick those out and read them right, was to see the implications of what I read in the neural pathways. What outside schol-ars come here to do, or what they ask us to tell them, mirrors the state of affairs on their worlds."

"In the neural pathways?" Hal turned to stare at Ajela.

"I haven't seen it there." Her face was pale. "But I told you no one could read the pathways like Tam."

"Time teaches anyone," said Tam. "Believe me."

The full strength of his grim and cantankerous spirit was in his voice; and Hal believed him. Looking at this man who had held the Final En-cyclopedia true to Mark Torre's dream for so long, Hal understood for the first time that to Tam the task had not been just like that of standing sen-tinel at a vault. It had been like the guarding of a living being. Not sim-ply the fierceness of a dragon crouching above a treasure had ridden in the other man, but an unthinking commitment like that of someone who defends and maintains a child of his or her body. It was not the machin-ery, but a soul, to which he had given the long years of his life.

"Then time's short," said Hal.

"Very short," said Tam. "What do you plan to do?"

Now that the decision was plainly taken, the strength that Hal had felt in the older man a moment before had given way once more to the great weariness in him.

"First," said Hal. "I've got to use the Encyclopedia to trace the roots leading to the emergence of the Others and the emergence of those who may successfully oppose them. It's the process by which knowledge gives birth to idea, and idea gives birth to art, that's the key to the way the En-cyclopedia is finally going to be used. But knowledge has to come first. Until I've got a full picture of how the present situation came to be, I'll have no hope of identifying the human elements that are the real things going to war, here. So, while Bleys mobilizes, I'm going to be tracing peo-ple and their actions back into the dust of the past. There's no other path I can take to what we need."

Chapter

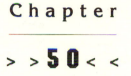

> > **50** < <

Nearly a standard year had gone by since Hal had come back to the Final Encyclopedia; and the knowledge he had dug out and forged in that time into new tools for his mind weighed far more heavily on his spirit than he could have imagined, twelve months before. It had enabled him to reach deeper into himself than he had thought possible in such a short time but it had also woken inner, sleeping gods and devils that he had not suspected himself of harboring. He understood now not only who he was, but also what he must do, and neither of those understandings were easy burdens to carry.

He sat, his chair-float seemingly adrift in space above the eastern hemisphere of the Dorsai. What he looked at was a simulation. No clouds were visible, but innumerable tiny white lights were scattered across the face of the numerous islands that made up the landmass of that sea-girt world; and it was these lights that Hal was considering.

Each of the lights stood for a pad on which a full-sized spacecraft could land and take off—always assuming there was a man or woman of the Dorsai, or an equivalently-skilled pilot, at the controls, to justify the risks in handling such a vehicle on and off surface. There were others besides Dorsai pilots who could bring deep-space vessels safely to a planetary surface, of course; but it was an uncommon skill.

The great number of pads he now looked at was therefore not surprising, considering the world they were on. Harmony, with its two fitting yards, of which one had been put out of action when he left, and with only two other pads where heavy spacecraft could be landed, was more typical of the other thirteen inhabited planets. Hal rotated the image of the Dorsai to show its western hemisphere; and the lights that signalled pads were as numerous there, as well.

The only other worlds that approached the Dorsai in their numbers of landing places were the two Exotic planets of Mara and Kultis; but both of these together did not have as many spacecraft pads as those he had just been observing. The large number on the Dorsai, of course, were attributable to the nearly three centuries in which the Dorsai had been not merely a supplier of professional soldiers, but full of training areas for them. Expeditionary forces were normally not only assembled but worked into shape close to the home areas of the officers who had undertaken the contract that would employ all of them.

Hal coded for a list of the pads he had been looking at, with their locations and their distances from nearby concentrations of the Dorsai populace; and as he did so, there was the sound of a single musical chime and a voice spoke to him from among the stars.

"Hal? Jeamus Walters. I can drop in now, if you're ready for me."

"Come ahead," said Hal.

He touched the invisible console at his fingertips, staying the list and re-evoking his normal working surroundings. The image of the Dorsai vanished and the small carrel off his own room in the Final Encyclopedia came into existence around him—walls, ceiling, floor, and furniture. The carrel was a tiny place—hardly more than a cubbyhole; and his main room beyond was not much more—almost a single-room office, with bedroom furniture recessed in the walls, and perhaps enough space to gather at most five or six people on floats in close conversation. A moment later, the door chimed on a deeper note than the phone had used to announce Jeamus Walters' call.

"Come on in," said Hal. The door opened to admit a short, broad man with thin blond hair on a round skull above a pleasant middle-aged face.

"Sit down," said Hal. "How much time have you?"

"As much as you want, now," said Jeamus. "We were just doing a periodic checkover when you called, earlier."

Hal touched his console and one side of the room blanked out to show the Final Encyclopedia from the outside; the image was enough to fill the space that had been between ceiling and floor, its gray, misty protective screen looking close enough so that either man could reach out and touch it.

"I haven't had time to learn much about it," said Hal, looking at the protective screen. "Periodic checkover, you said? I thought the screen was self-sustaining?"

"It is, of course," said Jeamus. "Once created, it's independent of anything else in the universe. Just as the same thing in phase-shift form would have to be independent of the universe, or it couldn't move spacecraft around in it. But one of the things that that independence means, is that if we constructed a screen around the Encyclopedia and did nothing more, we'd immediately begin to move out from inside it, as we travelled along with the rest of the solar system, here. So we have to arrange to have it move with us; or we'd destroy ourselves trying to go through it, just like anything else would destroy itself trying to get through it at us. Consequently, we arrange for it to move with us; which takes a certain amount of controlling—as does making irises available, opening and closing them, and all the rest of that business—"

He broke off, looking at Hal.

"You didn't ask me in just to hear me lecture on the phase-screen, though, did you?"

"As a matter of fact, yes," said Hal. "I've got some questions about it. How large can you make it? I mean, how large an area can you enclose and protect?"

Jeamus shrugged.

"Theoretically, there's no limit," he said. "Well, yes, of course there's the limit imposed by the size of the power source needed to create the protective sphere and keep adjusting it; and you have to keep adjusting, even if you're creating it to be set adrift in the universe; because sooner or later it'd begin to break down under the anomalies inherent in being a timeless system existing in a temporal universe."

"What's the practical limit, then, approximately?" Hal asked. "Suppose we just wanted to expand the sphere around us now and keep expanding it as far as we could."

Jeamus ruffled the thin hair on the back of his head, thoughtfully.

"Well," he said, "theoretically, we could make it a number of times as large as the solar system, given the power of our available sun—but actually, as soon as we reached the size of Earth's orbit we'd have the sun inside it with us—" He broke off. "I'd have to figure that."

"But," said Hal, "there'd be no problem in making it large enough to enclose a single world—practically speaking?"

"Well, no . . . there shouldn't be," said Jeamus. "You'd run into some control problems. Something like that's never been considered. We've got some pretty interesting problems even now, just with the Encyclopedia here, as far as ingress and egress go. Also, we have to open irises toward the sun, for example, at regular intervals, to draw power. . . . What I mean to say is, the controls for a sphere any larger would have to be very complex, not only for maintenance, but for making irises when and where you wanted them. I suppose you're assuming just about the same proportion of in and out traffic as we have here? Because any differences—"

"No different, for now," said Hal. "Could you run me up some figures for a world, say, just a little larger than Earth?"

"Of course," said Jeamus. He was staring at Hal. "I suppose I shouldn't ask what all this is about?"

"If you don't mind."

"Oh, I mind." Jeamus ruffled his back hair again. "I'm as curious as the next person. But . . . give me a week."

"Thanks," said Hal.

"Don't need to thank me. This is interesting. Anything else?"

"No. And thanks for coming by," said Hal.

"Honored." Jeamus got to his feet. "If you don't hear from me in a week, it'll be because I got sidetracked and bogged down on some maintenance problem. So if I don't get back to you in that time, give me a call; and I'll let you know how I'm coming with this. I suppose you realize, any time this stops being theoretical you're going to have to tell me exactly what you've got in mind if you want any really correct answers."

"Of course. I understand. Thanks again," said Hal; and watched the other man leave.

As the door shut, Hal dismissed the image of the Final Encyclopedia and called Ajela.

"How are things?" he asked, when she looked out of the phone screen at him. "Is now a good time for me to come up and give you both the whole story?"

"Just fine," she said. "You'll find us both in Tam's suite."

"I'll be right there."

When he stepped through the door into Tam's suite, he found her with Tam, seated in an obviously already prepared group of three old-fashioned chairs facing each other. He came on in, took the empty float and smiled at Tam.

"How are things?"

"I'm fine," said Tam. "Don't waste time worrying about me. You've got the chain of consequences worked out?"

Hal nodded.

"At least as far back as the fourteenth century," he said. "Where, for practical purposes, this present historical phase begins with a pivotal figure named John Hawkwood."

"Ajela told me about him from the time you were here before and wanted to look up Conan Doyle's novelistic hero, Nigel Loring." Tam's gaze sharpened. "But Loring was different. He was one of the original Knights of the Garter under the Black Prince, wasn't he? Hawkwood's barely mentioned in Froissart—I know that much."

"After the Peace of Bretigny, when the Black Prince captured King Jean at Poitiers and England and France were at peace, Hawkwood was one of the leaders of the White Company that went over the mountains into Italy," Hal said. "He ended as Captain General of the forces of Florence, two decades later; and he was at least in his forties when he went into Italy."

"They call him 'the first of the modern generals,' Ajela tells me," Tam said. "Anyway, how'd you get to him? And why've you been so close-mouthed about your progress until now?"

"It was one of those situations where I had to have all the pieces before it fell together," Hal said. "Until a week ago I was still going largely on faith. That's why I didn't have anything solid to tell you."

"Faith in yourself," murmured Ajela.

Tam glanced at her.

"All right," he said to her. He looked back at Hal. "Tell us in your own way. I won't interrupt."

"As you know, I started working from the present backward," Hal said. "The Others are crossbreeds between different Splinter Culture individuals. So they, too, are products of elements in the Splinter Cultures. The Splinter Cultures were a product of elements in the society of Old Earth just before and during the period when the phase-drive began to work and we had the explosion of emigration over less than a hundred years to the presently-occupied worlds. The Exotics came from an organization that named itself the Chantry Guild in the twenty-first century. The Friendlies were originally colonies sponsored by the so-called marching societies—and so on and so forth. These, in turn, had their roots in the breakout century—the Chantry Guild of that time grew out of the twentieth century's apocalyptic upsurge of interest in Eastern religions, the occult, and paranormal abilities. The marching societies developed from the re-emergence of religious fundamentalism."

"An apocalyptic time, generally," Tam grunted. "In any time of social stress, you've got this sort of hysteria cropping up in biblically-rooted societies. It isn't just with western Christians—the same thing happens with Jews and Moslems, when conditions are right. Lots of historical instances before the twentieth century."

"But there's a special historical pivot point in the twentieth century," said Hal. "It was the time of the acknowledgment of space. The great mass of humanity up until then had ignored, even when they knew of it, the size of the universe outside Earth's air envelope and the insignificance of their little planet compared to it. Suddenly, they couldn't do that anymore, and the psychological shock was profound. Earth had suddenly ceased to be a safe, warm protective shell for the race. They were suddenly naked to the stars. The shock of that made their century unique in human history and pre-history, and they were forced to be aware of that uniqueness. I know—to those people who live in it, their own time is always the supremely important one; but the people in the twentieth really had some reason to think that way. The idea of space shook them up hard, down to the unconscious levels; and consequently, it shook up the then-existing forms of society—all over Old Earth. Those same forms had been shaped by five hundred years of technological development that really became explosive in the mid-nineteenth century . . . and so on. But I'm covering ground too fast, maybe—"

"Did I say you were?" growled Tam.

"No," Hal smiled at the old man. "Of course not. What I meant was, I was getting ahead of myself. What I did, working from the present backward, was to key on shifts in historical development, tied to unique individuals. For example, a necessary precursor to the development of the present social conditions that have provided a breeding ground for the rise to power of the Others was the achievement of Donal Graeme in pulling all the worlds together under one legal system; and putting an end to exploitative opportunities that gave rise to the interstellar barons like William of Ceta—"

"I saw Graeme only once." Tam's harsh old voice, with its antique way of referring to an individual by surname only, rang oddly on Hal's ears. "It was at a party for him on Freiland. He wasn't particularly impressive to look at."

"But in any case," said Hal, "what Donal did wouldn't have been possible without the emergence of a unique group like the Dorsai who in the beginning were nothing but a supply of cannon fodder for the intercolony wars of the early centuries of interstellar expansion. And, in turn, what they became, and what Donal achieved would never have been possible without the unorthodox military science developed by Cletus Grahame."

"Runs in the family, doesn't it?" said Tam, smiling grimly.

"The Dorsai is a strongly hereditary Culture," said Hal. "It's less surprising on a place like the Dorsai that Donal and Cletus should turn out to be related, than it might have been someplace else. But the interesting thing is that Cletus could not have done what he did without the financial backing of the Exotics, even at that early time, and the Exotics became the Exotics almost exclusively because of—"

"Walter Blunt," said Tam.

"I don't think so," said Hal, slowly. "Walter Blunt was apparently wholeheartedly sincere about his gospel of a cleansing destruction as his cure for whatever ailed the human race. I've got a lot more to learn about Walter Blunt and the Chantry Guild. On the face of it that theory of his is the very antithesis of the search for the evolved human, which the Exotics developed; and yet the Chantry Guild became the Exotics. No, there's another man who comes out of nowhere suddenly, in the late twenty-first century, a mining engineer with one arm who suddenly becomes involved with the Chantry Guild Walter Blunt had founded and rises to essentially challenge Blunt's leadership in a very short time—only to drown almost immediately after that challenge becomes successful, in a small sailboat he was sailing in the Pacific Ocean, offshore. But his brief interaction with the Chantry Guild changes everything about it. After this man—Paul Formain—had been involved, Blunt was left essentially as nothing more than a figurehead; and Jason—"

The chime announcing a phone call interrupted him.

"What's that?" said Tam. "Ajela, I thought you told them—"

"I said we weren't to be bothered, except for something of the gravest importance," she answered, reaching for the console on the arm of her float. "They wouldn't call us unless it was that. . . . Chuni?"

"Ajela? We've got a request from Bleys Ahrens to come for a talk with Hal Mayne."

Ajela's finger lifted from the phone connection. Her eyes, and Tam's as well, went to Hal.

"Yes," said Hal, after a moment. "I suppose it was bound to happen. I'll talk to him, of course."

"Tell Bleys Ahrens he can come on in," Ajela said over the phone circuit. "Hal will see him."

"All right," answered the voice at the far end. "And—Ajela?"

"What?"

"We've got another request that came in at almost the same moment, from a jitney that's just docking in B chamber now. An Exotic named Amid; doesn't have a pass, but he also wants to talk to Hal. Bleys Ahrens is holding distance in a private spacecraft. I don't think they know about each other."

Ajela looked again at Hal.

"Amid first," said Hal. "Then Bleys. Amid may have some information for me that'd be useful before I meet Bleys. I told you about Amid; he's the one I mailed my papers to when the Militia caught me finally on Harmony; and he passed the word to the local Exotic Consulate to help me if I could get to them, then took care of me on Mara."

"Let them both in, Chuni," said Ajela. "Hal's going to see Amid first. Take him to Hal's room; and if you think they don't know about each other, better keep the two of them separate."

She glanced at Hal and Hal nodded. She closed off the phone circuit.

"Well," said Hal, "I think, under the circumstances, I'd better cut this short. There's too much to tell you to try to rush through it now. The essential point is, the chain leads back to a John Hawkwood, in the fourteenth century. Or rather, it leads back to the Renaissance; and it if hadn't been for John Hawkwood, we might not have had a Renaissance."

"That's rather a large statement, isn't it?" said Tam. "You aren't trying to tell us that history goes the way it does not simply because of a chain of social developments, but because of a chain of unusual individuals?"

"No," said Hal. "Pressures within the river of historical forces determine the bends and turns in that river; and the unusual individuals are thrown up by those same pressures at the turning points. A different turn or bend would have thrown up a different individual. At least, that's the way it always was in the past. But, beginning about a thousand years ago, the race started to move into an area where certain individuals began to develop a consciousness of the river; and, depending upon how great that consciousness is, each one since has been consciously able to make some at least partially successful attempt to bend the river to his or her will. That's why someone like Bleys with his great awareness of what's now happening can be many times more effective than he could have been in any past period of history."

He stood up.

"I should go," he said. "I want time to talk to Amid without Bleys knowing that I've kept him waiting."

"What difference would it make if he knew?" Ajela said.

"I don't know. With anyone else I wouldn't be so concerned," said Hal. "But I'm cautious about exposing even the corner of any potentially useful data to that mind of Bleys'. I'll talk to you again as soon as I've seen these two."

Amid, looking almost toy-like in a silver-gray robe, was waiting for him when Hal stepped back into his own room. The small Exotic was standing by Hal's desk.

"Sit down," said Hal, taking a seat himself, away from the desk. "It's good to see you."

Amid smiled wryly, and settled himself in a float.

"It's good of you to say so," he said. "Are you sure you're that pleased to see me?"

"Of course," said Hal. "How long will you stay?"

Amid's face sobered.

"Forever," he said, quietly. For a moment the lines of his face were sad and older than Hal had ever seen them. "Or, in practical terms, as long as I can be of any use to you."

Hal considered him thoughtfully for a moment.

"Should I take it opinions about me have changed on the Exotics?"

"In a sense," said Amid. "I'm afraid we've given up. That's why I'm free to come to you."

"Given up?" Hal sat looking at him. "That's a little like saying an elephant has given up being an elephant—it makes no sense at all. You don't mean it literally?"

"Literally? Of course not," said Amid. "No more than any healthy-minded person means it when he says he's going to give up living. Death is unthinkable; and since the Others mean to kill us off, to acquiesce in that is impossible. No, it's only that our best calculations show us no way out. Effectively, the contest is over. The Others have already won."

"You can't mean that either," said Hal.

"No other answer's possible. How much do you know, about what they've been doing lately?"

"Not much," said Hal. "With Tam Olyn's understanding of the Encyclopedia to help us, we take in all the information we can get from all the worlds and make cross-connections that help us analyze it. That has given us a general picture of the fact that they're mobilizing very rapidly, and that it's all under Bleys Ahrens' leadership. But it's all inference drawn from circumstantial evidence—even if very high-level inference. Specific, detailed information is something we don't get very much of; and when we do, we have to suspect it, since the Others have been putting out a lot of disinformation."

"That's why I'm here. I can help you with that." Amid sat with Exotic stillness in his chair, but Hal felt a tenseness in him. "For example, the situation isn't just that the Others are mobilizing against you; it's that they've already achieved mobilization—past the point where it looks as if they can be stopped. But, about me. With no visible way to go, we're all left free to do what we choose. So, I decided to humor my natural inclinations, and offer you my services, while the Others can still be fought. That's what I meant when I said I could stay forever, if you want. I can stay with you until the end."

Hal sat back in his float, thoughtfully.

"Oh," said Amid. "And, incidentally, we admit now that you and the Dorsai were right. The attempt to assassinate the Others, individually, wouldn't have worked. Each one of them's now got a large partisan population around them, on all the worlds they control. Even if they all could be killed, their deaths would only make those populations determined to destroy us in revenge."

"This is interesting," said Hal, slowly. "When I got here, some twelve standard months ago, all I could learn, through Tam Olyn, was that Dahno was dead, and that Bleys had taken over and started to mobilize."

"Not true, of course," said Amid. "Another piece of Dahno's campaign. When you got away from Bleys on Coby, I think you might have brought the report closer to being the truth. We'd known for years that Dahno and Bleys had very different ideas of what the destiny of the Others should be. Dahno's a genius in his own right. He's older than Bleys, so we never expected them to work well together. Also, Dahno has always been difficult to read clearly, but we think he's more interested in simple peace and prosperity in his own lifetime. Bleys appears to take a somewhat longer view."

Hal looked more closely at him.

"You sound as if you're giving me more credit for alarming Bleys than I'd suspected you would."

"I'm free now to say and do what I want," said Amid.

"How could Bleys move so fast with this mobilization that all of you on the Exotics would be sure he'd already won?"

"Not—already won," Amid answered, "but certain to win. Because of that tremendous leverage on other people that the Others seem to be able to bring to bear. What he's done, in effect, is start a popular movement against all of us who might oppose him."

"How? On what basis?" Hal said.

Amid smiled, almost wistfully.

"The man's a genius," he said. "He simply turned everything inside out. He made the Others' enemies the villains who'd destroy civilization. The popular opinion now becomes that there's a plot on the part of those same people on Earth who always wanted to control the Younger Worlds and their populations. The plot is supposed to be masterminded by those like yourself on the Final Encyclopedia; who, as everyone knows, for generations have been busy developing scientific black magic of great power—the variant of the phase-drive that gives you your protective envelope here is visible proof of that. The story goes that the main business of the Encyclopedia has been the development of awesome weaponry all these years and with these they can sweep all human life from the other worlds, unless those worlds surrender to them. The only hope of the Younger Worlds is that the Encyclopedia isn't quite ready to act; and if they move fast, they can kill the dragon before it gets out of its cave."

Hal sat for a moment.

"I see," he said at last.

"The Others have advertised themselves as leaders and organizers of the effort to save the Younger Worlds. According to them, all the historical henchmen of the Encyclopedia, such as the Dorsai, Exotics, and the wrong kind of Friendly, are known to be in with the Encyclopedia in this, helping to soften up the Younger Worlds for Earth's final attack; and so they must also be rooted out at the same time, once and for all."

Amid paused.

"You'll notice," he said, "how neatly this line is set up to be developed later into one that says that, if all people are to have lasting safety, all knowledge, science and related demons must be done away with or strictly controlled; so that they can never rise again in the future, to threaten the ordinary human."

"How large a proportion of the formerly uncommitted on those nine worlds seem to have been recruited by this, at the present time?" Hal asked.

"Perhaps twenty per cent," said Amid, "and that's why we've calculated that there's no hope for us. Effectively, twenty per cent is more than enough to commit an overwhelming supply of cannon fodder for the Others to throw against us. For all practical purposes, twenty per cent might as well be a hundred per cent. It represents so many individuals that they could march upon us, twenty abreast, forever. They'd be self-renewing down the generations, if the war against us could last that long."

"The Others may have the people," said Hal. "But it's something else to mount an attack between worlds with a force that massive, logistically."

"True," said Amid. "So we do have some time. But on the Exotics, our best calculations see the attack eventually, and our destruction, as inevitable."

His eyes were steady on Hal's.

"So you see," he went on, after a second. "Oh, I know. Ten years ago, anything like such a military attempt of worlds upon worlds would have sounded as wild as a fairy tale come to life. But what everyone took for granted was that no people would consider such a tremendous wastage of life and material as would be necessary to gain such an end. But to the Others, the costs don't matter as long as they get the results they want."

Hal nodded.

"Since that's the case," he said, "and since I assume you don't find any flaws in the Exotic calculations—"

"No," said Amid.

"Why bother coming to me?" finished Hal. "According to what you say, what you and I can do isn't going to make any difference. Under those circumstances I'd expect a mature Exotic to give up philosophically."

"Possibly then I'm not a mature Exotic," said Amid. "In spite of my wrinkles. As I say, I'm free now to do what I want; and, being free, I'm allowing myself to indulge an irrational, unprovable hope that, just as the Others with this charismatic talent of theirs pulled a rabbit out of their hat which nobody'd ever suspected, you just might be able to pull out an equally-unsuspected counter-rabbit. Consciously, of course, I have to realize that such a hope is nonsense. But I believe I'll feel better if I go down resisting, so to speak, until the bitter end. So, I'd like to stay as long as I can and be of as much use to you as possible."

"I see," said Hal. "You don't happen to have some Dorsai blood in your ancestry, by any chance?"

Amid laughed.

"I just think I can be useful to you," he went on. "You've got your inferences; but I can give you access to specific, hard information, much of it through a network of communication the Exotics have developed and improved over the centuries. If I could set up a communication center for you, here, I think you'd find what I could bring in would be very useful to you."

"I'm sure I would," said Hal. "All right, thanks; and welcome."

He stood up. Amid in response got to his own feet.

"I'm sorry to cut this short," said Hal. "But we'll have time to talk later. I've got someone else to see, now."

"Perfectly all right," said Amid.

Hal reached down to the console on the arm of the float he had just left and touched for Ajela.

"Hal?" Her voice came clearly into the room, but without picture on the phone screen.

"I'd like Amid to stay with us," Hal said. "Can we arrange quarters for him?"

"If one of the regular rooms for visiting scholars will do, certainly," said Ajela. "Tell him to turn right when he steps out of your room and he'll find me through the first door he comes to."

"Thank you, both of you," said Amid.

He left. Hal sat down again and touched the phone. This time the face of Chuni, the reception leader who had spoken to them in Tam's office, came on the phone screen.

"Hal?" said Chuni.

"Where's Bleys now, Chuni?"

"He's waiting in the private lounge here by the dock."

"He's alone?"

"Yes," said Chuni.

"Send him—no, bring him up yourself, would you please?"

"All right. Is that all?" Chuni looked tensely out of the phone at Hal.

"That's all," Hal said.

He sat down again. After only a few minutes, the door opened and he got to his feet again.

"Here you are, Bleys Ahrens. . . ." the voice of Chuni was saying; and the two of them came through the door, with Bleys in the lead. Chuni stopped just inside the threshold, nodded past Bleys at Hal and went out again, closing the door behind him.

Bleys stopped, three steps inside the room. He stood, lean and tall in a short black jacket and narrow gray trousers tapering into his boots. His straight-boned, angular face with its penetrating brown eyes under straight black brows studied Hal.

"Well," he said, "you've grown up."

"It happens," said Hal.

They stood, facing, little more than a meter of distance between them; and, strangely, the sight of the Other brought back the memory of Amyth Barbage, facing the other Militia Captain who had not wanted to keep pursuing Rukh's Command. The feeling struck Hal that the room seemed suddenly to have grown small around them; and he realized that for the first time he was looking at Bleys without the stark emotion of his memory of the day on the terrace, held like a drawn sword between them. It surprised Hal now—but not as much as he would have been surprised before he had discovered that his head had touched the same top of the doorway as had Ian Graeme's—to discover that he now stood eye to eye, on a level with Bleys. From nowhere, a strange poignancy took him. This individual before him was, in a reverse sense, all he had left of what he had once known; the only one to whom he had any connection from before the moment of his tutors' deaths.

Bleys turned and stepped to Hal's float-desk, sitting down on the edge of it, almost as if Hal was the visitor, rather than he.

"A big change to take place in a year," Bleys said.

Hal sat down in his chair. Perched on the desk, Bleys sat a little above him; but that advantage in position no longer mattered between them.

"The biggest change took place in that Militia cell in Ahruma, in the day or two after you left me," said Hal. "I had a chance to sort things out in my mind."

"Under an unusual set of conditions," Bleys said. "That Captain deliberately misinterpreted what I told him."

"Amyth Barbage," said Hal. "Have you forgotten his name? What did you do to him, afterward?"

"Nothing." Bleys sat still, watching him. "It was his nature to do what he did. Any blame there was, was mine, for not understanding that nature, as I should have. I don't do things to people, in any case. My work is with events."

"You don't do anything to people? Even to those like Dahno?"

Bleys raised his eyebrows slightly, then shook his head.

"Even to those like Dahno. Dahno may have created the conditions that could lead to his destruction. All I did was give the Others an alternative plan; and in refusing to consider it, Dahno put himself in other hands than mine. As I say, I work with larger matters than individual people."

"Then why come see me?" The almost painfully brilliant, hard-edged clarity of mind that had come on Hal as he sat at the head of the long dining table at Foralie, talking to the Grey Captains, was back with him now.

"Because you're a potential problem," said Bleys. He smiled. "Because I hate the waste of a good mind—ask my fellow Others if I don't—and because I feel an obligation to you."

"And because you have no one to talk to," said Hal.

Bleys' smile widened slowly. There was a short pause. "That's very perceptive of you," he said, gently. "But you see, I've never had anyone to talk to; and so I'm afraid I wouldn't know what I was missing. As for what brings me here, I'd like to save you if I could. Unlike Dahno, you can be of reliable use to the race."

"I intend to," said Hal.

"No," said Bleys. "What you intend is your own destruction—very much like Dahno. Are you aware the struggle in which you've chosen to involve yourself is all over but the shouting? Your cause isn't only lost; it's already on its way to being forgotten."

"And you want to save me?" Hal said.

"I can afford what I want," said Bleys. "But in this case, it's not a matter of my saving you but of you choosing to save yourself. In a few standard years an avalanche will have swallowed up all you now think you want to fight for. So, what difference will it make if you stop fighting now?"

"You seem to assume," said Hal, "that I'm going to stop eventually."

"Either stop, or—forgive me—be stopped," said Bleys. "The outcome of this battle you want to throw yourself into was determined before you were born."

"No," said Hal, slowly. "I don't think it was."

"I understand you originally had an interest in being a poet," said Bleys. "I had inclinations to art, too, once; before I found it wasn't for me. But poetry can be a personally-rewarding life work. Be a poet, then. Put this other aside. Let what's going to happen, happen; without wasting yourself trying to change it."

Hal shook his head.

"I was committed to this, only this, long before you know," he said.

"I'm entirely serious in what I say," went on Bleys. "Stop and think. What good is it going to do to throw yourself away? Wouldn't it be better, for yourself and all the worlds of men and women, that you should live a long time and do whatever you want to do—whether it's poetry or anything else? It could even be something as immaterial as saying what you think to your fellow humans; so that something of yourself will have gone into the race and be carried on to enrich it after you're gone. Isn't that a far better thing than committing suicide because you can't have matters just as you want them?"

"I think," said Hal, "we're at cross purposes. What you see as inevitable, I don't see so at all. What you refuse to accept can happen, I know can happen."

Bleys shook his head.

"You're in love with a sort of poetic illusion about life," he said. "And it is an illusion, even in a poetic sense; because even poets—good poets— come to understand the hard limits of reality. Don't take my word for that. What does Shakespeare have Hamlet say at one point . . . '*How weary, stale, flat, and unprofitable seem to me all the uses of this world*'?"

Hal smiled suddenly.

"Do you know Lowell?" he asked.

"Lowell? I don't believe so," answered Bleys.

"James Russell Lowell," said Hal. "Nineteenth-century American poet."

He quoted:

"When I was a beggarly boy,
And lived in a cellar damp,
I had not a friend nor a toy,
But I had Aladdin's lamp. . . ."

He sat, matching his gaze with Bleys'.

"You've been researching my childhood, I see," said Bleys. He got to his feet and Hal rose with him. "You're better at quoting poetry than I am." He stopped, his face a mask of stillness.

"I think," he went on, "that those events that took place at your Estate keep you from listening to me now. So I believe I'll have to accept the fact I can't save you. So I'll go. What is it you've found here at the Encyclopedia—if anything—if I may ask?"

Hal met his eyes.

"As one of my tutors would have said," he answered, "that's a foolish question."

"Ah," said Bleys.

He turned toward the door. He had almost reached it, when Hal spoke again behind him; his voice suddenly different, even in his own ears.

"'How did it happen?'"

Bleys stopped and turned back to face him.

"Of course," he said, gently, "you'd like to know more, would you? I should have seen to your being informed before. Well, I'll tell you now, then. The men we normally use to go before us in situations like that had found two of your tutors already on that terrace and the third was brought to join them a minute or two after I stepped out onto the terrace myself. It was the Friendly they brought. The Dorsai and your Walter the In-Teacher were already there. Like you, he seemed to be fond of poetry, and as I came out of the library window, he was quoting from that verse drama of Alfred Noyes, *Sherwood*. The lines he was repeating were those about how Robin Hood had saved one of the fairies from what Noyes called The Dark Old Mystery. I quoted him Blondin's song, from the same piece of writing, as a stronger piece of poetry. Then I asked him where you were; and he told me he didn't know—but of course he did. They all knew, didn't they?"

"Yes," said Hal. "They knew."

"It was that which first raised my interest in you above the ordinary," Bleys said. "It intrigued me. Why should they be so concerned to hide you? I'd told them no one would be hurt; and they would have known my reputation for keeping my word."

He paused for a second.

"They were quite right not to speak, of course," he added, softly.

Hal stood still, waiting.

"At any rate," said Bleys. "I tried to bring them to like me, but of course they were all of the old breed—and I failed. That intrigued me even more, that they should be so firmly recalcitrant; and I was just about to make further efforts, which might have worked, to find out from them about you, when your Walter the InTeacher physically attacked me—a strange thing for an Exotic to do."

"Not," Hal heard his own voice saying, "under the circumstances."

"Of course, that triggered off the Dorsai and the Friendly. Together, they accounted for all but one of the men I had watching them; but of course, all three of them were killed in the process. Since there was no hope of questioning them, then, I went back into the house. Dahno had just arrived; and I didn't have the leisure to order a search of the grounds for you, after all."

"I was in the lake," Hal said. "Walter and Malachi Nasuno—the Dorsai—signalled me when they guessed you were on the grounds. I had time to hide in some bushes at the water's edge. After . . . I came up to the terrace and saw you and Dahno through the window of the library."

"Did you?" said Bleys.

The two of them stood, facing each other for a moment; and Bleys shook his head, slowly.

"So it had already begun between us, even then?" he said.

He opened the door and stepped through it, closing it quietly behind him. Hal turned back to the nearest float and touched the phone controls.

"Chuni," he said. "Bleys Ahrens is on his way out. See that he doesn't go astray."

Chapter

> > **51** < <

Cutting the connection to Chuni, Hal called Ajela.

"I'd like to talk to you and Tam right away," he said. "Something new's come up. And I'd like to bring Amid with me, unless there's an objection to it."

"I'll ask Tam." Ajela's face looked at him curiously out of the screen. "But I can't imagine any objection. Why don't you just bring him along to Tam's suite? If there's any problem with that, I can meet you at the door and explain to Amid."

"I'll be there as soon as I can collect him, then," said Hal.

When the two of them reached the suite, Ajela was waiting, holding the door open. Inside, Tam waved them to chairs.

"I'm afraid this is going to disrupt things," said Hal, sitting down. "I'm going to have to leave for a while—"

He glanced at Amid.

"—Taking Amid if he'll go."

He had said nothing of this to the old Exotic. Amid raised his eyebrows, very slightly, but said nothing.

"Also, I'm going to suggest we tighten security on the Encyclopedia right away. I'm afraid that means all visitors—visiting scholars included—should leave."

Tam frowned.

"The Encyclopedia's never been closed," he said. "Even back when it was on Earth's surface, down in St. Louis, it was always open to those who needed to use it and were qualified to come in."

"I don't think there's any alternative now, though," said Hal. "Otherwise, one of these days a human bomb is going to be walking through an entry port. Bleys can find people willing to give their lives to destroy the Encyclopedia. Closed, we're invulnerable. Only, we'd have to look to the supply situation."

"That was taken care of long ago," said Ajela. "Even in the beginning, Mark Torre considered the chance that the Encyclopedia, being what it is, might be isolated one day. We're an almost perfect closed system, ecologically. The only thing we'd lack for the next half century is enough energy to see us through that much time. Closed up, we might go half a

year to a year on stored power . . . but at the end of that time, we'd have
to open irises to collect a fresh supply of solar energy. Of course, I can
put Jeamus Walters to work on a way to get solar energy through the
shield without opening up. . . ."

"I don't think we need to worry about obvious physical attack from outside for some time, yet," said Hal. "But for everything else, the available
time looks a lot shorter than I'd thought."

"That's what you found out from Bleys, was it?" Tam asked. "What did
he say?"

"What he told me, effectively, was that he'd like me to resign myself
to the fact that his people had already won—"

"Won!" said Tam.

"Unfortunately," Hal went on, "what he had to say about it agrees with
what Amid came to tell me. Amid, why don't you tell Tam and Ajela?"

Amid did. When he was done, Tam snorted.

"Apologies, and all that," he said to Amid. "But I don't know you. How
can I be sure you're not someone who belongs to Bleys Ahrens?"

"He isn't, Tam," said Ajela, softly. "I know who he is. He's the kind of
Exotic who wouldn't be able to work on Bleys' side."

"I suppose," Tam growled, looking from her to Amid and back again.
"You Exotics should know each other, of course. But as far as the Others
already having won goes, though—well, what did you have in mind to
do, Hal?"

"I'm going to have to go back to Harmony, to Mara or Kultis, and the
Dorsai. It's become time to get our forces organized," said Hal. He turned
to the small Exotic. "Amid, you were going to help me with communication. Can you get a message, now, to Harmony ahead of our own landing there? A message arranging a meeting for me with a leader of one of
the resistance Commands named Rukh Tamani?"

Amid frowned.

"The Encyclopedia can put me in phone communication with the Exotic Embassy in Rheims, down on Earth, can't it?"

"Of course," said Ajela.

"Good. Let me see what I can do, then," Amid said. "If you'll excuse
me, I'll go to that room you gave me and do my calling from there."

"Thank you," said Hal.

Amid smiled a little grimly, and went out.

"He's a sensitive listener," said Hal, after the door had closed behind
the small man in the gray robe. "I think he understood I needed to talk
to the two of you, alone."

"Of course he did," said Ajela. "But what was it you didn't want him to hear?"

"It's not exactly that I had a specific reason for not wanting him to hear," said Hal. "It's just that there's no particular reason for including him, yet; and until there is—"

"Very good. Quite right," said Tam. "When we know him better maybe it'll be different. But for now, let's keep private matters among the three of us. What was it you were going to tell us, Hal?"

"My conclusions about Bleys, and his visit," said Hal. "Bleys said he came here to see if I couldn't be brought to accepting the fact that his side had won; and I believe that actually was one of his reasons for coming. From which I judge that he's now ready to move against Earth; and that's why I feel the Encyclopedia's now in danger."

"Why?" demanded Tam. "What makes you suddenly think he's ready to move against Earth; and why should that suddenly put the Encyclopedia in danger?"

Hal looked from one to the other of them.

"I thought it was obvious. You don't see it?" he said. Ajela, beside Tam, shook her head. "Well, to begin with, you've got to realize that Bleys is completely honest in anything he says; because he feels he's above any need to dissimulate, let alone lie outright. He told me he'd hate to waste what I could do for the race; and since that's what he said, that's the way he must feel."

"How," demanded Tam, "do you know he's above any need to dissimulate?"

Hal hesitated.

"In some ways I understand him, instinctively," he answered. "In some ways, even, I think he and I are alike. That's one of the things I was forced to recognize in the Militia cell on Harmony, when I came to understand other things. I can't prove it to you—that I understand him. All I can do is ask you to take my word for it. What I'm sure of, in this instance, is that if he ever needed to dissimulate, he'd cease, in his own eyes, to be Bleys Ahrens. And being Bleys Ahrens is the most important thing in the universe to him."

"Again," said Tam, "why?"

Hal frowned a little.

"Because he's nothing else. Surely that much has always been obvious about him?"

Tam was silent.

"Yes," said Ajela, slowly, "I think it always has been."

"So," said Hal. "Since he doesn't dissimulate and therefore he really was interested in saving me if he could, we're faced with the fact that that reason alone isn't strong enough to bring him here, now. Also, his main reason for coming, whatever else it is, isn't likely to have to do with the Encyclopedia, which he respects but doesn't fear. So it must have to do with Earth. Earth's always been the one world where the Others have been inexplicably ineffective with a majority of the populace."

"As opposed to the Exotics, the Friendlies and the Dorsai, you mean?" said Ajela. "Where the reasons are plain why most of the people there manage to resist that charismatic talent of the Others?"

"Exactly," said Hal. "The people of Old Earth as a whole never have had the sort of commitment to the ideals of their Cultures as members of the three great splinter groups have. But in spite of this a majority of the people on Earth seem to be able to shrug off the charisma. The Others know they'll have to control Earth, eventually; but in spite of this mobilization of theirs for what looks like an orthodox military movement against their enemies, their natural preference isn't for that way of doing things. Neither Bleys nor any others of his kind want to spend any large part of their lifetimes playing at being generals. What they really want is to sit back among worlds already conquered and enjoy themselves. So, since Bleys is here now, it has to mean two things at least. One, that he's planning to move soon on Earth, in a non-military manner—since any military effort they could mount is at least logistically unready; and two, Bleys, himself, wanted a firsthand look at the situation there before that effort got under way."

"All right," said Tam. "I still don't see what in this sends you off to Harmony, the Exotics and the Dorsai."

"The fact that Bleys is different."

"That's what 'Other' means," said Tam dryly.

"I mean," said Hal, "different from the rest of the Others. He heads their cause for a reason of his own I don't yet fully understand; and until I do, I've got to dig for every possible understanding of the situation."

He stopped and looked at Tam, who nodded slowly.

"And the situation right now requires that understanding," Hal went on, "if we're to get any clear idea of what Bleys and the Others are planning for Earth."

"All right, then," said Tam, "just what are they planning, do you think?"

"Well," answered Hal, "they know they aren't as successful at stampeding individuals there as they are elsewhere; but on the other hand, Old Earth's people have always been ripe for any emotionally powerful appeal, particularly in an apocalyptic time. You heard Amid. The argument they're already beginning to use in their mobilization on the other worlds is that individuals on Earth with a traditional desire to dominate all other civilized planets, and armed with new, dark weapons from the Encyclopedia, are about to try to conquer the Younger Worlds. Note that the blame's being laid on individuals."

"Why's that important?" said Ajela.

"Because, since it's easier to paint individuals as villains than all those on Earth, the most obvious deduction is that Bleys plans to send charismatics to Earth, to preach a crusade in which the common people there will be urged to rise against the Encyclopedia and those supposedly-evil individuals who're pushing the plan to take over the Younger Worlds. If they can get a popular movement of any size going down there, then the Younger Worlds can be asked to send help, to take power by force. Meanwhile, it's a good argument to use on Earth's people; and a good plan to gain power for the Others, there. It's using their special talent at one remove; but, given the special character of the old world's full-spectrum peoples, that makes it all the more likely to work."

He paused.

"Am I making sense to you both?" he asked.

Tam nodded.

"Go on," his deep, hoarse voice rattled against the walls of the room.

"So it's necessary I carry what we know and what I deduce to the Exotics and the Dorsai; and show the Exotics, in particular, that victory for the Others isn't a foregone conclusion—that they can be fought, if they try what I believe they're going to try. They can be fought and checked right here on Earth."

"And how are you figuring on fighting them, right here on Earth as you put it?" asked Tam.

"With counter-preachers." Hal's eyes met the dark old ones levelly. "What I finally realized in that cell on Harmony was that, at base, those charismatic abilities of the Others are derived from a talent evolved on the Friendlies; where the urge to proselyte has always been strong, powered by the quality of their faith. Rukh Tamani, if I can get to her, can tell me who the Harmonyites are who're available and would want to come to Earth and oppose those who'll preach this doctrine of the Others. We'll need people who can oppose it with the same sort of force and faith that fuels the charismatic talent. Then, if the Exotics and the Dorsai see reason to hope, we may be able to get all those who ought to be united against the Others working together effectively as a unit—in time to stop Bleys."

Tam said nothing for a second.

"I see." He glanced at Ajela. "The minute you begin fighting him on

Earth, successfully or otherwise, you'll force Bleys to fall back on the use of force to win. That's why you think we've got to start protecting the Encyclopedia right now?"

"Yes," said Hal.

Tam nodded.

"All right," he said, heavily. He turned to Hal. "I suppose you've taken into consideration the possibility that Bleys might already have someone, a saboteur, already here, at the Encyclopedia."

"Yes," said Hal. "But it's a long shot. The plans of the Others are too recent for it to be one of the regular personnel; and there've been none of the regulars who've been away from the Encyclopedia in recent years long enough and under conditions where they could be permanently corrupted, by even someone as capable as Bleys himself. That leaves the visiting scholars, as I say; and while it's unlikely one of them could have been gotten at—considering the general level of their ages and reputations—in the last year, we shouldn't take chances. In any case, there's no way I can see that we can check those we've got here now for possible intent to sabotage us, and be sure of what we find."

"Perhaps there is," said Tam. "Come along to the Academic control chamber. Let me take a look at the neural chart there and see what our current visitors have been working on in the last twelve months."

They went. The control chamber was as Hal had remembered it from his first visit to the Encyclopedia when he had been brought to it by Ajela. The room, which was large as rooms in the Final Encyclopedia went, was still banked on each wall with the control consoles, with half a dozen technicians in white shirts and slacks moving softly about it, recording the work done by the visitors and surveying it for what was new to the master files and should be added to them.

Tam led Ajela and Hal directly to the mass of red, cord-thick lines apparently hovering at waist-level in the center of the room. The one technician beside it moved discreetly back out of view as the old man came to a halt and stared down at the intermittently-glowing sections that came and went in the mass of lines. He stood, studying it for a long moment.

"Rotate this overall view forty-five degrees," he said, almost absently.

"Rotate . . . ?" The technician who had retreated came forward, staring. "But then all our present charting is going to be thrown off—"

He checked himself before Tam's suddenly raised head and the glare of his eyes. Tam opened his mouth, as if to speak, then closed it again.

"Of course. Right away—" The technician hurried to a console and Tam looked back at the display of the Encyclopedia's neural circuits, as they seemed, not so much to rotate, as to melt and twist into different patterns. After a second, the changes stopped taking place, and Tam considered the shapes before him.

After a moment he sighed and looked at Ajela, then beyond her to the technician, now standing well back by the console he had gone to to rotate the display.

"Come here," said Tam.

The technician came forward. The other white-dressed figures in the room were not looking, not watching what was going on at the center of it; but they were very still and Hal thought he could see their ears tensed.

"I do my best nowadays," said Tam quietly to the technician, "not to lose my temper, but sometimes I'm not too successful. Try and remember that the rest of you don't know all the things I've learned in the last century; and that I get weary of having to make the same explanation over and over again to new people every time I want something done."

"Of course, Tam," said the technician hastily. "I shouldn't have spoken up."

"No, you shouldn't," said Tam. "But now you should also know why you shouldn't have; and from now on you should tell other people, so they know, too. Will you do that?"

"Yes, Tam. Of course."

"Good." Tam turned back to Hal and Ajela. "Jaime Gluck and Eu San Loy. I think both those visitors may have used up their welcome here."

"Tam—" began Ajela.

"Oh, I can't be sure," Tam said. "But let's go on that assumption that I'm right. Better safe than sorry, as Hal pointed out."

"All right," said Ajela. She turned to Hal. "I'll tell them, right away. How soon will you be leaving?"

"On the first available deep-space transport. . . ." But Hal's eyes were on Tam, who had turned back once more to studying the neural display. Ajela's attention followed his and they stood in silence, watching the old man as the seconds slipped past. But Tam was paying attention only to what held his gaze. Finally, slowly, he looked back and around, at Hal, with an expression on his face Hal had never seen before.

"You're doing it," he said, on a long exhalation of breath.

"Not really," replied Hal. "Not yet. I'm just beginning to investigate the possibilities—"

"You're doing it—at last!" said Tam, in a stronger voice. "What Mark Torre dreamed of—using the Encyclopedia as a pure thinking tool. Using it, by God, the way he planned it to be used!"

"You have to understand," said Hal, "this is just a beginning. I'm only trying out poetry as a creative lever. I was waiting to show you until I had some firm results—"

Tam's wrinkled gray-skinned hand closed with remarkable strength on Hal's sleeve.

"This trip," said Tam. "Put it off. You've got to stay here, now. Stay, and work with the Encyclopedia."

Hal shook his head.

"I'm sorry," he said. "I'll get at it again just as soon as I can get back. But there's no one else to do what needs to be done on the Friendlies, the Exotics and on the Dorsai. I have to go, if the worlds are to be saved."

"Damn it, the worlds can take care of themselves, for once!" snapped Tam. "This is the doorway, the dawn of a new beginning! And you're the only one who can lead us into it. You can't be risked, now!" The technicians about the room were staring. Tam ignored them. "Hal!" he said. "Do you hear me?"

"I'm sorry." Gently, Hal pulled his sleeve out of the other's grasp. "I meant what I said. There's no one else to talk to the people who have to be talked to if the worlds are going to survive."

"Well, and what if they don't—as long as the Encyclopedia survives with what you can learn to do, now—what does the rest matter, then?" raged Tam. "Let Bleys and his friends have the other worlds, for fifty years—or a hundred years—or whatever. They can't touch you and your work here; and here's where the future lies. Isn't it the future that counts?"

"The future and the people," said Hal. "Without the people there wouldn't be any future. What good's a gift with no one to give it to? And you know as well as I do it's only if what I might find here turned out to be no use to anyone else, that Bleys'd leave the Encyclopedia alone. While if he already had all the other worlds and was really determined to get the Encyclopedia, eventually he would. With Newton, Cassida, and the stations on Venus, he'll have some of the best scientific and technological minds in his service. They'd find a way eventually to break through to us. Nothing ever made by humans stops other humans forever. Tam, I have to go."

Tam stood still. He did not say anything further. But his whole body seemed to hunch into itself, to become less. Ajela stepped to him and put her arms around him.

"It's all right," she said softly to him. "It'll work out, Tam. Hal'll come back safe. Believe him—believe me."

"Yes . . . ," said Tam, harshly. He turned slowly away from her and toward the doorway that would take him back to his own suite. "You don't give me much choice, do you?"

Chapter

> > **52** < <

The first deep-space vessel available to carry Hal and Amid in the right direction took them both only as far as New Earth City on New Earth, from which point they went different ways. Amid, to Mara to talk to his fellow Exotics there in preparation for the message Hal was planning to bring them; Hal, to the city of Citadel on Harmony.

Hal had half a day to himself in New Earth City after seeing Amid off; and he spent it taking note of the differences that had come over that metropolis since he had paused there as a boy, on his way to Coby almost seven years before. The larger differences were ones that seven years of time alone could not account for. It was the same city, on the same world; and business within it was proceeding much as it had proceeded when he had seen it before; but in the people there, those Hal saw on the streets and in the buildings, a change had come for which ten times seven years would hardly have been enough to account.

It was as if a darkening sense of limited time had moved in upon them like some heavy overcast of cloud, to interdict whatever hope and purpose had formerly shone into their daily lives. Under this gathering darkness, they seemed to scurry with the frantic energy of those who would deny a rapidly-approaching deadline when all their efforts would become useless. Like ants who appear to redouble their dashing about in the fading light of sunset, the people of New Earth City seemed obsessed with an urgency to accomplish all their usual activities, both with great dispatch and with a denial that there was any need for that urgency.

But, behind that denial, Hal felt a penetrating and overwhelming fear of an approaching night in which all they had done to prepare would turn out to be useless.

He was glad at last, therefore, to ride up to the ship into which he now transferred. Arriving in orbit around Harmony, he rode a jitney down to the Citadel Spaceport; and landed shortly after a storm had passed, a rare heavy rain which had washed the city clean. A watery, but clear, sunlight from the large orangish orb of Epsilon. Eridani, one of the stars Hal had picked out of the night sky back on Earth as a boy, gilded the stolid brick and concrete buildings of the city outside the Port.

He took an automated cab and directed it to a destination on the city's northern outskirts, to a dome-roofed building in the midst of a large, rub-bled, open lot among dwelling places set at some little distance from each other. Releasing the cab, he entered the building.

There was nothing to show that time had not stood still since his last visit. The air inside, barely a degree or two above the temperature of that outside, was as before heavy with the banana-like lubricant smell. Several elderly surface vehicles, their propulsive units exposed or partially dismantled, sat about the unpartitioned interior, lit by the pale light that came through the translucent dome. A stocky, older man in work clothes was head-down into the works of one of the vehicles.

Hal walked over to him.

"Hello, Hilary," he said.

The head of the stocky man came up. Amber eyes from under a tight, oil-streaked skullcap looked at Hal, dryly.

"What can I do for you?" the other man asked.

"You don't recognize me?" said Hal, caught halfway between humor and sadness.

It was not surprising. In the two years since the other had last seen him, Hal had crossed the line into physical maturity. He had been a tall, lean, intense stripling when Hilary had seen him last. Now, although there were no sudden age lines on his face and the twenty extra kilograms of flesh and muscle he now carried on his bones had only reasonably increased his apparent weight, a world of difference had overtaken him. He was no longer just very tall. He was big. Indeed, as he had fully realized at last only when Ajela had confronted him with his own image on his return to the Final Encyclopedia, he was very big.

He read the message of that size in Hilary's response—in the fact that Hilary seemed to tighten up slightly at the first sight of him, then settle in, become even more compact by comparison. It was an unconscious reflex of the other man, part of an indefinable, automatic measuring instinct in him, like that which causes one male dog to bristle at his original glimpse of a strange and larger other, only to lower the hair on back and shoulders when a second glance discovers that the difference in size between them was too great to make any thought of challenge practical.

Hal had encountered similar reactions from time to time, this past year, at the Encyclopedia; and once, turning a corner to find himself face-to-face with a mirror, in one of those unguarded moments where, for a second, the viewer fails to recognize himself—he had felt it himself. In that moment, before recognition and ordinary personal self-consciousness came back, he had seen someone who was not only large physically, but big beyond that size in some indefinable quality that was at once quiet, isolated and forever unyielding. For a fraction of a second there he had seen himself as a man he did not know, and when the recognition had come, it had brought not only a kind of embarrassment, but unhappiness; for until that moment he had been telling himself that he had at last learned to live with that inner difference and isolation of his, some time since. But now, here again with someone who had met him before, he had seen the mark of that difference, unerasable still upon him.

"Hilary, don't you know me?" he said. "Howard Beloved Immanuelson? Remember when Jason Rowe brought me around and you took us to join Rukh Tamani's Command?"

Hilary's eyes cleared to recognition. He held out his hand.

"Sorry," he said, "you've changed a bit. Who are you now?"

Hal gripped hands with him.

"My papers say I'm a Maran named Emer—commercially accredited to trade on Harmony by the Exotic Ambassadorial Office here."

"You could have fooled me," said Hilary, dryly, as their hands released. "Particularly wearing those ordinary clothes."

"You know Exotics don't always wear robes," said Hal. "Any more than Friendlies always dress in black. But, for your information only, you'd better have my real name. It's Hal Mayne. I'm of Earth."

"Old Earth?"

"Yes," said Hal. "Old Earth—and now, of the Final Encyclopedia, as well. I'm up to my ears in something larger than fighting the Militia, nowadays."

He looked closely at Hilary to read the other man's reaction.

"It isn't just here, or on Association, any longer," he went on, when Hilary said nothing. "Now, the battle against the Others is on all the worlds."

Hilary nodded. The wraith of a sigh seemed to tremble in him.

"I know," he said. "The old times are ending. I saw it coming a long time back. What can I do for you?"

"Just tell me where I can find Rukh," said Hal. "Some people were looking for me, but they haven't had any luck. For the sake of all the worlds, I've got to talk to her as soon as I can. There's a job only she can do for us."

Hilary's face became grim.

"I'm not sure I'd tell you unless you had someone to vouch for you. A year can move some people from one side to another. But in this case, it makes no difference. Whatever you've got in mind, you'd better find someone else to take it on," he said. "Rukh Tamani's dead—or if she isn't,

I'd be sorry to hear it. The Militia have her. They caught up with her three weeks ago."

Hal stared at the older man.

"Three weeks ago . . . where?"

"Ahruma."

"Ahruma? You mean she's been there ever since she blew the Core Tap?"

"They had it almost repaired. She was reconnoitering to see if the repair work could be sabotaged. There's a limb of Satan named Colonel Barbage—Amyth Barbage—who's been devoting his full time to running her down. He got word she was in the city, made a sweep, and two of the people he picked up knew where she could be found—"

Hilary paused, shrugged.

"They talked, of course, after he got them back to the Militia Center. And he caught her."

Hal stared at him.

"I'm going to have to get her out as soon as possible," he said.

"Get her out?" Hilary stared at him for a long moment. "You're actually serious, aren't you? Don't you think if prisoners could be got out of Militia Centers, we'd have been doing it before this?"

"And you haven't, I take it," said Hal, hearing his own voice echoing harshly off the curved walls and roof that were one and the same.

Hilary did not even bother to answer.

"I'm sorry," said Hal. "But there's too much at stake. I'll have to get her out, and as soon as possible."

"Man," said Hilary softly. "Don't you understand? Odds are a hundred to one she's been dead for at least a couple of weeks!"

"I've got to assume she isn't," said Hal. "We'll go in after her. Who do I see in Ahruma to get help? Are there any of her old Command around here?"

Hilary did not move.

"Help," he said, almost wonderingly. Moving as if by their own volition, his hands picked up a tan square of saturated cleansing cloth from the mainframe below the windshield of the vehicle he had been working on and started to wipe themselves. "Listen to me, Hal—if that's really your name—we can't just pick up a phone and call Ahruma. All long distance calls are monitored. It'd take three days to find a courier, a week to pass him or her on through friends who can make transportation available between here and Ahruma, another week to get people there together to talk about trying a rescue—and then they'd all go home an hour later after they heard what you had in mind, because they all know, like me, that any such thing's impossible. You were in a Command. What do you think a handful of people with needle guns and cone rifles can do against a barracks-full of police inside a fortress?"

"There are ways to deal even with fortresses," said Hal, "and as far as a phone message to Ahruma goes, I can probably make use of Exotic diplomatic communications, if the message can be coded safely. Why a week to get a courier there, anyway, when air transportation makes it in two hours?"

"God has afflicted your wits," said Hilary, calmly. "Even if we had someone locally who could show airport checkpoints an acceptable reason to make such a trip, it'd cost a fortune we don't have. Remember your Command, I say. Remember how you had to make do with equipment and weapons that were falling apart?"

"Credit's a problem?" Hal reached into his jacket and came out with a folder. He opened it to show the vouchers of balances in interstellar credit within it to Hilary. "I'm carrying more in interworld credit than you'd need for even a small army—given the exchange rate to Harmony currency. This is mine, and the Final Encyclopedia's. But if necessary, I'm pretty sure I could get more yet through Exotic diplomatic channels."

Hilary stared at the vouchers. His face became thoughtful. After a second, he walked around the vehicle across which he had been talking to Hal all this time.

"Coffee?" he said.

"Thanks," answered Hal.

Hilary led the way to a desk some twenty feet away, with a small cooker holding a coffee pot and a stack of disposable cups. They sat down and the older man poured a couple of cups. He drank slowly and appreciatively from his own, while Hal put his cup to his own lips, then set it down again. He had almost forgotten what Harmony coffee tasted like.

"I'm going to trust you," said Hilary, putting his own cup back down among the cluttered paperwork on the worn surface of the desk. "It's impossible, just as I say, but with that kind of credit we can at least daydream about it."

"Why is it still impossible? What makes it impossible?" Hal asked.

Hilary stared at him without answering.

"You say you're from Old Earth," he said. "Not from Dorsai?"

"Old Earth."

"If you say so." Hilary nodded slowly. "All right, then, to answer your questions, weren't you held in the Center here for a day or so before you and Jason came to see me? So do I need to tell you what they're like inside?"

"I didn't see much of it," said Hal. "Besides, you said Rukh's in the Center at Ahruma, not the one here at Citadel."

"They're all built the same," said Hilary. "It'd need an army to force its way into one, let alone bring someone out, let alone the Militia'd probably kill any prisoner they suspected we were about to try and rescue."

"If it needs an army, we'll get an army," said Hal. "This is something that concerns all the fourteen worlds. But maybe that much won't be necessary. Draw me a plan of a Center, if they're all alike as you say. Who'd I talk to in Ahruma to help me organize this?"

"Athalia McNaughton—I'd heard you'd met her," Hilary said briefly. He pushed the paperwork on the desk aside, drew a stylus and a blank sheet from the drawer below the desk's surface. He pushed both things across to Hal. "I can't draw worth a hoot. I'll tell you, and you draw. There's three main sections inside each Center, the Clerking section, the Militia Barracks, and the Cells section. . . ."

"Just a minute," said Hal. "What about finding a courier? We can't spare three days for that—"

"You won't need a courier. I'll go with you," said Hilary. "You can try and convince Athalia; and while you're doing that I'll see who I can round up in the local territory to help you, just in case. Now, draw this the way I tell you. The three sections of the Center are always in a single brick building on the end of a city block, as long as the block is wide, and about half that, in its width. The building in Ahruma is going to be less than six stories high, but with at least three levels underground. The Cells section, as you might expect, takes up the bottom levels. . . ."

Together, they caught a late-afternoon flight to Ahruma, three hours later; and Hal found himself sitting in the combination outer office-living room of Athalia McNaughton on the outskirts of Ahruma as the summer twilight outside gave way to night. Hilary was in Athalia's small working office, off to the right of this larger room, phoning people from Athalia's records of local resistance members, calling them to a conference. Athalia had remembered Hal but he found her even less ready to entertain the idea of rescuing Rukh than Hilary had been.

". . . Those funds you've got are all very well," the tall, brown-haired woman told him, after he had made his initial argument. They were sitting in overstuffed chairs in one corner of the room, facing each other almost like enemies. "But you're asking me to put the lives of a number of good and necessary local people in danger for a wild-goose chase. Hilary told you the straight of it. She's undoubtedly dead by now. The only reason she wouldn't be, would be if someone there had some special use for her."

"She wouldn't talk easily," said Hal.

"Don't you think I know that?" Athalia flared. "No Commander of a Command talks easily—and I've known her since she was a baby. But she'd either talk, and they'd kill her when they thought she had no more to tell them; or they'd have killed her by this time trying to make her talk. They aren't set up for keeping prisoners more than a few days—they just don't do it."

"All right," said Hal. "Then let's find out if she's still alive. Don't tell me you don't have some line of contact going inside that Center?"

"Into the Center, yes. Into the Barracks, yes. But into the Cells . . ." Athalia's words slowed as his eyes remained steady on hers. Her voice became almost gruff. "All we've ever been able to do as far the Cells go is sometimes smuggle suicide materials to one of our people who's been caught."

Hal sat watching her. With Rukh's life or death possibly hanging in the balance, he found himself very quiet within, and certain. As he had when he had come at last to the moment of having to win over the Grey Captains of the Dorsai, he was conscious of tapping skills until now locked away from him. One of these was a sort of intuitive logic that made him very sure of the answers that had come to him. He felt now something like an inner strength that had for a time slumbered, but was now awaking to take hold of him. Athalia, unchanged since he had seen her last, sat as one who has every confidence in her ability to win the argument. Her large-boned, thin-lipped face, strikingly attractive under the dark hair, in spite of her age, waited for him to do the impossible job of convincing her; and watching her, he considered with the recently-reawakened part of his mind what would reach her, what would touch her, what would prove what he had to say beyond the possibility of any further disagreement—as he had facing the Grey Captains.

"I know Rukh's alive," he said.

Only a slight widening of Athalia's eyes signalled that he might have found the right thing to say.

"How?" she demanded.

"Simply take it that I know," he said, meeting her eyes. And it was true; the feeling was a sureness in him. Although even if he had not felt it, he would have spoken the same words to Athalia, anyway. "But certainly we ought to be able to find out, if you want outside proof. I can't believe you don't have some way to check on that, at least."

"I suppose . . . ," said Athalia slowly, "yes, I think we could check that much."

"Then there's no point in wasting time, is there?" said Hal. "While you're doing that, everything else can be going forward on the assumption that we're going to hear that she's alive; then we'll be ready to move as soon as possible when we do hear she's alive. Suppose I make an agreement with you?"

He went on before she could have a chance to speak.

"As you know, I've been with a Command. I wouldn't think of trying to buy you, or anyone else. But will you do this much for me? Organize and push forward the preparations for a rescue, including using anyone who'd be involved with that, and if it turns out Rukh isn't still alive I'll reimburse everyone concerned for any time or expense lost they've been put to—if you want to, I'll also donate five hundred credits of interstellar units to the use of your local people—and you know what that works out to in terms of local exchange."

He paused to take a breath and she began to speak, coldly.

"I don't think—"

"But," he said, overriding her, "if Rukh is alive, we'll forget about any reimbursement or donations—except for the matter of any expenses your people couldn't afford. Otherwise I'll assume that what this might cost them is no more than what they'd undertake for Rukh's sake, in any case."

He stopped then and waited for her to speak. But she only looked at him, almost as an enemy might look, for a long second.

"All right," she said. "Within reason and within the bounds of what I think is safe for those I'm responsible for, all right."

"Good," he said, swiftly, "then, since I'm willing to pay for it if I'm wrong, there's some things I'd like put in motion right away. I'll need to know a great deal about that Militia Center, everything you can find out for me, including how many Militiamen and officers they've got there at the moment—I know you won't be able to give me an exact count, but I need to know the approximate number on hand at the time we go in after Rukh. Also, I want to know about deliveries and traffic, in and out of the building. Also, when they unlock the public areas, who those are who don't belong there but are occasionally allowed to go in and out anyway, such as when the building gets its garbage picked up; and what the arrangements are for repair calls by outside workmen, in case they need services of any kind. I need to know the hours of the various shifts on duty, the personalities of the officers in command and the kinds of communication going into the building."

He stopped.

"You don't want much," she said. She smiled slightly, grimly.

"There ought to be local people you can ask to find out these things," he answered. "Naturally, we also need to know about armament, and locks and security measures. But there's one thing I'd like you to start right now—and it won't commit you or your people to anything. That's to spread the word around the city that Rukh might—just might—still be alive. Then, when we find out she is, that rumor will have the general public ready to accept the information and maybe mount some shielding demonstrations for us."

Athalia hesitated, then nodded.

"All right," she said, "that much can be done."

"And as soon as we get definite word Rukh's still alive," he said, "I want to meet with everyone and explain to them how we can get her out."

"If you can," said Athalia.

"We'll see," he answered.

"All right." She got to her feet. "I'll go right now and set the machinery working to find out—if I can get Hilary off that phone for five minutes."

"How soon do you think we might hear?" he called after her as she headed toward the small office.

"I don't know. Forty-eight hours at least, I'd say," she answered over her shoulder.

But it was not forty-eight hours. Before noon the next day Athalia heard from the fish dealer who supplied the Barracks section kitchen in the Center and was on easy speaking terms with the mess cook and his staff. Rukh, he had been told, was in an isolation cell; but, as of the previous day, she had been alive.

Eight hours later, as soon as darkness had cloaked the streets for an hour, sixteen people gathered in Athalia's warehouse, around a table of boards set up on trestles for the occasion.

Chapter

> > **53** < <

Hal sat at one end of the table looking down its length at Athalia and at all those between them. Again, as when he had talked to her the evening before, he was strongly reminded of the moment in which he had faced the Grey Captains in the dining room at Foralie. Outside of Athalia herself and Hilary, those at the table were all faces he did not know, with the exception of two from Rukh's Command, the perky, aggressive features of Tallah, and the long face of Morelly Walden. Morelly had evidently healed from his wound, but he had lost weight and now his body was as thin as his limbs. He had supported himself with a stick as he had walked into the warehouse, and he looked twenty years older than the man Hal had known.

If any of the other twelve people Athalia had invited were also members or former members of Commands, they showed no sign of it. It seemed to Hal that with the exception of Tallah and Morelly, he looked at all city faces; hard faces, in some instances, but city ones nonetheless; and his instincts told him that he could expect no help from either of his former comrades, or from Hilary—if Hilary had indeed come to the point of wanting to help—in convincing these others.

Athalia began matters by briefly rehearsing Hal's credentials as a former member of Rukh's group and stating what he wanted.

". . . and as you all know," she wound up, "we did hear earlier today that Rukh was still alive in the Cells at Center—in an isolation cell, but alive. He's made certain offers to us you know about. Now, I'll let Hal have his chance to tell you what he's got in mind."

"Thanks," said Hal.

He looked at the men and women he did not know; and their expressions were not encouraging.

"I take it for granted," he said, "that there's no one here who'd hesitate at anything I've got to propose, if he or she thought there was a real possibility of getting Rukh free from the Militia. But I'm going to have to ask one uncomfortable question before I start talking to you—is there anyone here who seriously feels that it's a waste of time even listening to me? I'm asking each one of you to examine your own conscience."

The eyes around the table stared back at him. No one stirred or spoke.

"I ask that," said Hal, "because I know many of you feel that simply because no prisoner has ever been recovered from a Center, no prisoner ever could be; and I'm here to tell you not only that that's a belief that's mistaken, but that bringing Rukh safely out of the hands of the Militia is the sort of thing that people like us have done down through history. It's not only possible, it's practical. However, there's not one of you here I can convince of that, if you've already made up your mind there's no point in listening to me. So, I'll ask you again, for Rukh's sake, are there any of you here who've got a completely-closed mind on this subject?"

There was a moment of silence and stillness. Then the people about the table looked at each other, and after several seconds there was a screech of metal on concrete, as a tall man in a dark leather jacket, near the far end of the table, pushed back the barrel-like metal container that had been serving him as a seat. He stood up; and at the sight of his rising, a shorter man in a business suit at the table's very end also stood up.

"Wait," said Hal.

They paused.

"I honor your honesty," he went on, "but please—don't leave. How about sitting in, with the rest of us, after all? Not to join in the discussion, but just to listen?"

The two standing men looked at him. The one who had been the first to rise was the first to sit down. The other followed.

"Thanks," said Hal. He paused to look around the table before going on. "Now, let me make one other point first. I've told Athalia, and I believe she's relayed what I said to the rest of you, that the main reason an effort has to be made to free Rukh is there's a job to be done by her no one else on any of the worlds can do."

"She belongs to Harmony," broke in a heavy man in a dark green, knitted jacket, seated next to Tallah.

"Right now," said Hal, "I could answer that statement by saying the only thing she belongs to is the Militia. But I know what you're talking about—that she's a Harmonyite, one of the Elect, and that she's got work here. That's true, she does have work here; but she also has it everywhere, now, as well. I'll ask you again, all of you, to keep listening to me with open minds for the moment."

He paused. Their faces still waited, without expression.

"Stay with me, first," he said, "while I go through something you already know, but something that's going to be important in this case. I can't emphasize too much that the Others are only a handful, proportionally speaking, compared to the rest of us, on all the settled worlds. By themselves, no matter what their abilities and powers, they couldn't be a real threat to the whole human race. What makes them a threat is that they're able to use other people, people like your closest neighbors, as a lever to multiply their original strength many times and make it possible to control the rest of us."

He paused again, waiting for anyone who might want to argue this point, but none of them said anything. He went on.

"They can use others as levers, because they're able to make these people into followers, into believers in them," he said. "Everyone knows there are many the Others can't do anything with—people like yourselves who're strong in faith, and the Dorsai, and the Exotics. What's not known so well is that there are also a lot of people the Others can't use among the people of Old Earth—"

"I've heard that," said the man in the knitted jacket. "It's hard to believe."

"The reason you find it hard to believe," Hal said, "is because, if true, it sounds like it makes a mockery of your own hard-won strengths, to say nothing of the strengths of those who can also resist on the Dorsai and the Exotics."

He looked around the table at them all.

"But really," he went on, "it doesn't do that at all. It's not even strange. Let me ask you a question. Your forebears, the ones who emigrated from Earth, and made the first settlements here on Harmony and Association, would you say that they had less faith than you here, and those of your generations of these two worlds, nowadays?"

There was an instant hum of negation around the table.

"More!" came the strong voice of a heavy, middle-aged woman with bright, dark eyes on Hal's left and about five faces down the table.

"Well . . . possibly," said Hal. "We tend to remember the best about our ancestors and forget what in any way diminishes them. Let me ask you another question, then. Do you all believe that every person capable of the special faith that you consider makes a Friendly left Earth and came here? Couldn't there have been some who, for personal reasons of anything from finances to a simple preference for Old Earth, stayed there, married and had children of their own there?"

Silence held the table, although he gave them time to speak.

"So," he said, gently at last, "is it so unreasonable to think that everyone from Old Earth who might have made a Dorsai went to that world? Or that everyone who could have made an Exotic went to Mara or Kultis? One more question; and then we'll leave this side matter and get back to the main business. Before any of those emigrants came to any of these worlds, were they any less than they showed themselves to be once they got there?"

Again he waited. Still they were silent.

"Then it's reasonable to assume, isn't it," he said, "that there were men and women of faith before Harmony or Association were dreamed of, that there were people of courage and self-reliance before the Dorsai was imagined to exist; and that both men and women dreamed of an ethical ideal and a philosophy for all people from that ethical ideal, when the worlds of Mara and Kultis were not even suspected?"

He paused—only a fraction of a second this time.

"In short, that there were Friendlies before there were Friendly Worlds, Dorsai before the Dorsai was found, and Exotics before the Exotic planets were settled; and that all these others were originally on Old Earth—and that there are people like that there still, part of that original gene pool that's the true reservoir of our race?"

"Granted," said Athalia sharply from the end of the table. "As you say, let's get on with the main business that's brought everybody here."

"All right," said Hal. "What all this leads to, is the important point, about Rukh's value to all the worlds. The reason she's needed is because she represents the best of what your Culture's been able to produce. People here should be proud of that, rather than jealous of it. But to get to what Athalia's just reminded me is the main business of this meeting . . ."

He looked around the faces at the table once more and saw some of them, at least, had backed off from their initial hard expressionlessness to looks varying from thoughtfulness to puzzlement. At least, he thought, he was reaching these few among his audience.

"As to how we get her out," he said—and those words wiped away once more all facial expressions but listening ones—"the idea that it's impossible to get a prisoner back out of a Center is actually our largest asset. Because that means that the Militia undoubtedly believe it, too; and so they won't be expecting a rescue attempt. That's of the greatest possible help, because to make the rescue we've got to set the stage for it ahead of time; and the Militia's belief in the Center's impregnability is going to work for us to keep them from getting suspicious. Without that, we could still do it, but it'd be a lot more difficult."

"You still haven't told us anything that makes it possible," said the man in the knitted jacket.

"It's possible because it's the sort of thing that's been done before," said Hal, "as I told you. Simply, it's a matter of creating situations to reduce the opposition we'll run into, once we're inside the Center; reduce it to the point where the rescue party we send in can handle it."

A thin, fiftyish man across the table and three faces down, with the lines of habitual anger on his face, gave a snort of disgust.

"That's right! All we need are miracles!" the thin man said.

"No," said Hal, without varying the tone he had used so far, "all we need is planning."

He looked at Athalia, at the end of the table.

"I've learned that the number of Militia barracked in your Center here isn't more than four companies of roughly two hundred men each, plus a couple of hundred office and related personnel. In short, the maximum number we can find ourselves up against isn't more than eleven hundred individuals at the outside."

"And that's a lot," said the middle-aged woman who had spoken up to deny that the first settlers on the Friendly Worlds had owned less faith than its present generations.

"I know it sounds like a lot," said Hal. "But actually, a city on any other world except Association, the Dorsai, or the Exotics would have up to three times that number of police normally, for a city this size. One of the factors working for us are the patterns of your Culture which, reduce the need for police."

"That's nice," said the woman. "It's a compliment, perhaps; but it doesn't help us in getting Rukh out."

"Yes, it does," said Hal. "Because what it means is that in their duties as police, the Militia here are actually very understaffed to handle a city as big as Ahruma. That was something that didn't matter as long as the Others weren't around and the local populace were cooperative. But now the local people—at least from what I saw the day Rukh spoke in the square, following up the sabotaging of the Core Tap—are anything but cooperative."

"I still don't see how that helps," said the man in the knitted jacket.

"Hush, Jabez," said the woman. "I think I see. You mean to use the people in the city to help us, don't you, Hal Mayne?"

Hal nodded.

"That's right. I want to use them to draw off the available manpower of the Militia from the Center until it's down to a skeleton crew, before we try going in to get Rukh out."

"How?" It was Athalia's voice from the head of the table.

"Yes," said the man in the knitted jacket. "How? Aside from anything else, if we get people in general involved in this, how are we going to keep the rescue secret? The Militia's got its spies and connections in the city, just like we've got some in the Militia."

"The people don't have to know—until we want to tell them," said Hal.

"If they don't know . . . ?" The man looked puzzled. "How can they help? How did you plan to have them help?"

"I want them to start fires, riots, street fights—you name it—" said Hal. "I want fifty different incidents scattered out all over the city so that the Militia has to keep sending men out to keep order until they're scraping bottom for people to dispatch."

"But there's no way to get people—I mean ordinary people who aren't Children of Wrath, or otherwise committed to fighting the Belial-spawn—to do all that for you without explaining why you want it done," half-shouted the thin man with the anger lines on his face. "And what about the Militia themselves? What's to keep them from getting suspicious when suddenly there're fires and riots erupting all over? They'll smell something rotten and end up by doubling security on the Center!"

Hal looked at him for a moment without speaking.

"When I was here on Harmony before, as Howard Beloved Immanuelson," he said, finally, "I was a member of the Revealed Church Reborn. What is thy church, brother?"

The man stared back at him; and the thin face hardened.

"I am of the Eighth Covenant," he said, harshly. "Why?"

"The Eighth Covenant . . ." Hal sat back thoughtfully, laying his hands on the table before him and knitting his fingers together. "Isn't that the Church that was founded by one Forgotten of God? One so steeped in sin and other filthiness that the church to which he was originally born cast him from its doors, forbidding him ever to return, so that he ended by founding his own church, which all know is therefore so steeped in evil and pernicious—"

There was a crash as the barrel that the angry man had been sitting on went over backward loudly onto the concrete floor; and the man himself was on his feet even as his neighbors grabbed and held him from plunging down alongside the table toward Hal.

"Peace! Forgive me! Forgive me, please!" said Hal, holding up his hand, palm out. "I just wanted to demonstrate what we all know—that arguments between people belonging to different churches can always break out, particularly in a city this size; and if those arguments lead to open fighting, then the Militia is going to have to send out squads to restore order wherever there's trouble, aren't they? So that if the spirit of disputation spreads, we can foresee a lot of Militia squads being sent out from the Center into the city to restore order."

"I don't understand," said the man in the knitted jacket; as the angry man slowly and stiffly reseated himself, glaring at Hal.

"I do, Jabez," said the middle-aged woman with the piercingly-dark eyes. "By starting street fights, we can gradually drain off the interior strength of the Center. All right, Hal Mayne, but the Militia officers'll have figured out ahead of time how many men they can safely spare and not send any more out than that."

"They'll try not to, of course," said Hal. "But our plan would be to give them a gradually-escalating situation to deal with, over about a fifty to seventy-five hour period; both to lead them gradually to overstretch themselves and to wear out both them and the men they send out into the streets with lack of sleep. Wear them out until the judgment and reflexes of all of them are less than the best. In fact, what we'll try to do is bring everyone in the Center to the ragged edge of exhaustion. For that, forty-eight to seventy-two hours is about the limit. More than that, and they'll have a chance to adjust. Also, of course, time's critical in getting Rukh out. We know she's alive now, but not what kind of condition she's in; and how much longer she can endure in there."

Hal paused and took a second to check the expressions on the faces around the table. If nothing else, he had their full attention now, although fury still showed in the expression of the thin man he had provoked earlier.

"It might work," said the man in the knitted jacket—not to Hal but to the table in general. He turned to Hal. "Assuming it would, at least to the extent of draining off most of the fighting personnel of the Center, and exhausting them, where do we go from there?"

"When the time's ripe, we send a team into the Center through a service entrance, securing a route as we go through whatever service ways are used to deliver meals to the Cells section or take out anything—from laundry to dead prisoners. This team liberates Rukh and brings her back out the way it went in."

"And everybody left in the Center is waiting for them when they try to go back out!" said the thin man, harshly.

"Not necessarily," said Hal. "Remember, the Militia are going to be thinking primarily in terms of the outside disorders, which by then are going to have escalated to where they begin to look like a potential city-wide riot. Their first thought, when the alarm reaches them that they've been invaded through the service area, will be that this is simply another uncoordinated outbreak of the rioting, a group aiming at damaging the Center, or stealing as much as possible, and then getting away again. There'll be no evidence available to make them suspect that all the rioting is an excuse to get one prisoner—one prisoner only—out of their Cells."

There was silence in the warehouse.

"A pretty large gamble—that they won't suspect," said Athalia.

"It shouldn't be," said Hal. "For one thing the odds are going to be pared by the fact that just before the team goes in after Rukh, we'll mount a diversionary attack on the front door of the Center. It should look—only look, of course—as if the attackers in front are trying to fight their way in; and that ought not only to draw off what Militia strength is left in the building to that front area, but explain any reports that a smaller party has broken in through the service area."

"You're still gambling on the way the Militia's going to think," said Athalia.

"We can help the way they think, considerably," said Hal. "For one thing, simply by properly dressing up our team going into the Cells and having its members act to give the impression that they're simply a bunch of looters taking advantage of the fact there's an attack going on out front to slip in and grab what they can while the grabbing's good—what's a Militia cone rifle and ammunition worth, sold under the table, nowadays?"

Athalia nodded grudgingly.

"A lot," she said.

"So," said Hal, "I think we can be pretty confident the Militia officers are going to send only a small part of their available strength to deal with what they think must be a lightly-armed, untrained bunch off the street, that will run at the first sight of a uniform. Meanwhile, if we move with proper speed, we can have reached Rukh, got her out and be on our way back. We ought to be able to shoot our way through the first opposition they send from the front of the building against us; and be outside the Center by the time reinforcements reach the area where we were. Remember, at least according to the information I've been given, all the important parts of the Center are up front—the Record sections, the Armory, and so forth. The first instinct of Colonel Barbage and his men is going to be to protect that area first, and get around to mopping up the incursion through the service area when they've got more time."

He stopped talking. His own first instinct had been merely to give them a moment to let them think over what he had just said. But a fine-tuned perception in him now told him that he had, in fact, achieved more than he had hoped for, at this stage.

"Excuse me a minute," he said. "I'll be right back."

He turned and walked out through the door that connected the warehouse proper with Athalia's living quarters. Even as he passed through and shut it behind him, he could hear their voices break out in sudden discussion, which came, blurred but unmistakable, through the wooden panel of the door behind him.

Let them discuss it among themselves, he thought. Let them talk. He glanced at the chronometer on his wrist. Give them five minutes and then he would go back in. . . .

He wandered about the main room of Athalia's home, killing time. His thoughts drifted, and he thought of Rukh in the Militia Center. The image of her as he had first seen her came back to him, the whole scene of it caught between the tree-shadow of the conifers by the little stream, and the sunlight; with the green moss and the brown, dead needles underfoot—and overhead the wind-torn clouds, black and white, against the startling blue of the open sky—and Rukh and he and all the rest standing looking at each other, in that moment.

He remembered how he had thought then that she had looked—tall, slim and erect, in her bush-jacket, woods trousers and gunbelt—like the dark blade of a sword in the sunlight. He thought of her again now, as he had seen her in that moment, and that image was followed by another, one of her in the hands of the Militia; and it was as if something broke in him, without warning, like a small, hard explosion high in his chest near his throat, that spread its effect outward through all his body and limbs, chilling him.

He stood, chilling. . . .

A door opened noisily behind him, and he whirled about like a tiger. Athalia stood framed in the opening to the warehouse.

"What's keeping you?" she said. "We're all waiting."

"Waiting?" he echoed. He glanced at his chronometer, but he could not remember what it had said when he had looked at it just a short while before.

"It's been more than ten minutes," said Athalia, and jerked her head toward the warehouse interior behind her. "Come along. We've got a lot of questions for you."

Chapter

> > **54** < <

Opening the door into the warehouse, he found a change in those waiting there; and a change in the very atmosphere of the wide, chill, echoing enclosure. For a second, the faces at the table looked up at him in a savage eagerness, with the glitter of excitement found in the eyes of starving people held back too long from food spread plainly before them. It came to him then that he had forgotten how many years people like these had suffered from the Militia, without a chance to strike back in equal measure. It was small credit to him after all, he told himself, that he should be able to move them now to the point of action for Rukh and against such an enemy.

They dropped their heads, turning their eyes away from him as he stepped through the door and began to approach the table; but the caution was useless. To anyone trained by life as he had been, the fire in those seated there could be felt as plainly as the radiation from a metal stove with a roaring blaze in its belly.

"The question is," said the man in the knitted jacket to Hal, as Hal retook his seat, "whether we've got anything like the number of people you've planned for to do something this big. How many men and women do you think you'll have to have?"

"For which part of the operation?" asked Hal. "To go into the prison section of the Center and bring Rukh out won't take more than a dozen people—and half of those are there only to be dropped off at points along the route, to give us warning if any force is sent against us from the front part of the Center. Any more than six people in on the actual rescue— that's five, including me—would get in each other's way in any small rooms or corridors. Our real protection's going to be in getting in fast and getting out again before the Center's officers realize what's happened."

"Only twelve?" said the tall man who had gotten up to leave, earlier. "But who's to back you up outside, once you've brought Rukh Tamani out?"

"Maybe a dozen more," said Hal, "but those don't need to have combat experience, like those I'll take inside; and in fact, the only really trained help I'll need are going to be the five with me. Give me five former Command members and the others can be anyone you trust to have courage and keep their heads under fire."

—Or give me just two Dorsai like Malachi or Amanda, the back of his mind added. He put the thought from him. Nothing was as useless as wishing for what was not available.

"But you want us meanwhile to staff a full-scale assault on the front of the Center—" began the man in the knitted jacket.

"Thirty people who can actually hit most of what they shoot at," said Hal. "Plus as many more as you've got weapons for and can be trusted not to kill themselves or their friends. But by the time the assault starts, you ought to be able to use those you put to work to stir up the riots and fights, earlier. I'll say it again—the attack on the Center from its front is only for the purpose of occupying the attention of the Militia in the building, for the twenty minutes or so it takes us to get Rukh out. Don't tell me a city area this size can't come up with a hundred hard-core resistance people."

He stopped speaking and looked down the table at all of them. For a moment none of them answered. They were all looking at the tabletop and elsewhere to hide their satisfaction with his answers.

"All right," said Athalia, once more from the far end of the table where she had reseated herself. "We'll have to talk over the details, of course. Why don't you wait in your room until I bring you our answer?"

Hal nodded, getting to his feet. He left the room and all of them to what he was fairly certain was already a foregone conclusion. But instead of going to his room, he stepped out the front door of Athalia's establishment into the darkness and the cool night air of the yard. Three low shapes, heads down and tails wagging solemnly, moved in on him. He squatted on the dirt of the yard and held his arms out to them.

Above them, the cloud cover of the night sky was torn here and there to show the pinpoints of stars. The dogs pressed hard against him, licking at his face and hands. . . .

The next day fighting broke out in the city, here and there, at first between individuals and then between the congregations of various churches. A few fires erupted. The day after there were more fires, fighting was more common and mothers did not send their children to school. By afternoon of the second day, the only people seen on the streets in Ahruma were adults armed with clubs, at the least, and squads of Militia, who ordered them back inside whatever buildings belonged to them, then went on to help the overburdened firemen of the city deal with the conflagrations that seemed to be erupting everywhere. The tempers of the

Militiamen had shortened with exhaustion; and the reactiveness of the civilians had risen to match.

"It's out of hand," said Morelly Walden, coming into Athalia's front room late on that afternoon. The slack skin of his aging face was pulled into a shape of sad anger. "We're not controlling it any longer. It's happening on its own."

"As it should," said Hal.

Athalia's front room had been made into a Command Headquarters; but she and Hal were the only people other than Morelly there at the moment. Morelly looked from Hal to her.

"The city doesn't have a single district left that doesn't have at least two or three fires," he said. "It could end with the whole area burnt down."

"No," said Hal. "The firebugs who've been tempted to go to work on their own are getting tired, just like the Militia and the rest of us. Dawn tomorrow, things will begin to slack off. There's a pattern to riots in cities that's existed since there were cities to riot in."

"I believe you," said Morelly, and sighed, "since I know you from the days in the Command with Rukh. But I can't help worrying, anyway. I think we ought to make our move on the Center now."

"No," said Hal. "We need darkness—for psychological as well as tactical reasons. If you want to worry about something, Morelly, worry about whether both the rescue teams and the ones who'll be attacking the front of the Center are getting some rest so as to be ready for tonight. Go check on them. The attackers shouldn't move into position until full dark; and the rescuers mustn't move until the fighting's been going on up front for at least a couple of hours; long enough to draw as many of the Militia in the building as possible up to the front of it."

"All right," said Morelly.

He went across the room and through the door leading back into the warehouse where the cots had been set up for those not presently needed on the streets.

As the door closed behind him, Athalia looked directly across the room at Hal.

"Still," she said, "isn't it about time you were waking those who're going in with you?"

"They already know all I know about what we'll run into," answered Hal, nodding at the plans on the table, plans drawn from the information they had been able to gather from Athalia's contacts with the Center, of the corridors and passageways leading to Rukh's cell. "From here on, it'll be a matter of making decisions, and their following the orders I give. Let them rest as much as they can—if they can."

Shortly after sunset, word came back to Athalia's front room that sniping at the front of the Center building had begun. Hal went into the warehouse to gather his two teams; the one that would penetrate the building and the one that would guard the service courtyard where deliveries were normally made, at the back of the building, where the first team would go in through the Barracks' kitchen entrance. Of the twenty-five men and women he sought, he found all but one of them awake, sitting up for the most part on the edge of their cots and talking in low voices. The exception was a slim, dark-skinned man dressed in the rough bush clothing that was the informal uniform of those in the Commands—a last-minute-replacement for one of the interior team, whom Hal had not met yet, slumbering facedown.

Hal shook a shoulder and the other sat up. It was Jason Rowe, who had led Hal originally to the Commands and to Rukh Tamani.

"Jase!" said Hal.

"I just made the last truck in," Jason said, yawning hugely. "Greetings, Brother. Forgive me, I've been a little short on sleep lately."

"And I was giving you credit for being the one person here with no nerves." Hal laughed. "How much sleep have you had?"

"Don't worry about me, Howard—Hal, I should say—I've had six"— Jason glanced at the chronometer on his wrist—"no, seven hours since I got here. I heard about you being here and thought you'd need me."

"It's good to see you—and good to have you," said Hal. Jason got to his feet. Hal looked around and raised his voice. "All right, everyone who's with me! Into the front room and we'll get ready to leave."

As the trucks that carried them got close to the Center, they heard the whistle of cone rifles from a couple of blocks away, and when they were closer yet, the tall faces of the buildings on either side of the street brought them echoes of the brief, throaty roars of power weapons, like the angry voicings of large beasts.

The trucks turned into a street along one side of the Center; and the metal gates to the service courtyard entrance, almost to the rear of the block-long building, stood wide open. Whatever Militia Guards had kept their post here, normally, there was now no sign of them. Instead, four men and one woman in civilian clothes and holding power rifles, with two still figures in uniforms lying against the rear courtyard wall, were waiting for them. Their trucks were waved into the courtyard, and the gates closed behind them.

"Everyone out!" Hal called as the trucks stopped.

He got out himself and saw the riders in the main bodies of the trucks dismount and sort themselves into two groups. He turned to the seven men and five women he would be taking inside with him; and saw that they had already congregated about Jason, as a recognized Command officer.

"Power sidearms and rifles, only, inside," he told them. "Who's got the cable?"

"Here," said one of the men, partially lifting the small spool of what seemed only thin, gray wire, at his belt. The wire was shielded cable for a phone connection between the invaders which the communication equipment in the Center would not register, let alone be able to tap.

"Stretcher?"

"Here," answered a woman. She held up what seemed to be only a pair of poles wrapped in canvas.

"Good," said Hal. He looked for the four people who had been guarding the black metal gates when the trucks arrived, and saw one of them, a man, standing a little apart from the two groups. "Anyone in the kitchen there, as far as you know?"

"We were inside," said the man, shifting his power rifle from one arm to the other. "There was just one person on duty. She's tied up in a corner of the main room."

That would mean, thought Hal, that the kitchen attendant on duty was a civilian. If she had been of the Militia, they would have killed her.

"All right." Hal turned back to his dozen people. "After me, then. If you fall out of touch with me, or something happens to me, take your orders from Jason Rowe, here. Keep together; and you observers take posts in the order we talked about earlier today. Report anything—anything at all out of the ordinary you see or hear—over the phone circuit. Come on."

They went in, with Hal in the lead. Inside, the kitchen was only partially lighted over the sinks at one end and smelled heavily of cooked vegetables and soap. Hal saw a bundle of dark blue cloth under the farthest sink that must be the bound and gagged attendant.

"First observer, here," he said. One of the women in his group, tall and lean and in her forties, stooped and took the end of the cable from the drum slung from the shoulders of the man beside her, clipping it to a wrist phone on her right arm. The detailed map of the Center's interior, which Athalia had provided for Hal to study, was printed in his mind. He led the rest off through a doorway in the wall to his left, down a long, straight corridor where the odors, by contrast, were dominated by the sharp smell of some vinegarish disinfectant.

Dropping off observers at the points already picked out on the map he had studied, Hal led deep into the interior of the block-square building and quietly down three flights of ramps. At the base of the last of the ramps, a man in black Militia uniform snored lightly on a cot beside a bare desk and just to the left of a barred door leading to a corridor lined with metal doors that could be seen beyond. The Militiaman slept the utter sleep of exhaustion, and only woke as they began to bind his arms and legs to make him a prisoner.

"How do I open the door to the cells?" Hal asked him.

"I won't tell you," said the Militiaman, hoarsely.

Hal shrugged. There was no time to waste in persuading the man, even if he had preferred doing so. With his power pistol he slagged the lock of the barred door, which had not been designed to resist that sort of assault. Kicking the still-hot bars of the door to open it, Hal led his team, including the man with the reel of cable, into the corridor. The last of the observers was left behind with the trussed and gagged Militiaman.

The doors of the cells, like the door on the cell Hal had shared with Jason, long before, in Citadel's Militia Center, were solid metal with only a small observation window which could be covered with a sliding panel. The observation windows on the cells they passed were uncovered; and as Hal glanced into each, he saw it was empty. They reached the end of the corridor where it ran into another corridor at right angles, running right and left.

"Shall we split up, Hal?" Jason asked.

"No," said Hal. "Let's try to the right, first."

The leg of the cross-corridor to the right offered more empty cells—but also three inhabited ones. They slagged the locks on these and released two men and one woman who turned out to have been arrested the day before in the course of the rioting. All three had been badly treated; but only one of the men required assistance to walk; and this the other two gave him. Hal sent them back to the room where the last observer waited with the bound Militiaman, with orders to follow the cable wire from there to the kitchen and freedom.

In the same way Hal and his team proceeded through eight more corridors and cross-corridors, releasing over twenty inmates, only one of whom had been there before the riot; and who had to be carried out by his fellow-rescued on a makeshift stretcher. Still, they had not found Rukh; and a coldness was settling into existence, deep inside Hal, at the thought that maybe they were half a day too late—perhaps she had died and her body had been taken out to be disposed of by whatever method was used in Centers like this one.

"That's the end of it," said Jason Rowe at Hal's left shoulder.

They had come to the end of a corridor and the wall that faced them was doorless and blank.

"It can't be," said Hal. He turned about and went back to the room before the entrance into the cell block.

"There are other cells," he said to the captured Militiaman. "Where?"

The white face of the bound man in the black uniform stared up into his and did not answer. Hal felt something like a breath of coldness that blew briefly through his chest. A living pressure went out from him and he saw the man on the cot felt it. He stared down.

"You'll tell me," he said; and heard—as a stranger might hear—a difference in his voice.

The other's eyes were already wide, his face was already pale; but the skin seemed to shrink back on his bones as Hal's stare held him. Something more than fear moved between the two of them. In Hal's mind there came back a long-ago echo of a voice that had been his, telling a man like this to suffer; and now, in front of him, the Militiaman stared back as a bird might stare at a weasel.

"The second door, in the first corridor to the right—it isn't a cell door," the man answered, huskily. "It's a stair door, to the cells downstairs."

Hal went back to the cell block. He heard the footfalls of Jason and the others on the concrete floor behind him, hurrying to keep up. He came to the door the Militiaman had mentioned and saw that the window shield of it was open. The view through it showed an ordinary, empty cell. He tried the door handle.

It was unlocked.

He swung it wide; and it yawned open to his left. Stepping through, he turned and saw a picture-screen box fastened over the window on the inside face of the door. Beyond were wide, gray, concrete stairs under bright illumination, leading downward. He descended swiftly, passed through the door at the bottom, and stepped into a corridor less than fifteen meters in length, with windowless cell doors spaced along both sides.

Where the windows might have been were red metal flags, and these, on all the doors but one, were down. Hal took five long strides to the one with the flag up and reached for its latch.

It was locked. He slagged the lock. Holstering his pistol, he tore off a section of his shirt, wadded it up to protect his hand, and, grasping the handle above the ruined lock, swung the door open.

A sewer stench struck him solidly in the face. He stepped inside, almost slipping for a second on the human waste that covered the floor. Inside, after the brilliance of the light in the corridor outside, he could see nothing. He stood still and let his senses reach out.

A scant current of moving air from some slow ventilation system touched his left cheek. His ears caught the even fainter sound of shallow breathing ahead of him. He stepped forward cautiously, with his arms outstretched and felt a hard, blank wall. Feeling down, at the foot of the wall, his hands discovered the shape of a body. He scooped it up; and it came lightly into his arms as if it weighed no more than a half-grown child. He turned and carried it out the doorway into the light.

For less than a second the thin, foul-smelling bundle of rags he held in his arms could have been someone other than Rukh. She was almost skeletal; bruises and half-healed lacerations and burns had distorted her features and her hair was matted with filth. But her dark eyelids, which had closed against the light as he stepped through the doorway, opened slowly, and the brown eyes that looked up at him were untouched and unchanged.

With effort, her dry lips parted. Barely, he heard the whisper that came from her.

"I testify yet to thee, my God."

A memory of a day in which he had stood to his neck in water, looking through the screening branches of a waterside bush, returned to Hal. Through the delicate tracery of brown twigs and small green leaves, he remembered seeing in the distance—now, for the first time, clearly—three old men on a terrace, surrounded by young men in black with long-barrelled pistols, and by a very tall, slim man; and his arms pressed the body he held close to himself, tenderly and protectively, as if it were something more precious than the universe could know. Deep within him, the breath of coldness that had awakened in him momentarily in Athalia's outer office came back, awakened, coalesced to a point, and kindled into icy fire.

"Here," he said, putting Rukh gently into Jason's arms. "Take her out of here; and give me your rifle."

His hand closed about the small of the butt of Jason's power rifle, as the other man's arms, holding Rukh, released the weapon. The feel of the polished wood against his fingers was strange—as if he had never touched such a thing before—and at the same time, unforgettably familiar and inescapable. He holstered his own power pistol and turned to one of the others who carried a rifle.

"And yours . . . ," he said.

He grasped the second rifle in his other hand and looked again at Jason. "If I'm not outside with the rest of you when you've loaded the trucks," he said, "don't wait for me."

He turned and went off before Jason had time to question him. He heard the footsteps of the others begin and follow. But the sound of their feet died away quickly behind him, for he was moving with long strides, up the stairs, out of the cell block and through the entrance room. He passed the final observer there without answering her as she tried to question him about the still-bound Militiaman, and went on up the corridor beyond.

The chart he had studied of the Center's interior layout was burned sharply into his memory. As he approached the next-to-last observer she stared at him and at the two rifles he carried nakedly, one in each hand.

"Monitoring equipment from the yard just called to say they think a party's been sent from the front of the Center to deal with us—" she began.

"Jason and the rest have Rukh," he interrupted, without breaking stride. "Go with them as soon as they reach you."

He continued straight down the corridor, parting company with the cable, which here made a ninety-degree turn into a cross-corridor, on its way back to the kitchen and its exit.

"But where are you going, Hal Mayne?" the observer called after him.

He did not answer; and the echoes of her question followed him down the corridor.

He went on, following the chart in his head now, turning at the second cross-corridor he came to, heading toward the front of the building. Inside him, the point of coldness was expanding, spreading out through all his body. All his senses were tuned to an acuteness wound to the edge of pain. He saw and remembered each crack and jointure in the walls that he passed. He heard the normally-silent breathing of air in the ventilating system through the gratings in the ceiling beneath which he stepped. His mind was focused on a single point that ranged ahead of him, reaching through the walls and corridors between the Center's front offices, where the majority of the black-clad Militia would be, their officers with them and Amyth Barbage, among those officers.

Now, the coldness possessed him totally. He felt nothing—only the purpose in him. He turned into a new corridor and saw, ten meters down it, three Militiamen pushing a small, wheeled, power cannon in his direction.

He walked toward them, even as they suddenly noticed him and stopped in stunned silence to stare at him, striding toward them. Then, as one of them roused at last and reached for the power cannon's firing lever, the rifles in his hands roared briefly, the one in his left hand twice—like the coughings of a lion—and the three men dropped. He walked up to them, past them, and on toward the front of the building.

"Report!" rapped a harsh voice from a speaker grille in the ceiling of the corridor. "Sergeant Abram—report!"

He walked on.

"What's happening there, Sergeant? Report!" cried the speaker grille, more faintly over the increasing distance between it and him. He walked on.

He was all of one piece, now; with the coldness in him that left no room for anything else. Turning into another corridor he faced two more Militiamen and cut them down also with his rifles; but not before one of the counter discharges from the power pistols both carried cut a smoking gash in the jacket sleeve of his upper left arm. He smelled the odor of the burned cloth and the burned flesh beneath, but felt no heat or pain.

He was getting close to the front of the building; and the corridor he was on ended a short distance ahead in another cross-corridor. Already, there was a difference in what he saw around him. The doors, that were now of glass, to the dark offices he passed had become more widely separated, indicating that the rooms they opened on were larger than those he had passed earlier. Half a dozen steps from its end, the corridor he was in abruptly widened, its walls now faced with smooth stone where up to this point they had been merely of white-painted concrete. The floor had also changed, becoming covered with a pattern of inlaid gray tiles in various shapes, highly polished; and his footsteps rang more sharply upon this new surface. To the abnormal acuteness of his vision, under the now-hidden but even brighter illumination from overhead, the invisible atmosphere about him seemed to quiver like the flesh of a living creature.

He had been moving under the impetus of something neither instinct nor training, which directed him from the back, hidden recesses of his mind. Now he felt this impetus, like a hand laid on one of his shoulders, stop him, turn him and steer him into one of the dark offices. He closed the door behind him and stood to one side in the interior shadows, looking out through the transparency of the door at the empty corridor ahead.

For a few seconds he heard and saw nothing. Then there came a growing sound that was the hasty beating of many feet, rapidly approaching; and, within a minute, a dozen heavily-armed Militiamen burst into sight around a corner and ran past him, back the way he had come. He let them pass. When they were out of sight, he stepped back into the passageway and continued, turning left into the cross-corridor from which they had just come.

A short dogleg in this direction, and then another turn, brought him to a final corridor busy with men in black uniforms hurrying back and forth between doorways. These glanced at him puzzledly as he walked among them, but no one stopped him until he came at last to an open doorway on his left. Looking in, he saw a large room with a long, fully-occupied conference table and blackout curtains over tall windows in a far wall. Two Militia privates with cone rifles stood guard, one on each side of the entrance; and when he turned to enter, they stepped to bar his way, the rifles snapping up to cover him.

"Who're you—" began one of them.

Hal struck out right and left at both men. The butt of a power rifle crashed into the forehead of one, the barrel end across the throat of the other, and they dropped. Hal stepped inside, closing the door behind him.

Those at the conference table within were already on their feet. Still moving swiftly, he saw clearly what his first glance through the doorway had made him suspect, that the uniforms of all of them there showed officer's rank.

Two reached for holstered pistols at their belts; and the rifles in his hands coughed. They fell; and the other officers stood staring. A hand turned the doorknob from the corridor, outside.

"Stay out!" shouted the officer at the far end of the table.

"Where's Amyth Barbage?" Hal asked—for the man he had come to find was nowhere in the room. As he spoke he continued to move around the walls of the room, so that he could cover with his weapons not only those at the table but the closed door through which he had just come.

No one answered. Still moving, and approaching the table, Hal swung the muzzle of the rifle in his left fist to center on the senior officer present, a squarely-built major in his fifties, at the end of the table farthest from the door, under the curtains of one of the windows.

"He's not here—" said the Major.

"Where?" demanded Hal.

The Major's face had been pale. Now the color came back.

"No one here knows," he said, harshly. "If anyone could tell you, even, it'd be me—and I can't."

"But he's in the Center," said Hal; for Athalia's people had reported Barbage returning to the Center some hours past, and that he had not gone out again.

"Satan take you!" said the Major. "Don't you think I'd tell you if I knew?"

But to Hal's hypersensitive hearing in this moment, there was a note of triumph in the officer's voice that convinced him not only that the other was lying and knew where Barbage was, but that something had been achieved by the other since Hal had entered the room.

The words of the second-to-last observer on the cable line came back to Hal, telling him that the monitoring equipment in the kitchen courtyard had called with the suspicion that an earlier party had been sent from the front of the building to deal with the team sent out to rescue Rukh. The Major's hands were in open sight on the tabletop, but he was standing with the middle of his body pressed against the table-edge before him. Hal moved swiftly forward and knocked the man backward. Cut at an angle of forty-five degrees into the table's edge and covered until now by the bottom edge of the Major's uniform jacket was a communications panel as long as Hal's hand, but hardly wider than a ruler.

The door to the room smashed open and armed Militiamen erupted inward.

"Take him now!" The Major's order came out more scream than shout. Around the table, the officers who had not yet drawn their sidearms were reaching for them.

Malachi Nasuno, or anyone who had ever had Dorsai training, could have pointed out their error. Their very numbers were the cause out of which their failure could be certainly predicted. Moving thinkingly and surely around the table, using the bodies of those who would kill or capture him as shields, Hal disabled or threw into the fire of the weapons aimed at him all those with whom he came in contact. Finally, as the room began to be empty of people still on their feet, panic took those of the Militia who were still unharmed; and there was a sudden, general rush for the still-open door.

Hal found himself standing alone, the passage beyond the open doorway empty.

But, caught still in the coldness that held him, he was aware that the victory was a transient one; and that the way out the still-open door was no safe escape route for him. Turning, he pointed his power pistol at one curtained window and blew out both curtain and window. The thick but ragged edge of the window material showed through the tatters of the curtain. It had been heavy sandwich glass, which would have frustrated even the energy of a power pistol at any greater distance than the point-blank range at which he had used the one he held.

He knew from the plan in his memory that the window from which he was escaping was near one end of the building's front, closest to that same side which, farther back, held the courtyard and the kitchen entrance. He dropped onto concrete sidewalk, behind the line of Militia cars parked along the front curb of the street. Having landed, he stayed flat on his belly at the foot of the front wall of the Center; and had this sensible decision rewarded by hearing the whistle and pock of impacts on the wall above him, of cones fired by the resistance people in buildings across the street.

Undoubtedly, among those rounded up to maintain a steady fire on the Center's front, there were responsible individuals who would realize that someone not in Militia uniform, exiting out a smashed window of the building, was hardly likely to be an enemy. But they would be too few and too scattered to get that understanding passed quickly to all the excited amateurs with weapons surrounding them.

The cone-rifle firing continued—but, as he had foreseen, the line of vehicles parked parallel to the curb shielded him from the direct view of the resistance people, and from any shots that came close. And his position up against the base of the wall, under the narrow outcropping of the decorative stone window ledge over which he had just come, protected him from observation and fire from atop the building. He began to wriggle along the base of the wall toward the corner of the building, only a few scant meters from him.

He reached it and turned the corner. Rising to his feet he ran down the empty, lamplit street toward the lights of the kitchen courtyard.

There was a silence about the courtyard as he got closer that made him slow his steps and begin to move more quietly, himself. There had not been time for the rest of the team to get loaded into the trucks and away, yet. He went swiftly but softly until he came to the beginning of the courtyard wall. Ignoring the gate, he found finger-cracks enough where the building wall joined that of the courtyard, climbed to the top of the wall and dropped down inside.

The trucks were still there, close enough to him so that they blocked his view of most of the rest of the courtyard. He drew the power pistol and went with it in his hand around the back of the nearest truck . . . and breathed out with relief.

The team was just now loading, ready to depart. But something—it may have been their first sight of Rukh as she now was—seemed to have impressed them to a degree he himself had not been able to, earlier. They were moving as silently as they could, and communicating by hand signals wherever possible.

Rukh was just now being brought to the back of the nearer truck. He holstered his gun and stepped forward into the midst of them. Ignoring the astonishment of the others, to whom he must have seemed to have appeared out of empty air, he walked to the side of the stretcher on which they carried her.

Her bearers checked themselves, just short of handing the stretcher up to those waiting to receive it, behind the raised tailgate of the truck; and Rukh herself looked up at him. The nurse they had had among those waiting with the backup team in the courtyard had possibly already given her medications to ease and strengthen her; but the eyes looking up into his were now more widely open and her voice, though still whispering, was stronger than he had heard it in the cell block.

"Thank you, Hal," she said.

For a moment the coldness moved back from him.

"Thank the others," he said. "I had selfish motives, but the others just wanted you out."

She blinked at him. Her eyes were moist. He thought she would like to say something more; but that the effort was too great. Hastily he spoke himself.

"Lie quiet," he said. "I'm taking you clear off-planet to Mara, where the Exotics can put you back together, body and mind, as good as new."

"Body only . . . ," she whispered. "My mind is always my own. . . ."

Hal felt his right sleeve plucked. He turned and saw Athalia standing just behind him with a face shaped by cold anger. He allowed her to pull him back out of earshot of Rukh.

"You didn't tell us anything about taking her off-world!" Athalia whispered savagely in his ear.

"Would you have risked lives to rescue her, if I had?" he answered grimly, but with equal softness. "I told you she had a value to the whole race, above and beyond her value to all of you here on Harmony. Now that she's free, do you suppose anything less than off-planet can be safe for her, or safe for anyone who might try to hide her?"

Athalia's hand fell from his sleeve.

"You're an enemy, after all," she said, bitterly.

"Ask yourself that a year from now," said Hal. "In any case, the Exotic Embassy can help get her off Harmony, which none of you can do; and once she's known to be on another world, the pressure from the Militia, turning you all upside down to find her, will let up."

"Yes," Athalia said. But she still looked at him savagely as he turned away from her.

They had begun to lift the stretcher's far end so as to pass it to those in the truck. There was a pause as they made the decision to lower the tailgate first, after all. In the moment of that pause, a voice struck at them from the kitchen entrance of the building.

"So!" it said, hard, loud and triumphant in the silence of the lamplit courtyard, "the Whore of Abomination has friends who would try to steal her from God's justice?"

Everyone looked. Amyth Barbage, stick-thin in his close-fitting black Militia Colonel's uniform, stood alone in the entrance to the kitchen. He carried a power rifle, generally pointed at all of them; and Hal's eyes, without moving, saw that—like himself—none of the rest had weapons in hand and ready for use.

Alone and apparently indifferent to that fact, Barbage walked three steps forward from the doorway. His power rifle pointed more directly toward the stretcher bearing Rukh, and those who stood closely around it.

"Carry her back inside," he said, harshly. "Now!"

The coldness returned to Hal with a rush; and from the same place that it came from in him, came other knowledge he had not known he had.

A wordless shout that erupted like an explosion in the stillness of the courtyard tore itself from him. It came from every nerve and muscle of his being, not merely from the lungs alone, the utmost in sound of which his body was capable; and it went out like a bludgeon against the thin, white-faced man, a wall of sound directed against Barbage alone. For a moment the other seemed stunned and frozen by it; and in that same moment, Hal leaped aside from the line of aim of the Militia officer's rifle, drew his own pistol and fired.

The knowledge, the actions, were all as they should have been. But Hal's body had not been trained relentlessly from birth and never allowed to fall out of the ultimate in fine-tuned conditioning. The early years with Malachi and a few years of self-exercise at the Encyclopedia could not give him what the years of his lifetime would have given a body born and raised on the Dorsai. The energy bolt from his power gun struck, not Barbage at whom it was aimed, but Barbage's rifle, spinning it from that officer's hands to skitter across the rough paving of the courtyard with the last few millimeters of its barrel's muzzle-end glowing a dull red heat.

And Barbage—where Hal had been less than he should, Barbage was more. Barbage, who should have been doubly immobilized, first by the killing shout, and then by the loss of his weapon, recovered before Hal had fully regained his balance. Bare-handed, he plunged toward the truck and Rukh on her stretcher.

Hal threw up the muzzle of his pistol to fire, found too many bodies in the way, and dropped his sidearm on the pavement. He leaped forward himself to meet Barbage, just as the other reached the tailgate of the truck. Hal's hands intercepted and closed on the furious, narrow body, at waist and shoulder, and lifted it into the air. It was like lifting a man of cloth and straw.

"No!" Rukh said.

The volume of her voice was hardly more than the whisper in which she had spoken a moment earlier; but Hal heard it and it stopped him. The coldness held him in an icy fist.

"Why?" he said. Barbage was still in the air, motionless now above the paving on which his life could be dashed out.

"You cannot touch him," said Rukh. "Put him down."

A quiver like that which comes from overtensed muscles passed through Hal; but he still held Barbage in the air.

"For my sake, Hal," he heard her say through the coldness, "put him back on his feet."

Slowly, the coldness yielded. He lowered the man he held and set him upright. Barbage stood, his face frozen, staring not at him, but at Rukh.

"He must be stopped," Hal muttered. "A long time ago, James Child-of-God told me he had to be stopped."

"James was much loved by God, and by many of the rest of us," said Rukh. With great effort she raised herself slightly from the stretcher and looked Hal in the face. "But not even the saints are always right. I tell you you cannot touch this man. He is of the Elect, and he hears no one but himself and the Lord. You think you can punish him for what he did to me and others, by destroying his body. But his body means nothing to him."

Hal turned to stare at the white face above the black uniform collar, that did not see him—only Rukh.

"Then what?" Hal heard himself saying. "Something has to be done."

"Then do it," said Rukh. "Something far harsher than destroying his mortal envelope. He will not hear his fellows. Leave him then to the Lord. Leave him, by himself, to the voice of God."

Hal was still staring at Barbage, waiting for the other man to speak. But to his wonderment, Barbage said nothing. Nor did he move. He simply stood, gazing at Rukh, as she sagged back onto the stretcher.

For a moment there was no movement anywhere in the courtyard. Then, slowly, the resistance people began to continue bringing Rukh fully aboard the vehicle and themselves mounting into it and the other one that waited for them. Hal stood, continuing to watch Barbage, waiting for him to make a leap for the fallen power rifle. But Barbage still stood motionless, his expression unchanged, staring into the darkness under the canvas hood of the truck into which Rukh had now disappeared.

The motor of that truck started. Then the motor of the other vehicle. "Hal! Come on!" called the voice of Jason.

Slowly, still keeping an eye on Barbage, Hal stepped back two paces and picked up his power pistol from where it had landed when he had flung it down. Careful not to turn his back on the Militia officer, he swung himself up into the back of the truck which held Rukh. Once up, he turned, and stood above the again-raised tailgate, holding the pistol ready at his side as the truck he was in slowly pulled out of the courtyard and until the wall about it finally cut off his view of its interior.

But Barbage had not moved from where he stood.

Chapter

> > 55 < <

The best ways between the stars were not always the direct ways; and after Rukh had recovered enough to travel, Hal accompanied her to Mara, where Exotic healers began their work. Eventually he left her to their ministrations, and took ship to Kultis, where he transshipped, to proceed from there to his own destination.

So it was that he landed once again at Omalu. There, in the Terminal after the long trudge across the Landing Pad, through cool air and the blinding sunlight from the white-hot dot in the sky that was Fomalhaut, he found someone waiting for him. It was Amanda; and he felt a sudden, great, rush of relief and love as without planning, thought or warning, his arms went around her.

Her body was slim and strong and real against him. In almost the same second, her own arms wrapped his body and she held him, strongly. They pressed together wordlessly, ignoring the rest of the universe. He had not realized until this moment how transient and uncertain by comparison were almost all the other things of his life. He did not want to let her go. But he could not, after all, stand in the middle of a busy Terminal forever, holding on to her. After a long moment, he released her. She released him, and stepped back.

"How'd you know I was coming?" he asked incredulously.

"The Exotics had sent us word of your possible travelling-names," she said. "And when the captain of your ship called in his manifest while still on approach to orbit, your identity was there on the list of possibles. We watch for you these days."

"You do?" he said. He had not been used to being afforded any special notice. The Exotics were hardly likely to fuss over anyone at all.

"Yes," she told him. She turned and they moved off through the Terminal together. She was wearing a knitted dress of brilliantly-white wool that clung to the narrowness of her waist. At her throat was a necklace, small, coiled with seashells, also a clean white outside, but with a delicate pink rimming the inner lips of each shell opening.

"You're dressed up," he said, with his eyes on her.

She smiled, looking straight ahead.

"I had some business in Omalu today, to get dressed up for," she answered. "You brought luggage, this time?"

"A travel case, that's all."

She walked with him toward the baggage-delivery section; and they did not quite touch as they went, but he was conscious of the living warmth of her body beside him.

"I wrote to Simon Khan Graeme—the senior living Graeme—about you," she said. "He's still on New Earth doing police organizational work; and his estimate was that he hasn't more than another few months before the influence of the Others squeezes him out of a job, even there. But he'll be staying as long as he can earn interstellar credits. Of the other two left in the family, the younger brother—Alistair—is consulting on Kultis, and their sister, Mary, is on Ceta for some border dispute, so Graemehouse is still empty. But Simon said you're welcome to stay there anytime you're on the Dorsai."

"That's good of him," said Hal.

She opened the small hand-case she was carrying and passed him a thumb-stall with a fingerprint reproed on the end.

"You can use my print to unlock the front door," she said. "But you'd better register your own when you get there, so you won't need to carry a copy of mine. You'll find the lock-memory just inside the front door to the left—look under the sweaters and jackets hanging up there, if you don't see it at first."

He smiled at her and took the stall, putting it in a breast pocket of his gray jacket. She moved along beside him, appraising him gravely as she went.

"You've come into your full size," she said. "The house will feel right, having you there."

There was a moment of silence between them.

"Yes . . . ," he said. "Will you thank Simon Khan Graeme for me?"

"Of course. But it's nothing unusual, his inviting you to stay." She smiled again, an almost secret smile. Her white-blond hair was longer now; and she shook it back over her shoulders as she walked. "Hospitality's a neighborly duty, after all. Besides, as I say, I told him about you. There's hardly a Dorsai home that wouldn't put you up."

"With its people not there?"

"Well . . . maybe not with their people not there," she said; and smiled back at him.

"I appreciate your thinking of my staying there," he said slowly. "I may not get another chance."

She sobered, looking away from him, toward the baggage area.

"I thought you'd want to," she told him. "Have the flyer you hire take you right to the house. There's no need to go in through Foralie Town unless you want to; and people there are busy. Everyone's busy, right now."

They walked on in silence. When they reached the baggage area, luggage from the ship Hal had come in on had not yet been delivered.

"When you're done in Omalu, today, you'll come by and visit me?" he said.

"Oh, yes." She met his eyes squarely for a moment. "Here comes your luggage, now."

The wall had dilated an iris in itself, to give entrance to an automated luggage carrier. It drove up to the distribution circle before them and the baggage began to feed off from it into the chutes that would sort their contents into the stalls where the passengers waited. Hal slid his passage voucher into the sensor slot of the stall in which he and Amanda were standing. Seconds later, the check stub attached to his case having shown that its torn edge matched the torn edge of Hal's voucher, the case slid up through a trapdoor before them, onto the floor of the stall.

Hal picked it up and moved away toward the local transportation desk. Amanda went with him. They did not talk as they walked. Hal felt himself full of words that would not sound right, said here and now.

But at the local transportation desk it developed that all the long-haul jitneys based at the spaceport had already been put under hire for the day. He would have to take ground transportation to Omalu and pick up one at the Transportation Center, there.

"We can go to town together, then," he said to Amanda, feeling suddenly as light as a reprieved prisoner. She frowned.

"I hitched a ride out," she answered. "I shouldn't—on the other hand it's your interstellar credit, if you want to buy me a seat on the bus."

"Of course I want to," he said firmly.

They rode in together, sitting in adjoining seats three rows back in an otherwise-empty surface bus. He put his hand on hers, and she squeezed his fingers briefly, then slid her arm through his and brought their hands together again, so that they sat with forearms on the armrest between them, arms intertwined and hands clasped. Their forearms pressed against each other, he thought, like those of two people about to take a blood oath, mingling the fluid in both their veins with the single cut of a knife.

But the knife and oath were unnecessary, here. It seemed to Hal, as they sat holding to each other in this unremarkable way, as if the life-sustaining conduits of their flesh had long since been joined into one system; so that each beat of his heart sent his blood through her arteries as well as his;

and that each of hers must direct that of both of them back through his own body.

There was still a great deal to say, but no hurry to say it now. The silence of the moment was itself infinitely valuable. He watched her clean profile etched against the windowed view of the countryside through which their vehicle was passing. There was a glow of a quiet peace and happiness in her that had not been present when he had been here before, a warmth independent of and at odds with the season of his coming. His last visit had been at the crisp end of summer. Now he was arriving early in the spring. Beyond the windows of the bus it was cold, clear and bright. The unsparing illumination of Fomalhaut lit all the landscape like a late and final dawn.

Under that light there was a northern look to what he could see outside the windows of the bus, that had not been there on his earlier visit. Now, in the nakedness of spring, it was clear that the land had just emerged from an icy winter and was hurrying to adapt to the march of seasons. In the earth and the growing things he read a race to survive under the sword of time. The few homesteads they passed were as neat as those he had seen before; but fields that had obviously been under cultivation the previous year had not been prepared this spring for sowing. Flower beds before the houses they passed were bare and empty.

Even in the wild fields the light green of the grass stems laid over toward the ground under the breeze, showing the brown tint of the earth through their own color. Against the dark branches and twigs of the trees, the young leaves were a darker green than the grass; but tiny and stiff, as if they huddled on the stems that held them. Above, the upper wind sent scattered clouds scudding forward visibly, harrying them toward the close, jagged horizon of the mountains surrounding. The little creeks that the bus occasionally crossed were gray-blue of surface and sharp-edged where their brown banks met the blue water, the earth not yet alive with new vegetation to soften the sharp line where dirt ended at streamside.

At the Transportation Center in Omalu, he arranged for a jitney and Amanda parted from him. He wanted to remind her of her promise to see him after her business here was done; but he was half-ashamed to make such a point of it. The jitney he had hired lifted him high above the surface of the world, into the blue-black of near space, and dropped him down again in the front yard of the home.

He let himself in, as the jitney took off again into the upper skies. Within, the house was as ready for habitation as ever; but the stillness of the air there shut out the strange wintriness he had seen everywhere on the way here and wrapped him with a feeling of suspended time. He reached, without looking, brushed aside jacket and put his hand on the plate of the lock-memory, his fingers coding it to remember his thumbprint. He walked through the house, dropped his luggage case on the white coverlet of the bed that had been Donal's and left it there, coming back to the living room.

He opened the door that led from the living room to the library and stepped into the opening. His head brushed the top bar of the frame; his shoulders brushed against the uprights on both sides of him. Amanda had been right—he had come into his full size. He was conscious of what was himself, small, silent, and alone, inside the big body.

"An odd boy. . . ."

He went into the kitchen, opened the storage units there and made himself a meal of bread, goat cheese and barley-like soup, which he ate seated at the kitchen table and looking out at the sky above the outbuildings. Afterward, he cleaned up the debris of his eating and went back to browse through the bookshelves of the library. They were old, familiar books, and he lost himself in reading.

He woke from the pages before him to see that the sun was low on the mountains and evening had grown long shadows. Loneliness stirred in him; and to put it away from him he got up, returned his book to its place, and went out through the front door of the house.

It would be sunset shortly and Amanda had not come. He turned away from the house and wandered toward the outbuildings. As he came close, a horse neighed from the stable. He went in and found two of them in the stalls there. Their long noses and brown eyes looked around at him as he came up behind them.

One was Barney, the gray Amanda had been riding when he had first seen her, and during their rides together afterward during his first visit. The other was a tall bay gelding, large enough to carry someone of his size and weight comfortably. Saddles, bridles and blankets were hung on the wall of an adjacent stall.

He smiled. Both horses whickered and moved impatiently, watching him over their shoulders for some sign that he would take one of them out for a ride. But he turned away and went back out again.

He moved about the grounds, stepping into each of the outbuildings in turn, standing and listening to the walled quiet inside them. As the sun was setting he went back to the house. It was time for the end-of-day news on any technologized world; and he sat watching that news on the communications screen in the living room. For the first few minutes, as on any unfamiliar world, what he saw and heard of people and their actions made little sense. Then, gradually, the forces behind what he watched became more apparent. The Dorsai world was mobilizing—it was as he had expected when he had decided it was time to come here once more.

He became engrossed in what he watched and followed, as the sunset moved on around the planet and the source of the broadcast moved with it. There was a uniqueness, an attention-compelling magic in the interior life of a people—any people. Waking at last from this, he suddenly realized it was almost ten P.M. and Amanda had neither come nor called. Outside, it had been dark for several hours.

He sat, recalled once more to the emptiness and silence of the house about him. He stood up and stretched. A fatigue he had not noticed until this moment sat between his shoulder blades. He dimmed the light in the living room to a nightglow and went to the room where his travel case waited.

Lying in bed, he thought at first that in spite of the fatigue he would not sleep. But he put disappointment from him and slumber came. It was at some unknown time later that he was roused by the faintest whisper of movement and opened his eyes on the darkened space around him.

He had swung wide the windows and left the drapes drawn back so that outside breeze could come freely through. In that moving air, the bottom ends of the glass curtains now flowed inward, moving between the dark pillars of the pulled drapes. In the time he had been asleep, the moon had risen and moved into position to shine strongly into the middle part of the room, away from his bed. The air was cool—he could feel it on face and hands, only, the rest of him warm under the thick coverlet; and in the center of the room stood Amanda, half-turned from him, undressing.

He lay, watching her. She would be too good at moving silently not to have deliberately made the slight sound that she knew would waken him. But she went on now with what she was doing as if unaware his eyes were on her. He lay watching; and the last piece of clothing dropped to her ankles and lay still. She straightened, and stood for a second like some warm and living sculpture of ivory, bathed in moonlight, drowned in moonlight. The light turned the curve of hip and buttock, outlining them against the further darkness of the room, and her breasts shone full in the moonbeams. Her hair was like a cloud with its own interior illumination, haloing her head. Beneath its light, her calm face was like the profile on some old coin; and from shoulder to feet the length of her body reflected the moonlight. She balanced there like a wild thing that has just raised its head from drinking at something heard far off; then he saw her hips seem to widen below the narrow waist as she turned toward him. Lifting the coverlet, she slid beneath it, turning to face him.

A harsh, ragged sigh of relief tore itself past the gates of his throat and his arms went around her, one hand closing about the soft turn of hip, one sliding beneath her to cradle her upper body, his forearm beneath her shoulder and his fingers in the softness of her hair. With one simple effort, he lifted her to him.

"You came . . . ," he said, just before their lips met, and their bodies pressed strongly together.

He returned, after a while, to the rest of the universe—he came back gradually, drifting back. They were lying side by side now on the bed, with no cover over them; and the moon had moved some distance in the sky, so that its light had abandoned the center of the room, and now shone full upon them.

"Now everything is different," he said.

He lay on his back, and she lay on her side, propped on her left arm, facing him. He could feel her eyes watching him even though he stared at the ceiling and the moonlight.

"Is it?" she said, softly. The fingers of her left hand wandered caressingly through his black, coarse hair. Her other arm lay across his chest, white against the darkness of the matted hair there. She moved closer to him, fitting her head into the hollow of his shoulder; and he turned toward her, laying his right arm over her. He saw his own thick wrist and massive hand lying relaxed upon the gentle rise of her breast and felt a wonder that she should be here, like this; that out of all times and places they should find each other in this moment when the worlds were beginning to burn about them.

The wonder grew in him. How was it that at a time like this he could feel so close to someone else and happy; when only a handful of days past on Harmony—

He shuddered suddenly; and her arms tightened swiftly about him.

"What is it?" she said.

"Nothing . . . ," he said. "Nothing. An old ghost walking over my grave."

"What old ghost?"

"A very old one," he said. "Hundreds of years old."

"It's not gone," she said. "It's still with you."

"Yes," he said, giving up. The core of him was still cold, even though she warmed him with her arms; and the words came from him almost in spite of himself.

"I've just come from the Friendlies," he said. "I'd gone there to get a Harmonyite named Rukh Tamani—did I tell you about her when I was here before? There's a work she's needed for on Earth, for all the worlds. But when I got there the Militia at Ahruma had her in prison."

He stopped, feeling the coldness grow within him.

"I know about the Militia on the Friendlies," Amanda said.

"I got the local resistance people to get her out. We went into the Militia Headquarters after her. When I found her, she'd been left in a cell. . . ."

The memory grew back into a living thing, about him. He talked on. The coldness began once more to grow in him, as it had then, spreading out through his body. The bedroom and Amanda seemed to move away from him, to become remote and unimportant. He felt himself reentering the memory; and he grew ever more icy and remote. . . .

"No!" It was Amanda's voice, sharply. "Hal! Come back! Now!"

For a moment he teetered, as on a sharp-crested rock, high above a dark depth. Then slowly, clinging to her presence, he began to retreat from the place into which he had almost gone a second time. He returned, farther and farther . . . until finally he was back and fully alive again. The coldness had melted from him. He lay on his back on the bed and Amanda had him in her arms.

He breathed out once, heavily; a sound too great to be called a sigh; and turned his head to look at her.

"You know about it?" he said. "How do you know?"

"It's not uncommon here," she said, grimly. "The Graemes had their share of it. It's called a cold rage."

"A cold rage. . . ." He looked back up at the shadowy ceiling overhead. The phrase rang with familiarity in his ears. His mind took what she had just told him and ran far into the interior of his own thoughts, fitting it like a key to many things in himself he had not yet completely understood. He felt Amanda releasing the fierce grip she had maintained on him until now. She let go the tension of her arms and lay back a little from him. He felt her watching him.

"I'm sorry." The words came from him in a weary gust of air. He was still not looking at her. "I didn't mean to put it off on you, that way."

"I just told you," she answered—but her tone was more gentle than her words, "it's not uncommon here. I said the Graemes had their share of it. How many nights out of the past three hundred years, do you think, has one of them, man or woman, lay talking to whoever was close enough to tell, as you did now?"

He could think of nothing to say. He felt ashamed . . . but released. After a little while, she spoke again.

"Who are you?" she asked softly.

He closed his eyes. Her question struck heavily upon him at his recognition of a knowledge he had not expected her to have. There was nowhere he could turn to hide the rest of things from her—now that he had just tried to go as far as human mind could take him from her and she had brought him back in spite of himself.

"Donal." He heard his voice say it, out loud in the night silence. "I was Donal."

His eyes were still closed. He could not look at her. After a long moment, he asked her: "How did you know?"

"Knowing runs in the Morgan line," she answered. "And the Amandas have always been gifted with it, even more than the others in the family. Also, I grew up with Ian around. How could I not know?"

He said nothing for a little while.

"It's Ian you look like," she said. "But you know that."

He smiled painfully, opening his eyes at last and gazing up at the ceiling. The relief in having it out in the open was so great that adjustment to it came hard.

"It was always Ian and Kensie I wanted to be like—when I was growing up—as Donal," he said; "and I never could."

"It wasn't Eachan Graeme? Your own father?"

He laughed a little at the thought.

"No one could be like Eachan Graeme, as I saw it then," he said. "That was too much to expect. But the twins—that seemed just barely possible."

"Why do you say you never were?" she said.

"Because I wasn't," he said. "As the Graemes go, I was a little man. Even my brother Mor was half a head taller than I was."

"Two lifetimes . . . ," she said. "Two lifetimes bothering over the fact that you were shorter than the other men in your family?"

"Three lifetimes," he corrected her, "and if you're male, it sometimes matters."

"Three?"

He lay silent again for a moment, sorting out the words to say.

"I was also a dead man for a time," he said at last. "That is, I used the body and name of a man who'd died. I had to go back in time; and there was no other way to do it."

It was the last thing he had meant to do, but he heard the tone of his own voice putting up a wall against further questions from her about that second lifetime.

"How long have you known who you were . . . this last time?" she asked.

He had been speaking without looking at her. But now he opened his eyes and turned toward her; and her own eyes, pure blue now in the moonlight, drew him down to her. He kissed her, as someone might reach out to hold a talisman.

"Less than these last two years—for certain," he said. "I grew up until I was nearly seventeen years old on Old Earth, not knowing. Then later, when I was in the mines on Coby, I began to feel the differences in me. Later, on Harmony, there began to be moments when I did things better than I should have known how to do. But it wasn't until I got here to Graemehouse on my first trip—when I was in the dining room there—"

He broke off, looking down into those eyes of hers.

"You must have known, then," he said, "or suspected, when you found me there when you came back, and saw how I was."

"No," she said. "It was the night before, that I felt it. I knew then, not who you were, but what you were."

He shook slightly, remembering.

"But I wasn't really sure then, myself. I didn't even understand how it could be," he said, "until this last year at the Final Encyclopedia. Then, when I began to use the Encyclopedia for the first time as a creative tool, the way Mark Torre had hoped and planned it would be used, I put it to work to hunt back and help me find out where I'd come from."

"And it showed you," she said, "that you'd come from the Dorsai?"

A coolness—different from the coldness she had rescued him from before, but equally awesome, blew through him.

"Yes," he said, "but also much more than that, very much, much further back than that."

She watched him.

"I don't understand," she said.

"I'm Time's soldier," he said softly. "I always have been. And it's been a long, long campaign. Now we're on the eve of the last battle."

"Now?" she asked. "Or can it still be sidestepped?"

"No," he said, bleakly. "It can't be. That's why everyone's in it who's alive today, whether they want to be or not. I'll take you to the Encyclopedia one day and show you the whole story as it's developed, down the centuries—as I've got to show it to Tam Olyn and Ajela as soon as I get back."

"Ajela?"

"Ajela's an Exotic—only about my age." He smiled. "But at the same time she's Tam's foster-mother. She's in her twenties now, and she's been taking care of him since she was sixteen. In his name she does most of the administrating of the Encyclopedia."

Chapter

> > **56** < <

Amanda asked nothing more, for the moment. A temporary silence closed around them and by mutual consent they turned back to each other and into the universe and language that belonged only to the two of them. Later they lay companionably quiet together on their backs, side by side, watching the last of the moonlight illuminating a far corner of the room; and Amanda spoke.

"You didn't expect it at all, then, that I'd be waiting at the Spaceport when you came back?"

He shook his head.

"I couldn't expect that," he said. "It would have been like expecting to grow up to be like Eachan Khan Graeme—too much to imagine. I just thought that when I came I'd look you up, wherever you were. I only hoped. . . ."

He ran down into silence. Amanda said nothing for a moment.

"I've had more than a year to think about you," she said.

"Yes," he smiled, ruefully. "Has it been that long? I guess it has, hasn't it? So much has been going on. . . ."

"You don't understand."

She raised herself up on one elbow and looked down into his face.

"You remember what I tried to tell you when you were here the last time?"

"That you were like the other two Amandas," he said, sobering. "I remember."

He looked up at her.

"I'm sorry I was so slow to realize what you meant," he went on. "I do now. You were telling me that, like them, you're committed to a great many people, too many to take on the possible conflict of an extra commitment to someone like myself. I understand. I've found out how little I can escape from my own commitments. I can hardly expect you to try to escape from yours."

"If you'll listen," she said, "I might be able to tell you what I'm trying to tell you."

"I'm listening," he answered.

"What I'm trying to say is that I had a chance to think about things after you were gone. You're right, I sent you off because I didn't think there was any room in my life for anyone like you—because I thought I had to be what the second Amanda had been; and she'd sent Ian away. But with time to think about it, I started to realize there was a lot there I hadn't understood about both the earlier Amandas."

He lay waiting, listening. When she paused, he merely continued to look up at her.

"One of the largest shocks was realizing," she said, almost severely, "how little I'd understood about my own Amanda, the second one, in spite of being raised by her. I told you I grew up with Ian around the house so much of the time that as a young child I thought he was a Morgan. He and Amanda were both at a good age then, his children were grown and had children of their own; and his wife, Leah, was dead. He and Amanda, eventually in their old age, had come to be what life and their own senses of duty had never let them be until then—a love match. This was all right there, under my nose, but I was too young to appreciate it. Being that young and romantic-minded, all I could see was Amanda's great renunciation of Ian when she was younger, because of her obligation to the people of the Dorsai."

She paused.

"Say something," she demanded. "You are following me, aren't you?"

"I'm following you," he said.

"All right," she went on. "Actually, when I began to see Ian and Amanda as the human beings they really were, I was finally able to see how there'd been a progression at work down the Amanda line. The First had her obligation only to her family and the people of this local community. My Amanda had hers to the Dorsai people as a whole. The obligation I carry, I think, is the same as yours, to the human race as a whole—in fact, I think that's one of the forces that's brought us together now, and would have brought us together, sooner or later, in any case."

He frowned a little. What she had last said was an obvious truth that had never occurred to him.

"I realized finally," she was going on, "that, far from our personal commitments making us walk separate roads, they probably do just the opposite. They were probably going to require us to walk the same road together, whether we wanted to do so, or not; and if that was so, then there was no problem—for me, at least."

She stopped and looked down at him with an almost sly smile he had not expected and did not understand.

"Are you still following me?" she demanded.

"No," he answered. "No, to be honest, now you've lost me completely."

"My, my," she said, "the unexpected limits to genius. What I'm telling you is, I decided that if it was indeed inevitable that the factors involved were going to bring the two of us together, then it was just a matter of time before you came back here. If you never did, I could simply forget about the whole matter."

"But if I did come back? What then?" he asked.

She became serious.

"Then," she said, "I wouldn't make the mistake I'd made the first time. I'd be waiting for you when you got here."

They stared at each other for a long moment; and then she took her weight off her elbow, lay down and curled up against him, her head in the hollow of his shoulder. He put his other arm over and around her, holding her close. For a moment or two neither of them said anything.

"The last thing in the universe I expected," he commented, at last, to the ceiling. "It took me two tries at life to realize I had to develop the ability to love, then a third try from a standing start to actually develop it. And now, when I finally have, at a time when it ought to have been far too late to do me any good—here you are."

He stopped talking and ran the palm of his hand in one long sweep down her back from the nape of her neck to the inner crook of her knee.

"Amazing," he said thoughtfully, "how you can fit yourself so well to me, like that," he said.

"It's a knack," she answered, her lips against his chest. There was a second's pause. "Except all these hairs you have here tickle my nose."

"Sorry."

"Quite all right," she said, without moving. Another momentary pause. "I won't ask you to shave them off."

"Shave them off!"

She chuckled into his chest. They held each other close for a little while.

"I shouldn't do that sort of thing," she said in a different voice, after the time had passed. "I don't know what makes me want to tease you. It's just that it's like being able to ride a wild horse everyone is afraid to get close to. But I can feel something of what it must have been like for you, all those years and all those lives. It's so strange it doesn't show on you more, now that you know who you were, and what you did."

"Each time was a fresh start," he said, earnestly. "It had to be. The slate had to be wiped clean each time so there'd be no danger of what had been learned before getting in the way of the new learning. I set myself up fresh each time. That way I could be sure I'd only remember what I'd known before after I'd progressed beyond needing it in my newer life. I've been learning—learning all the way."

"Yes, but hasn't it been strange, though?" she said. "Everybody else starts at the bottom and works up. Actually, what you've done is start at the top and work down. From Donal, controller of worlds, you've struggled your way down to being as much like an ordinary person as you can."

"It's because the solution's got to be for the ordinary-person level—or it's no solution. Donal started out to mend the race by main force; and he learned it didn't work. Force never really changes the inner human. When Genghis Khan was alive, they said a virgin with a bag of gold could ride from one border of his empire to the other end and no one would molest her, or it. But once he was dead, the virgins and the gold started moving again under heavy armed guard, as they always had before. All anyone can ever do for even one other human being is break trail for him or her, and hope whoever it is follows. But how could I even break trail for people unless I could think like them, feel like them—know myself to be one of them?"

His voice sounded strange in the quiet nighttime room and his own ears.

"You couldn't, of course," Amanda said gently. "But how did Donal go wrong?"

"He didn't really," Hal said, to her and the shadowy ceiling. "He went right, but without enough understanding; and it may be I don't have enough understanding, even yet. But his start was in the right direction and what he dedicated me to as a child is still my path, my job."

"Dedicated you?" she said. "You mean, as Donal, as a child, you dedicated yourself to what you're doing now? How—so early?"

A remembered pain moved in him. A memory of the cell on Harmony closed around him once more.

"Do you remember James Graeme?" he asked her.

"Which James?" she asked. "There've been three by that name down the Graeme generations since Cletus."

"The James who was Donal's youngest uncle," he answered. "The James who was killed at Donneswort when I—when Donal was still a child."

He paused, looking at her calm face, resting now with the one cheek against his chest, looking back at him in the remains of the moonlight.

"Did I tell you the last time I was here about my dreaming about a graveyard and a burial, while I was in the cell on Harmony?" he asked.

"No," she said. "You told me a lot about the cell and what you thought your way through to, when you were there. But you didn't mention any dream of a burial."

"It was when I was just about to give up," he said. "I didn't realize it then, but I was just on the brink, finally, of finding what I'd sent myself out as Hal Mayne to find. What I'd come to understand began to crack through the barrier I'd set up to keep myself as Hal from knowing what had happened to me before, and what came through was a memory of the ceremony at Foralie held over James' grave, when I was a boy. . . ."

His voice was lost in the pain of remembering for a moment, then he brought it back.

"That was the moment of Donal's decision, his commitment," Hal went on. "James had been closer to him than his own brother—it sometimes happens that way. Mor was between us in age, but Mor—"

His voice did not die this time, it stuck. Mor's name blocked his throat.

"What about Mor?" Amanda asked after a moment. Her hand moved gently to touch his, her fingertips resting on the skin at the back of his hand as it lay on the bed.

"Donal killed Mor," he said, from a long distance away.

He could feel her fingertips as if they touched the naked nerves below the skin and reached up along them to touch the innermost part of his identity.

"That's not the truth." He heard her voice a little way off. "You're making more of it than it is, somehow. It's right, but not that right. What is true?"

"Donal was responsible for Mor's death," he answered, as if she had commanded him.

The feeling of her reaching into him withdrew.

"Yes," she said. "That's all right, then, for now. You were telling me about James' death and how it brought about Donal's commitment to what's driven you all these lifetimes and all these years. What happened?"

"What happened?" His mind pulled itself back from the vision of Mor, as the finally-insane William of Ceta had left him, and came back to the vision of James' burial. "They just accepted it. Even Eachan—even my father—he just accepted James' being killed, reasonlessly, like that; and I . . . couldn't. I—he went into a cold rage—Donal did. The same sort of thing you brought me back from a little while ago."

"He did?" Amanda's voice broke on a note of incredulity. "He couldn't—he was far too young. How old was he?"

"Eleven."

"He couldn't at that age. It's impossible."

Hal laughed, and the laugh rang harshly in the quiet bedroom.

"He did. Kensie felt the same way you're feeling . . . when Kensie found him, in the stables where he'd gone after the ceremony, when all the rest had gone up to the house. But he could and did. He was Donal."

With the last word, as if the name had been a trigger, he felt within him a return, not only the coldness, but of a sweep of power that woke in him without warning, threatening to carry him off like a tidal bore sweeping up in its wall of water anything caught in its naked channel at high-water time.

"I am Donal," he said; and the power took and lifted him, irresistible, towering—

"Not Bleys."

Amanda's quiet voice reached out and cut the power off at its source. Clear-mindedness came back to him, in a rush of utter relief. He lay for a few seconds, saying nothing.

"What have I told you about Bleys?" he asked her, then, turning to look through the gloom at her.

"A great deal," she answered, softly, "that first night you were at Fal Morgan, when you talked so much."

"I see." He sighed. "The sin of the Warrior, still with me. It's one of the things I still have to leave behind, as you saw . . . when I remembered Rukh's rescue. No, thank God, I'm not Bleys. But at eleven years old, I wasn't Bleys either. I only knew I couldn't endure that nothing be done about James' unnecessary death, about all such unnecessary evils in the universe—all the things people do to each other that should never be done."

"And you committed yourself then, to stop that?"

"Donal did. Yes," he said. "And he gave all his own life to trying. In a sense, it wasn't all his fault he went wrong. He was still young. . . ."

"What did he do?" Her voice gently drew him back onto the path of what he had been about to tell her, earlier.

"He went looking for a tool, a tool to make people not do the sort of things that had caused James' death," Hal said. "And he found one. I call it—he called it—intuitive logic. It's either logic working with the immediacy of intuition, or intuition that gets its answers according to the hard rules of a logic. Take your pick. Actually, he was far from the first to find it. Creative people—artists, writers, composers of music, musicians themselves, had used it for years. Researchers had used it. He only made a system for it and used it consciously, at his will and desire."

"But what is it?" Amanda's voice prodded him.

"It can't be explained—in the same sense a mathematics can't be explained—in words," he said. "You have to talk the language in which it exists to explain it—and even before that, your mind has to begin by making the quantum jump to a first understanding of that language, before you can really start learning what it is. I can give you a parallel example. You'll have seen, at one time or another, some great painting that reached out and captured you, heard a piece of music that was genius made audible, read a book that was beyond question one of the everlasting books?"

"Yes," she said.

"Then you know how all those things have one element in common: the fact you can come back and back to them. You can look, and look again, at the painting without ever exhausting what's to be found in it. You can listen to the music over and over, and each time find something new in it. You can read and reread the book without ever getting out of it all that's there for you to discover and enjoy."

"I know," she said.

"You see," he told her, "what makes all your returning to these things possible is their capability of triggering off in you an infinity of discoveries; and they can do that because there is an infinity of things to be discovered, put into them by the creator. That infinity of possibilities could never be marshalled together consciously by one human mind and put to work in one piece of canvas, one succession of sounds, one succession of printed words. You know that. But still, there they are. They did not exist before, and now they do. There was no way they could have come into existence except by being put there by the human being who made each of them. And there was only one way he or she could have accomplished that—the maker had to have built not only with his conscious mind, which is precise but limited in how much it can conceive at anyone time, but also with the unconscious, which knows no limits, and can bring all life's observations, all life's experience, to bear on a single rendered shape, sound, or word, placed just so among its fellow shapes, sounds or words."

He stopped speaking. For a second, she did not reply.

"And that," said Amanda then, "is what you call intuitive logic?"

"Not quite," said Hal. "What I was talking about there was creative logic, which is still operating under the control of the unconscious. If the unconscious is displeased with the task, it refuses to work, and no power of will can make it. What Donal did was move that control fully into the conscious area, that's all, and put it to work there manipulating the threads of cause and effect. Then, when he was still so young, he didn't realize how much he was drawing on what he had learned from reading the works on strategy and tactics by his great-grandfather."

"By Cletus Grahame, you mean?"

Hal nodded.

"Yes. You remember, don't you, that Cletus had actually started out with the idea of being an artist? It was only later on he became caught up in the physics of military action and reaction. He used creative logic to build his principles; and in fact, from what's there to be seen in his work, he may have crossed the line himself from time to time, into a conscious control of what he was making."

"I see." Amanda seemed to think for a moment. "But you don't know if he ever did? You seem to know that Donal did."

"I was never Cletus." Hal smiled, more to himself than to her. "But I was Donal."

"And you say creative logic was why Cletus was able to win the way he did, against Dow deCastries and an Earth so rich in everything all the Younger Worlds seemed to have no chance against it? And it was symbolic logic then that brought Donal to the title of Secretary of Defense of all the worlds, including Earth, before he was in his mid-thirties?"

"Yes," said Hal, somberly. "And having done it, Donal understood the lesson of the virgin with the bag of gold, after the death of Genghis Khan. He looked at the peace and law he had enforced on all the civilized planets and saw that he'd done nothing. He hadn't changed a single mind, a single attitude in the base structure of the human animal. It was the nadir of everything he had reached out for since that moment when he was eleven years old."

Her hand reached out and caressed his arm.

"It was all right." He smiled again, this time ruefully. "He lived through it. I lived through it. Being who I am, I can't give up. That's really what operated in that Militia cell. My conscious mind and body were ready to give up and lie back to do just that—but they weren't allowed to. That that's in me pushed me on, anyway. Just as it pushed Donal on, back then. As Donal, I saw I'd been wrong. The next step was to amend that wrongness—to correct, not an errant humanity, but the overall historic pattern that had made humanity errant."

"And how did he think he could do that?" Her voice led him on to talk, and the talking was the slow unloading of an intolerable burden he had carried for so long he had forgotten that he had ever been without it.

"By turning his tool of intuitive logic not just upon the present, but on what made it, the causes behind the effects he saw around him and the causes behind those causes, until he came back to a point at which something could be done."

"And he found it."

"He found it." Hal nodded, "But he also found that what needed to be done was not something he could do as he had done things up until then. It wasn't something he was yet equipped to do. To operate upon what he needed to operate upon, he himself had to change, to learn. To grow."

"So," Amanda said. "And your second life came from that. Can you tell me about that, now?"

He was conscious of all the burdens he had already laid aside for the first time in his life, in talking to her here and now.

"Yes," he said. "Now I can."

He reached his free hand across to lie on the living incurve of her belly. He could feel her ribs rise and fall, slowly and fully with her breathing. He stared into the shadows above him.

"The problem had several sides," he said. "Humanity couldn't, as he thought he saw it then, be changed from where he stood at the moment, just like you couldn't do much about a tree that was already grown. But if you went back to the time of its planting and made changes that would be effective upon the environment in which it would grow to what it would be in the present . . ."

He stopped.

"Go on," Amanda said.

"I'm trying to work out the best way of telling you all this briefly," he answered. "And it takes a little thinking. You'll have to take my word for it that by using intuitional logic and working back from the then-present effects to the causes he already knew for them, or could discover, he found he could trace back to the closest point in history where all the elements he hoped to alter were available at a single time and place for changing. He found that first point in the twenty-first century, just on the eve of the practical development of the phase-drive, just before the diaspora to the Younger Worlds, in a time when all the root stocks of what would later become the Splinter Cultures were to be found together within a single environment—that of Old Earth."

Amanda rose on her elbow again to look down into his face.

"You're going to tell me he actually went back in time, to change the past?"

"Yes and no," Hal said. "He couldn't physically travel back in time, of course. He couldn't actually change the past. But what he found he could do was work his consciousness back along the chain of cause and effect to the time he wanted and there try to make the necessary changes; not in what actually happened then, but in the possible implications of what happened. He could open up to the minds living in that time possibilities that otherwise they might not have seen."

"How did he think he was going to communicate these possibilities—by stepping into people's dreams, then, or speaking to them, mind to mind?"

"No," he said, "by interacting—but as someone who actually did not exist at the time. To make the story as short as possible, he ended by reanimating a dead body, a mining engineer of the twenty-first century who had drowned, named Paul Formain. As Paul Formain, he influenced people who were the forerunners of the Dorsai, the Friendlies and others—but most of all he influenced the people making up something that was then called the Chantry Guild."

"I remember that from history," said Amanda. "The Exotics came from the Chantry Guild."

"Yes," said Hal. "In the Chantry Guild and seed organizations of other Splinter Cultures, he introduced possibilities that were to have their effect, not in Donal's time, but in our present day. Now."

"But when did Donal manage to do this?" Amanda said. "He was in the public eye right up to the moment of his death—when he took that courier ship out alone and was caught by the one-in-a-million chance of not coming out of phase-shift."

"He didn't die," said Hal. "It was simply assumed he'd died, when he didn't arrive where and when he was supposed to and no trace of his ship could be found. He hid in space for many years, until it was time to let the ship be found, drifting into Old Earth orbit."

She said nothing for a long moment.

"With a baby aboard," she said. "A very young child—that was you?"

"Yes." Hal nodded. "It's something the mind can do with the body, if it has to. Even Cletus mended his crippled leg with his mind."

"I know that story," said Amanda. "But the Exotics helped him."

"No," said Hal. "They just provided the excuse for him to believe in his own ability to do it."

She said nothing, looking at him.

"We've had miracle cures reported all down the centuries," he said. "Long before the Exotics. They, themselves, have quite a library on such incidents, I understand. So, I hear, has the Final Encyclopedia. I believe I was dying in that cell from the pneumonia or whatever it was I had, until I realized I couldn't afford to die. Shortly after that realization, my fever broke. Of course, it could have been coincidence. But mothers have stayed untouched in the midst of epidemics as long as they were needed to care for their sick children."

"Yes," she said, slowly. "I do know what you mean."

"That, and taking over a dead body as life leaves it, are only two aspects of the same thing. But I don't want to get off on that business now. The main point is, Donal went back and became Paul Formain, so as to change the shape of things to come—and to change himself."

"Will you sit up?" Amanda said. "Then I can sit up, too. I can't lie propped on one elbow indefinitely."

They arranged themselves in seated position, side by side, with their backs protected by pillows from the carved walnut of the bedstead behind them. The narrow width of the single bed left them still close, still touching.

"Now," said Amanda. "You said—'and to change himself.' Change himself how?"

"Donal'd seen how he'd gone astray in his own time," Hal said. "He felt it was because he had failed to feel as he should for those around him—and he was right, as far as that went. At any rate, he went out to learn the ability to feel another's feelings, so that he could never again fall into the trap of thinking he had changed people when actually all he'd done was change the laws that controlled their actions."

"Empathy? That was what he wanted?"

"Yes," said Hal.

"And he found it?"

"He learned it. But it wasn't enough."

Amanda looked at him.

"What is it bothers you so about this time Donal—no, not Donal— when you were this animated dead man . . . what was his name?"

"Paul Formain," Hal said. "It's not easy to explain. You see, as Formain, he—I—did it again. Donal'd played God. He hadn't done it just for the sake of playing God, but that's what the effect he'd had on the populations of fourteen worlds had amounted to. Then when he saw what he'd done it sickened him, and he decided whatever else he did, he wouldn't be guilty of doing it again. Then, as Paul Formain, he went and did just that."

"He did?" Amanda stared at him. "I don't see why you say that—unless you call it playing God to plant the possibilities of our present time. . . ."

Her own voice ran down.

"No!" she said, suddenly and strongly. "Follow that sort of reasoning and you end up with the fact that to try to do anything for people, even for the best of reasons, is immoral."

"No," Hal said. "I don't mean that. What I mean is that once again, he realized he'd acted without sufficient understanding. As Donal he hadn't considered people at all, except as chess pieces on a board. As Paul Formain, he considered people—but only those with whom he learned to empathize. He was still trying to work with humanity from the outside—that was what hadn't changed in him."

He paused, then went on.

"He faced that, after he'd done what he'd gone back to the twenty-first century to do. He'd set in motion the very factors that are now bringing the internal struggle of the race-animal out into the open and forcing everyone to take sides, with the Others or against, for the survival of us all. But he'd done it, in a sense, with a certain blindness; and it was because of that blindness that he couldn't foresee someone like Bleys and the growth of power behind him. After he returned Paul Formain's body to the ocean bed from which he had lifted it, he realized how he had gone wrong—although he couldn't yet foresee the consequences, that hold us in a vise right now. But he understood enough finally to see what his great fault had been."

"His great fault?" said Amanda, almost harshly. "And what was that great fault?"

"Just that he'd never had the courage to give up the one apart corner of himself, to abandon standing apart from everyone else." Hal turned his head to look directly at her. "He'd been the 'odd boy,' according to his teachers. He'd been the small and different ugly duckling among the Graemes. He'd been born with the same sort of mind that led Bleys Ahrens to put himself light-years apart from the rest of the race. Donal, too, had been born an isolated individual, suffered from that isolation, and come to embrace it, as Bleys had embraced it. With his development of empathy, Paul Formain could begin to feel what someone else might be feeling, but he felt it as any human being might feel a frog's hunger for a passing fly. The soul of him still stood alone and apart from all those he had thought early had cast him out."

Again, he paused.

"I was afraid to be human, then," he said. He did not look at her, but he felt her arm go around his waist and her head come to rest on his shoulder.

"Not anymore," she said.

"No." He heaved a very deep sigh. "But it was literally the hardest thing I ever had to do. Only there was no choice. There was the commitment. I had to go forward—and so I did."

"By coming back as a child," she said.

"As a child," he agreed. "Starting all over again without memory, without strength, without the skills of two lifetimes to protect myself with in an arena I'd built and didn't know I'd built. So I could finally learn, once and for all, to be like everybody else."

"Was it so absolutely necessary to do that?" he heard her asking from the region of his shoulder.

"It was critical," he said. "You can lead or drive from the outside, but you can only show the way from inside. It's not just enough to know how they feel—you have to feel it with them. That was the mistake I made being Formain and thinking empathy alone was going to give me what I needed to get the work done. And I was right—all the years of being Hal Mayne have proved how right I was, this last time. I was born Donal, and nothing I can do can ever leave him behind, but I can be a larger Donal. I can feel as if I belong to the community of all people—and I do."

He stopped and turned his head to look down into her face.

"And, of course," he said, "it brought me you."

"Who knows?" she said. "You might've come to it anyway by a different route, eventually. I still feel things—the historic forces, as you call them—would've brought us together in the long run, one way or another."

"I thought you'd thought it could go either way, and you'd just left it up to fate," he said.

"I did," she answered. "But looking back on it, I was certain you'd be back. I've learned to trust myself in things like that. I know when I'm right. Just as I know . . ."

She did not finish the sentence.

"Know what?" he asked.

"Nothing. Nothing worth talking about, right now, anyway. Nothing to worry about." He felt her shake her head, briefly. "In ancient times they would have called feeling like that second sight. But it's not giving me anything you ought to be concerned about. Tell me something else. When you talk about the race-animal, do you really mean some entity, actual and separate from us all?"

"Not separate," he said. "Oh, I suppose you could call it separate in that it might want something that you or I as part of it don't want. No, as I say, it's just the self-protective and other reflexes of the race as a whole, raised to the level of something approaching a personality because it's now the reflex-bundle of an intelligent, thinking race, as opposed to the same sort of thing in the case of the race of, say, lions or lemmings—or you name them."

"And that's all it is?" she said. "Then how do you justify talking about it as if it were a sort of wilful individual personality that had to be dealt with?"

"Well, again, that's the difference that's come into it because we, who make it up, while we're a race of intelligent individuals, are also a conglomeration of willful individuals. Because we think, it thinks—after our fashion. Try this for an explanation. It's a sort of collective unconscious, as if all our individual unconsciousnesses were wired together with something like telepathy—again, there's been evidence for that sort of wired-togetherness in the past."

"Yes," she said thoughtfully. "The empathy between twins. Or between parent and child, or any two adults in love, that allows them sometimes to feel at a distance what's happening to the other. I can agree with that. You know, we—you and I—have that, I think."

"All right, then," he said. "But there's one difference from us in the lower orders—particularly in the examples of the beehive or the anthill—in our case. It's that we can not only want something different from what the race-animal wants—we can actually try to change its mind and its course, by convincing the unconsciousness of our fellow individuals. If we can get enough of them wanting what we want, the race-creature has to turn that way from whatever other route it's chosen."

"How do you convince the unconsciousnesses of others, though? There's nothing there to take hold of. The conscious mind of someone else you can talk to. All right, I know the Exotics do a beautiful job of mending sick minds by talking to the conscious and getting the corrections filtered down to the unconscious. And, for that matter, Bleys' charisma and that of the Others—that's working directly with the unconscious of people. So's hypnosis. But none of those things have a lasting effect unless what's being put into the subject really agrees with what was there in the unconscious in the first place. There's no direct way to hold converse with other humans' unconscious."

"Yes, there is," he said, "and it's a way that's been used at least since a prehistoric people lived in the caves of the Dordogne, back on Old Earth—you can talk to the unconsciousnesses of other people through the mediums of art."

"Art . . . ," she said, thoughtfully.

"That's right," he said. "And you know why? Because art—real art—never tells anyone something. It only lays it out there for whoever comes to pick it up."

"Perhaps. But it certainly makes whatever it has to say as attractive as possible to whomever comes along. You have to admit that."

"Yes, all right. If it's good. And if it isn't good, it doesn't offer anything to the unconscious of a viewer, reader, or listener. But the difference between that and conscious attempts to persuade is the difference between an order and a demonstration. The maker of the piece of art doesn't convince the person experiencing it—the person experiencing it convinces himself or herself, if they decided what's laid out in the art is worth picking up. That's why I worked my way back down the ladder from Donal, as you put it. All of Donal's strength couldn't move the race one millimeter from its already-chosen path. But if I go first and leave footprints in the snow, some may follow, and others may follow them."

"Why?" she said. "I'm not against you, my love, but I want to see the reasons plainly. Why should anyone follow you?"

"Because of my dreams," he said. "Donal dreamed at James' death of a time when no more Jameses would be killed for stupid or selfish reasons. I've come to dream further—I see the old dream of the race as a whole, now possible."

"And what does a race dream of?" she asked, so softly that anywhere but in this quiet and private room he would not have been able to hear her.

"It dreams," he said, "of being a race of gods. From the beginning, the individual part of the race, shivering in the wet as a stone-age savage, said, 'I wish I was a god who could turn the rain off,' and, finally, generations and millennia later, he was such a god—and his godlike power was called weather control. But long before that the urge to command wetness to cease had produced hats, and roofs and umbrellas—but always the push in the human heart went on toward the original dreams of being able to just say, 'Rain, stop!' and the rain would stop."

He looked down through the dimness at her.

"And that's how it's been with everything else the individual, and therefore the race-animal, dreamed of—warmth when it was cold, coolness when it was too hot, the ability to fly bird-like, to cross great distances of water dry-shod, to hear and talk at as great or even greater distances, to block pain, defy disease and death. In the end, it's added up to one great desire. To be all-mighty. To be a god."

He paused, having heard his voice grow loud in the room and went on more quietly.

"And always the way to what was wanted's been found in a dozen small and practical ways before the single command, the wave of a godlike hand, was developed that could simply make it happen. But always the dream has run in advance. Hunters and cities, conquerors and kings, all succeeded in being and were superseded. The dream was always achieved first in art, time and again, and never forgotten until it was made real. Slowly, the human creature was changing, from a being that lived and died for what was material, to one who lived and died—and fought and died—and fought and died—for what was immaterial; for faith and obligation and love and power, power over the material first and then power over fellow-creatures, and finally, last and greatest, the power over self.

And the dreams have gone always ahead, picturing what was wanted as something already possessed; until it became a truism to the race-animal that what could be conceived, could be had."

He stopped talking, finally.

"And you say these dreams were kept in the language of art?" she said.

"Yes," he answered, "and still are. The footprints I want to leave in the snow lead off toward the reality of what has only been barely dreamed of yet. The universe in which to understand a thing is to have it. Do you want a castle? You can have it merely by wanting it—but you have to know and own the materials it'll be built of, the architecture that'll ensure it'll stand, not fall, once it's built, and the very nature and extent of the ground on which it stands. If you know that much, you can have your castle right now, by means already known. But you want more than just the physical structure. Your castle must have those immaterial qualities that made you desire its castleness in the first place. These are not to be found in the physical universe, but in the other one that we all know and reach for, unconsciously. So, such a universe offers much more than the fulfillment of material dreams; it offers satisfaction of that original dream to be a god—the chance to cure all ills, to learn all mysteries, and finally to build what has never been dreamed of by any of us before now."

"You want everyone to dream your dream," Amanda said.

"Yes," he said. "But my dream is their dream, already—unless they shut it out as Bleys and his kind have done. I just articulate it."

"But maybe it never will be articulated, except in your own individual mind," she went on. "And when you're gone, it'll be gone."

"No," he said, strongly. "It's there in other minds as well, too strongly for that. It's there in the race-creature itself, along with the fear of trying for it. Haven't you felt it yourself—haven't you always felt it? It's too late now to hide it or kill it. Four hundred years ago, the race-animal was forced to face the fact that the safe, warm world it was born on was only an indistinguishable mote in a physical universe so big that anything conceivable not only could, but almost certainly must, exist in it. It could try to close its eyes to what it had been brought generally to know, or it could take the risk and step out into the alien territory beyond its atmosphere."

"It hadn't any choice," she said. "Overpopulation of Old Earth, for one thing, drove it out."

"Overpopulation was a devil it knew. The unlimited universe was one it didn't. But it went—in fear and trembling, talking of things 'man was not meant to know,' but going; and it scattered its bets as best it could by turning loose all the different cultural varieties of itself society had produced up until then, to see which, if any, would survive. Toward whatever survivors there were, it would adapt. Now that time of adaptation is on us; and the question is, which of two choices is it going to be? The type that'd stop and keep what we have—or the type that'd go on risking and experimenting? Because the human equation that's involved can stand for only one solution. If the dominant survivor is the Bleys type, with its philosophy of stasis, then, for the first time since we lifted our eyes above the hard realities of our daily lives, we stop where we are. If it's yours and mine, and that of those like us—we go on reaching for what may make us or destroy us. The race-creature waits to see which of us will win."

"But if the choices are either-or," she said, "then maybe the race-creature—you know, I've got trouble with that clumsy double word you thought up, you really should try to come up with something better— would be doing the right thing in going with Bleys and the Others if they win."

"No," said Hal, bleakly, "it wouldn't. Because it's a creature made up of its parts, and its parts aren't gods—yet. They and it can still be wrong. And they'll be wrong to choose the Others, because neither they nor it seem to realize that the only end to stasis is eventual death. Any end to growth is death. Never having stopped growing from the beginning, the race-creature's like a child who can't really believe he'll ever come to an end. But I know we can."

"You could still be the one who's wrong."

"No!" he said again. He stared down at her. "Let me tell you about this last year. You know I went back to the Final Encyclopedia; and with what I know now as Paul Formain and Hal Mayne, this time I used it as Mark Torre dreamed of it being used—I made poetry into a key to unlock the implications of the records of our past—and the dream of godhood I've been talking about, personal godhood for every individual human, is there in the record. It explodes for the first time, plainly, in the constructs of the Renaissance. Not just in the art, but in all the artifacts of human creation from that period on."

He stopped and looked hard at her.

"You believe me?" he asked.

"Go on," said Amanda, quietly, "I'm still listening."

"Even today," he said, "there's a tendency to think of the Renaissance only in terms of its great art works. But it was a time of much more than that. It was a time of a multitude of breakings-out, in the forms of craft innovations and social and conceptual experimentation. I told you about the Theater of Memory which prefigures the Final Encyclopedia, itself.

It wasn't just by chance that Leonardo da Vinci was an engineer. Actually, what we call the technological age had already begun in the pragmatic innovations of the later Middle Ages—now it flowed into a new consciousness of what might be possible to humans. From that, in only six centuries came the step into space . . . and everything since has followed. In each generation there were those who wanted to stop where they were, like Bleys, and consolidate. But did we? At any time along that uncertain and fearful upward way, did we stop?"

He himself stopped.

"No," said Amanda. "Of course, we didn't."

She turned and darted upward slightly at him—and he jerked his head away from her. He stared grimly at her.

"You bit my ear!" he said.

"That's right." She looked at him wickedly. "Because that's enough of that for now. There'll be time yet to worry about the enemy before he starts beating at our gates. For now, I'm hungry and it's time for breakfast."

"Breakfast?"

Involuntarily, he glanced at the window and what she had just said was true. They—or rather he, he thought ruefully—had talked the moon down; and the darkness outside was beginning to pale toward day. He could see the grayish scree of the slope behind the house more clearly, looming like a slightly more solid ghost of the future.

"That's what I said." She was already out of bed, had seized his wrist, and was hauling him also to his feet. "We've had a large night and we've got a large day ahead of us, starting not many hours off. We'll eat, clean up, and then if you can nap, you take a nap. Your meeting with the Grey Captains is set for noon."

"Meeting?" he echoed. He watched her begin to dress and mechanically reached for his shorts to follow her example. "I didn't even ask you yet about setting one up."

"A notice was sent out to all of the Captains while you were still in orbit," she said. "That was what kept me in Omalu yesterday, putting the last-minute finish to the paperwork for the meeting. I brought some meat up here with me, Hal Mayne. Not fish this time—meat! How about a rack of lamb for a combination breakfast and the proper dinner you probably didn't get around to having last night?"

Chapter

> > **57** < <

Amanda lifted her little air-space jitney off the ground with the two of them aboard; and Hal watched Foralie fall and dwindle swiftly away below them, feeling an emptiness in him. It was a moment before he associated that emptiness with how he had felt on his first days on Coby, and how he had felt as Donal, leaving this same house to go out to the stars.

"I'd thought I'd be staying at least a week," he said. Her profile was sharply sculpted against the steel-blue sky beyond the jitney's side window. "But if I can settle things with the Grey Captains today, I'd better get moving as soon after that as possible. Can we stop at the Spaceport by Omalu long enough for me to find out when the next ship is due to be headed back toward Sol and the Final Encyclopedia?"

"That won't be necessary," said Amanda. She was wearing a dark blue linen suit of skirt and jacket, light blue blouse and a single strand of small blue-gray coral beads; and somehow her dress today gave her distance from him and authority. "We're giving you a courier ship and pilot."

He was jolted. It was not the cost of a private ship to Earth that startled him. He could draw interstellar funds to handle that, from the Encyclopedia or probably even from the Exotics, if necessary. Very soon, such funds would have little use, in any case. It was the realization that other people had already begun to think of him in terms of someone whose work was now important enough not to be slowed down by the delays of commercial spaceship schedules. As he was still absorbing that idea, Amanda reached forward to the hand-luggage compartment in the firewall of the jitney; and, without looking down, brought out a sheaf of papers which she tossed into his lap.

"What's this?" he asked, picking it up. The set of pages made a stack at least three centimeters thick.

"A copy of the contract for you to read on the way to Omalu," she answered, with her eyes on the cloud layer ahead above which the jitney was now climbing.

Contract . . . he smiled sadly to himself. Laying the paper on his knees, he started to read. Such documents would also soon have as little use and purpose as funds of interstellar credit. But at the same time it was touching and a little awesome to hold the commitment of a world of people in his hands, in so small a form as a handful of printed sheets.

When they got to Omalu, Amanda landed the jitney beside others in the parking lot of the Central Administrative Offices. Here, rain had moved in once more; and the skies above them were an unbroken, dull-colored mass. They went in the wide, double-doored main entrance and Hal, looking up, saw the two stanzas of A. E. Housman's poem, "Epitaph on an Army of Mercenaries," cut into the stone of the wall just above the doors. The four somber lines of the first stanza caught in his mind, as always, as he passed underneath them.

> "*These, in the day when heaven was falling,*
>   *The hour when earth's foundations fled,*
> *Followed their mercenary calling*
>   *And took their wages and are dead. . . .*"

The room in which the meeting was to be held turned out to be one of the general audience rooms, where matters of concern to large areas of the Dorsai, if not to the planet as a whole, were debated. It was a chamber that could hold at least several hundred people and it was needed for the number who had come this day.

"That many Grey Captains?" Hal said softly to Amanda, as she led him to the platform at the center of the semicircular room; from which he looked out at the curved ranks of seats, each with a continuous table running in front of it, lifting to the back of the room.

"Active, reactivated, and also all those others who may not be Captains but have become responsible in what we're to do now," she answered, as quietly. "There's no one here who's not involved."

She stood with him on the platform at the lectern, until the conversation in the room died and all eyes came on them.

"I think you all recognize Hal Mayne," she said; her voice reaching clearly to the walls under the excellent acoustics of the chamber. "Rourke di Facino is Chairman of this meeting. I'll leave it to him, now."

She stepped down from the platform and went to sit in the only seat left empty in the first row. Hal recognized the pink, older face of Rourke di Facino in the center of the second row, directly opposite him. He also saw that the second row, and therefore Rourke himself, was directly level with him, leaving the first row, where Amanda sat, slightly below him and all rows from the third upward, above.

For a moment, a touch of impatience stirred in Hal. He could see so clearly now what must be done, without other choice, that meeting like this seemed redundant, a waste of valuable time. Then, surging up in him,

came the understanding that this gathering was no less important a rit-
ual than the service and the bagpipe music at the grave of James. He
realized that he was listening to the deathsong of a people and his impatience was lost in shame.

He was still standing at the lectern. To his left was also a table and chair,
the chair pulled back invitingly, the table empty. But he continued to
stand. He put his copy of the contract, which he was still carrying, on
the lectern's sloping face before him, and waited. Surprisingly, Rourke did
not leave his seat in the audience area, but spoke from there.

"This meeting is now in session," said the small man; his tenor voice
beat sharply upward upon the general silence of the room. "I'll announce
the time for general discussion when that time comes. Until then, matters will proceed according to the schedule set up by your steering com-
mittee."

He stared at Hal.

"We're honored to have you with us again, Hal Mayne," he said.

"Thank you," said Hal.

"Is there anything in particular you want to say before we get into the
planned business?"

Hal looked at him and around the room.

"Just . . . that I see you've anticipated me," he said.

There was a difference in attitude about those he now watched from
the lectern, a difference from what he had seen and felt, facing the smaller
number of Grey Captains he had talked to at Foralie. What he sensed
now was part of the larger difference he had observed earlier in the unplanted fields and all the other changes he had noticed on the Dorsai
since he had arrived.

The awareness of it struck him with a sharpness and a poignancy he
had not expected to feel. It drew him to identify it and the source of its
power upon him; and so, in that moment between his answer to Rourke
and Rourke's response to it, he saw more clearly the details of what was
before him.

It was as if the moment put itself on pause; as if time held its hand,
briefly. But it was not really time holding or being held, but his own mental processes that had been enormously speeded up. Donal had known
how to do that; and with the reawakening of Donal inside him, the ability came back to him.

So on that stretched-out second he noticed the clothes worn by those
there, while still individual and casual for the most part, were, like
Amanda's this morning, yet more formal than what he had seen the last
time he had faced the Captains.

In a subtle way, although what they were dressed in varied from individual to individual, there was a preponderance of quiet earth colors, blues, and grays, and a majority of open-throated upper garments with collars that laid down neatly, and a fresh cleanliness showed about everything they had on, that gave the impression that they were in a common uniform.

But then he saw that the impression had deeper roots than clothes alone. There was also an innate commonality in the way they sat and in the state of their bodies. All of them, even the older ones present, had the appearance of being healthy and in good physical condition. There was no excess fat to be seen, even on the more thick-boned and thick-chested of those present. They sat easily, upright and square-shouldered in their seats; and they sat still, with the relaxed stillness of those who have their selves under complete control.

. . . And there was also something even deeper in them than clothes and bodies that made them seem alike, for all that their faces were the most varied, one from another, of the faces in any gathering he had seen on the Younger Worlds or Old Earth. No two, from the pink of Rourke's, to the hard black of Miriam Songhai's, to the lightly-turned whiteness of Amanda's, were in any way the same. But still the likeness sat on them all; and he recognized its source finally in a similarity of attitude that gave them all a kinship.

For the first time, then, he saw something he had not caught earlier. A bleakness lived in them all, a bleakness that was so deep in each that it lay buried, below actions, below appearance, even below speech.

It was a bleakness hiding a silent and dry-eyed grief. A grief so intense and personal that they did not even speak of it to each other. A grief so fenced apart by custom and responsibility that it could be more easily seen in an unplowed field and unplanted flowers, than by anything said or done by these people. He felt it also in his own soul, recognizing it with that powerful empathy which he, as Donal, had gone through time to acquire.

Feeling it, he suddenly understood why he had shrunk from talking even to Amanda about that second existence of his as Paul Formain. Each time he had needed to start life again, either as Paul or as Hal, the process of abandoning the life in him that had been—even to begin again—had been traumatic.

The first time, when he had become Paul Formain, had been hardest of all. To strip the mind naked of knowledge and recollections, to throw the body into an unknown environment, trusting it to survive without all that had been a familiar anchor in reality—to accept the very universe as a plastic and changeable thing—had taken more courage than even

Donal had realized, until the actual moment of his changing. He had gone on, then, only because there had been no other choice.

Remembering that pain, he came abruptly to a full understanding of the pain in those he faced. It was not from what they would lose personally, or the destruction of their world and way, that they had labored to build for nearly three hundred years. It was from something even harder to bear; the knowledge that what they had lived with, and once thought of as secure for all foreseeable time, was now passing, would never come again, would in time be all but forgotten and buried forever.

The pride and dream of the Dorsai, like the dream of the Round Table before it, was to pass; and they were witnesses to its passing.

"We will proceed." The voice of Rourke was dry and emotionless in the room.

He shuffled together the papers lying before him on his section of the long table.

"We've lived by contracts for three centuries, here on the Dorsai," he said, briskly. "We'll die, if necessary, by proper contract. I take it you've had a chance to read the copy Amanda Morgan furnished you?"

"Yes," said Hal. "I should say, to begin with—"

The uplifted hand of Rourke stopped him.

"We can discuss the actual contract in a moment," Rourke said. "As it happens, this isn't an ordinary coming to terms; but an agreement which goes in many ways beyond anything any of us have entered into before. So, with your permission, we'll ask you a few questions first; and if the answers to those are satisfactory, we can move to direct discussion of the contract, itself."

"By all means," said Hal.

"Good," said Rourke.

He glanced right and left, as if he would have paused to gather the eyes of all his fellow Dorsai there, if that had been possible without his standing up and turning around. Then his gaze came back to Hal's.

"There are provisions in the contract," he said, "to require operating income for those engaged in the work of the contract, for the care of their dependents, and for themselves in case of death or disabilities received in the course of work, as well as some further provision for everyone from this world who's to be engaged in that work. But in the ultimate sense, there's no currency or credit in which payment can be made for the kind of service that's being asked of us, here. I believe you can agree with me on that?"

"Yes," said Hal. "It's true."

"Then," said Rourke, "on behalf of all of us, let me ask you the soldier's question. Under that circumstance, why should we risk everything we've ever had, to fight and die for people who can't or won't fight for themselves?"

"I don't think you'll find them unwilling to fight," said Hal slowly. "Some, right from the start, and more, as time goes on, are going to come and join you. In fact, I'd be surprised if you hadn't already made provision for that."

"We have, of course," said Rourke. "But my question still needs an answer."

"I'll try to answer it . . . ," said Hal. He stepped back mentally to let that in him which was Donal respond, and—as had happened involuntarily to him on his previous meeting with the Grey Captains—felt his earliest self take over.

"It's an old question, isn't it?" he heard himself say. "Never answered once and for all. The Classical Greek who drank hemlock, the Roman who fell on his sword, had reasons for what they did. More to the point, the blind king, John of Bohemia, had his reasons a thousand years ago when, at fifty-four, he went to help King Philip of France against the English at the battle of Crécy; and had his squires lead him into the thick of battle, that August day in 1346—a battle in which he had to know he would be killed."

He paused, searching the faces before him. But there was no puzzlement or uncertainty there, only a waiting.

"In my own case . . ." he went on, "it's clear to me why I'm going to give everything that I've got—not just my life and all I've ever had, but any future there is for me—to what has to be done, now. I could give you my own reasons for doing that. Or I could make out a list of reasons for that ancient Greek I talked about, that old Roman, and the blind king of Bohemia. But in the end, each set of reasons would total up to the fact that what was done was done because the person doing it was who he or she was. I do now what I do because I am what I am. You, all of you, will do what you choose to do because as individuals and as a community you are what you are; and have been what you are, since the race began."

He stopped speaking.

"That's all the answer I've got for you," he said.

"Yes," said Rourke unemotionally. "The other question is—where are you going to want us to fight?"

Hal's eyes met his on the level.

"You know I can't answer that," he said. "In the first place, that 'where' is going to be decided by what happens between now and the moment in which we all commit ourselves to action. In the second place—you know that I don't doubt your security. But in a matter like this, with the life and future of people on a number of worlds concerned, that's one piece of information I can't share with anyone until the time is right. When the moment comes for your involvement, I'll tell you; and at that time, if you want, you can make your decision to go along with it or not, since there'll be no way in any case that I could make you agree to go along with my plans if you didn't want to."

There was silence in the general audience room. Rourke had a stylus in hand and was making notes on the screen inset in the table-surface before him. A strange feeling of having been through this before took Hal, followed by another, even stranger sensation. Abruptly, it seemed to him that he could feel the movement of this small world around its distant sun, the movement of Fomalhaut amongst its neighboring stars, the farther movements of each of the human-inhabited worlds under their suns; and beyond even these he seemed to feel the great sidereal movement of the galaxy, wheeling them all inexorably onward to what awaited them further in time and space.

"I've so noted that in the contract," Rourke said, looking up again at Hal; "and that ends the questions we had for you, at this moment. Do you have any to ask us?"

"No," said Hal. "I'm sorry, but yes. You've made this a contract between all of you and me, with only the Final Encyclopedia to back me up. You'll have to understand that there's no way I'd ever be capable of ensuring the obligations this contract requires me to have toward you all. Even the Encyclopedia doesn't have the kind of resources that would allow it to guarantee what's set down there as due you in certain eventualities. Matters like rehabilitating this entire world, for example, if parts of it should be destroyed or damaged by enemy action in retaliation for your work under the contract; that's beyond the capabilities and wealth of several worlds, let alone something like the Encyclopedia—to say nothing of being beyond the resources of an individual like myself."

"We understand that," said Rourke. "But this contract is made for the historical record, as well as for legal reasons. It's the whole human race we're serving in this instance; and there's no legal machinery that would be capable of binding the human race as a whole, to these obligations. But an opposite party to a contract is a necessary element in an agreement like this. We consider that what's set down here will bind both you and the Final Encyclopedia morally, to the extent of what resources you do have, to observe its provisions. More than that, we can't expect—and don't."

"I see." Hal nodded. "On that basis, of course. Both Tam Olyn, for the

Final Encyclopedia, and I will be more than willing to agree to it."

"Then," said Rourke, "it only remains for this assembly to go through the contract itself with you, paragraph by paragraph, and make sure that the language of it means the same thing to you as it does to us."

So they did. The procedure took over three hours, and when Hal at last stepped down from the lectern, he found himself stiff-legged and light-headed. Amanda collected him from a number of the Captains who had come up to clasp hands with him; and led him toward the back of the room.

"I've got someone to introduce you to," she said.

She preceded him through the crowd of rising and departing people, many of whom also interrupted his passage to clasp his hand as he went up the levels toward the back of the chamber. As they got toward the back, the crowd thinned, and he saw a man standing by one of the entrances, looking in their direction. For a moment Hal's gaze sharpened; for it was almost as if he was seeing one of the Graeme twins alive again, as his Donal memory recalled them.

But when he got closer, he saw the differences. The man waiting for them was undeniably a Graeme—he had the straight, coarse black hair, the powerful frame and the dark eyes; but he was shorter than Ian or Kensie had been—shorter by several centimeters, in fact, than Hal himself. His shoulders sloped more than had Ian's or Kensie's and there was a more solid, less mobile, look about him. The impression he gave was of power and immovability, rather than of the rangy agility that had belonged to the twins, for all that this latter-day Graeme stood with all the balance and lightness of his lifetime's training. He was perhaps in his early thirties; and his eyes watched Hal with a controlled curiosity that Hal could understand, knowing how he, himself, must look to the other man.

But whatever his curiosity, the other was clearly too polite in Dorsai terms to ask direct questions of Hal when Amanda halted the two of them before him.

"Hal," said Amanda, "I want you to meet the driver of your courier ship. This is the current head of the Graeme household I told you about— Simon Khan Graeme. He just got in from New Earth, after all."

Simon and Hal clasped hands.

"I'm indebted to you for letting me be at Foralie," Hal said.

Simon smiled. He had a slow, but strongly warming smile.

"You did the old house honor by stopping there," he said, softly.

"No," Hal shook his head. "Foralie is something more than any single person can honor."

Simon's grip tightened briefly again before he released Hal's hand.

"I appreciate your saying that," he said. "So will the rest of the family."

"Maybe a time will come when I can meet the rest of the family," said Hal. "You'll be Ian's great-grandson, then?"

It was an incautious question, coming from someone who bore the family resemblance as plainly as Hal; and Hal saw a certainty wake and settle permanently in Simon's eyes.

"Yes," Simon answered. The words he did not speak—*and your own relationship to Ian, is . . . ?* hung on the air between them.

"I'm ready to go this moment if you want," Simon said. "There's nothing in particular for me to stop home for. Would you want to lift right away?"

"I'm afraid time is tight," said Hal. "I need to leave for Mara as soon as possible, now things are settled here. Now, about the costs involved in your services and this ship—"

"No, Hal," said Amanda, "any costs are part of the Dorsai's obligations under the contract, now. Simon'll take you where you need to go and stay with you from now on. Any expenses concerned with him or the ship should be routed back through our Central Accounting."

"Why don't all three of us have lunch, then," said Hal, "and after that, you can take care of whatever last-minute details there are with the ship? It'd give us a chance to talk, Simon."

"You did say you wanted to leave as soon as possible?" Simon asked.

"I'm afraid so."

"Then I think I'd better go directly to see about the vessel," said Simon. "I had a late breakfast in any case, and we'll have time to talk on our way, Hal Mayne. You two don't mind eating by yourselves, do you?"

Hal smiled.

"Of course not. Thank you," he said.

"Not at all," said Simon. "I'll see you at the ship, then. Excuse me."

He swung away. Hal felt Amanda's hand close on his, down between their bodies.

"He's thoughtful," said Hal. "I think he knew I wanted you to myself for a little longer."

"Of course," said Amanda. "Now, come along. I know where we'll eat."

The place she took him to was within the Terminal itself; but except for the occasional, muted sound of a liftoff or landing and the sight of the Spacepad beyond the one wall that was a window, the small room was as remote from the business of travelling as any restaurant they might have found in Omalu. It held only four tables; but whether because of arrangement by Amanda, or chance, the other tables were all empty.

The four tables sat next to a balcony on a sort of terrace which occupied most of the room; and looked down across a small reflecting pool at the window wall that showed the Landing Pad and space vehicles ready to lift. Among them, in the middle distance, Amanda pointed out the small silver shape of the courier ship assigned to Hal.

"I was found in a ship that size," said Hal, half to himself, "a much older model, of course."

He looked back to her from the field in time to see her draw her shoulders slightly into her body, as if she had felt a sudden chill.

"Will you ever have to do it again, do you think?" she asked.

Her voice was very nearly a whisper; and her eyes were focused not on him but past him. She gazed at some point in infinity.

"No," he answered, "I don't think so. This time I should go on being Hal Mayne until I die."

Her eyes were still fixed on that far, invisible point. He reached across the table and took her hand, that lay on the table's surface, into his own.

Her fingers tightened about his and her eyes came back to his, watching him strangely and longingly, like someone watching a loved one on a ship which is at last pulling out from shore.

"It's going to be all right," he said. "And even if it shouldn't, it wouldn't make a difference for us."

Her fingers tightened, and his.

They held together, as in the night just past, building a moment around themselves that made time once more seem to stand apart. And so they continued to sit, their fingers interlocked, with the clean air, the reflecting water and the field beyond the window's transparency enclosing them.

Again, as he had sensed it standing before the Grey Captains just a little while past, he felt the turning of the universe, the inexorable sweep of events forward into a future. That sweep was all about them now but it did not reach them. They stayed, as two people standing upon a floating hub might stay, unmoved by the spinning of the great wheel surrounding the place on which they were temporarily at rest.

Chapter

> > **58** < <

In the sunlight of Procyon, Mara floated below the courier ship like a blue-green ball, laced with the swirling white of clouds. Its resemblance to Earth, and the thought of Earth, itself, touched off a loneliness and sadness in Hal, mingled with the secret and bitter knowledge of guilt. If it had not been for the lack of a moon there would be little to identify Mara as not being Earth, the two worlds were so close in appearance and Mara so slightly larger. Even knowing it was not Earth, Hal was tempted to imagine that he was watching the planet on which, only a handful of years back, he had grown to physical maturity; and it came to him for the first time how deep was the emotional bond that tied him to the Mother World.

They had been holding on station for some twenty minutes; now the vessel's speaker system woke with the voice of a surface traffic-control unit.

"Dorsai JN Class Number 549371, you're cleared for self-controlled descent to referenced intersection, access code Cable Yellow/Cable Orange, private landing pad. Link for coordinates, please."

Simon Khan Graeme tapped the white access button of the vessel's navigation equipment to link it to the control unit's net; and under his hands, the small ship began to drop toward the surface far below. Hal had all but forgotten the advantage of a Dorsai ship and pilot that could take him to the very doorstep of his destination on any world, rather than hanging in orbit around a world and making him wait for shuttle service. He looked at the long, powerful fingers of Simon, resting their tips lightly upon the direct-control keys, touching . . . pausing . . . touching again.

The face of Mara came up toward them. Then they were suddenly through a high cloud layer, over blue ocean and slanting in toward a coastline. They were over land and dropping, and without warning, there was snow in the air about them. Below, dusted with snowcover, were rolling woodlands from horizon to horizon, with only the occasional white patch of a meadow-clearing to interrupt them; and their ship fell at last toward the still, ice-held ribbon of a minor river, and to what looked like an interconnected clump of graceful, pastel-colored buildings sitting back a small distance from its bank.

They sat down at last on a small weather-controlled Pad, showing the bare concrete of its surface to the clouded sky. Hal stepped out, followed by Simon, and found Amid, in a light gray robe, waiting for them.

"Amid, this is Simon Khan Graeme," Hal said, stepping aside to let Simon come forward. "He's driving me around these days, courtesy of the Dorsai."

"Honored to meet you, Simon Khan Graeme," said Amid.

"And I, you," said Simon.

In the Exotic fashion, Amid did not offer his hand; and Simon did not seem to expect it. Hal had forgotten how tiny the older man was. Seeing him now, as he stood looking up at Simon's face, Hal registered their difference in size with a mild emotional shock. It was almost as if Amid had aged and dwindled since Hal had last seen him. Standing together on the pad there was only still, dry, warm air surrounding them; but, beyond, about the house, over the river and above the trees, the snow was quietly sifting down in large, soft flakes.

It was strange to see it. Somehow, Hal had always thought of the two Exotic Worlds as caught in an endless summer of blue skies and green fields. With Simon, now, he followed Amid off the pad and into the house—if that was really the right word for such a wandering and connected collection of structures—and almost immediately found himself, as usual, without any way of telling whether he was indoors or outdoors, except for an occasional glimpse of snowy surface beyond a weather shield.

Simon was left behind in a suite of rooms that would be his until he left; and Amid took Hal on to find Rukh.

They located her after a little while, wrapped in what looked more like a colorful, antique quilt than anything else, seated by the side of a free-form pool surrounded by tall green plants that arched long, spade-shaped leaves over the lounging float upon which she was stretched out.

She threw off the quilt and sat up when she caught sight of them, her float adjusting to her new posture. She was wearing an ankle-length Exotic robe of maroon and white, the ample folds of which helped to hide how she had lost weight. Her olive skin looked sallow, but her face, in its gauntness, was more beautiful than ever. They came up to her and Hal reached down to kiss her. It was still a wire-strong young body that his arms enclosed; but thin, thin. . . .

He let go of her as Amid brought up floats for the two of them; and they sat down together.

"Thank you, Hal," she said.

"For what?" he asked.

"For being God's instrument to set me free."

"I had reasons of my own for doing it." His voice sounded roughly over the quiet pool—but hid, and effectively reburied, the chill of fury momentarily reawakened in him by the sight of how frail she was. "I needed you—I have plans for you."

"Not you, only." She looked at him closely. "You're a lot older, now."

"Yes." A soberness in him had replaced the first stirrings of remembered emotion. "I still need to explain to you, though, why it was I did something different than I told you I was going to do—back when the Militia was after us all, there outside Ahruma."

"You don't have to explain." She smiled. "I understood it, later. How you'd taken the only way there was to protect the rest of us and get the explosives safely into Ahruma, out of the Militia's reach. Once I understood, we scattered, and lost them. We stayed scattered until it was time to gather together again to destroy the Core Tap. But by doing what you did for us, you delivered yourself up to the Militia."

And she put one narrow hand softly on his arm.

"They carried me around on a silver platter in that jail—" he said, suddenly and bitterly, "compared to what they did to you!"

"But I was enguarded of God," her voice reproved him, gently. "You were not. There was no way they could touch me with anything they might do; any more than anything you might have done could have touched Amyth Barbage in the courtyard there, afterward."

An uncomfortableness moved in him—something as yet not understood, as the scene she spoke of came back to him. But she smiled at him again, gently and tolerantly, the way a mother might smile at a child who did not yet understand some completely ordinary matter, and the uncomfortableness was forgotten.

"You say you had reasons for doing what you did?" Her brown eyes watched him gravely. "What reasons were these?"

"I've still got them," he said. "Rukh—there's a place that needs you more than Harmony does."

He had expected her to object to that, and he paused, waiting. But she merely continued to look at him, patiently.

"Go on," she said.

"I'm talking about Old Earth," he told her. "The Others have been holding back from an all-out effort at getting control of the people there, because so many show that strong, apparently-innate resistance to their charismatic talent. You know about that. So Bleys and the rest have been marking time, hoping they could figure out a way around the problem, before trying to move in. But time's getting short for them, as well as us. They'll have to start pushing onto Old Earth, any time now."

"But they've already got people there, haven't they?" Rukh asked. "We were told on Harmony that a secret group of unknown but influential Earth locals are afraid of them; and that these've been running a campaign to prejudice the general mass of Earth's people against them?" She looked at him closely. "Or was that report just a divide-and-conquer technique, on Bleys' part?"

Hal nodded.

"But if they're not going to be able to convert any important percentage of the populace there, in any case," she went on, "why worry about them? Even if they put on what you call a push, it wouldn't look as if they'd have much luck."

"I'll tell you why." Hal sat back on his float. "When they had me in the Militia cell, I was running a high fever, and I hit a decision point in my life. The result was, I went into what you might want to call a sort of mental overdrive; and I realized a number of things I hadn't been able to see earlier."

She reached out to put her hand on his, softly, for a moment.

"You don't need to feel for me," he told her gently in return. "I told you they carried me around on a silver platter there, compared to what they did to you."

"No one seems to understand you—how you fight in a battle larger than any of ours," she murmured. "But I know."

"Some of us have some idea, I think," murmured Amid.

Hal curled his fingers around hers.

"One of the things I suddenly understood, then," he went on, "was that the charismatic talent, instead of being some special gift of genetic accident, given only to those who were Others, was really just a developed form of an ability that had been already sharpened to a fine edge on your own worlds, Harmony and Association. It was the ability to proselyte and convert—worked over, refined, and raised to a slightly-higher power. The only ones among the Others who really have it are those like Bleys Ahrens who are at least partial products of the Friendly Worlds."

"Friendly? The records say Bleys is a mixture of Dorsai and Exotic," Amid put in.

"I know that that's what the records say, as far as they say anything about him," answered Hal; "and I've got no hard evidence to the contrary. But I've met him; and in some ways I think I know him better than anyone else alive. He's all three Splinter Cultures—"

He broke off, abruptly. He had been about to say—just as I am myself—and had stopped just in time. Somehow, since the night with Amanda, he was not only more open to the universe, but also less self-guarded. But neither Rukh nor Amid seemed to notice the check in what he had been about to say. He went on.

"The point is," he said, "your Culture, Rukh, like the Cultures of the Exotics and the Dorsai, ties back into Old Earth Cultures at their roots; and there've been times in history before this when the Faith-holders have managed to stampede the general Culture around them. Look at the rise of Islam in the Near East in the seventh century, or the Children's Crusade, in the thirteenth. The Others won't need to control the Exotics directly, any more than they'll need to control the Dorsai, as long as the rest of the inhabited worlds are under their direct control. But Old Earth is a different problem than the Dorsai or the Exotics. It's like the Friendlies in that the Others can be satisfied there with a division of opinion about them that effectively keeps the world as a whole from organized opposition. But on Earth, unlike Harmony or Association, the Others can't afford open civil war. A peaceful Old Earth is still necessary as an economic pivot point for interworld commerce—which will have to go on. But if they can prevent Earth from becoming a potential enemy, short of crippling her economic roles, they'll control absolutely the interworld trade in skills—the base of the common interplanetary credit system that's let all our worlds hold together in one society this long."

He looked at Amid.

"The Exotics have always known that, haven't they, Amid?"

The wrinkles in Amid's face rearranged with his smile.

"We've known it for three hundred years," he said. "That's why, from the first, we made it our major effort—in a secular sense—to dominate interplanetary trade, so as to protect ourselves."

He sobered.

"That's why, Hal Mayne," he said, "you'll find us probably more hardheaded about this situation with the Others than anyone else. We know what it'll mean to have them in power, and we've known it from the first move they began to make as a group."

Hal nodded, turning back to Rukh.

"So," he said, "you see. The one world it's absolutely necessary for the Others to neutralize is Earth. The reason they've got to do that goes beyond the obvious fact that, in spite of the way the Old World was plundered and wasted in the early centuries of technological civilization, it's still far and away the most populous and resource-rich of the inhabited planets. The further reason's that, quite literally, it's the storehouse of the original gene pool, the basic source of the full-spectrum human being, from which we all came."

He stopped, and waited to see if she wanted to respond to all this he was saying, but she simply sat, relaxed and still, waiting for him to go on.

"If successful opposition to the Others is possible from any people at all, in the future," he went on, "it's most possible from the people of Old Earth. They've got their past all around them—there's no way they can be blinded to what the Others would take from them. Also, as their history shows, they're intractable, imaginative and—if they have to be— capable of giving their lives for what they consider a necessary goal, practical or otherwise. For the Others, the necessity is obvious—Earth is the one citadel which must be taken and controlled, to ensure a permanent end to all opposition to them. As a last resort—but only as a last resort—they'll destroy it rather than have it go against them. They've got no choice, if it comes to that." He paused. Rukh watched him. Amid watched him.

"In the long run, the Dorsai can be starved to death. The Exotic Worlds can be rendered helpless. The Friendlies can be kept fighting among themselves to the point where they'll never emerge as a serious threat. But Earth has to be either cancelled out or destroyed, if it's to be taken out of the equation at all. Nothing less's going to answer for what the Others need."

He stopped talking, hearing the echo of his own words in the following silence; and wondering if he had gone too far into rhetoric, so that Rukh would instinctively recoil from him and from what he was about to ask her to do. But when he paused she still merely sat silent, her gaze going a little past him to the greenery around the farther bend of the pool, then turned her eyes back a little to look into his.

"There's only one way for them to do this, as things stand," he told her. "They've got to work inside the social structure and pattern of Earth if they want to bring about a large enough division of opinion there to keep its people as a whole stalemated. And that's what they've been trying to do from the start with the individuals they've already got there, talking up their cause. But with things on all the other worlds moving to a showdown—"

He paused and shrugged.

Somewhere in the depths of the garden a soft chime rang once, and a small sound in Amid's throat intruded on the silence. Hal turned to look at the smaller man.

"I'm afraid I've been waiting for a chance to tell you something," Amid said. "You remember, you wanted it arranged for you to talk to the Exotics as a whole. A gathering of representatives from both Mara and Kultis are here, now; and they're ready to listen to you as soon as you can talk to them; by using single-shift phase, color-code transmission, we're going to try to make it possible for everyone on both worlds to see and hear you as you talk—this may not work, of course."

"I understand," said Hal. As phase-shifting went, the distance between the two worlds under the sun of Procyon was easily short enough to be bridged in a single shift. But the problem here would be the tricky business of ensuring that the distance between disassembly point and reassembly point of the transmitted data was bridged exactly at all moments during transmission. Even with no more than a single shift, and orbital points whose positions were continuously calculated from outside referents like that of Procyon itself, keeping precise contact over that distance for any period of time at all would be a staggering problem.

"However, what I really have to tell you is that Bleys Ahrens is here, here on Mara—here with us." Amid's voice held no change of expression. "He seems to be remarkably lucky at making guesses; because he apparently assumed you'd be coming to speak to us at this time. Under the circumstances, the sooner we finish talking here and let you go to that talking, Hal, the better. Everyone's ready, including Bleys. He's asked for a chance to address us, himself. We said yes."

"I wouldn't expect you to do anything else," answered Hal. "As far as his ability to guess my being here to talk, he could be using an intuitional logic, like the one Donal worked with."

Amid's eyes narrowed, and his gaze sharpened.

"You think the Others have that, too, now?"

"No . . . not the Others as a group," Hal said. "Bleys alone might—but almost certainly no one else. Or, he could just have made a lucky guess, as you say. It doesn't disturb me that he's going to talk. Before me—or after me?"

"Which would you prefer?" Amid's voice was still expressionless.

"Let him speak first."

Amid nodded; and Hal turned back to Rukh.

"As I was saying," he went on, "there's no real alternative for the Others, then. They're going to have to send to Earth some of their own number, plus as many disciples as they can who seem to be able to use something of the charismatic talent. With these they can try to make an all-out effort to enlist enough of Earth's population to build a division of opinion large enough to block anything that might be done by Earth people who could realize what the Others' control of the civilized worlds will mean."

She nodded.

"So," he said, "Bleys knows he's got people with the talent to do that; and his assumption will be we've got no one to stop them. But we do—

we've got you, Rukh; and those like you. I escaped from the Militia by getting out of an ambulance that was taking me to the hospital; and the reason I could escape was because the ambulance was caught in the crowd listening to you speak in that square at Ahruma. I heard you that day, Rukh—and there's nothing in the way of changing minds Bleys or any of his people can do, talking to an audience, that you can't match. In addition, you know other true holders of the Faith who could join you in opposing the crowd-leaders Bleys will be sending to Earth. Those others like you are there—on Harmony and Association. They'd never listen to me, if I tried to convince them to come. But you could—by coming yourself first and sending your words back to those who're left behind you as well as those you'll be speaking to on Earth."

He stopped speaking.

"Will you?" he asked.

She sat, looking at and through him for a little while. When she did begin to speak, it was so softly that if he had not been straining to hear her answer, he would have had difficulty understanding her.

"When I was in my cell alone, there, near the end of the time I was prisoner of the Militia," she said, talking almost as if to herself, "I spoke to my God and thanked Him for giving me this chance to testify for Him. I resigned myself once more to His will; and asked Him to show me how I might best serve Him in the little time I thought I had left."

Her eyes came back and focused penetratingly only on him.

"And His answer came—that I should know better than to ask. That, as one of the Faith, I already knew that the way I must travel at any time would always become plain and clear to me, once it was time for me to take it up. When I accepted this, a happiness came over me, of a kind I hadn't felt since James Child-of-God left the Command to die alone, so the rest of us might survive. You remember that, all, because you were the last to speak to him. I understood, then, that all I had to do was wait for my path to appear; for I knew now that it would do so, in its own good time. And I've been waiting, in peace and happiness, since then—"

She reached out to take Hal's hand.

"And it's a special joy to me, Hal, that you should be the one to point it out to me."

He held her hand; wasted, weak and fragile within his own powerful fingers and wide palm; and he could feel the strength that flowed between them—not from him to her, but the other way around. He leaned forward and kissed her again, then got to his feet.

"We'll talk some more as soon as I've done what I came here for," he said. "Rest and get strong."

"As fast as I can." She smiled; and smiling, she watched them go.

The amphitheater into which Amid brought Hal was deceptive to the eye. Hal's first impression was that it was a small place, holding at most thirty or forty people in the seats of the semicircle of rising tiers. Then he caught a slight blurring at the edges of his vision and realized that in any direction in which he looked, the faces of those in the audience directly in focus were clear and sharp; but that beyond that area of sharpness and clarity, there was a faint ring of fuzzily-visible faces. He seemed to be looking across an enormous distance at mere dots of people. With that he realized that the smallness of amphitheater and audience was a deception; and that a telescopic effect was bringing close any area he looked at directly to give the impression of smallness to an area that must hold an uncountable number of individuals—who each undoubtedly saw him at short distance.

Padma, the very aged Exotic he had met before, was standing on the low platform facing the seats of the amphitheater. The slim, erect, wide-shouldered shape of Bleys, in a loose, light gray jacket, over dark, narrow-legged trousers, towered over the aged Exotic. The illusion Hal had noticed before—that Bleys stood taller than human—was here again; but as Hal himself approached the two men, it was as if Bleys dwindled toward normal limits of size. Until at last when they were finally face-to-face, as had happened the last time they had met, he and the leader of the Others stood level, eye to eye, the same size.

It registered in Hal's mind that Bleys had changed since that last meeting, in some subtle way. There were no new lines of age in his features, no obvious alterations in any part of his features. But nonetheless there was an impression about him of having become worn to a finer point, the skin of his face drawn more taut over its bones. He looked at Hal quietly, remotely, even a little wistfully.

"Hal Mayne," said Amid at Hal's elbow, as the two of them reached Padma and Bleys, "would prefer that Bleys Ahrens speaks first."

"Of course," Bleys murmured. His eyes rested for a moment longer in contact with Hal's. It seemed to Hal that in Bleys' expression, there was something that was not quite an appeal, but came close to being one. Then the Other's gaze moved away, to sweep out over the amphitheater.

"I'll leave you to it, then," said Hal.

He turned and led the two Exotics back off the platform to some chair-floats that were ranked on the floor beside it. They sat down, the back of their floats against the wall that backed the platform. They sat, looking out at the amphitheater and the side and back of Bleys.

Standing alone on the stage, he seemed once more to tower, taller than any ordinary human might stand, above audience and amphitheater, alike.

Unexpectedly he spread his long arms wide, at shoulder height, to their fullest extent.

"Will you listen to me?" he said to the Exotic audience. "For a few moments only, will you listen to me—without preconceptions, without already-existing opinions, as if I were a petitioner at your gates whom you'd never heard before?"

There was a long moment of silence. Slowly, he dropped his arms to his side.

"It's painful, I know," he went on, speaking the words slowly and separately, "always, it is painful when times change; when everything we've come to take for granted has to be reexamined. All at once, our firmest and our most cherished beliefs have to be pulled out by the roots, out of those very places where we'd always expected them to stand forever, and subjected to the same sort of remorseless scrutiny we'd give to the newest and wildest of our theories or thoughts."

He paused and looked deliberately from one side of the amphitheater to the other.

"Yes, it's painful," he went on, "but we all know it happens. We all have to face that sort of self-reexamination, sooner or later. But of all peoples, those I'd have expected to face this task the best would have been the people of Mara and Kultis."

He paused again. His voice lifted.

"Haven't you given your lives, and the lives of all your generations, to that principle, ever since you ceased to call yourselves the Chantry Guild and came here to these Exotic Worlds, searching for the future of humankind? Not just searching toward that future by ways you found pleasant and palatable, but by all the ways to it you could find, agreeable or not? Isn't that so?"

Once more he looked the audience over from side to side, as if waiting for objection or argument; and after a moment he went on.

"You've grown into the two worlds of people who dominated the economies of all the inhabited worlds—so that you wouldn't have to spare time from your search to struggle for a living. You've bought and sold armies so that you'd be free of fighting, and of all the emotional commitment that's involved in it—all so you'd have the best possible conditions to continue your work, your search. Now, after all those many years of putting that search first, you seem ready to put it in second place to a taking of sides, in a transient, present-day dispute. I tell you frankly, because by inheritance I'm one of you, as I think you know, that even if it should be the side I find myself on that you wish to join, at the expense of your long struggle to bring about humanity's future, I'd still stand here as I do now, and ask you to think again of what you have to lose by doing so."

He stopped speaking. For a long moment there was no sound at all; and then he took a single step backward and stood still.

"That's all," he said quietly, "that I've come here to say to you. That's all there is. The rest, the decision, I leave to you."

He stopped speaking and stood in silence, looking at them a moment longer. A long moment of silence hung on the air of the amphitheater. Then he turned and walked off the platform to the chairs from which Hal, Amid and Padma rose to face him.

Behind him, in the amphitheater, the silence continued.

"I'd like to speak privately to these people," said Hal.

Bleys smiled, a gentle tired smile, nodding.

"I'll see to it," said Amid, answering even before Bleys had nodded. He turned to the Other. "If you'll come with me?"

He led the tall man out by the door in through which he had brought Hal, a short few minutes earlier. Hal stepped up on the platform, walked to the front of it and looked at the audience.

"He doesn't hope to convince you, of course," Hal said to them. "He does hope he might be able to lull you into wasting time which his group can put to good use. I know—it's not necessary to point that out to you; but having been in the habit of being able to take the time you need to consider a question sometimes makes it hard to make decisions in little or no time."

He was searching his mind for something to say that would reach them as he had finally reached the Grey Captains at Foralie; and he suddenly realized that what he was waiting for was some response from them to what he had already said. But this was not a single room with a handful of people all within easy sight and sound of his voice. Here, he must simply trust to his words to do the job he had set them, as Bleys had been forced to do a few moments before. He remembered the mental image that had come to him in his final moments before parting with Amanda— of being for a brief time at the hub of a great, inexorably-turning wheel. But this place in which he now stood was no longer at that hub—nor were these who sat here as his audience.

"The river of time," he said, "often hardly seems to be moving about us until we see the equivalent of a waterfall ahead or suddenly find the current too strong for us to reach a shore. We're at that point now. The currents of history, which together make up time's current as a whole, have us firmly in their grip. There's no space left to look about at leisure for a solution, each in his own way. All I can do is tell you what I came to say.

"I've just come from the Dorsai," he said. "They've made their preparations there now for this last fight. And they will fight, of course, as they've always fought, for what they believe in, for the race as a whole—and for you. What I've come to ask you is whether you're willing to make an equal contribution for the sake of what you've always believed in."

He suddenly remembered the first stanza of the Housman poem, carved above the entrance to the Central Administrative Offices in Omalu on Dorsai. He shook off the memory and went on.

"They've agreed to give up everything they have, including their lives, so that the race as a whole may survive. What I've come to ask of you is no less—that you strip yourselves of everything you own and everything you've gained over three hundred years so that it may be given away to people you do not know and whom you've never spoken to; in the hope that it may save, not your lives, but theirs. For in the end you also will almost surely have to give your lives—not in war, like the Dorsai, perhaps—but give them up nonetheless. In return, all I have to offer you is that hope of life for others, hope for those people to whom you will have given everything, hope for them and their children, and their children's children, who may—there can be no guarantee—once more hope and work for what you hope now."

He paused again. Nothing had changed, but he no longer felt so remote from his audience.

"You've given yourselves for almost three hundred years to the work and the hope that there's a higher evolutionary future in store for the human race. You haven't found it in that time; but the hope itself remains. I, personally, share that hope. I more than hope—I believe. What you look for will come, eventually. But the only way to it now is a path that will ensure the race survives."

The feeling of being closer to his audience was stronger now. He told himself that he was merely being moved by the emotion of his own arguments, but nonetheless the feeling was there. The words that came to him now felt more like words that must move his listeners because of their inarguable truth.

"There was a time," he said, "in the stone age, when an individual who thought in terms of destruction could possibly smash in the heads of three or even four human beings before his fellows gathered about him and put it beyond his power to do more damage. Later, in the twentieth century, when the power of nuclear explosives was uncovered and developed for the first time, a situation was possible in which a single person, working with the proper equipment and supplies, could end up with the capability of destroying a large metropolitan area, including possibly several millions of his fellow human beings. You all know these things. The curve that measures the destructive capability of an individual has climbed from the moment the first human picked up a stick or stone to use as a weapon, until now we've come to the point where one man—Bleys—can threaten the death of the whole race."

He took a deep breath. "If he achieves it, it won't be a sudden or dramatic death, like that from some massive explosion. It will take generations to accomplish, but at its end will be death, all the same. Because for Bleys and those who see things as he does, there is no future—only the choice between the present as they want it, or nothing at all. He and those like him lose nothing, in their own terms, by trading a future that is valueless to them, for a here and now that sees them get what they want. But the real price of what they want is an end to all dreams—including the one you all have followed for three hundred years. You, with all the wealth and power you still have, cannot stop them from getting what they want; the Dorsai can't stop them; nor, by themselves, can all the other groups and individuals who are able to see the death that lies in giving up dreams of the future. But all together we can stop them—for the saving of those who come after us."

He let his eyes search from one side of what he saw as the amphitheater to the other.

"So I'm asking that you give me everything you have—for nothing in return but the hope that it may help preserve, not you, but what you've always believed in. I want your interstellar credit, all of it. I want your interstellar ships, all of them. I want everything else that you've gained or built that can be put to use by the rest who will be actively fighting the Others from now on—leaving you naked and impoverished to face what they will surely choose to do to you in retaliation. You must give it, and I must take it; because the contest that's now shaping up can only be won by those who believe in the future, if they work and struggle as one single people."

He stopped talking.

"That's all," he said, abruptly.

He turned and left the platform. There was no sound from the audience to signal his going. Amid was standing waiting for him, but Padma had already left, apparently.

In silence they left the amphitheater through a doorway different from the one by which they had entered. Hal found himself walking down a long, stone-walled corridor, with an arched roof and a waist-high stretch of windows deeply inset in the full length of wall on his right. They were actual windows, not merely open space with weather control holding the cold and the wind at bay; and their glass was made up of diamond-shaped panes leaded together. The stone was gray and cold-looking; and beyond the leaden panes, he could see in the late-afternoon light that the white flakes were still falling thickly, so that the snow was already beginning to soften and obliterate the clear outlines of trees, paths and buildings.

"How long, do you think, before the vote will be in, from both worlds?" Hal asked Amid.

The small, old face looked sideways and up at him.

"It was in before you landed."

Hal walked a few steps without saying anything.

"I see," he said, then. "And, when Bleys appeared, it was decided to hold up the results until everyone had heard what he had to say."

"We're a practical people—in practical matters," said Amid. "It was that, of course. But also, everyone wanted to see and hear you speak, before a final announcement of the decision. Wouldn't you, yourself, want to meet the one person who would deal with the end of everything you'd ever lived for?"

"All the same," said Hal, "the option was reopened for them to change their minds, if Bleys was able to bring them to it. Well, was he?"

"Except for a statistically-insignificant handful, no, I'm told." Amid's eyes rested on him as they walked. "I think that in this, Hal Mayne, you may fail to understand something. We knew there was nothing Bleys Ahrens could say that would change any of us. But it's always been our way to listen. Should we change now? And do you really think so badly of us that you could believe we'd fail to face up to what we have to do? We here have our faith, too—and our courage."

Amid turned his gaze away from him, looking on ahead to the end of the corridor, to the double doors of heavy, bolted wood, standing ajar on a dimness that baffled the eye.

"It'll take a day or two for our representatives to get together with you on details," the small man went on. "Meanwhile, you can be discussing with Rukh Tamani your plans for her crusade on Old Earth. In three days, at most, your work will be done here, and then you'll be free to go on to wherever you've planned to, next. Where is that, by the way?"

"Earth . . . ," said Hal.

But his mind was elsewhere; and his conscience was reproaching him. He had felt a small chill on hearing that Bleys was here; and that chill had come close to triggering an actual fear in him when he saw the man standing before those assembled in the amphitheater, and heard him speak. It was no longer a fear that Bleys might have the talent and the arguments to out-talk him; but a fear that the Exotics, even recognizing the falsity of Bleys' purpose, would still seize on what the Other said as an excuse not to act, not to join the fight openly until it was too late for them and everyone else.

He had been wrong. From the time he had been Donal, he thought now, one failing had clung to him. With all he knew, he could still find it in him to doubt his fellow humans; when, deeply, he knew that anything that was possible to him must be possible to them, as well. For a little while, there in the amphitheater, he had doubted that the Exotics had it in them to die for a cause, even for their own cause. He had let himself be prejudiced by the centuries in which they had seemed to want to buy peace at any price; and he had forgotten their dedication to the purpose for which they had bought that peace.

Now he faced the unyielding truth. It was far easier for anyone simply to fight, and die fighting; than to calmly, cold-bloodedly, invite the enemy within doors and sit waiting for death so that others might live. But that was what the people of Mara and Kultis had just voted to do.

Amid had been right in what he had just said.

With this last act, all of them, including the unwarlike little man now walking beside him, had demonstrated a courage as great as any Dorsai's, and a faith in what they had lived for during these last three centuries as great as that of any Friendly. Out of the corner of his eyes he watched Amid moving down the corridor; and in his mind he could see—not himself—but the ghosts of Ian and Child-of-God walking on either side of his ancient and fragile companion.

"Yes," he said, breaking the silence once more as they came to the double doors. "Earth. There's a place there I've been trying to get back to for a long time now."

Chapter

> > 59 < <

They went on together, passing from the light of day into the relative obscurity of the space lying beyond the double doors, which closed behind them.

Within, warmly lit by an artificial illumination that in here was more than sufficient, but which had been unable to compete with the cloudy brightness of the late winter afternoon beyond the leaded windows, was a hexagonal room with a slightly-domed ceiling, under which nine Exotics were seated about a large, round table. Their robes warmed the interior space with rich earth colors in the soft light. Two chair-floats at the table sat empty; and it was to these that Amid brought Hal and himself.

Sitting down, Hal looked about at those there, four of whom he recognized. There were the old features of Padma, the small, dark ones of Nonne, the dry ones of Alhanon and the friendly expression of Chavis— all of those who had talked to him on his last visit here, sitting with him and Amid on a balcony of Amid's home. The others he saw were strangers to him; strangers with quiet Exotic faces having little to make them stick in the mind at first glance.

"Our two worlds are at your disposal now, Hal Mayne," said the age-hoarsened voice of Padma; and Hal looked over at the very old man. "Or has Amid already told you?"

"Yes," said Hal, "I asked him, on the way here."

Nonne started to say something, then stopped, looking at Padma.

"I won't forget," said Padma, looking briefly at her. "Hal, we feel you ought to understand one thing about our future cooperation with you. We don't sign contracts like the Dorsai, but three hundred years of keeping our word speaks for itself."

"It does," said Hal. "Of course."

"Therefore"—Padma put his hands flat on the smooth, dark surface of the table before him as if he would summon it to confirm his words— "you have to understand that we've chosen to go your way in this struggle, simply because there was no other way we could find to go. What's ironical is that the very calculations we'd been using to find out if you ought to be followed, now unmistakably show that you should be—primarily because of the effect of our own decision on the situation."

The hoarseness in his voice had been getting worse as he talked. He stopped speaking and tapped the tabletop before him with a wrinkled forefinger. A glass of clear liquid rose into view; and he drank from it, then continued.

"It's only right to tell you that there was a great feeling of reservation in many of us about following you," he said, "—not in me, personally, but in many of us—and that reservation was a reasonable one. But you should know us well enough to trust us, now that we've voted. Effectively, those reservations don't exist any longer. Irrevocably and unchangingly, we're now committed to follow wherever you lead, whatever the cost to us."

"Thank you," said Hal. "I know what that voting has to have meant to you all. I appreciate what you've done."

He leaned forward a little over the table, becoming suddenly conscious of how his greater height and width of shoulders made him seem to loom over the rest of them.

"As I said out there, what I'll probably have to ask your two worlds to give me," he said to them all, "to put it simply, is everything you have—"

"One more moment, if you don't mind," Padma broke in.

Hal stopped speaking. He turned back to Padma.

"We know something of what you've got to tell us," Padma said. "But first, you ought to let us give you some information we can share with you now; we couldn't tell you, earlier, before we were committed to working with you."

There was a small, tight silence about the table.

"All right," said Hal. "Go on. I'm listening."

"As I just said, what we have is yours, now," said Padma. "That includes some things you may know we have, but which are possibly a great deal more effective than you might have guessed."

His old, dry-throated voice failed him again. He reached for the filled glass on the table before him and sipped once more from its contents. Putting the glass down, he went on more clearly.

"I'm talking," he said, "of our ability to gather information—and our techniques for evaluating it. I think you'll be interested to hear, now, what we've concluded about both you and Bleys Ahrens."

"You're right." Hal stared hard into the old eyes.

"The result," Padma went on with no change in his tone, "of that gathering and evaluating gave us a pattern on each of you that could help you now to define the shape of the coming conflict."

He paused.

"The pattern on Bleys shows him aware of his strength and deter-

mined to use it in economical fashion—in other words, in such a way that
he and the Others can't lose, since they'll simply operate by maintaining
their present advantage and increasing it when they can, until there's no
opposition to them left. This is a sort of dealing from strength that seems
particularly congenial to Bleys' temperament. He seems to believe he and
his people are fated to win; and, far from glorying in it, he seems to find
a sad, almost melancholy pleasure in the inevitability of this that suits
his own view of himself and reality. Apparently, he regards himself as
being so isolated in the universe that nothing that happens in it can either much raise or lower his spirits."

"Yes," murmured Hal.

"This isolation of his bears an interesting resemblance to your own iso-
late character," said Padma, gazing at Hal. "In many ways, in fact, he's remarkably like you."

Hal said nothing.

"In fact," Padma went on, "to a large extent he's justified in his ex-
pectations. The ongoing factors of history—the forces that continue from
generation to generation, sometimes building, sometimes waning—now
seem to be overwhelmingly on the side of the Others. Our own discipline
of ontogenetics, which we evolved to help us solve such problems as this,
instead simply produces more and more proofs that Bleys is right in what
he believes."

Hal nodded, slowly; and Padma took a moment to drink once more.

"If Bleys is the epitome of all that is orthodox aiming to win and moving to that end," Padma went on, "you, who should in any sane universe
be the champion of what has been tried and established, are just the opposite. You are unorthodoxy personified. We have no real data on you
before the time you were picked up as a mystery infant from a derelict
ship in Earth orbit. You show no hard reason why you should emerge as
the leader of an effort to turn back something like Bleys and the Others; but somehow all those opposed to Bleys have enlisted to follow
you—even those of us on our two worlds, who've striven to think coolly
and sensibly for three hundred years."

He paused and drew a deep breath.

"We," he said, "of all people, don't believe in mysteries. Therefore,
we've had to conclude that there must be some mechanism at work here
in your favor that we can't see and don't understand. All we can do is
hope that it's equally invisible to, and equally beyond the understanding
of, Bleys Ahrens."

"Assuming you're right," said Hal, "I'll join you in that hope."

"Which brings us to your pattern—what we know of it," said Padma.

"What we have, in fact, concluded from the information we've processed—and we assume that someone like Bleys must have also come to the same conclusions—is that the only course open to you is to use the Dorsai as an expeditionary force against whatever military forces the Others may be able to gather and equip."

He paused and looked at Hal.

"Go on," said Hal, levelly. "What you've said so far is only an obvious conclusion in the light of the present situation. It doesn't call for any special access to information, or a Bleys-like mind, to read that as a possibility."

"Perhaps not," said Padma. "However, it's equally obvious then that, either way, such a use on your part can't end in anything but failure. On the one hand, if you hold back your Dorsai until the forces that the Others are capable of gathering are ready to move, then not even the Dorsai will be able to handle that much opposition. Am I right?"

"Perhaps," said Hal.

"On the other hand," Padma went on, "if you spend this irreplaceable pool of trained military personnel in raids to destroy the Others' forces while those forces are forming and arming, the gradual attrition of even such experienced fighters as the Dorsai in such encounters will eventually reduce their numbers to the point where there won't be enough of them left to pose any real opposition to the Others' strength. Isn't that also an inescapable conclusion?"

"It's a conclusion, certainly," Hal answered.

"How, then," said Padma, "can you hope to win?"

Hal smiled—and it was not until he saw the faint but unmistakable changes of expression on the other faces around the table that he realized how that smile must appear to them.

"I can hope to win," he said slowly and clearly, "because I will not lose. I know those words mean nothing to you now. But if it was possible for you to understand what I mean by that, there'd be no war facing us; and the threat posed against us by the existence of the Others would've already been solved."

Padma frowned.

"That's no answer," he said.

"Then let me offer you this one," said Hal. "The forces of history are only the internal struggles of a human race that's determined, above all, to survive. That much you ought to be able to understand yourselves, from your own work and studying to understand what is humanity. Apply that understanding equally to the large number of forces that seem to operate in favor of the Others and to the relatively-small number that seem to operate in the favor of the survival of us—we who oppose them—and you'll see which forces must wax and which must wane if survival for the race as a whole is to be achieved."

He stopped, and his words echoed in his own ears. I'm talking like an Exotic myself, he thought.

"If what you're saying is the truth," Nonne broke out as if she could not hold herself silent any longer, "then the situation ought to cure itself. We don't need you."

He turned his smile on her.

"But I'm one of those forces of history I mentioned," he said, "—as Bleys is. We're effects, not causes, of the historical situation. If you got rid of either one of us, you'd simply have a slightly-different aspect of the same problem with someone else in replacement position. The truth is you can't get rid of what each of us represents, any more than you can get rid of any of the other forces at work. All you can do is choose your side; and I thought I'd just pointed out to you that you've already done that."

"Hal," said Amid softly at his side, "that was an unnecessary, if not somewhat discourteous, question."

Hal sobered, turning to the small man.

"Of course. You're right. I withdraw it—and apologize," he said to Nonne. He looked at Padma. "What else have you got to tell me from this body of information you've gathered and evaluated?"

"We've got detailed data from all the sites on the worlds where the Others are gathering and training their soldiers," said Padma, "and from all the areas where work is going on to produce the spaceships and matériel to equip them. Hopefully, this will be sufficient for your needs, although of course there's information we can't get—"

"It's not that so much," said Hal, almost unthinkingly, "as that there's other information I have to gather for myself."

"I don't understand," said Padma.

Around the table they were regarding him oddly.

"I'm afraid," said Hal slowly, "I'd have trouble explaining it to your satisfaction. Basically, it's just that I'll have to see these places and the people working in them for myself. I'll be looking for things your people could never give me. You'll just have to take my word for it, that it's necessary I go and see for myself."

The concept of the Final Encyclopedia had been forming like a palpable mass in his mind as he spoke and the sense of the immeasurably-vast, inchoate problem with which he had been wrestling these last years crouched like a living thing before him. There was no way of explaining to Exotics that the battleground he now envisioned encroached literally upon that territory which encompassed the human soul.

"You'll simply have to trust me," he repeated, "when I say it's necessary."

"Well," said Padma heavily, "if you must . . . we still have courier ships making the trips back and forth between these two worlds of ours and our embassies on the other worlds. We can supply you with a ship."

Hal breathed out evenly and lowered his gaze to the polished pool of darkness that was the tabletop.

"A ship won't be necessary," he heard himself say, as if from some distance. "The Dorsai've already given me one—and a driver."

He continued to stare into the darkness of the tabletop for a moment longer, then slowly raised his eyes and looked back once more at Amid. He smiled again, but this time the smile faded quickly.

"It seems that trip of mine to Old Earth is going to have to wait a little longer, after all," he said.

His perception was correct. Months later, standard time, he had still not stepped within the orbit of Earth; and he was running for his life through back alleys of Novenoe, a city on Freiland.

The months of visiting most of the Younger Worlds, slipping in with his Dorsai courier ship and going secretly to make firsthand observations at the factories and installations in which the Others were putting together the soldiers and matériel they would use in their war effort, had worn him thin—almost as thin as he had been on Harmony when the Militia had caught him.

But this was a different thinness. With his admission at last to Amanda of his first identity as Donal Graeme—that identity that had been withheld from him deliberately by his Donal-self until he should pass through the learning process of growing up as Hal Mayne—he had finally come very close to replicating Donal's old physical abilities and strengths, though he still necessarily fell short of the strength and skill of an adult Dorsai who had maintained his training daily since birth. Still, what he had accomplished flew in the face of all physiological experience among the Dorsai. That after twenty-odd years of living untrained by Dorsai standards (even giving him credit for what Malachi Nasuno had taught him up into his sixteenth year) it was simply beyond reason that in only a few months he had been able to achieve reflexes and responses that came at all close to being as effective as Simon Graeme's, for example.

Simon himself had commented on it. It had been impossible to hide the development in Hal from the other man, under the conditions of the close-knit existence they shared aboard the courier vessel with Amid. The old Exotic had been riding with them as a necessary living passport for Hal to the Exotic embassies from which they drew information and assistance. That development was, as Simon hinted, at once impossible and an obvious fact, and Simon had compared the achievement with that of some of the martial artists down through history who had become legendary in their own times. Beyond that comment, the current titular head of the Graeme family seemed content to leave the matter for later explanation. Hal had no choice but to do the same; although to him, too, it was a cause for wonder and a puzzle not as easy to accept as it seemed to be for Simon.

His own temporary conclusion was that it could be some sort of psychic force at work upon him in response to Donal's emergent identity; a psychic force that could shape even bone and muscle, if necessary. Cletus Grahame, nearly two hundred years before, had been supposed to have rebuilt his damaged knee by some such means. At the same time, something in Hal strongly insisted that there was more to it than the simple term "psychic force" implied; and the unknown element nagged at him.

But there had been no time to ponder this up to now, and there was certainly none at this present moment. Running easily but steadily, like a hunger-gaunted wolf dodging through the dark and odoriferous passages that hardly deserved the names of streets and alleys in this quarter of ruined buildings, Hal felt the intuition that had been Donal's numbering and placing in position about him the pursuers that were now closing in.

He had gotten inside the spaceship yards he had gone to Freiland to see, and identified the vessels being built there as military transports. But after these many months, the forces controlled by the Others on all their worlds were alerted and on watch for him; and he had been both identified and pursued by the so-called executive arm of the Novenoe police. His only hope of escape from them lay in the courier ship waiting for him in the yard of a decayed warehouse. He was leading his pursuers toward it now, simply because he had no other choice. The invisible calculations of intuitive logic that had woken in him from the Donal part of himself told him there was no way he could reach the vessel before those hunting him would close in on him.

His estimate was that there were between thirty and forty of the "executives"—and they would know this part of Novenoe better than he did.

He ran on—steadily, still at three-quarter speed, saving his strength for the moment in which he would need it. The last leg of his journey led over broken, but still high, security fences; and across forgotten yards full of abandoned equipment rusting in the darkness. As, still running, he reached the last fence but two, flung up a hand to catch its top edge and vaulted over, he heard ahead of him the small, impatient sounds of at least two police in wait for him in the darkness of the littered yard.

He crouched down and went like a ghost, feeling his way ahead and around the debris, large and small, that littered his way. His aim was to bypass those in wait for him if he could; but one of them—evidently cramped and weary with waiting—rose and blundered directly into his way as Hal tried to pass.

Hal felt the heat of the body approaching and both smelled and heard the other's breath. There was no time to go around, so he rose from the ground and struck out, swiftly.

The "executive" dropped, but grunted as he fell; and immediately a thin, rapier-like guide-beam of visible light, of the sort used to direct the night-firing of a power weapon, began playing about the yard like a child's toy searchlight. Hal snapped a shot with the silent, but low-powered, void pistol that was the only weapon he carried, at the source-point of the light, and the beam vanished. But the damage was done. The darkness now would be alive with the electronic screaming of alarms and communications, pinpointing his position to his pursuers.

He went to full speed. Even then, clearing the fence before him into the yard next to the one where the courier ship waited, his senses of hearing and smell counted five of those who sought him, on hand to block his way. They were too many to slip by. He could hear each now, plainly, while they would not be able to hear him; but they would have heat-sensing equipment and with it could see him as a glow amidst the scattered junk filling the yard; a glow imprecise in outline and occulted by the shapes of the junked vehicles and trash filling the yard, but establishing his general position, nonetheless.

The choice was no choice. If he wanted to reach the ship, there was no way to do it unobserved. He must fight his way through those who were here to take him. He dropped to the gritty earth underfoot to catch his breath for a second.

It needed little enough thought to see how he had to do it. His position was hardly different from that of a man in a river, and about to be swept over a waterfall, who calls to a friend safe on the bank to jump in and help him. But the hard facts of the matter were, he knew he was more important to the large work yet to be done than was Simon Graeme. Nor would Simon—or any other Dorsai—thank him for not calling for help when it was needed, under such circumstances.

Savagely, he pressed the button at his waist that would send out a single gravity pulse to the ship's sensors and summon Simon to his aid.

Having called, he gave himself wholly over to survival, dropping flat in the dirt of the yard and squirming his way forward toward the farther fence. He could hear the five men closing in upon him; and knew that they would shortly be reinforced. He stopped, suddenly, finding himself boxed. To move in any direction from the ruins of a tractor behind which he was presently sheltering was to put himself into the open field of fire from one of the "executives." Now, he must make gaps in their circle about him, if he wanted to pass through.

He did not need a visible guide-beam for the weapon he carried. He could aim accurately by ear; and the silentness of the void pistol in use would help to hide the point of origin of its killing pulse. He shot one man, and shifted quickly into the gap this made, only to find himself boxed again. And, so it began. . . .

It was an ugly little battle, fought in the dark, at point-blank range, with his opponents' numbers being reinforced faster than his accurate fire could clear them out of his way. A bitterness stirred inside him; the bitterness of someone who has had to fight for his life for too many years, on too many occasions, and who is weary of the unceasing attacks that give him no rest. Crouching and moving through the dark, he felt for the first time in his experience the burden he carried—not the physical but the emotional weight of his three lifetimes.

He had fought his way now for half the remaining distance between him and the last fence. He was less than five or six meters from it; and the number of his enemies in the yard had grown to more than fifteen. He stopped in passing over the body of one of those he had just taken out of the action and picked up the heavy shape of the power rifle the man had been using. And at that moment, Simon came over the wall from the ship.

Hal heard him come; and knew who he was. The "executives," hearing nothing, suspecting nothing, were caught by void-pistol fire from a new angle and assumed that Hal had reached the fence. They changed direction to move in on the position Simon now held.

Hal gave them a slow count of five. Then, standing up in the darkness and holstering his nearly depleted void pistol, he triggered the power rifle he had picked up onto continuous fire; and swept it like a hose of destruction across the front of those making the sounds of movement through the yard.

There was sudden, appalled inactivity among the weapons of those still left unhurt among the attackers. In that moment, Hal threw the power rifle from him, far across the yard, to where the clatter of its fall would draw any fire well away from Simon and himself—and ran for Simon's position, hurdling the barely-seen obstacles in his path.

They were suddenly together, two patches of darker dark in the gloom. "Go!" grunted Simon.

Hal went up and over the fence, without pausing, checked on the far side, and swung about, void pistol held high over the fence to cover Simon as the other followed, landing beside him. They ran together for the courier ship. The outer-airlock door yawned before them, with Amid ducking hastily back out of their way, then closed behind them. Simon hurled himself at the controls; and the courier ship bucked explosively into motion—upward into the night sky.

There were police craft holding station overhead, in positions up to four kilometers of altitude. But barely above the rooftops, Simon went into phase-shift; and suddenly the silence of orbital space was around them. Hal, who had been standing, holding to the back of the copilot's seat against the savage acceleration off the ground, let go and sagged limply backward into one of the backup seats of the control compartment.

He felt a touch on his elbow, turned his head to look into the face of Amid, standing beside him.

"You need sleep," said Amid.

Hal glanced again at Simon, but Simon had already finished his plot for a second shift, and the stars jumped as they watched, to a new configuration in the screens about them. Ignoring them, Simon reached to the plotting board for the next shift and Hal stood up.

"Yes . . . ," he said.

He let Amid lead him back into his own compartment and stretched out in the bunk, unprotestingly letting Amid pull off his boots and his heavy outer jacket. Exhaustion was like a deep aching, all through his body and mind. He lay, staring at the gray metal of the compartment ceiling, a meter and a half above his bunk; and Amid's head moved into his field of vision, between him and it, looking down.

"Let me help you sleep," said Amid; and his eyes seemed to begin to grow enormously as Hal watched.

"No." Hal shook his head, fractionally. It was a great effort even to speak. "You can't. I have to do it for myself. But I will. Just leave me."

Amid went, turning out the compartment lighting, closing the door behind him. Hal stared up into sudden lightlessness; feeling again the weight of his lifetimes, which had come upon him in the darkness of the yard. He turned his mind like a hand holding up the stone of consciousness, letting that stone fall from the grasp that held it, fall into darkness . . . and fall . . . and fall . . . and fall. . . .

It took them five days, ship's-time, to make Earth orbit. Most of that time Hal slept and thought. The other two left him alone. When they parked at last in Earth orbit, Hal called up a jitney to take him down to the planet's surface.

"And Amid and me?" asked Simon. "What do you want us to do? Wait here?"

"No. Go and wait for me at the Final Encyclopedia," answered Hal. "I'll be a day—at most two. No more."

Chapter

> > **60** < <

Riding the upcurrent above the brown granite slope of the mountainside in the late afternoon, high above the grounds of the Mayne Estate, the golden eagle turned his head sharply to focus his telescopic vision on the flat area surrounding the pool behind the building. There had been movement there—animal movement different from the movement of grass and twigs in the wind—where there had been no movement for a very long time.

His eyes fastened on a dark-clad, upright man-shape, tiny with the distance between them. There was no profit to be found in this, then, for a knight of the air like himself. The eagle cried harshly his disappointment and wheeled off, away from the Estate and the mountainside, out over the thick green of the upland conifer forest.

Hal watched him go, standing on the far edge of the terrace overlooking the lake. A little, cold breeze rippled the gray surface of the water; and, above him, in the declining afternoon light, the blue of the sky was the blue of ice. Here, in this northern temperate zone of Old Earth, summer still held to the lowlands; but up in the mountains the first cutting blasts of winter's horn could be faintly heard. The cold, moving air chilled the exposed skin surfaces of his body and out of old days and memories came a piece of a poem to fit itself to the moment. . . .

> *"O what can ail thee, knight at arms*
> *Alone and palely loitering?*
> *The sedge has withered from the lake,*
> *And no birds sing! . . ."*

It was the first verse of the original version of "La Belle Dame sans Merci"—"The Beautiful Lady Without Mercy"—a poem by John Keats about a mortal ensorcelled by a fairy, but without the limiting term to that ensorcelment found in its poetic ancestor—*"True Thomas."* The older poem had been written by Thomas of Erceldoune back in the thirteenth century, from even older versions of the legend passed down by word of mouth.

For that matter, he thought, the coming of the technological age five hundred years ago had brought the old tale to a newer version still; the concept of the Iron Mistress, that artifact of work that could capture a human soul and never let it loose again to live naturally among its own kind.

It was an update of an Iron Mistress, that historic purpose, which held him captive now; and had held him from his beginning.

He shook off the self-pitying notion. Ever since he had been last on the Dorsai, he had been missing Amanda, deeply and unyieldingly. The pain of not having her within sight and hearing and touch was a feeling of deep wrongness and loss, like the pain of an amputated limb that would not grow again. No, he corrected himself, it was as if the pain and sense of loss from an earlier amputation had finally made him aware of it. The feeling was something that could be buried temporarily under the emergencies of the moment, during most of his waking hours. But at times when exhaustion stripped him down to bones and soul, as aboard the courier ship leaving Freiland recently, or when he was alone, as now, it came back upon him.

What were the later six lines in Keats' poem—about the hillside and the pale kings and warriors, with their warning? Oh, yes . . .

"*. . . The latest dream I ever dreamed*
    On the cold hillside.

"*I saw pale kings, and princes too,*
    Pale warriors, death-pale were they all
They cried—'La Belle Dame sans Merci
    Hath thee in thrall!' "

"*. . . The Iron Mistress hath thee in thrall! . . .*"
Once more, he pushed the feeling of depression from him. There was no need for this. The time would not be too long before he and Amanda would be together, permanently. It was not like him to waste time on gloomy thoughts, fantasies of despair summoned up out of old writings. He made an effort to examine why he should be acting like this, now; but his mind shied away from the question.

It was only his coming back here and finding the Estate so empty, he told himself. For that matter, when poetry could hurt, poetry could also heal. The heart of the same ancient story had been dealt with less than thirty-four years later by another poet, Robert Browning, in the first volume of his *Men and Women*. Browning had written "*Childe Roland to the*

Dark Tower Came," a poem similar in subject—but with all the difference in the universe, in theme. As an antidote to the earlier verse, Hal
quoted the last verse of Browning's poem to himself aloud, softly, into the
face of the chill river of air coming at him across the cooling water of the
lake—

> ". . . *There they stood, ranged along the hillsides, met*
> *To view the last of me, a living frame*
> *For one more picture! in a sheet of flame*
> *I saw them and I knew them all. And yet*
> *Dauntless the slug-horn to my lips I set,*
> *And blew."*
> —*Childe Roland to the Dark Tower Came*

Browning had been a Childe all his life—an aspirant to a greater
knighthood—although that part of him had passed, invisible before the
conscious eyes of almost everyone, with the exception of his wife. As Hal
was, himself, a Childe now, though in a different time and place and way,
and never as a poet. It was no Iron Mistress that drove Browning, and
perhaps even himself, after all, but the fire of a hope that would not let
itself be put out.

At the same time, even with this small bit of understanding, the emptiness inside him that reached from Amanda echoed back the emptiness
of this place he had known so well, but from which the three old men
who had given it life and meaning were now departed. The Estate had
not become strange to him. He had become a stranger within it.

But an instinct had drawn him back to spend the night here; and
spend it, he would. He turned back from the terrace and toward the
french windows that would let him into the house, glancing through
them, instinctively, down into the library where already the automatic
lighting had gone on; and where, the last time he had looked in, he had
seen Bleys and Dahno standing toe-to-toe.

He opened one of the windows and stepped through, closing it behind
him. The warmth of the atmosphere within, guarded by that same automatic machinery that had kept the place so well that all these years its
caretaker had needed only to glance occasionally into the surveillance
screens in his own home, five miles away, to make sure all was well,
wrapped itself around him. He was enclosed by the still air, the smell of
the leather bindings on the hundreds of old-fashioned books, dustless and
waiting still on their long shelves of polished, honey-colored wood. He

had read them all in those early years, devouring them one after the other, whenever he had the chance, like some starving creature fallen into a land of plenty.

Now that he was within doors, he was made aware of the darkening of the day beyond the windows. In just these last few moments the sun had gone behind the mountains. He walked to the fireplace at the end of the room. It, too, was waiting; laid ready for firing. He took the ancient sparker from its clip on the mantelpiece and with it touched the kindling under the logs alight.

Flames woke and raced among the shavings and the splinters beneath the kindling, reaching up to make the bark on the logs spark and glow. He seated himself in one of the large, overstuffed, wing-backed chairs flanking the hearth and fastened his eyes on the growing fire. The flames ran like small heralds among the dark structure of the wood, summoning its parts to holocaust. The heat of the burning reached out to warm him; but he could still feel the emptiness of the house at his back.

He had not been so conscious of being alone since he had run for the Encyclopedia, after the killing on the terrace beyond these windows. In all the time since he had headed for Coby, except for the moment in the Harmony prison when they would not come, he had never made the fully necessary effort to summon up self-hypnotically the images of his three dead tutors. But now, feeling the hollowness and darkness at his back, he reached within himself, keeping his eyes on the fire, and let the mental technique, in which Walter the In Teacher had coached him as a child, channel the force of his memories into subjective reality.

When I lift my eyes from the fire, he thought, they will be there.

He sat, gazing at the fire which was now sending flames halfway up inside the squared central pile of logs; and after a bit, he felt presences in the room behind him. He lifted his head, turned and saw them.

Malachi Nasuno. Obadiah Testator. Walter the InTeacher.

They sat in other chairs of the room, making a rough semicircle facing him; and he turned the back of his own chair to the fire, in order to look directly at them.

"I've missed you," he told them.

"Not for a long time," said Malachi. The massive torso of the old Dorsai dwarfed the tall carved chair that held him; and his deep voice was as unyielding as ever. "And before that, only now and then, at times like this. If you'd done anything else, we'd have failed with you."

"And that we did not," said Obadiah, scarecrow thin, looking taller than he was by virtue of his extreme uprightness as he sat in his chair.

"Now you've met my own people, as well as others, and you understand more than I ever could have taught you."

"That's true," said Hal. He looked at Walter the InTeacher and saw the Exotic's old, blue eyes quiet upon him. "Walter? Aren't you going to say hello?"

"I was thinking, only." Walter smiled at him. "When I was alive, I would have asked you at a moment like this why you needed us in the first place. Being only a figment of your imagination and memory, I don't have to ask. I know. You needed us to help you do the kind of learning that was only possible to the open, fresh mind of someone discovering the universe for the first time. But do you even know now where the end of this journey of yours lies?"

"Not where," said Hal. "But in what. Like all journeys, it has to end in accomplishment—or I've gone nowhere."

"And if it should turn out you have?" asked Walter.

"If he has," Malachi broke in harshly, "he did well—he did his best while he could, at the trying of it. Do you always have to make things difficult for him?"

"That was our job here, Malachi," said Walter, "to make things difficult for him. You know that. He knows that—now. When he was Donal Graeme he saw himself growing away from the soul of humankind. He had to come back—and the only way was a hard way."

He smiled at his two fellow tutors.

"Otherwise why arrange with your intuitive logic that your trustees would choose three like us?"

"I'm sorry," said Hal. "I used you all. I've always used people."

"Maudlin self-pity!" snapped Obadiah. "What weakness is this, after all we taught you, and now that you're face-to-face at last with what you set out to do?"

Hal grinned, a little wanly.

"You sent me out to become human, after you were killed," he answered. "But you also put me on the road even before you sent me out. Can't you let me be a little human now, from time to time?"

"As long as you get your job done, boy," rumbled Malachi.

"Oh," Hal sobered. "I'll get it done, if it can be done. There's no changing or stopping the juggernaut of history, now. But, you know what the real miracle is? I wanted to start Donal over again, to get him right this time. But what I did worked even better than I could have dreamed. I'm not Donal, redone. I'm Hal; and even all of what Donal was, is only a part of me, now."

"Yes," said Malachi, slowly. "You've put away all armor. I suppose you had to."

"Yes," said Hal. "The passage ahead's too narrow for anyone wearing armor." He lost himself for a moment in thought, then went on. "And all those who come after me are going to have to come naked, likewise, or they won't get through."

He shivered.

"You're afraid," said Walter, quickly, leaning forward intently in his chair. "What are you afraid of, Hal?"

"Of what's coming," said Hal; and shivered again. "Of my own testing."

"Afraid," said a new voice in the room, "of me. Afraid I'll prove him wrong about this human race of ours, after all."

The tall figure of Bleys moved out of an angle in the bookcases and stepped forward to stand between Obadiah's chair and that of Malachi.

"Playing with your imagination, again?" he said to Hal. "Making up ghosts out of the images of your memory—even a ghost of me; and I'm still very much alive."

"You can go," said Hal. "I'll deal with you another time."

But Bleys continued to exist, standing between the chairs holding Malachi and Obadiah.

"Your unconscious doesn't want to dismiss me, it seems," he said.

Hal sighed and looked again into the fire. When he turned back to the room, Bleys was still there with the rest of them.

"No," Hal said. "I guess not."

None of the subjective images replied. They stayed; the three sitting, the one standing, looking at him, but without words.

"Yes," said Hal, after a time, looking back at the fire. "I'm afraid of you, Bleys. I never guessed there would be someone like you; and it shocked me to find you, in real life. If I've evoked your image now, it is to make me see something in myself I don't want to see. That's why you're here."

"My similarity to you," said Bleys. "That's what you don't want to see."

"No." Hal shook his head. "We're really not that similar. We only look that way to everyone else. But that doesn't make us alike. If all the people on all the worlds had in common what you and I have, we wouldn't look alike. Our differences would show, then; and we'd look as unalike—as we actually are."

He glanced briefly into the fire again.

"Unalike as two gladiators pushed into a ring to fight each other," he said.

"No one pushed either of us," said Bleys. "I chose my way. You chose to fight it. I offered you all I had to offer, not to fight me. But you decided to anyway. Who could push either of us, in any case?"

"People," said Hal.

"People!" There was a strange note of anger in Bleys' voice. "People are mayflies. It's no shame or sin in them; it's only fact. But will you die— and that magnificent, unique engine that's yourself be lost, for a swarm of mayflies? Leaving aside the other fact that the only one who can certainly kill you is myself; and you know I won't do that until it's plain you've lost."

"No," said Hal. "You know you'd lose, not gain, by killing me before that. As a dead martyr either one of us would make sure of victory for our side—and perhaps wrongly, by that means. No, it's the contest that's important, not ourselves. A chess Grand Master could shoot his opponent dead before the game between them was done. But the fact the other couldn't finish would prove nothing to the watchers, when it was vital to know whose game was best and who should have won. The watchers might even assume that the one who shot did because he knew he was going to lose—and that might not be true."

He paused. Bleys said nothing.

"I've understood you couldn't afford to kill me," Hal went on, more gently. "You admitted that when you didn't take advantage of my being your prisoner, back in the hands of the Militia on Harmony. You talk of mayflies; but I know—maybe I'm the only one who knows—that you care for the race as a race, in your own way, as much as I do."

"Perhaps," said Bleys, broodingly. "Perhaps you and I only need them to fill the void around us. In any case, the mayflies aren't us. Tomorrow there'll come another swarm of them, to replace what died today, and tomorrow after that, another. Give me one reason you want to sacrifice yourself for what lives only for a single day."

Hal looked at him, bleakly.

"They break my heart," he said.

There was silence in the room.

"I know you don't understand them," Hal said to Bleys. "That's the one great difference between us, the one reason I'm afraid. Because you represent only one part of the race; and if you win . . . if you win, the part I know is there can be lost forever, now that the race-animal's decided it can't live divided any longer. I can't let that happen."

He stopped speaking for a moment, looking at all four of his subjective images, then back at the shade of the tall Other.

"You don't see what I see," he said. "You can't see it, can you, Bleys?"

"I find it," said Bleys slowly and quietly, "inconceivable. There's nothing in them—in us—to break any heart, even if hearts were breakable.

We're painted savages, nothing more, in spite of what we like to think of as some thousands of years of civilization. Only our present paint's called clothing, and our caves called buildings and spaceships. We're what we were yesterday, and the day before that, back to the point where we dropped on all fours and went like the animals we really are."

"No!" said Hal. "No. And that's the crux of it. That's why I can't let the juggernaut go the way you want. It's not true we're still animals; it's not true we're still savages. We've grown from the beginning. There was never a time we weren't growing; and we're growing now. Everything we face in this moment's only the final result of that growing, when it broke loose into consciousness, finally, a thousand years ago."

"Just a thousand?" Bleys' eyebrows lifted. "Not five hundred or fifteen hundred—or forty, or four thousand?"

"Pick the when and where you like," said Hal. "From any point in the past, the chain of events run inescapably forward to this moment. I've chosen the nexus in the fourteenth century of western Europe, to count from."

"And John Hawkwood," said Bleys, smiling thinly. "The last of the medieval captains, the first of the modern generals. First among the first of the condottieri, you'd say? Sir John, in northern Italy. You see, like these others here, I can read your mind."

"Only the shade of you I summon reads my mind," said Hal. "Otherwise, perhaps I could make you see some things you don't want to see. It was John Hawkwood who stopped Giangalleazo Visconti in 1387."

"And preserved the system of city-states that made the Renaissance possible? As I just said, I know your mind." Bleys shook his head. "But it's only your theory. Do you really think the only thing that made the Renaissance possible was one summer's military frustration of a Milanese Duke—who was still in pursuit of the kingship of all Italy when he died, about a dozen years later?"

"Probably not," said Hal. "Giangalleazo's later tries didn't work. Nonetheless, the historic change was in the wind. But history's what happened. The causal chain I picked to work with links forward from Hawkwood. If you see that much, why can't you see people as I do?"

"And have them break my heart, too?" Bleys watched him steadily. "I told you I found that inconceivable. And it's inconceivable to me that they can breaks yours—or that hearts can break, as I said, for any reason."

"It breaks mine, because I've seen them in actions you don't believe exist." Hal met the other man's gaze. "I've been among them and I've watched. I've seen the countless things they do for each other—the extraordinary kindnesses, the small efforts to help or comfort each other, the little things they deny themselves so that someone else can have what they might have had. And the large things—the lives risked and laid down, the lifetimes of unreturned effort, the silent heroisms, the quiet faithfulnesses—all without trumpets and flags, because life required it of them. These aren't the actions of mayflies, of animals—or even of savages. These are the actions of men and women reaching out for something greater than what they have now; and while I live I'll help them to it."

"There's that," said Bleys, remotely. "Sooner or later, you'll die. Do you think they'll build a statue to you, then?"

"No, because no statues are needed," Hal answered. "My reward never was supposed to be a recognition of anything I've done; but only my knowing I'd done it. And I get that reward every day, seeing the road extend, seeing my work on it and seeing that it's good. There's a poem by Rudyard Kipling, called 'The Palace'—"

"Spare me your poems," said Bleys.

"I can spare you them, but life won't," said Hal. "Poems are the tool I've been hunting for all these years, the tool I needed to defeat those who think the way you do. Listen to this one. You might learn something. It's about a king who was also a master mason, who decided to build himself a palace like no one had ever seen before. But when his workmen dug down for the foundations, they found the ruins of an earlier palace, with one phrase carved on every stone of it. The king ordered them to use the materials of the earlier palace and continued to build—until word came to him one day that it was ordained he should never finish. Then, at last, he understood the phrase the earlier builder had carved on each stone; and he told his workmen to stop building, but to carve the same phrase on each stone he had caused to be set in place. That phrase was—'*After me cometh a builder. Tell him I too have known!*' "

Hal stopped talking. Bleys sat still, silent, watching him.

"Do you understand?" Hal said. "The message is that the knowing is enough. No more is needed. And I have that knowing."

"*Shai* Hal!" murmured Malachi.

But Hal barely heard the old Dorsai praise-word. His mind was suddenly caught up by what he had just said; and his mind wheeled outward like an eagle, seeing farther and farther distances lifting over the horizon as his wide wings carried him toward it.

The fire crackled and burned low behind him, unnoticed.

When he looked up, all four of the shades he had summoned from the depths of his mind were gone.

Chapter

> > **61** < <

Sometime in the hours of the night, he exploded into wakefulness, sitting up, swinging his legs over the side of the bed and getting to his feet in one swift, reflexive motion.

He stood utterly still in the darkness, his senses stretched to their limits, his eyes moving in steady search of the deeper shadows, the muscles behind his ears tensed for the faintest sound.

As he stood, his recently-sleeping mind caught up with his already-roused body. The hard electric surge of adrenalin was suddenly all through him. There was an aching and a heaviness in his left side and shoulder, as if he had slept with it twisted under him so long that a cutoff of circulation had numbed it. He waited.

Nothing stirred. The house was silent. Slowly, the ache and heaviness faded from his side and shoulder, and his tension relaxed. He got back into the bed. For a little while he lay awake, wondering. Then sleep took him once more.

But this time he dreamed; and in his dream he had come close at last to that dark tower which he had been approaching in his earlier dreams, across a rubbled plain that had become a wild land of rock and gullied earth. Now, however, he was in a place of naked rock—a barren and blasted landscape, through which wound the narrow trail he was following.

He came at last to a small open space in which stood the ruins of a stone building with a broken cross on top of it. Just outside the shattered doorway of the building was a horse with a braided bridle, a saddle with a high cantle and armor on its chest and upper legs. It stood tethered to the lintel. When it caught sight of him, it threw up its head, struck its hooves on the broken paving beneath them and neighed three times, loudly. He went to it and mounted it; and rode on, for now the tail had widened. It led him along and between the rocks, sometimes by way of a scant ledge with sheer stone to his right, a sheer drop to his left; and then again between close rocky walls on either side. As he rode, the day, which was gloomy already, darkened even further until it was as if he rode at twilight.

What little illumination there was seemed to come from the sky in general. It was more light than starglow or moonglow, but not much more; and no trace of sun was visible, so that the dimness enclosed everything. Down among the rocks as he was, he could no longer see the tower, and the trail wound backward and forward, turning to every quarter of the compass. But he did not doubt that he was still headed for the tower, for he could feel its presence, close now ahead of him.

He let the reins lie slack because the horse seemed to be determined to carry him on, whether he controlled it or not; and in any case there was only one route to follow. From the first moment he had seen it at the chapel it had shown its eagerness to be ridden by him, and in this one direction.

Together, they continued a little ways; and then he saw, ahead and on his right, a break in the rock wall filled by a pair of locked gates, made of dark metal bars overgrown with green vines. Through the bars was revealed an area of stony wilderness in which nothing seemed to live or move; and pressed against the far side of the gates, gazing through them at Hal as he approached, was a slim figure that was Bleys Ahrens.

Hal checked his horse opposite the gate. It tossed its head impatiently against the pull of the bit, but stood; and for a moment the two men were face-to-face.

"So," said Bleys, in a remote voice, "we have the ghosts of those three tutors of yours, do we, raised again by you, and crying out against me for vengeance?"

"No," said Hal. "They were only creatures of history, just as you and I are. It's everyone who lives now, crying out to be freed from the chains that always held them."

"There's no freedom for them," said Bleys, still in the remote voice. "There never was."

"There is, and always has been," said Hal. "Open the gate, come through, and let me show you."

"There is no gate," said Bleys. "No trail, no tower—everything but this land about us here is illusion. Face that, and learn to make the best of what is."

Hal shook his head.

"You're a fool," said Bleys, sadly. "A fool who hopes."

"We're both fools," said Hal. "But I don't hope, I know."

And he rode on, leaving Bleys standing, still leaning against the other side of the locked gate, until a turn in the narrow trail lost him to sight.

. . . Hal was roused again, this time by the chiming of a call signal, and opened his eyes to the phone screen at his bedside glowing white. Groggily he pushed himself to full awareness; and with that, suddenly, he was fully alert. No one except a few people at the Final Encyclopedia, such as Amid, Simon, Ajela and Tam, knew that he was here—or even had any reason to think that the Estate was occupied.

He flung out an arm and punched on the phone. The screen cleared to show Ajela's face, tight with an unusual tension.

"Hal," she said. "Are you awake? They've tried to assassinate Rukh!"

"Where? When?" He pushed himself up on one elbow and saw himself screen-lit, imaged in a mirror across the room, the dark hair tumbled forward over his forehead, the strong-boned features below it scowling away the last numbness of slumber. The hard-muscled, naked torso above the bedcovers was the brutal upper body of a stranger.

"A little over forty minutes ago, standard time," said Ajela. "The word is she's only wounded."

"Where is she?" Hal swung his legs over the edge of the bed, throwing the bedcovers back. "Will you get Simon down here to the estate for me right away?"

He got up and stepped past the screen, reaching for his clothes, from long automatic habit laid close and ready. He began dressing.

"We can't get traffic clearance down there for a courier ship," Ajela's voice came from the screen, behind him. "Not even for you, under Earth's regulations. An aircar'll pick you up and take you to Salt Lake—a shuttle'll be held there for you. It'll bring you straight to the Encyclopedia."

"No." He was almost dressed now. "I'll go directly to Rukh."

"You can't—where are you now?" Ajela said—and he moved back to sit on the bed and face the screen. "Oh, there you are! You can't just go to her. Her own people with her rushed her off and hid her after it happened. We don't know yet where they've taken her."

"I'd still be better on the scene, helping to find her."

"Be sensible." The tone of Ajela's voice was hard. "The most your being there could mean would be finding her a few minutes earlier. Besides, you've been out of touch with us and Earth, except for messages, for too long. You're needed here, to catch up. No one grudged you a day to make the trip you're on; but if it gets down to hard choices, your duty's here, not with Rukh."

He took a short breath.

"You're right," he said. "I need to talk to you all as soon as I can. The aircar's on its way?"

"Be with you in fifteen minutes. It'll land on that small lake behind your house."

"I'll be out there waiting," he said.

"Good." Ajela's voice softened. "It's all right, Hal. I know she'll be all right."

"Yes," said Hal, hearing his voice as if it came from someone else. "Of course. I'll be outside waiting for the aircar when it comes."

"Good; and we'll all be waiting for you when you get here. Come right to Tam's quarters."

"I will."

The screen went dark. He rose, finished dressing and went out.

In the open air behind the house, frost held the grounds and mountain areas beyond. In a cloudless, icy sky, the stars were large and seemed to hang low overhead. A nearly-full moon was bright. The cold struck in at him, and his breath plumed straight upward from his lips in the moonlight as he stood by the dark water's edge at the house end of the lake. After a while a dark shape scudded across the sky, occulting the stars, and dropped vertically to land on the water at the center of the lake. It turned toward him and slid across the watery surface to where he stood. The passenger door opened.

"Hal Mayne?" called a male voice from the lighted interior.

"Yes," Hal said, already inside the car. He dropped into a seat behind the driver as the door closed again and the vehicle leaped upward.

"We ought to make Salt Lake Pad in twenty minutes," said the driver, over his shoulder.

"Good," said Hal.

He sat back, letting his mind slip off into a calculation of the probabilities involved in Rukh's situation, using all of Donal's old abilities in that area. It was true enough, if she had not been killed outright and there was any decent sort of medical help available, she was almost sure to survive.

If.

He forced his mind to turn, coldly and dispassionately, to what it would mean to the confrontation with the Others if she had not lived; or had, but would no longer be able to lead Earth's people to an understanding of the cost of an Others' victory. The messages about her of which Ajela had just now spoken had, he knew, been painting a picture of strong successes, for Rukh and for those others she had recruited from Harmony and Association to speak elsewhere about Earth. He had been counting on those successes, taking them for granted.

If her help was now to be lost . . . it was true that he had fallen out of touch with the situation here on Earth, while he had been out scouting Bleys' military preparations on the Younger Worlds. What he had seen out there had not only confirmed his worst forebodings but driven the more immediate problem of controlling Earth from his mind. His losing touch with the Encyclopedia and Earth had, in a sense, been unavoidable—he could not be in two places at once—but its unavoidability did not alter the danger in which it had possibly put them all. The open contest with the Others here at humanity's birthplace was one in which lack of knowledge could guarantee defeat. Now that he knew what he knew, there was nothing for it but to move as swiftly as he could.

Ajela had been more right than she knew, in insisting he come back to the Encyclopedia just now. The breakpoint was upon them. How close upon them, he had not realized himself until the past evening. But the full implications of the realization were something to be explored later, when time was available. For now, even if Rukh had been no more than scratched, it was not. Every standard day now that he delayed in putting to work the information he had gained, more of its usefulness would leak away.

The shuttle, empty of passengers except himself, slid into the metal-noisy, bright-lit entry port of the Encyclopedia. Simon Graeme was waiting for him as he stepped out of the vehicle.

"I'm to take you to Tam Olyn's quarters," Simon said.

"I know."

They went quickly, bypassing the usual passage that led past the center of the Encyclopedia and stepping almost immediately through a side door into a quiet corridor that, by the internal magic of the Encyclopedia, led them only a dozen steps to Tam's entrance door.

Within, Tam's office-lounge was as Hal had remembered it, with the illusion of the little stream and the grove of trees. But both the temperature and humidity of the place were higher; and Tam, seated in one of the big chairs, looked further shrunken and stilled by the hard hand of age, into a final motionlessness in which there seemed to be no energy left for any movement or emotion.

Besides Tam, the office held Ajela and Jeamus Walters, the Engineering Chief of the Encyclopedia, standing facing Tam, one on either side of his chair. They turned together at the sound of the door-chimes; and both their faces lit up.

"Hal!" Ajela turned quickly to Tam. "You see? I told you. Here he is, now!"

She turned back to hug Hal as he reached her. But almost immediately she let him go again and pushed him toward the chair with the old man in it.

"Hal!" said Tam. His voice rustled like dry paper; and the fingers he put out for Hal to grip were leathery and cold. "It's good to have you here. I can leave it to you and Ajela, now."

"Don't," said Hal, brusquely. "I'm going to need you, for some time yet."

"Need me?" Tam's darkened eyes found a spark of life and his papery voice strengthened.

"That's right," Hal said. "I've got something specific to talk to you about as soon as there's a minute to spare."

He turned to Ajela.

"No more word on Rukh?" He saw the answer in her face before she could speak. "All right. What's the situation here that I need to catch up on?"

"Amid, Rourke di Facino and Jason Rowe were to be signalled the minute you landed," she answered. "They'll be here in minutes. Then we can go over the full situation. Meanwhile, sit down—"

"If you don't mind." The interruption by the short, broad Chief Engineer was soft-voiced, but insistent. "While you've got a minute to give me, Hal, I've got something wonderful to tell you. You know this phase-shift-derived communication system of the Exotics? The one by which they've been able to transmit simple messages via color-code across interplanetary distances with at least forty per cent effectiveness—"

"Jeamus," said Ajela, "you can tell Hal about that later."

"No," said Hal, watching the serious, round face under the thinning, blond hair, "if you can tell me in just a few words, go ahead, Jeamus."

"We didn't know about their method, here," said Jeamus; "because they were so good at keeping it secret; and they didn't appreciate the fact that here on the Encyclopedia we know more about collateral uses for the phase-shift than anyone else, including them. Also, they didn't have experience or the capacity to do the running calculations necessary to maintain a steady contact over light-years of distance; which is why they'd never succeeded in using it across interstellar space. After all, the problems involved were like trying to make a spaceship hop the distance from here to any one of the Younger Worlds in a single shift—"

"Jeamus," said Ajela, gently, "Hal said—'a few words.'"

"Yes. Well," Jeamus went on. "The point is, we took what they already had; and in seven months here, we've come up with a system by which I can link with an echo-transmitter on one of the Younger Worlds and give you this-moment, standard-time, sight and sound of what the echo-transmitter's viewing. Do you understand, Hal? It's still got some problems, of course; but still—you can actually see and hear what's going on there with no time lag at all!"

"Good!" said Hal. "That's going to be a lifesaver, Jeamus. It's something that'll be useful—"

"Useful?" Jeamus took an indignant step toward Hal. "It'll be a miracle! It's the greatest step forward since we put the shield-wall around the Encyclopedia, itself. This is doing the impossible! I don't think you appreciate quite what—"

"I do appreciate it," Hal said. "And I realize what you and your people've done, Jeamus. But right now we're under emergency conditions when other things have priority. We'll talk about this communication system in a little while. Now, what progress have you made on setting up that planet-sized shield-wall I asked you to work up?"

"Oh, that," said Jeamus. "It's all done. There's nothing to doing something like that, as I told you, except to make the necessary adjustments for the difference in size between the Encyclopedia and a planet. But this phase-shift communication—"

"Done?" said Hal. "In what sense done?"

"Well," there was an edge in Jeamus' voice, "I mean done—it's ready to go. I've even got the support ships equipped for it and their crews trained, ready to take station. It turned out we needed fifteen spaceships for a wall the size you wanted; and they've been set up. They'll take position around whatever world you want . . . and then it's done. Once the wall's up, they'll act as inner control stations to open irises, just as the Encyclopedia does—only of course larger and more of them—to the star around which the planet is orbiting, for energy input. They're parked now in close proximity orbit, staffed and ready to go, as soon as you tell them where. Not that they haven't got a pretty good idea where. They had to practice taking station, and everyone knows there's only one world larger than Earth that fits the specifications you gave me—"

The door to Tam's quarters chimed and opened. Nonne came in, moving swiftly in a dark brown robe that swirled about her feet as she strode forward. Her face was thinner and older-looking; and she was followed by both Jason Rowe and Rourke di Facino. Jason was wearing a thin blue shirt and the sort of light-gray work slacks common in the unchanging, indoor climate of the Encyclopedia; clothes which had obviously never been fabricated on either Harmony or Association. In them, rather than his Harmony-checked bush shirt and trousers, he looked, by contrast with Nonne, even smaller and younger than Hal remembered him. Rourke, however, was unchanged—still in his Dorsai wardrobe; as dapper, as crisp of manner and as unchanged as ever.

"Good," said Hal, turning from Jeamus. "I'm sorry to have been gone so long. Sit down and we'll talk. Jeamus, I'll catch up with you a little later."

Jeamus nodded dourly, and went out.

Ajela had pulled up one of the antique, overstuffed chairs. Nonne took the only other such one, turning it so that she faced Hal, as he pulled in a float from behind him and sat down next to Tam. Jason took another float, a little back from Nonne's and alongside it. He smiled at Hal and sat back in the float. Only Rourke continued to stand, behind and between Nonne and Jason. He folded his arms and looked keenly at Hal.

"I'm honored to see you all again," Hal said, looking about at them, "and my apologies for being out of touch with everyone this length of time. There wasn't any other way to do it; but I appreciate what it's been like for the rest of you. Why don't we go around the circle; and each of you tell me what you most want to talk to me about?"

Silence gave assent.

"Tam?"

"Ajela can tell you," said Tam hoarsely.

"Ajela?"

"The Final Encyclopedia's as ready as we're ever going to be, for whatever you've got in mind," said Ajela. "Earth's another matter. Rukh and her people have been working miracles I honestly didn't expect, myself. They've already raised a powerful wave of popular opinion all over the world that's ready to back us. But there's still a majority down there who're of a few thousand other sets of minds, or who're blithely ignoring the whole situation on the basis that whatever happens Earth always comes out all right—by which I mean they simply assume there won't be changes in their backyards."

"What's your opinion of what's going to happen, now that Rukh's been at least hurt and maybe killed?" Hal said.

"Now . . ." Ajela hesitated and took a deep breath. "Now, until we can find out about her, and until word of how she is reaches the general Earth populace, it's anyone's guess."

She stopped speaking. Hal waited for a moment.

"Anything more?"

"No," said Ajela. "That's it. If you want anything more, you ask the questions."

Hal turned to Nonne.

"Nonne?"

"Both Mara and Kultis are prepared," she said gravely. Her hands smoothed the gown over her knees. "We've turned over to the Dorsai, the Encyclopedia here and to those Friendlies who oppose the Others, anything they said they needed and we had to give, as you told us to do. Those on both our worlds now are waiting for the next step—ready and waiting. It's up to you now to tell us what's next. Beyond that, as Ajela said, if you want details you've only to ask me."

Hal nodded; and was about to move his gaze to Jason when she spoke again.

"That doesn't mean there aren't a multitude of things I've got to discuss with you."

"I know," said Hal softly. "I'll get to that with all of you, in time. Jason?"

Jason shrugged.

"Those who oppose us still hold the cities and much of the countryside, on both Harmony and Association," he said. "But you don't need to be told that the Children of Wrath aren't ever going to stop fighting. There's little we can do for you, Hal, but go on fighting. I can tell you what we hold and where our strengths are; and if you can give me specific targets to aim at, we'll aim at them. As everybody else here says, beyond that you'll have to ask me questions—or let me ask you some."

Hal nodded again and looked finally at Rourke di Facino. But the spare, dandified little man answered before Hal could speak his name.

"We're ready to move," he said.

His arms were still folded. He stood, unaltered, as if the four words he had just brought forth were the sum total of anything that he could contribute to the conference.

"Thank you," answered Hal.

He looked at the others.

"Thank you all," he said. "To give you my own information in capsule form, Bleys has going what'll amount to an unending capability to attack us. He's got more than enough bases, more than enough matériel, more than enough people to arm and throw at all our capabilities for resistance. It's only a matter of a standard year or less; then he can begin that attack anytime he wants; and, if pushed, he could begin it this moment. Being Bleys, I expect him to wait, until he's fully ready to move."

"I take it," said Nonne, "you want to force his hand, then?"

Hal looked soberly at her.

"We have to," he said.

"Then let me ask you a question," Nonne said. "I said there were a multitude of things I wanted to discuss with you. Let me ask you about one."

"Go ahead." Hal looked at her thoughtfully.

"We seem to be heading inevitably for the point," said Nonne, "where it's going to boil down to a personal duel between you and Bleys. For the sake of my people I have to ask you—do you really think you can win a duel like that? And if so, what makes you think so?"

"I'm not sure at all I can win," answered Hal. "There're no certainties in human history. As an Exotic, of all people, you should realize that—"

He checked himself. Ajela had just made a small sound in the back of her throat as if she had begun to speak and then changed her mind. He turned to her. She shook her head.

"No," she said. "Nothing." She was looking hard at Nonne.

"We've got to go with what advantages we've got," Hal went on, "and in most cases that means turning the advantages of the Others to our use. Did you ever read Cletus Grahame's work on strategy and tactics?"

"Cletus—? Oh, that early Dorsai ancestor of Donal Graeme," said Nonne. "No. My field was recordist—character and its association with activity or occupation. Military maneuvers didn't impinge."

"I suppose not," said Hal. "Let me explain, then. Bleys is the most capable of the Others—you know that as well as I do. Otherwise he wouldn't be leading them. Someone more capable would have taken the leadership from him before this. So we've no choice who we've got to fight— we either defeat him, or lose. All I can tell you about my winning any duel with him is that if it ever comes down to that, I intend to be the winner; and as to why I think I might, it's because I've at least one advantage over him. My cause is better."

"Is that all?" Nonne's face was completely without expression.

"That can be all it takes," said Hal, gently. "A better cause can mean a better base for judgment; and better judgment is sometimes everything in a close contest."

"Forgive me," said Nonne, "if I boggle at the word 'everything.' "

"Think of two chess masters playing opposite each other," said Hal. "Neither one's going to make any obvious mistake. But either one can misjudge and make an obviously-right move a little too early or a little too late. My job's going to be to try to avoid misjudging like that, while trying at the same time to lead Bleys into misjudgments. To do that, I'll be taking advantage of the difference in our characters and styles. Bleys has all the apparent advantages in this contest of ours. He can lead from strength. Earlier than anyone else among the Others, I think, he perceived that about the situation from the beginning. Certainly, his use of that fact has been the major factor in his being accepted by the rest of the Others as their most capable member. Since his recognition of this has worked for him so far, I believe his perception of it is going to continue to lead him, as I said earlier, to wait until he's fully ready before he moves against us."

He broke off.

"Am I making my point clear to you?" he asked.

"Oh, yes," said Nonne.

"Good," answered Hal. "Now, then, it'd be bad strategy for him to change tactics that are winning for him without a strong reason, in any case. But I think we can count on this other factor in his thinking, as well. So, this leaves the initiative with us—which he will be aware of, but doesn't worry about. However, that same initiative can give us an advantage he may not suspect, if we can use it either to lull him into waiting too long to make a move, or startle him into moving too soon. It'll all depend on how good the plans are we've made."

"Then I take it you feel you've made good plans?"

He smiled gently at her.

"Yes," he said. "I do." He turned to Ajela. "I shouldn't have sent Jeamus away," he said. "Could you get him back here?"

Ajela nodded and reached to the control panel set in the arm of her chair. She touched one of the controls, murmuring to the receptor in the panel. Hal had turned back to the others.

"When you say you're ready to move," he said to Rourke, "do you mean just combat-ready adults, or all adults, or the whole population?"

"Nothing's ever unanimous," said Rourke, "and least of all, on the Dorsai, as I'd expect you to appreciate, Hal Mayne. A fair percentage of the population is going to stay. Some because age or sickness gives them no choice, some because they'd rather wait in the place they were born for whatever's going to happen to them. Nearly all of those of service age are ready to go."

"Yes," said Hal, nodding, "that was pretty much what I'd expected."

The voice of Jason sounded almost on the echo of his last word.

"Go where, Hal?" asked Jason.

"You didn't know?" Nonne looked across at the young Friendly.

"No," said Jason slowly, looking from her to Hal. "I didn't know. What was it I was supposed to have known?"

Instead of answering, Nonne looked at Hal.

"In a minute, Jason," Hal said. "Wait until Jeamus gets here."

They fell silent, looking at him. For a moment, as they sat waiting, Hal's mind went away from the immediate concerns.

He was aware of the four of them as individual puzzle-boxes, unique individual universes of thought and response, through which must be communicated what those they represented would need to understand. Once, as Donal, he would have seen them only as units, solid working parts of an overall solution to an overall problem. His greatest interest in

them would have been that they should execute what he would direct
them to do or say. Their objections would have been minor obstacles, to
be laid flat by indisputable logic, until they were reduced to silence. The
tag end of some lines from the New Testament of the Bible, spoken by
the Roman Centurion to Christ, came back to his mind, *"I say to one,
go, and he goeth and to another come, and he cometh. . . ."*

That sort of thinking could indeed produce a solution on the Donal
level. But he had lived two lives since then to find something better,
something more lasting. It had been his awareness of the need for that
which had bothered Donal near the end of his time, as he stood, finally
in charge of all the worlds and their workings, looking out at the stars beyond the known stars. He had seen the future clearly, then, and the fal-
lacy in the idea that it could be won, even to a good end, by strength
alone.

It had never been enough to make people dress neatly, walk soberly
and obey the law. Only when the necessary improvement had at last been
accepted by the inner self, when the law was no longer necessary, had any
permanent development been accomplished. And if he could not show
to these people here in this room with him now what would need to be
done and achieved, then how was he going to show it to the billions of
other individual human universes that made up the race?

It was not that they were not willing, any of them, to move to a higher
and better land. But each of them, one by one, individually, in their billions, would have to make the trip by himself or herself when the time
came; and for that, they would need to be able to see the way clear and
the goal plain and desirable before them, so that each would move freely
and on a personal determination to find it. Because the goal was not one
that could be reached by intellectual decision alone. In the case of each
person, it would require a combined effort of the conscious and the unconscious minds, of which only a handful of people in each past century
had been capable. But now the way would be marked. Those who really
desired to reach it could do so—they could all do so. Only, they would
first have to see the marking of the way; and grow into a belief in their
own abilities that would make them set their feet with utter confidence
upon it.

And as yet that way was cloudy, even to him. He must go first, like a
pioneer into new territory, charting as he went, making a road for the rest
to follow—and that road began with these here, with Rukh and these others who had shown some desire to listen to him and follow him—

The chiming of the annunciator and the opening of the door to Tam's
suite to let in Jeamus interrupted that train of thought.

"Come in, Jeamus," said Hal. "Take a seat if you like. I want to explain to these people what I asked you to design, in the way of a planetary shield-wall."

"Isn't this wasting valuable time?" Nonne broke in. "We all know he's been working on a shield-wall, and where it has to go—"

"I don't," said Jason, interrupting in turn. The eyes of the rest turned to him, for there was a strength and firmness to his voice that none of them, except Hal, had ever heard before. "Let's hear that explanation."

Jeamus had reached the circle by this time. His eyes rested for a second on the standing figure of Rourke, and he ignored the float that was within arm's reach of him.

"More than a standard year back," he said, "Hal asked me to look into making a phase-shift shield-wall, like the one we have around the Encyclopedia here to protect it, but large enough to protect a world. He specified a world slightly larger than Earth. We've done that. Once the ships to effect it are in proper position about that world, and in proper communication between themselves, it can be created instantly."

He looked at Hal.

"Do you want me to go into the principle of it and the details of its generation?"

"No," said Hal. "Just tell them what it'll do."

"What it'll do," said Jeamus to the rest of them, "is enclose what it surrounds in essentially a double shell which from either side will translate anything touching it into universal position—just as a phase-shift drive does. Only, in this case, the object won't be retranslated into a specific position again, the way a phase-drive does. I suppose all of you know that the phase-drive theory was developed from the Heisenberg Uncertainty Principle—"

"Yes, yes," said Nonne. "We know all that. We know that the Principle says it's impossible to determine both the position and velocity of a particle with full accuracy; and the more accurate the one, the more uncertain the other. We know that in phase-drive terms this means, for all practical purposes, that in the instant of no-time in which velocity can be absolutely fixed, position becomes universal. We know this means anyone or anything trying to pass a shield-wall like the one around the Encyclopedia would be effectively spread out to infinity. We know that Hal Mayne plans to set up a garrison world with such a shield-wall around it—as no doubt Bleys Ahrens also does—and defend it with the Dorsai, and that world is to be our Exotic World of Mara—"

"No," said Hal.

Jeamus' head came around with a jerk. Ajela leaned forward, her face suddenly intent. Nonne stared at him.

"No?" she said. "No what? No, to which part of what I said?"

"It won't be Mara," said Hal gently. "It's to be right here—Earth."

"Earth!" burst out Jeamus. "But you told me larger than Earth! The dimensions you gave me—"

He broke off, suddenly.

"Of course!" he said wearily. "You wanted to enclose the Encyclopedia in it. Of course."

"Earth?" said Nonne.

"Earth," Hal repeated.

He touched the control panel on the edge of his float and one side of the room dissolved into a view of the Earth as seen from the orbit of the Encyclopedia. A great globe, blue swathed with white, it hung before them. Hal got up and walked toward it until he stood next to the view, seeming to the rest of them almost to stand over the imaged world, as someone might bend above something infinitely valuable.

"But this makes no sense!" said Nonne, almost to herself. "Hal!"

At the sound of his name he turned from the screen to face her across the small distance that now separated them.

"Hal," she said. "Earth? What's the point of defending Earth? What kind of a strong point can it make for you when more than half the people there don't care if the Others end up in control? You haven't even got their permission, down there, to put a shell around them, like the one we've been talking about!"

"I know," said Hal. "But asking first would've been not only foolish, but unworkable. They'll be surprised, I'm afraid."

"They'll make you take it down."

"No," said Hal. "Some will try, of course. But they won't succeed. The point is, they can't. And in time they'll come to understand why it has to be there."

"Wishful thinking!" said Nonne.

"No." He looked at her for a second. "Or at least, not wishful thinking in the sense you mean. I'm sorry, Nonne, but now, for the first time, we're at a point where you're going to have to trust me."

"Why should I?" Her answer was fierce.

He sighed.

"For the same reason," he said, "that's been operative from the time you first heard of me. You, your people, and everyone else who hopes to escape the Others haven't any other choice."

"But this is madness!" she said. "Mara's willing to have you put a shield-wall around it. The people on Mara are even expecting it. The people on Mara are behind you to a person. They're ready for sacrifice; they've faced the need to sacrifice in order to survive. Hardly enough individuals to count on Earth have even thought of opposing the Others, let alone the cost of it."

"Something more than that, Nonne," put in Ajela. "Rukh's crusade has been a real crusade. They've been flocking in their thousands and hundreds of thousands to listen to her and the other people she brought in to carry the message."

"There're billions of people on Earth!" said Nonne.

"Give Rukh time," said Ajela. "The process is accelerating."

"There's no more time," said Hal; and the eyes of all of them came to him. "Bleys has moved faster than any of you realize. I've just spent months seeing the evidence of that. A decision has to be made now. And it has to be for Earth."

"Why?" demanded Nonne.

"Because Earth holds the heart of the race," said Hal, slowly. "As long as Earth is unconquered, the race is unconquered. A man once said, talking to an Irishman in a hotel at five o'clock in the morning, back in the twentieth century, 'Suppose all the poets, all the playwrights, all the songmakers of Ireland were to be wiped out in an instant. How many generations would it take to replace them?' And before he could answer his own question, the Irishman held up one finger, as the answer the man had been about to give."

He looked at them all.

"One. One finger. One generation. And they were both right. Because not only the children who were still young would grow up to have poets and playwrights and songmakers among them; but those adults presently alive who'd never written or sung would suddenly begin to produce the music that had always been in them—in response to the sudden silence about them. Because the ability to produce such things never was the special province of a few. It was something belonging to the people as a whole, in the souls of every one of them, only waiting to be called forth. And what was true at the time of that conversation, and before and since, with the Irish people, is true as well, now, for the people of Earth."

"And not for the people of the other worlds?" asked Jason.

"In time, them too. But their forebears were sent out by the hunger and fear of the race, to be expendable, to take root in strange places. For now, they stand—all of you stand, except Tam—at arm's length from the source of the music that's in you, and the future that's in you. You'll find it—but it would come harder and more slowly to any of you than it would for any of those down there—"

He gestured at the blue and white globe he had displayed.

They sat watching him, saying nothing. Even Nonne was silent.

"I told the Exotics," Hal went on, in the new silence, "I told the Dorsai—and I would have told your people, as well, Jason, if I'd had the proper chance to speak to them all—that in the final essential, they were experiments of the race. That they were brought into being only to be used when the time came. Now, that time's come. You all know the centuries of the Splinter Cultures are over. You know that, each of you, instinctively inside you. Their day of experimentation is done. Your kind lived, grew, and flourished for the ultimate purpose of taking one side of the great survival question of which road the race as a whole is going to follow into its future among the stars. Not to you and your children, unique and different, but to the children of the race in general, the future belongs."

He stopped. They still said nothing.

"And so," he said, tiredly, "in the end it's Earth we have to protect. Earth with all its history of savagery, and cruelty, and foolishness and selfishness—and all its words and songs and mighty dreams. Here, and no place else, the battle's finally going to be lost or won."

He stopped again. He wanted them to speak—if only so that he would not feel so utterly alone. But they did not.

He looked back at the blue and white globe of Earth.

"And it's here the question of the future is going to be decided," he said, softly, "and such as you and I will have to die, if that's our job, to get the answer needed for that decision to be made."

He stopped speaking and looked again at the imaged Earth. After a second or two, he was conscious of another body close behind him, and turned, lifting his eyes, to see that it was Ajela.

She put her arms around him; and merely held him for a minute. Then she let him go and went back to her seat by Tam.

"You give us reasons," said Nonne to him, "which aren't military reasons, and may not even be pragmatic, practical reasons. My point remains that Mara's a better base for a stonewall defense than Earth is. You haven't really answered me on that."

"This isn't," said Hal, "exactly a war we've entered into for pragmatic and practical reasons—except in the long run. But the fact is, you're wrong. Mara's a rich world, as the Younger Worlds go; but even after centuries of misuse and plundering of its resources, Earth is still the richest inhabited planet the human race knows. It's entirely self-supporting, and

it still maintains a population many times larger than any other inhabited world, to this day."

He broke off abruptly, holding all their eyes with his. Then he went
on.

"Also, there's a psychological difference. Enclose any other world, cut
it off from contact with the other inhabited worlds, and emotionally it
can't escape the feeling that it may have been discarded by the community of humanity, left behind to wither and die. As time goes on, it'll become more and more conscious of its isolation from the main body of the
race. But Earth still thinks of itself as the hub of the human universe. All
other worlds, to it, are only buds on its branch. If all those others are cut
off, whatever the cost may be otherwise, emotionally the most Earth will
think of itself as having lost are appendages it lived without for millions
of years and can do without again, if necessary."

"That large population's no benefit to you," said Nonne, "particularly,
if—as it is—it's full of people who disagree with what you're doing.
They're not the ones who're rallying to the defense of Earth. You're planning to defend that world with the Dorsai."

"In the beginning," said Hal, "certainly. If the battle goes on, I think
we'll find people from Earth itself coming forward to man the barricades.
In fact, they'll have to."

He turned to the old man.

"Tam?" he said. "What do you think?"

"They'll come," said Tam. The rattly, ancient voice made the two
words seem to fall, flat and heavy in their midst, like stones too weighty
to hold. "This is where the Dorsai came from, and the Exotics, and the
Friendlies—and everyone else. When defenders are needed from the people, they'll be there."

For a moment no one said anything.

"And that," said Hal, with a deep breath, "is another reason for it to
be Earth, rather than Mara. In time, even your Marans would produce
people to stand on guard. But they'd have to go back into what lies below
their present character to do it."

"But they could and would," said Nonne. "In this time, when everything that's been built up is falling apart, even Maran adults would do
that. Even I'd fight—if I thought I could."

A little smile, a not-unkindly smile, twitched the corners of Rourke di
Facino's lips.

"Dear lady," he said to her. "That's always been the only difference."

The remark drew her attention to him.

"You!" she said. "You stand there, saying nothing. Did your people bargain to defend Earth where the people have never understood or appreciated what the Younger Worlds mean—least of all, your kind? Are you simply willing to be their cannon fodder, without at least protesting what Hal Mayne wants? You're the military expert. You speak to him!"

The little smile went from Rourke's lips, to be replaced by an expression that had a strange touch of sadness to it. He came slowly around from behind the chairs of the rest where he had been standing and walked up to Hal. Hal looked at the erect, smaller man.

"I've talked to Simon about you," Rourke said. "And to Amanda. Who you are is your own business and no one discusses it—"

"I don't understand," interrupted Nonne, looking from one of them to the other. "What do you mean—who he is, is his own business?"

For a second it seemed that Rourke would turn and answer her. Then he went on speaking to Hal.

"But it's the opinion of the Grey Captains that we've got to trust your judgment," he said.

"Thank you," said Hal.

"So," said Rourke, "you think it should be Earth, then?"

"I think it always had to be," said Hal. "The only question has been, when to begin to move; and as things stand now, Bleys gets stronger every standard day we wait."

"I repeat," said Nonne. "You don't have a solid Earth at your back— you don't begin to have a solid Earth at your back. Rukh may have been gaining ground fast—as you say, Ajela—but now she's out of the picture and the job she set out to do isn't done. If you move now, you're gambling, Hal, gambling with the odds against you."

She looked back at Hal.

"You're right," said Hal. He stood for a second in silence. "But in every situation a time comes when decisions have to be made whether all the data's on hand, or not. I'm afraid I see more harm in waiting than acting. We'll begin to garrison Earth and lock it up."

Rourke nodded, almost as if to himself.

"In that case," he said, "I'll get busy."

He looked over at Jeamus.

"I can use that new communications system of yours now, Chief Engineer," he said, turning and heading for the door. Jeamus looked at Hal, who nodded, and the balding man hurried after the small, erect back of the Dorsai.

Before either one reached the door, however, a phone chime sounded. They stopped, as Ajela reached out to touch the control panel on the arm of her chair and all of the rest of them turned to look at her. A voice spoke from the panel, too low-pitched for the others to hear.

She lifted her head and looked at Hal.

"They've located Rukh," she said. "She's at a little place outside Sidi Barrani on the Mediterranean coast of Africa west of Alexandria."

"I'll have to catch up with the rest of you later, then," Hal said. "Everything down below depends to some extent on how much she's going to be able to go on doing. Ajela, can you set up surface transportation for me while I'm on my way down to the shuttle port nearest Sidi Barrani?"

Ajela nodded. Hal started toward the door, looking over at the young Friendly.

"Jason," he said, "do you want to come?"

"Yes," said Jason.

"All right, then," Hal said, as Rourke and Jeamus stood aside to let him out the door first. "We'll be back in some hours, with luck. Meanwhile, simply begin what you'd planned to do, once the decision to move was taken."

He went out the door with Jason close behind him.

Chapter

> > **62** < <

Sidi Barrani lay inland from the shore of the Mediterranean, across one of those areas which had been among the first to be reclaimed from the North African desert, over two hundred years before. Tall still-towers had been built and water from the Mediterranean had been pumped into them, to be discharged within their tops and allowed to fall some hundreds of meters to great fans in their bases, which then blew the moistened air back up and out the tops of the towers to humidify the local atmosphere.

That humidity had made lush cropland out of the dry earth surrounding; and, as the years went by, a resulting climatological change had altered the fertile areas, pushing inland from the shoreline the edge of the desert Rommel and Montgomery had fought over in the mid-twentieth century. The desert's edge had been forced to retreat some hundreds of kilometers, until it had been finally overwhelmed and vanquished entirely against the green borderland surrounding the newly formed Lake of Qattara; a large body of water formed when the Nile, backed up by the massive Aswan Dam, had at last found a new channel westward into the Qattara Depression.

It was to the shore of that lake and to a hotel called the Bahrain, therefore—an inconspicuous, low, white-walled structure in a brilliantly-flowered and tropically-aired landscape—that Hal and Jason came finally in their journey to find Rukh.

But for all the peace and softness of the physical surroundings, stepping through the front door of the hotel was like stepping out into a bare field when lightning is in the air. Hal shot a quick glance at Jason, who, after his years in the Harmony resistance, could be sensitive enough to feel the field of emotional tension they had just entered, but might not yet be experienced enough to react wisely to it.

However, Jason's face was calm. Possibly a little more pale than usual— but calm.

The sunken lobby under the high-arched white ceiling before them showed no one occupying the overstuffed chair-floats hovering around a small ornamental pool. The only visible living figure to be seen was what, here on Earth, must be a desk clerk hired for purely-ornamental purposes.

His gaze was directed downward behind the counter of the reception desk, as he appeared busy, or pretended to be busy, at something. Otherwise there was no sign of anyone human within sight or hearing—but the feeling of tense, if invisible watchers, all around them, was overwhelming.

The desk clerk did not look up until they had actually reached the counter and stopped on their side of it. He was a slight young man with a brown, smooth skin and a round face.

"Welcome to the Bahrain," he said. "Can I be of assistance?"

"Thanks, yes," said Hal. "Would you tell the lady that Howard Immanuelson is here to see her?"

"Which lady would that be, sir?"

"You've only got one lady here that message could be for," said Hal. "Please send it right away."

The clerk put both hands on the counter and leaned his weight slightly on them.

"I'm afraid, gentlemen," he said, "I don't understand. I can't deliver a message until I know who it's for."

Hal looked at him for a second.

"I can understand your position," he said, gently. "But you're making a mistake. We'll go and sit down by the pool, there; and you see that message I gave you gets delivered. If it doesn't . . . perhaps you'd better ask someone who'd know who Howard Immanuelson is."

"I'm sorry, sirs," said the clerk, "but without knowing who you want to contact, I've no way of knowing if that person is even a guest here, and—"

But they had already turned away, with Hal in the lead, and the voice died behind them. Hal chose a float with his back to the desk; and Jason moved to sit opposite him so that between them they would have the whole lobby in view. Hal frowned slightly; and, after a split second of hesitation, Jason took a float beside him, facing the same way.

They sat without talking. There was no sound from the desk. Hal's eyes and ears and nose were alert, exploring their surroundings. After a moment his nose singled out a faint, but pervasive and pleasant, scent on the air of the lobby; and an alarm signal sounded in his mind. Out on one of the Younger Worlds such a thing would have been highly unlikely; but here on Earth, where riches made for easy access to exotic weapons, and disregard for even the most solemn local laws and international agreements were not to be ruled out, it was not impossible that an attempt was being made to drug them by way of the lobby atmosphere.

It would not call for a drug capable of making them unconscious. All that would be needed would be to slightly dull one or more of their senses, or blunt the fine edge of their judgment, to give the unseen watchers a dangerous advantage.

On the other hand, the scent could be no more than it seemed. One of the services, or grace notes, a place like this might provide to make its lobby pleasant to guests.

There was only one way to find out which it was. The single ability most vulnerable to any kind of drugging was the meditatively-creative one. The gossamer bubbles of memory or fantasy, blown by the mind, and all the powerful release of emotion these could entail, were invariably warped or inhibited by anything alien to the physiological machinery supporting them.

He let the meditative machinery of his mind sink momentarily below the surface level of that watchful awareness which still continued to be maintained automatically by the outward engine of his consciousness; and allowed himself to slip back into recall of his childhood years, to a time when all emotions had been simple, pure and explosive.

It had been, he remembered, a time when excitement had had the power to almost tear him apart. Sorrow had been unbearable, happiness had lit up the world around him like a sheet of lightning, and anger had swallowed up all things—like one sheet of flame devouring the universe.

There had been a time, once, when he had been about five years old, that Malachi Nasuno had refused him something. He could not now remember what it had been without digging for the information, and for present purposes, so much was not necessary. He had wanted to handle some tool or weapon that the old Dorsai had considered beyond his years and ability; and Malachi had refused to let him have it. A fury at all things—at Malachi, at rules and principles, at a universe made for adults in which he was manacled by the unfairness of being young and small, had erupted in him. He had exploded at Malachi, shouting out his frustration and resentment, and run off into the woods.

He had run and run until breath and legs gave out together; and he had dropped down at last at the narrow edge of a stream which had cut its way through the mountain rock, bursting into unexpected tears. He had cried in sheer fury; determined never to go back, never to see Malachi or Walter or Obadiah again. Wild visions of living off the land in the mountains by himself billowed up like smoke from the bitter fires of frustration inside him.

And gradually a new despair came over him; so that he lay by the stream, silent in the misery of the thought that it seemed he could never be either what he wanted to be or what Malachi and the others might want him to be. Inwardly, he accused them of not understanding him, or not caring for him—when they were all he had, and when he had tried with every ounce of strength he owned to be what they wanted.

. . . And in that moment, as he huddled lost on the ground, two massive, trunk-like arms closed around him and brought him gently against the wide chest of Malachi. It was infinitely comforting to be found after all, held so; and he sobbed again—but now in relief, wearing himself out into peace and silence against the rough fabric of Malachi's jacket. The old man said nothing, only held him. He could hear, through jacket and chest wall, the slow, powerful beating of the adult heart. It seemed to him that his own heart slowed and moved to match that rhythm; and, just before he slipped into a slumber from which he would not wake until hours later, in his own bed, he felt—as clearly as if it had been in himself—the pain and sorrow that was in his tutor, together with an urge to love no less powerful than his own. . . .

He came back to full awareness of the Bahrain lobby, still wrung by the remembered emotions, and the achievement of that first rung on the ladder of human understanding, which had made life different for him from that moment on; but reassured, by the successful summoning up of that ancient emotion, that whatever perfumed the air around him was nothing with any power to inhibit either his body or his mind.

There was the sound of shoe soles on the hard, polished surface of the floor, approaching behind them. They turned to see the desk clerk.

"If you'll go up to room four-thirty-nine, gentlemen?" said the clerk. "It's the fifth door, to your right as you step out of the lift tube."

"Thanks," said Hal, rising. Jason was also getting to his feet; and they went toward the bank of lift tubes that the clerk was indicating with one hand.

The soft white walls of the corridor of the fourth floor stretched right and left from the lift tube exits there, but bent out of sight within a short distance in either direction. Clearly the corridor was designed to wander among the rooms and suites available. They went to their right; and, as they passed each door, it chimed and lit up its surface. As they went by, the number faded.

"Vanities!" said Jason under his breath; and Hal glanced at him, smiling a little.

Perhaps thirty meters from the lift tubes, a door glowed alight with the number 439 as they came level with it. They stopped, facing toward it.

"This is Howard Immanuelson," said Hal, clearly, "with someone who's an old friend of all of us. May we come in?"

For a moment there was no response. Then the door swung silently in-ward; and they entered.

The room they stepped into was large and square. The whole of the side opposite the door by which they had come in was apparently open to the weather, with a balcony beyond; but the coolness and stillness of the atmosphere about them told of an invisible barrier between room and balcony. Green-brown drapes of heavy material had been pulled back from the open wall to their limit on each side. Framed by these were the blue waters of Lake Qattara, with three white triangles that were the sails of one-person pleasure rafts, seeming to look inward to the room.

There was no one visible, only a closed door in the wall to their left. The entrance, which had opened behind them, closed again. Hal turned toward the closed door in the side wall.

"No," said a voice.

A thin, intense figure with a long-barrelled void pistol, favored for its silence and deadliness on an Earth where there was little call for long-range accuracy, and where the destruction of property could have a higher price tag than that of human lives, stepped from behind the bunched folds of the drape three steps down the wall from the side door. Bony of fea-ture, frail and deadly, incongruous in khaki-colored, Earth-style beach shorts and brightly-patterned shirt with leg-of-mutton sleeves, was Amyth Barbage; and the pistol in his hand covered both Hal and Jason with utter steadiness.

Hal took a step toward him.

"Stop there," said Barbage. "I know of what thou art capable, Hal Mayne, if I let thee come close enough."

"Hal!" said Jason, quickly. "It's all right. He's Rukh's now!"

"I am none but the Lord's, weak man—nor ever have been," replied Barbage, dryly, "as perhaps thou hast. But it's true I know now that Rukh Tamani is of the Lord and speaks with His voice; and I will guard her, therefore, while I live. She is not to be disturbed—by anyone."

Hal stared with a touch of wonder.

"Are you sure about this?" he said to Jason, without taking his eyes off the thin, still figure and the absolutely-motionless muzzle of the gun. "When did he change sides?"

"I changed no sides," said Barbage, "as I just said. How could I, who am of the Elect and must move always in obedience to His will? But in a courtyard of which you know, it happened once to be His will that a cer-tain blindness should be lifted from my eyes; and I saw at last how He had vouchsafed that Rukh should see His Way more clearly than I or any other, and was beloved of Him above all. In my weakness I had strayed, but was found again through great mercy; and now I tell you that for the protection of her life, neither you nor anyone else shall disturb her rest. Her doctor has ordered it; and I will see it done."

"Amyth Barbage," said Hal, "I have to see her, now; and talk to her. If I don't, all the work she's done can be lost."

"I do not believe you," said Barbage.

"But I do," said Jason, "since I know more about it than you, Old Prophet. And my duty to the Lord is as great as yours. Count on that, Hal—"

"Wait!"

Hal spoke just in time. He had read the sudden tensing in the man at his side, and understood that Jason was about to throw himself into the fire of Barbage's pistol so Hal might have time to reach the other man and deal with him. Jason slowly, imperceptibly, relaxed. Hal stared at the man with the gun.

"I think," he said slowly, "a little of that blindness you talked about is still with you, Amyth Barbage. Did you hear what I said—that if I didn't see and talk to Rukh now, all her work here could be lost?"

His eyes matched and held those of Barbage. The seconds stretched out in silence. Then, still holding the void pistol's muzzle steadily upon them, still watching them unvaryingly, Barbage moved sideways to the door in the side wall they had been facing, softly touched and softly opened it, then stepped backward through it. Standing one step inside the farther room, he spoke in so low a voice they barely heard him.

"Come. Come quietly."

They followed him into a curious room. It was narrow before them as they stepped into it and completely without furniture. Its far end was closed by drawn draperies of the same material and color as those in the room they had just left; and the wall to their right seemed to shimmer slightly as they looked at it.

As soon as they were inside and the door had closed automatically behind them, Barbage held up his free hand to bring them to a halt.

"Stay here," he said.

He turned and walked through the wall with the shimmer, revealing it for the projected sound-barrier image that it was. Hal and Jason stood silently waiting for several slow minutes; then suddenly the imaged wall vanished to show a large, pleasant hotel bedroom with the drapes drawn back and a bed-float contoured into a sitting position—and, propped up in it, Rukh.

Barbage was standing by the bedside, frowning back at them.

"Her strength must not be wasted," Barbage said. "I do this only because she insists. Tell her briefly what you have to say."

"No, Amyth," said Rukh from the bed, "they can talk until I ask them to stop. Hal, come here—and you, too, Jason."

They stepped to the bedside. Clearly, Hal saw, Rukh had never recovered from the thinness to which her ordeal at the hands of the Harmony Militia had reduced her; and now, with her upper left side and shoulder, farthest from them, bulky with bandages under the loose white bed dress she wore, she looked even more frail than when Hal had seen her last. But her remarkable beauty was, if anything, more overwhelming than ever. In the green-blue light reflected into the room by the vegetation and water outside, there appeared to be a translucency to her dark body, framed by the pale buttercup shade of the bed coverings.

Jason reached out to touch the arm of her unwounded side, gently, with the tips of his fingers.

"Rukh," he said softly. "Thou art not in pain? Thou art comfortable?"

"Of course, Jason," she said, and smiled at him. "I'm not badly hurt at all. It's just that the doctor said I was needing a rest, anyway—"

"She hath been close to exhaustion for some months, now—" began Barbage harshly, but checked himself as she looked at him.

"It's all right," she said. "But Amyth, I want to talk to Hal alone. Jason, would you forgive us . . . ?"

"If this is thy wish." Barbage lowered the pistol, turned to the shimmering image-wall and passed through it. Jason turned to follow.

"Jason—I'll be talking to you, too. Later," Rukh spoke hastily. He smiled back at her.

"Of course. I understand, Rukh—whenever you want to, I'll be here," he said, and went out.

Left alone with Hal she lifted her good right arm with effort from the bedspread covering her and started to reach out to him. He stepped close and caught hold of her hand with his own before hers was barely above the covers. Still holding it, he pulled a chair-float up to her bedside with his other hand and sat down close to her.

"It occurred to me you'd be showing up here," she said, with a smile. Her hand was warm but narrow-boned in his own much-larger grasp.

"I wanted to come the moment I heard," he said. "But it was pointed out to me that there were things to do, decisions I had to make. And we didn't know where you were until a few hours ago."

"Amyth and the others decided I ought to vanish," she said, "and I think they were probably right. This is an area where the people like me."

"Where they love you, you mean," said Hal.

She smiled again. For all its beauty, it was a tired smile.

"Duty kept you from searching for me right away, then," she said. "Did duty bring you now?"

He nodded.

"I'm afraid so," he said. "Time can't wait for either of us. Rukh, I had to make a decision to start things moving. We're out of time. I've sent word to the Dorsai they're to come here; and a phase-shield-wall, like the one about the Final Encyclopedia, is going to be thrown around the whole Earth—including the Encyclopedia, in orbit. From now on, we're a fortress under siege."

"And the Exotics?" she said, still holding his hand, and searching his eyes. "All of us thought it would be one of the Exotics you'd choose to fortify and defend, with the help of the Dorsai."

"No." He shook his head again. "It was always to be here, but I had to keep that to myself."

"And Mara and Kultis, then? What happens to them?"

"They die." His voice sounded unsparing in his own ears. "We've taken their space shipping, their experts and valuables, and whatever else we could use. The Others will make them pay for giving us those things, of course."

She shook her head slowly, her eyes somberly upon him.

"The Exotics knew this would happen?"

"They knew. Just as the Dorsai knew they'd have to abandon their world. Just as you and those others from Harmony and Association who came here knew you came here not for a few months or years, but probably for the rest of your lives." He gazed for a long second at her. "You did know, didn't you?"

"The Lord told me," she said. She drew her hand softly from within his fingers and put it around them, instead. "Of course, we knew."

"All things were headed this way from the beginning," he said. His voice had an edge like the edge found in the voice of someone in deep anger. He knew he did not have to lay the cold truth out for her in spoken words, but his own inner pain drove him to it. "In the end, when the choosing of sides came, the Dorsai were to fight for the side of the future, the Exotics were to make it possible for them, at the cost of everything they'd built. And those of you from the Friendlies who truly held faith in your hands were to waken the minds of all who fought on that side so they could see what it was they fought for."

Her fingers gently stroked the back of his hand.

"And Earth?" she said.

"Earth?" He smiled a little bitterly. "Earth's job is to do what it has always done—to survive. To survive so as to give birth to those who'll live to know a better universe."

"Shh," she said; and she stroked his hand gently with her thin fingers. "You do the task that's been set you, like us all."

He looked at her and made himself smile.

"You're right," he said. "It doesn't change how I feel—but you're right."

"Of course," she said. "Now, what did you come to ask from me?"

"I need you back at the Encyclopedia," he said, bluntly, "if you're able to travel at all. I want you to make a broadcast to all of Earth from the Encyclopedia; and I want all of Earth to know you're speaking from the Encyclopedia. I need you to help explain why the Dorsai are coming here and why a phase-shield-wall's been put around this planet, both without anyone asking the Earth people's permission. I can talk to them at the same time you do and take any responsibility you'd like me to spell out. But no one else can make them understand why these things had to be done the way you can. The question is—can you travel?"

"Of course, Hal," she said.

"No," he replied deliberately. "I mean exactly what I say—are you physically able to make the trip? You're too valuable to risk losing you for the sake of one speech, no matter how important it is."

She smiled at him.

"And if I didn't go, what would happen then, when the Dorsai start arriving down here and they discover the shield-wall?"

"I don't know," he said. His eyes met hers on a level.

"You see?" she said. "I have to go; just as we all have to do what we have to do. But don't worry, Hal. I really am all right. The wound's nothing; and otherwise there's nothing wrong with me a few weeks of rest won't cure—once the Dorsai are here and the shield-wall's up. There's no reason I can't have time off then, is there?"

"Of course there isn't."

"Well, then—"

But what she had started to say was cut off by the sudden eruption through the wall of a man of ordinary height with thin, fading brown hair, a bristling gray mustache and a face that seemed too young for either. He was wearing a sand-colored business suit that looked as if he had been sleeping in it and had just been wakened. The expression on his face was one of bright anger. Amyth Barbage was right behind him.

"You!" he said to Hal. "Get out of here!"

He swung to face Rukh, on the bed.

"Am I your doctor or not?" His voice beat upward under the pale white ceiling of the quiet room. "If I'm not, tell me now; and you can find yourself someone else to take care of you!"

"Of course you are, Roget," she said.

Chapter

> > **63** < <

Dawn came up bright and hard on the waters of Lake Qattara, with a little chop to the waves and an onshore breeze. With dawn came also a man in his fifties with a tanned, sharp-boned face and bright, opaque eyes, who wore his civilian suit like a uniform and was called Jarir al-Hariri. It appeared he was the equivalent of Police Commissioner for the large district surrounding the lake. With his coming the hotel began to swarm with activity. The instincts of Hal and Jason on entering the hotel had not lied to them. The great majority of guests who now appeared were plainly Earth-born and non-military; but their protective attitude toward Rukh was more like that of the members of her old Command on Harmony than that which might have been expected from casual converts to the message she had been preaching.

Hal himself was up before dawn. He had sat with Rukh until her breathing deepened into heavy slumber, then eased himself gently and with great slowness from the position in which he sat holding her. Detached, finally, he had laid her gently down in the bed and covered her up, leaving her to sleep.

Back in the room to which the clerk in the hotel led him after Amyth had called down to the lobby, he dropped onto his own bed; and slept heavily for nine hours—coming awake suddenly with a clear mind, but a drugged feel to his body that told him he was still far from normally rested. He rose, showered, ran his clothes through the room cleaner, and ate the breakfast he had ordered up to his room.

Then he went in search of Jason and Amyth, found them deep in consultation with Roget the physician over the problem of moving Rukh safely, and was himself drawn into the talk. But by nine in the morning, local time, the move was underway. They would go from the hotel to the Spacepad outside Alexandria, some two hundred and seventy-three kilometers distant, by surface transportation. Medically, Roget had reservations about an air trip. These were slight, but existed nonetheless. There were, however, very strong security reasons for sticking to the ground. Any atmosphere craft could be vulnerable to destruction by a robot drone with an explosive warhead—something any wild-eyed fringe group could put together in an hour or so—given the materials—out of any number of industrial atmosphere-operating robots, doing the work in any handy back room or basement.

Spacepad security would destroy any such drone automatically at its perimeters, so there would be no worries once the Spacepad was reached; and beyond the umbrella of that security any shuttle on its way to the Encyclopedia would be either too high or moving too swiftly for a drone to reach it.

Once in the Encyclopedia, of course, Rukh would be utterly safe.

"I take it," Hal had said to Jarir al-Hariri, early in this discussion, "security's been strict about letting the information spread beyond these walls that Rukh's leaving today?"

The stony, bright eyes had met his almost indifferently across the table at which they sat with cups of coffee—real Earth coffee, pleasant but strange now to Hal's taste buds.

"There has been no leak through my people," Jarir had said.

The pronunciation of the words in Basic was noticeably mangled on the Commissioner's tongue; surprising in the case of anyone speaking a language that had been the majority tongue of Earth as well as that of the Younger Worlds for three hundred years; particularly when teaching methods had been in existence at least that long which made it possible for nearly everyone to learn any new language quickly, easily and without accent.

Jarir was evidently one of those rare linguistic exceptions who had trouble with any tongue he had not been born to. The Commissioner turned to Roget and spoke to him rapidly in what Hal recognized as Arabic. Hal did not speak that particular language himself, but he caught the word *"Es-sha'b,"* which he identified by the Exotic cognate methods Walter the InTeacher had taught him, as meaning "people" in Arabic.

Roget answered with equal rapidity in the same language, then broke back to Basic, looking at Hal.

"I go in and out of this hotel all the time," he said. "None of those with Rukh have left it since you came in; and the hotel staff is as loyal to her as anyone else."

There was a casualness with which both of them seemed to dismiss the problem of necessary secrecy that disturbed Hal. No doubt what both had just said was true enough. Nonetheless, he had seen people beginning to congregate there at first light, outside the low white stone wall with its wide, low gates, that marked the limits of the hotel's grounds before its entrance.

Later, when their convoy of vehicles finally drove out through those same gates, the crowd assembled there was several hundred people in size, standing closely massed on both sides of the road. As the gates opened and the convoy of vehicles moved out, they waved—silently—at the opaqued windows of the ambulance in the center of the convoy line. While their appearance was friendly, it was impossible that so many should have known to gather there unless there had been little or no attempt to keep word of the trip from them; and if Jarir's security was so lax in that respect, what did that promise for the other areas of possible danger they might encounter on their way to the Alexandria Spacepad?

The waving hands were clearly directed at Rukh; but in fact, Rukh was not in the ambulance. She rode on the curved banquette seat of the rear compartment of one of the following police-escort cars, seated between Hal and Roget, with Jason occupying the single facing seat. The transparent safety window between the rear and driving compartments was up and locked, additional and effective enough shield against any small-arms fire short of that from power rifles or handguns—which were unlikely to be found outside the hands of the military or paramilitary here on Earth.

Through the window as the convoy left the hotel, Hal could see the countryside before them, framed between the backs of the heads of the police driver and Jarir. As they went through the gates, Jarir glanced back for a second at Rukh, and through the transparency, Hal saw the stony eyes go soft and dark. Only half a kilometer or so down the road the wayside was free of people watching and waving, and the convoy speeded up. Ahead, the roadstead was a wide strip of closely-growing dwarf grass, green as spring leaves between the low white siderails that warned off pedestrians. Hal could see even this short, thick grass flatten beneath the supporting air cushions of the vehicles as they picked up speed.

The green road ran in a long curve steadily toward the horizon, bordered on each side by open fields interspersed with the low transparent domes of hydroponic farms. Occasionally a few people were to be seen, standing waiting for the convoy to pass and waving as it did so.

"So much for security about Rukh's leaving the hotel," commented Hal.

"I can sympathize with those who leaked the word, though," said Jason. "Particularly after those news broadcasts last night."

"What news broadcasts?" Hal looked at him.

"You didn't—no, that's right, you went to bed early." Jason's face lit up. "You don't know, then!"

"That's right," said Hal, "I don't. Tell me."

"Why," Jason said, "evidently it took about ten hours for news about the assassination attempt to sink in around the world. Then some groups in a few of the major cities—you know, it's just like back home, here. The people outside the cities are all on our side. It's in the cities that they don't care—but as I started to tell you, some of these groups who'd picketed Rukh's talks and spoken and written against her came up with the idea of celebrating the fact that someone'd tried to kill her. And that triggered off the landslide."

"In what way?" demanded Hal.

"Why, it brought out all the people who'd heard her, and understood her, and had faith in her!" Jason's face was alight. "More people than anyone'd imagined—more people than we'd believed or imagined. News services came out with large stories on her side. Government bodies started to debate resolutions to protect people like her from other assassination tries like that. Hal—you actually hadn't heard about this until now? Isn't it unbelievable?"

"Yes," said Hal, numbly.

He felt like someone who had been preparing to move a mountain out of his way by sheer strength of muscle, only to have it slide aside under its own power before he could lay a finger on it. He had gambled, making the decision to move the Dorsai in and put up the shield-wall, hoping only that enough of Earth's population could be brought to listen— only listen—when Rukh spoke, so that she would have a reasonable chance of convincing them that what had been done had needed to be done.

Now, apparently, there was to be little problem in getting a majority of them to listen. He sat back on the banquette, his mind teeming with wonder and sudden understandings. No wonder Jarir, and even Roget, had seemed to dismiss so lightly his concern over keeping secret Rukh's drive to the Alexandria Spacepad. Given the kind of attention that had erupted all over the world, it would have been foolish to imagine that all of those there, including the staff of the hotel, could be kept from letting out word of the trip to those closest to them. Also, those now lining each side of the roadstead were security themselves, of a not inconsiderable kind.

As they approached the coast the number of people on either side of their way, held back by the white barriers, became more and more numerous; until there was an unbroken double band of humanity ahead of them as far as the eye could see. When they began at last to come into the built-up areas surrounding the Spacepad, so that storefronts and other structures enclosed the route, leaving only a narrow walkway between themselves and the barriers, that space was filled four and five bodies deep—all that the walkway would hold—with those waving as they passed.

But it was when finally they passed out from between the buildings, into the open space required by law in a broad belt outside the high-fenced perimeter of the Spacepad itself, that the shock came. The tall structures had held them in shadow; so that they burst out at once into sunlight and into the midst of a gathering of people so large that it took the breath away.

Looking out across the heads of this multitude, Hal saw the brilliantly-cloudless sky overhead dim fractionally and a gray sparkle seem to come into it.

"Jason," he said. "Take a look at the sky."

Jason withdrew his staring eyes reluctantly from the crowd of faces on his side of the vehicle and glanced upward.

"What about it?" he asked. "It's as clear and fine a day as you'd like—and nothing up there that looks dangerous. Besides, we're practically inside the perimeter, now."

Rukh had been dozing quietly most of their trip. Like Morelly and others Hal remembered from the Command on Harmony, her faith led her to avoid medication if at all possible. She was no fanatic about it; but Hal had noticed that apparently the same kind of discomfort touched her that he had seen in people raised under strict dietary laws and who no longer lived by them but could not bring themselves to eat with any relish what had once been forbidden. So she had refused the mild sedative Roget would have given her for the trip; and the physician had not insisted. Her general exhaustion, he had told Hal, would keep her quiet enough.

But now, the sudden glare of the sunlight through the one-way windows of the vehicle on her closed eyelids, plus the excitement in Jason's voice, roused her. She opened her eyes, sat up to look up and saw the crowd.

"Oh!" she said.

"They're here to see you pass, Rukh!" said Jason, turning to her exultantly. "All of them—here for you!"

She stared out the windows as the convoy slid along through the air, plainly absorbing what she saw and coming fully awake at the same time. After a moment she spoke again.

"They think I'm in the ambulance," she said. "We've got to stop. I've got to get out and show them I'm all right."

"No!" said Roget and Hal together.

The doctor glanced swiftly at Hal.

"You promised to save your strength!" Roget said, almost savagely. "That was your promise. You know, yourself, you can't step outside there without going right into full gear. Is that saving your strength?"

"Besides that," said Hal. "All it takes is one armed fanatic there, willing to die to get you first; or one armed idiot who hasn't thought beyond killing you if the chance comes; and the fact that all these other people'll tear someone like that to pieces afterward won't bring you back to life."

"Don't be foolish, Hal," said Rukh. Her voice had strengthened. "How would any assassin know we'd stop along here, when we didn't know we were going to do it, ourselves? And Roget, this is something I have to do— something I owe those people out there. I'll just get out, let them see me and get right back in. I can lean on Hal."

She was already reaching forward to press the tab that signalled the front compartment of the vehicle. Jarir's head turned back and the window slid down between him and them.

"Jarir," said Rukh. "Stop the convoy. I'm going to get out just long enough for these people to see I'm all right."

"It's not wise—" Jarir began.

"Wise or not, do what I tell you," said Rukh. "Jarir?"

The Commissioner shrugged. Once more the stony eyes had gone liquid and soft.

"*Es-sha'b,*" he said to the driver, whose inquiring face was turned toward him. He turned to the panel in front of him, touched a stud and spoke in Arabic.

The convey slowed and stopped, the vehicles which composed it settling to the bright turf underneath them.

"Now," said Rukh, to Hal. "If you'll give me your arm, Hal. Open the door, Jason."

Reluctantly, Jason unlocked and swung open the rear compartment door on Hal's side of the car. Hal stepped out, turned and reached back in to help Rukh emerge. She stepped out and down to the ground, leaning heavily on his arm.

"We'll step out between the cars where they can see me," she said.

He led her in that direction. For the first three steps she bore most of her weight upon him; but as they left behind the vehicle they had been riding in and passed out into the thirty meters of space that separated it from the next car in line she straightened up, stretched her legs into a firmer stride, and after a pace or two let go of him entirely to walk forward by herself and stand straight, alone and a little in advance of him, facing the crowd on that side of the roadstead.

All along the route the people had waved at their passing in silence. At first this had felt strange to Hal, even though he realized those along the way must think that Rukh in the ambulance could not easily hear them if they did call out to her, and that in any case she should have to endure as little disturbance as possible. But he had grown accustomed to the lack of shouting as they went along and all but forgotten it, until this moment. But now, standing beside Rukh and looking out at those thousands of faces, the waving hands together with the quiet was eerie.

For a moment after they stopped and stood waiting, there was no change in those out at whom they looked. The eyes of everyone had been fastened on the ambulance; and few of them had even noticed the two figures that had come from one of the escort cars.

Then, slowly, the waving hands of those nearest Rukh and Hal began to hesitate, as the people became aware of them. Faces turned toward them; and gradually, like a ripple going over some wide and fluid surface, the attention of each one in the crowd was brought, one by one, to fasten upon them—and at last Rukh was recognized.

The hands had fallen now. It was a sea of faces only that looked at Rukh; and with that recognition, starting with those closest to her, the first sound was heard from the people as a whole. To Hal's ears it was like a sigh, that like a wave washed out and out from them until it was lost in the farthest part of the gathering, then came rushing like a wave back in again, gathering strength and speed, rising to a roar, a thunder that shook the air around them.

Rukh stood facing them. She could not speak to them with the noise they were making. She could not even have spoken to them if they had stopped making it. The closest were twenty meters from her; and few of them would have come equipped with repeaters to pick up her words and rebroadcast them to those farther back. But she slowly raised both her arms, stretched at full length before her, until they were at shoulder level, and then slowly she spread them wide, as if blessing them all.

With the lifting of her arms, their voices began to die; and by the time she had finished sweeping them wide, there was no sound at all to be heard from that vast gathering before her. In the new quiet, she turned about to face the other side of the roadstead; and repeated the gesture there, bringing these, too, into silence.

In that silence, she turned back toward the car and Hal moved quickly to catch her as she almost staggered once more, leaning heavily against him. He helped her back and half-lifted her into the vehicle, following close behind her.

With the closing of the door after them, and the starting up once more of the vehicles of the convoy, the voices broke out again; and that thunder beat steadily upon them, now, following them as they moved down the road past those who had not yet seen them up close, until they passed through the entrance in the high fence, past the unusually heavy perimeter guard of the Spacepad in their trim blue uniforms and heavy power rifles, and went on into the relative emptiness of the Pad, heading not for the Terminal but for the shuttle itself, better than four kilometers distant across the endless gray surface of the Pad.

Hal leaned forward and spoke to Jarir through the openness where the window between the compartments remained rolled down.

"You'll have to take my word for this," he said. "It's something I just noticed. A protective shield we've been planning to put around all of the Earth at low orbit level's just been set in place. The world is going to be hearing all about it in a few hours. But for now, if we don't get Rukh aboard that shuttle, and it off the ground in minutes, its pilots may find themselves ordered by the Space and Atmosphere authorities not to lift."

Jarir's eyes met his from a distance of only inches away, and held for a long moment. They had gone back to being bright stones again.

"She will be aboard," he said. "And it will lift."

Chapter

> > **64** < <

As *Roget had* predicted to them all in their pre-dawn session in the hotel, by the time the shuttle entered a bay at the Final Encyclopedia, Rukh was exhausted and sleeping heavily. Hal carried her off in his arms, into the clanging noise and brightness of the bay, and handed her over to two of the people from the Encyclopedia's medical clinic, who had brought a float stretcher. Almost beside him, the Number One pilot of the shuttle was close to shouting at the bay commander.

"I tell you I got word from the surface to turn around, to head back!" he was saying, "and I talked them out of it! I was the one who told them if they let me go on, I could get some answers up here. We could see it plain as day, coming in at this altitude—like a gray wall above us, stretching everywhere, out of sight. If it isn't all around the world and if it isn't the same thing you've got around the Encyclopedia, I'll eat it—"

"Pilot, I tell you," said the bay commander, a small, black-haired woman in her thirties with a quiet, oriental face, "everything's on emergency status here at the moment. If you want to wait, I'll try to get someone down from the Director's staff to talk to you. But I can't promise when anyone'll come—"

"That's not good enough!" The pilot's voice lifted. He was a large, heavy man and he loomed over the commander. "I'm asking you for an answer in the name of the Space and Atmosphere Agency—"

Hal tapped the man on the shoulder, and the pilot pivoted swiftly, then stopped and stared upward as he found himself facing Hal's jacket collar tab.

"There'll be broadcasts from here explaining this to the whole world, shortly," Hal said. "There's nothing you can be told now that you and your superiors won't be hearing in a few hours, anyway."

The pilot found his voice again.

"Who're you? One of the passengers, aren't you? That's no good. I want someone who knows what's going on, and I want whoever that is, now!" He swung back to the bay commander. "I'm ordering you, if necessary, to get someone here in five minutes—"

"Pilot," said the bay commander, wearily, "let's be sensible. You've got no authority to order anyone here. Neither has Space and Atmosphere, or anyone else from below."

Hal turned away, his leaving ignored by the pilot. With Jason close behind, he headed toward Tam's suite, pushing his way gently through the turmoil and confusion he encountered along the way.

As he stepped through the door of the suite he found a broadcast of the sort he had promised the pilot already underway. The room was crowded. Not only were Amid and Nonne there, as well as the head of every department in the Encyclopedia except Jeamus, but there were at least half a dozen technicians, apparently concerned with the technical details of the broadcast.

It was Tam who was speaking. A desk-float had been moved into position in front of his favorite non-float armchair and he looked across the unyielding gleam of the oak-colored surface as he spoke. Ajela stood to one side, behind him, just out of picture range. Her head turned to the door as Hal and Jason entered; and when she saw who it was she smiled at them. A smile, it seemed to Hal, of strong relief.

He went quietly to her along one wall of the room. It was neither a quick nor a steady journey. Everyone else in the room, it seemed, was utterly caught up in what Tam was saying in his deep and age-hoarsened voice. Hal would move a step or two, find his way blocked, and whisper in the ear of whoever was in the way. Whoever it was would turn, start, smile at him a little strangely, then move aside with a matching whisper of apology.

". . . times without precedent sometimes require actions without precedent," Tam was saying to the picture receptors—and the whole Earth beyond.

". . . And because we have access here at the Encyclopedia to equipment that does not, to my knowledge, exist anywhere else, I've been forced to make an emergency decision on the basis of information which we'll shortly be making available to all of you; but on which I felt I had to act at once.

"In brief, that information is that Earth is in danger of being attacked without warning and finding itself stripped of its historic freedom as an independent and autonomous world. My decision was that an impregnable barrier should be placed in position without further delay around our Mother World to make sure this could not happen.

"Accordingly, I gave an order which has since been carried out by personnel of the Encyclopedia: that a phase-shield-wall, similar to the one that's preserved the independence of this Encyclopedia itself for more than eighty years, be placed completely about our planet, to lock out any possibility of armed attack from other human worlds.

"This phase-shield-wall, as it's now configured, has been structured with all the necessary irises—or openings to outer space—that may be needed by space shipping to enter or leave the territory of Earth's space and atmosphere. These irises can be closed at will; and they will be, at a moment's notice, in the case of any threat against us. Once they are closed, nothing in the universe can penetrate to us without our permission.

"Even fully closed, however, this phase-shield-wall, which is an improved model of that which guards the Final Encyclopedia, has been designed to allow through it all necessary sunlight or any other solar radiation required for normal and customary existence. The physical condition of the space it occupies and the space it separates us from has been in no way altered by its existence.

"It's also within the capabilities of our crews generating this shield-wall to open irises at any other points that may be necessary, now or at any time in the future. Eventually they will do so in accordance with the desires of the general population of Earth.

"In short, nothing has been imposed upon, or taken away from the ordinary quality of life on our Earth by the establishment of this protective barrier. As you know, this world of ours is a closed and self-sustaining system that requires only the solar energy which will continue to reach us in order to exist indefinitely as we know it.

"Additional details on both the shield-wall and the threat that caused me to order it constructed will be made available to you shortly. There is no intention here on the part of those of us who staff the Final Encyclopedia to set ourselves up in any way as a form of authority over Earth or its peoples. In any case, we lack the skills and numbers of personnel to do so, even if this community of scholars and researchers were so inclined. Simply, we have been required by circumstances to take a single, vitally necessary, specific action without having time to consult with the rest of you first.

"For that action, I take sole and individual responsibility. For taking it without consultation with you all, I apologize, repeating only that the necessity existed for doing so. I ask you all to wait until all the information that led us to generate it is also in your possession; and you are individually in a position to judge the emergency that led us to take this action.

"Having said that much, I have only one more thing to tell you. It's that this is my last official act as Director of the Encyclopedia. As I imagine most of you know, I have held this post far longer than I'd planned, while the search has gone on for a qualified successor. Now, I'm happy to say, one has finally been found—I should, more correctly, say the Encyclopedia itself has found one, since the man I speak of has passed a test by the Encyclopedia itself that only two other human beings in its history have passed—those two being myself and Mark Torre, the founder of this great tool and storehouse of human knowledge.

"The individual who now replaces me is a citizen of Old Earth, named Hal Mayne. Some of you have already heard of him. The rest of you will shortly, when he speaks to you from here in the next day or two."

He stopped. His voice had been weakening steadily; and now it failed him. After a second, he continued.

"Bless you, people of Earth. I think more than a few of you know me by reputation. I'm not given to compliments or praise unless there's no doubt it's been earned. But I tell you, as someone who's watched you for over a century and a quarter now, that as long as you remain what you've been no enemy can hope to conquer you, no threat can hope to intimidate you. I have been greatly privileged, through a long life, to guard this precious creation, this Encyclopedia, for you. Hal Mayne, who follows me as its guardian, will keep it as well and better than I have ever been able to. . . ."

For a moment he stopped, and occupied himself only with breathing. Then he went on, raggedly.

"To you all, good-bye."

He sank back into his chair, closing his eyes, as the operating lights on the picture receptor went out. The room erupted with voices, all talking to each other around him and for a moment he was ignored, sitting shrunken and still in the big armchair.

Hal had reached Ajela's side, behind Tam's chair, some seconds back. At the sudden introduction of his own name into the speech he had looked down into Ajela's face and had been answered by something that could only be described as a hard grin.

"So," he said, as the talk rose around them. "You and Tam just went ahead and appointed me."

"You've been doing what's necessary without asking, when there wasn't any time to ask," she retorted. "So now we've done the same thing. You knew Tam's finally gone as far as he can—"

A shadow of pain darkened her eyes for a second.

"You're drafted," she said. "That's all. Because there's no one else around for the job."

He nodded slowly. It was true; moreover, he had been expecting Tam and Ajela to do some such thing as this. They knew as well as he did that he had to take on the title of Director of the Encyclopedia eventually; and that he would need it to give him a position from which to deal with the people of Earth in the future now upon them. Reflexively, he had left it to the two of them to push the job upon him, so that it would come to him only at the time when Tam was fully ready to let go. He had, he thought, been fully prepared for this moment.

But now that it had come, he felt a sudden chill to the mantle of authority that had just been draped about his shoulders. He tried to push the feeling away. He had always wanted to be a part of the Encyclopedia; and the work he had still to do required him to be here. But still, with Ajela's words, it was as if a shadow had fallen across his soul and he looked up to see tall walls closing about him. He felt an ominous premonition that he imagined as somehow being connected with Amanda.

"I won't have time to run it," he said, as he had known he would say at this time to either Tam or Ajela.

"I know," she answered, as he had known she would. "I'll do that part of it, as I—as I'm used to doing."

The door to the suite opened and Rourke di Facino came quickly in, followed by Jeamus. Hal, whose height allowed him to see over the heads of others in the room, caught sight of them immediately; and Ajela, following the sudden shift in direction of his gaze, turned and saw them also.

"Hal—" Rourke had caught sight of him. "Jeamus' system is working, and we've just got a picture of the first transports beginning to lift from the Dorsai—"

He had needed to speak across the room and over the sound of the crowd. His words reached everyone; and he was suddenly interrupted by a cheer. When it died, Rourke was still talking to Hal.

". . . come and see for yourself?"

"Pipe it in here!" shouted a female voice; and the room broke out in a noise of agreement.

"No!" Ajela's clear voice rode up over the voices of them all. "Everybody out, please. You can watch it in one of the dining rooms. Out, if you don't mind."

"Hal—" It was Tam's voice, unexpectedly. "Wait."

Hal checked his first movement to leave and stepped around to face the chair. Ajela had already moved around on the other side of it. Behind them, the suite was clearing quickly. Tam reached out and Hal now felt his hand taken between the two dry knobby ones of the old man, the bones of which felt too large for the skin enclosing them.

"Hal!" said Tam. He seemed to struggle for words a moment, then let the effort go. ". . . Hal!"

"Thank you," said Hal softly. "Don't worry. I'll take good care of it."

"I know you will," said Tam. "I know you will. . . ."

He let Hal's hand slide from between his own, which dropped back down on his knees. He sighed deeply, the burst of energy gone, sitting back in the chair with his eyelids sagging almost closed. Hal's eyes lifted and met those of Ajela. She moved her head slightly and he nodded. Quietly, he turned and went toward the door as she sank down on her knees beside Tam's chair.

As he went out, Hal looked back. Tam sat still, his eyes completely closed now. Still kneeling, she had put her arms around his waist and laid her head against his chest.

Hal closed the suite door and went off down the corridor outside. The second dining room he tried held everyone who had been in Tam's suite and a great many more of the people momentarily off duty in the Encyclopedia, all of them watching the one side of the room Jeamus had used as a stage for the projection equipment of his communications system.

Jason was standing just outside the entrance to the room, obviously waiting for him.

"Hal?" he said, as Hal came up to him. "There's a lot to be done. . . ."

"I know," said Hal. He closed one hand briefly about the nearer of Jason's lean shoulders. "I'll only step in for a minute."

He went past the other man through the doorway, and stepped aside from it to put his back to the wall and watch the projected scene over the heads of those between him and the stage area. The images projected were not perfect. A halo of rainbow colors encircled the pictured three-dimensional action, which it seemed was being recorded from some distance. The images went in and out of focus as the Encyclopedia's capacity to calculate strove to keep pinpointed the exact distance between it and the light-years-distant transmitter, continually correcting with small phase-shifts, as a ship might have to do to hold a constant position in interstellar space, relative to any other single point. The sound was irregular also—one moment clear and the next blurred.

The scene showed the large Pad at Omalu where Hal had last parted from Amanda. The Pad was full of spaceships, now; most of them obviously Dorsai but a fair number identifiable as having been built to Exotic specifications. The ship in closest focus at the moment had a large group of people slowly boarding it; mostly young adults and children, but here and there an older face could be seen among them. The scene blurred in, blurred out of focus, the sound wavering; and Hal found himself caught by what he watched as if he had been nailed to the wall behind him.

"They're singing something, but I can't catch the words," whispered the man just in front of him to the woman beside him. "Clea, can you make out the words?"

The woman's head shook.

Hal stood listening. He could not make out the words either, but he did not have to. From the tune he was hearing he knew them, from his boyhood as Donal. It was the unofficial Dorsai anthem, unofficial because there was no official anthem, any more than there was an official Dorsai flag or the armies the anthem spoke of; the Dorsai they were singing about was not the Dorsai they were leaving, but the Dorsai each one of them was carrying within them. He turned and went back out the door to find Jason waiting for him.

"All right, now," he said to the other man, as they went off down the corridor together. "What's most urgent of the things you've got in hand?"

Chapter

> > **6 5** < <

"*The things I* had in mind can wait," Jason said. "I just got a call from Jeamus. He's been trying to locate you, quietly."

"Jeamus?" Hal glanced toward the dining room where people were still watching the images from the Dorsai.

"Jeamus isn't there," Jason said. "It seems he got called back to Communications as soon as he stepped out of Tam Olyn's suite. He had a crew with him to set up the reception—he'd hoped to do it in the Director's suite, too—and he just left it to them to carry on to the dining room with it. He went back down to Communications himself, and he's just called me from there."

"He didn't say what about?"

"Just that he wanted you to come down there as quickly as possible, without telling anyone he'd called you."

Hal nodded, and led off down the corridor in which they were standing with long strides.

Within the door of the Communications Department, Jeamus, his face tight, caught sight of them the minute they entered, and came to hurry them into the privacy of a small office.

"What is it?" asked Hal.

"A signal," said Jeamus, "from Bleys. It just came in, via orbit relay private for me. I don't have a written copy because he asked me not to make one. The call came in without identification, to me, by name. I didn't even know he knew I existed. He said you'd know the call was authentic if I referred to him as one of the two visitors you once had in your library; and he gave me a verbal message for you."

Jeamus hesitated.

"You're Director now," he said. "It's only fair to tell you that fifteen minutes ago I'd have checked with Tam before passing this message along to you."

"That's all right," said Hal. "I assume you thought there might be something in it that might affect the security of the Encyclopedia. Fine. I'll appreciate your having the same sense of responsibility toward me now that I'm Director. What's the message?"

Jeamus still hesitated. He looked at Jason.

"It's all right," said Hal. "Jason can stay."

"Forgive me," Jeamus said. "Are you sure . . . I mean, this might affect more than the Encyclopedia. It might affect everything."

"I know Bleys; better, I think, than anyone else." Hal's eyes fastened on Jeamus' brown ones. "Any secrecy he's concerned about is only going to matter with those who're uncommitted—to being either for or against him. Jason can stay. Tell me."

"If you say so," said Jeamus. He took a deep breath. "He wants to meet you, secretly—here."

"Here in the Encyclopedia?"

"No. Close to it," Jeamus said.

"I see." Hal looked about the small, neat office. "Tell him yes. Have him signal you, personally, once he's here. Then you yourself see to it that an iris no bigger than necessary to let him, personally, in, is dilated in the shield-wall close to here. I'll meet him inside the shield-wall."

"All right," said Jeamus.

"And of course you'll tell no one," Hal said. "Including Ajela. Including Tam."

"I—" began Jeamus, and stuck.

"I know," said Hal. "The habits of years aren't easy to change in a minute. But I'm either Director or not; and you're either the head of my Engineering Department, or not. You expected me to go to Tam or Ajela as soon as you'd told me this, didn't you?"

"Yes," said Jeamus, miserably.

"Tam's out of it now," Hal said. "And Ajela I'll tell myself, in my own time. If you're tempted to go to either one in spite of what I've just said to you, stop first and think who'll take the Encyclopedia over if I don't. Ajela can keep it going; but I think you've heard Tam say often enough it's meant for more than this."

"Yes," Jeamus sighed. "All right, I won't say anything to either of them. But"— he looked suddenly up into Hal's face—"you'll tell me when you've told Ajela?"

"Yes," said Hal. He turned to Jason. "Come on. Didn't you have a whole list with you of things you wanted me to attend to?"

Jason nodded.

"Thanks, Jeamus," said Hal; and led Jason out of the Communications Section.

In the corridor outside, Jason stared at him as they walked.

"Can I ask?" he said. "What does it mean, this business of Bleys wanting to talk to you secretly?"

"I think it means he discovered he'd made a misjudgment," Hal answered. "Now, weren't you the one who told me how much work we had to do?"

The work was real enough. It was nearly four days before Rukh was strong enough to make her address to the world; and Hal chose to put off his own first speech as Director until it could also act as an introduction to what Rukh would say. Meanwhile, the days were frantic ones, with the Encyclopedia like a fortress under siege. A full third of the non-specialist staff was busy in shifts around the clock, fielding queries from the surface of Earth, from governmental bodies or planetary agencies like Space and Atmosphere.

The primary difficulty for the staff was the keeping of tempers. From sheer habit the various governments and authorities below had begun by demanding attention and answers. Only slowly had they come to realize that not merely was there no way they could force or threaten the shield-walled, independently-powered and fully-supplied Encyclopedia to do anything, but there had not been for the last eighty years. So they had finally backed off the path of bluster to the highway of diplomacy; but by that time the damage to the frayed patience of the Encyclopedia's relatively-tiny staff had been done.

"Who'd have thought it'd be like this?" Ajela said exhaustedly to Hal at mid-morning of that fourth day. Like everyone else, she had been operating on little food and less sleep since Tam's speech. "Ninety per cent of this is unnecessary. If some of those people in control down there would only face reality—but I suppose there's no hope of that."

"They actually are facing reality; and, in fact, it actually is necessary," said Hal.

They were in Ajela's office suite, and Ajela had just been talking to the Director of the planet's Northwest Agricultural Sector, who had been only the latest of a large number of officials needing to be reassured that the interposition of the shield-wall between the particular area of his responsibilities and the sun would not somehow have an adverse effect on the ripening grain of that year's upcoming harvest. It was clear he had no idea what kind of adverse effect this could be, but rather, hoped Ajela could tell him of one.

She frowned at Hal; suddenly he was emphatically conscious of how exhausted she was. In anyone but a born Exotic that frown would have been an emotional explosion. He hurried to explain.

"A man like that one you just heard from," Hal said, "is struggling to make an adjustment to the concept of the Encyclopedia as not only a politically-potent, but a superior entity. This is a situation that even a week ago was so far-fetched it was inconceivable. But now we've become the main power center, up here. So it's necessary for each member of the power network below to make contact with us and make sure we know they, personally, are also on the political map."

"But we haven't got the staff to play those kinds of games!" said Ajela. "That isn't what's important, anyway. What's important is handling four million Dorsai as they get here and seeing to their resettlement; and even if that was all we were trying to do, we don't have staff enough for it, now that the ships have started arriving; even if we do have all that wealth from the Exotics and can use the Encyclopedia as if it was an automated bureaucracy!"

"All right," said Hal. "Then let's have a communications breakdown." She stared at him.

"I mean a breakdown as far as conversations with the surface are concerned," Hal said.

Ajela was still staring. She was, Hal realized, more tired than he had thought.

"We can simply simulate an overload, or a power failure—Jeamus'll know what to do," he said. "Either respond to all calls from below as if our phones were tied up, or simply not answer at all with anything but static. We can have the difficulty clear up just as soon as I've made my speech and Rukh begins hers; and that leaves you free to fold up, from now until I start talking. That ought to be good for at least four hours' sleep for you."

"Four hours," she echoed, as if the words were sounds in some peculiar, unknown tongue. Then her gaze sharpened and she frowned at him again.

"And are you going to fold up too?"

"No," he said. "I don't need to. You've been running things, not me. All I am is ordinarily tired. In fact, it'll give me the chance I haven't had to work on my speech—which is my main concern."

She swayed a little as she sat at her desk, puzzling over what he had said, instinctively feeling the deception in it; but too dulled by fatigue to pinpoint the lie.

"You really think . . . ," she began at last—and ran down.

"I do," he said. He rose and went to her; and over her protests literally lifted her from her float by her elbows. Setting her on her feet, he steered her into her adjoining personal suite and made her lie down on her bed. He sat down in a chair-float beside her.

"What are you doing there?" she demanded, drunk with the exhaustion that was taking her over completely, now that she had let herself admit to it.

"Waiting to make sure you fall asleep."

"Don't be ridiculous," she said. "I'm wound up like a spring. I'm not going to fall asleep just like that. . . ."

She stared at him fiercely for all of twenty seconds before her eyes fluttered, closed, and she slept. He set the temperature control above her bed and left.

He went directly to his own quarters, now enlarged into a suite to provide space for the kind of conferences his new obligations as Director required; and sat down to put in a call to Rukh, Nonne, Rourke, Amid and Jason.

"Conference in two hours," he told them. "Here."

Having passed that message he went to the same bay into which he, Rukh and Jason had arrived less than a week before. The same bay commander was on duty.

"Chui," he said to her, "I need a skidder to go visit the Dorsai transports parked in orbit."

A shuttle was unloading; and a man in a pilot's uniform had just stepped out of the airlock among the passengers. She broke off to shout at him.

"No, you don't! Back in there! Passengers only. No crew allowed off the transport at this end!"

Her voice was considerable. He would not have thought it of her. She turned back, saw him watching her and looked, for a second, a little flustered.

"We've all changed, I guess," she said. "You want a driver?"

"No."

"If you want to go up to the front of the bay, out of the passenger area, I'll have one unracked and brought up to you right away."

Five minutes later Hal drove out of the Encyclopedia in his mosquito of a one-man craft and headed toward the parking area of the spaceships from the Dorsai. The gray orb of the Encyclopedia dwindled swiftly behind him at steady acceleration until his instruments warned him he was at midpoint from the nearest of the still-invisible ships. Then he flipped the power segment beneath his seat and rode in toward his destination on metered deceleration; as, with his viewscreen ranging ahead on normal telescopic setting, the first of the spacecraft which had just crossed twenty-three light-years of interstellar emptiness began to come into view.

These, lying ahead of him at protectively-spaced intervals, were some of the largest vessels, troop transports of the Dorsai and luxury spaceships that had followed regular schedules between the stars under Exotic ownership. The hundreds of smaller craft that would also be making the trip would lift later from the outlying, smaller community centers like Foralie; and even from personal Spacepads built by Dorsai families such as the Graemes, who had mustered and trained soldiers on their own land for specific off-Dorsai contracts. But first had come the big ships, loading up from the few cities and larger population centers.

They were fully visible now in his screen on a scan that compensated for the distance they covered, their parked ranks stretching away from him in a long curve that was part the illusion of distance and space, part actuality. They lay in sunlight translated through the shield-wall, next to the great, apparently-vertical wall of it on his right, that stretched upward and downward from his viewpoint until all view of it was lost in the blackness of space.

To his left, also in bright sunlight, floated the white-swatched blue orb of the Earth, looking close enough in the compensated view of the screen so that he could reach out at arm's length and touch it. Unimportant in the space that went also between them, and seeming only to crawl along, his tiny skidder crept up on the nearest of the huge vessels. Far ahead, and far behind, where the gray of the shield-wall seemed to vanish, the blackness of space showed the lights of stars, which from that angle and distance were perceptible through it.

A stillness took him. He felt the presence of the universe that dwarfed not only men and women but ships, planets and stars—even galaxies that were no more than scatterings of dust across its inconceivable face. The universe that knew nothing and cared less for the microscopic organism called the human race, that in its many parts tried so hard for survival. It was all around him, and its remoteness and vastness confirmed the isolation of his own spirit. Not on Earth, nor in sky nor space, he floated apart, even from his own kind. A crushing loneliness closed around him; but the call of what he had seen, what Donal had seen, gazing out at the unknown stars in that moment when Padma had at last had a chance and failed to recognize him for what he was, drew him on. With the failure of Padma, he had set aside all hope of being touched again by human understanding as one touched one in the race of his birth; and he had left it set aside through two lives since . . . until this one. Until now. . . .

He had come close enough finally to the first of the parked ships—a wide-bodied transport—to hit its metal skin with a spot communicator beam of light.

"*Sea of Summer!*" he said into his phone grille. "*Sea of Summer*, this is Hal Mayne of the Final Encyclopedia, en route from the Encyclopedia by skidder to the *Olof's Own*. I'm transmitting my personal image for iden-

tification. Repeat, this is Hal Mayne. Can you direct me to *Olof's Own?*
I ask, can you direct me—"

His screen lit up suddenly with a lean-faced young man wearing a
ship's officer's jacket, who seemed to peer at him through the screen.

"Hal Mayne?" he said. He glanced briefly off-screen then back at Hal.
"I'm third officer, duty shift. Mika Moyne. Want to identify yourself by
telling me where you last outvisited on the Dorsai?"

"Foralie Town, Mika Moyne," said Hal. "Honored."

"The honor's mine." The lean face grinned. "Hal Mayne, the *Olof's
Own* was the next to the last arrival last time I checked. We're going
through Fleet Locator now . . . all right, she's now in Station 103—not
far down the line at all."

"Thank you, Mika Moyne."

"My pleasure, Hal Mayne."

He signed off and went on. Fourteen hundred kilometers down the line,
he found the *Olof's Own,* identified himself and was invited aboard.

"I understand one of your passengers is Miriam Songhai," he said,
when he was inside. "I'd like to talk to her for a moment if she wouldn't
mind."

"We'll find her and ask," said the *Olof's Own* captain. "Do you want
to wait in the Officer's Duty Lounge? It shouldn't take more than a few
minutes to find her for you."

He took Hal into the Duty Lounge. Less than ten minutes later, Miriam
Songhai pushed open the door of the lounge and stepped in. Hal and the
captain stood up from the floats on which they had been seated.

"Excuse me," said the captain. "I've got to get back to the control area."

He left them in the empty lounge.

"It's good of you to see me," said Hal. "Honored."

"Nonsense," said Miriam Songhai. "I was only twiddling my thumbs,
anyway, and I'm the one who's honored. What did you want to see me
about?"

She sat down and Hal reseated himself.

"I've been watching for Amanda Morgan to turn up," he said. "So far
I haven't found anyone who knows when she'll be coming. I've talked to
a few of the Foralie area people, but they say she's been spending all her
time in Omalu these last weeks—which makes sense. She mentioned
once that you, too, had duties that put you in Omalu, a lot. So I thought
I'd ask you if you knew anything."

Miriam shook her head.

"I haven't seen her for a couple of weeks, at least," she said, "and then only to talk business about ways and means of getting official records packed and shipped. I've no idea when she was leaving. But the responsibilities of most of us in Omalu are over, now that the ships are actually lifting. She ought to be along any time now."

"I hope so," said Hal, and smiled.

He stood up. She stood up, also.

"Well, thank you," he said. "It was a long shot—but I appreciate being able to ask you."

"Nonsense, again," she said. "I'm just sorry I didn't have anything definite to tell you. But, as I say, she'll be along."

They went to the door of the lounge together. As it slid back automatically for them both, they stepped through; and just outside, she stopped—and checked him also with a hand that closed on his arm. He felt a strange shock go through him at her touch, as if a powerful electricity charged her. Her blunt, dark fingers held his arm strongly.

"Don't worry," Miriam Songhai said, firmly. Her gaze was direct and unyielding. "She'll be all right."

"Thank you," he said.

She released him; and he watched her go off down the corridor toward the aft section of the ship. He turned back into the control area and was greeted by the captain.

"Had your talk?" said the captain. "Anything else we can do for you, Hal Mayne?"

"No. Thanks very much," said Hal. "I'd better be starting back for the Encyclopedia."

Once more in the little skidder, he increased his acceleration to shorten the trip back. But when he finally reentered his suite, it was almost time for the conference he had called—and Ajela was waiting for him there in one of the non-float chairs, which, like Tam, she favored.

"That's interesting," he said, closing the door behind him. "Can you let yourself into anyone's living quarters whether they're home or not?"

"I can to yours," she said. "Because you're the Director; and I'm Special Assistant to the Director; and in case of emergency I have to have access to any place the Director might be."

She stared at him.

"—And as a matter fact, yes," she went on, "I could let myself into the quarters of anyone here at the Encyclopedia, only I wouldn't."

"Only into the Director's quarters?"

"That's right."

He sat down opposite her and looked at her critically.

"How much sleep did you get?"

"An hour—an hour and a half. Never mind that," she said. "What's this conference you'd have had me miss out on?"

He shook his head at her.

"The most important topic for discussion," he said, "is undoubtedly going to be my announcement that I'll be insisting on being a free agent; so I can do my own work in my own carrel, here. The rest of them are going to have to run matters without my looking over their shoulders. But this is something you already know about. The others are going to find it something of a shock, I think."

"That—and what else?"

"That and a few other things. The most important of those is that Bleys is coming secretly to have a talk with me."

She sat up suddenly in the armchair.

"What about?"

"I'll find out when he gets here."

The door annunciator spoke with the voice of Rourke di Facino.

"Hal, I'm here."

"Open," said Hal to the door; and Rourke walked in to take a seat with them.

"Nonne's on her way. So is Jason," Rourke said. "I haven't seen Amid."

He looked penetratingly at Ajela.

"You need rest," he said.

"Later," she answered.

"Then close your eyes and lean back until the rest get here," said Rourke. "You won't think it's helping, but it will."

She opened her mouth to answer him, then smiled a little and did as he had just suggested. Almost immediately, her breathing slowed and deepened.

Hal and Rourke looked at each other and said nothing by mutual consent. Hal got up, walked to the door and set it wide open. As the others he had called in appeared at it, one by one, he held his fingers to his lips and beckoned them in. Finally, however, they were all there—including Amid; and it was not possible to put off conversation any longer.

"We've just got time," said Hal, "to go over a few things before I go on general broadcast to the Earth to announce I've taken over as Director up here and introduce Rukh."

He looked across the seated circle of their gathering at Rukh, who returned his gaze calmly. The few days of rest for her here at the Encyclopedia had been absolute, simply because there was no means by which news that might disturb or rouse her could reach her without the active cooperation of the Encyclopedia's Communications Center, which Hal had refused to allow. Roget had all but danced in the corridors at the results that now showed. She was still as thin and fragile in appearance as she had been when Hal had seen her down at the hotel beside Lake Qattara. But the look of transparency had vanished from her. She was fully alive once more; and the aura of personal strength that had always been part of her was back.

He paused to look over at Ajela; but she had not woken at the sound of his voice. She continued to slumber, half-curled up with her head tucked into the angle between one of the wings and the back of the chair.

"I want to make sure you all understand fully what that appointment is going to mean, both for me and for the rest of you," Hal went on. "To begin with, I take it I don't have to explain why there's no question of my refusing it? There's no one else; and Tam isn't up to continuing other than under ordinary conditions. If Ajela was awake, she'd tell you that Tam first spoke to me about taking over here eventually some years ago; and both of us knew it had to happen eventually."

He looked around at them for possible comment. No one said anything, although Nonne's face was absolutely expressionless.

"Why you, especially, Hal?" asked Rukh.

"I'm sorry," he answered. "With all else that's been going on, I took it for granted Ajela or someone else might have told you. They didn't? But they did take you all past the Transit Point as you came in here the first time?"

All other heads, except Ajela's, shook.

"I didn't know that," Hal said. "There's a spot in the Encyclopedia at its centerpoint. I invite you all to ask one of the staff to show you where it is and go and stand there for a second. If you hear any voices speaking, get in touch with me at once; because it means you've also got one of the qualifications that's needed in whoever takes over the Encyclopedia. In all the years since it became operative, everyone who's come here's been led past that centerpoint; and I apologize for the system breaking down now. You all should have been tested as a matter of routine. In nearly a century only Mark Torre, Tam Olyn and myself have heard voices at that spot."

"You heard voices," said Nonne. "When, if you don't mind my asking?"

"The first time I came here, when I was not quite seventeen years old," said Hal.

"And not since?"

"Yes." Hal smiled at her. "I went back and stood there for a moment, as soon as I could get off by myself after Tam announced I'd be succeeding him."

"And the voices were still there?"

"Still there," said Hal.

Nonne's expressionlessness of face did not change.

"And this is supposed to mean . . . what?"

"That the Encyclopedia was meant to be something more than a supremely-effective library and research mechanism," he answered. "Mark Torre, who planned and built it, had a conception of something greater; a tool for the innate improvement of mankind. He built the Encyclopedia on the faith of that idea and nothing more; but the faith was justified when Tam also heard the voices. Until then Mark Torre had kept quiet about his reasons for running everyone who came through the centerpoint. After that he spoke up. It was the one proof that came in his lifetime, that there was a greater purpose and use for the Encyclopedia than anyone else had believed; a purpose and use we can't see clearly even yet, but that send out signals of its possibilities in something more than ordinary physical terms."

"And you'd like to be the one who puts it to that greater purpose?" Nonne asked.

"Nonne," said Rukh. "It strikes me at this point that Ajela'd have a question for you. Since she's still sleeping, I'll ask it for her. Amid—"

She glanced across at the older Exotic.

"You told me Nonne'd been one of those Exotics who'd originally been against Hal being trusted and backed by your people. From what I've been told by Ajela, so far, and from what I've seen in the short time I've known you, Nonne, you seem to have gone from having reservations about everything Hal's done to an outright antagonism toward him. Maybe it's time you tell the rest of us why."

Nonne's expressionlessness vanished. A little color tinted the smooth skin over her cheekbones.

"I didn't approve of Hal being given a blank check by my people, no," she said. "Amid was the one who did, as you say. As a result, it was decided by the rest of us studying the matter that since Amid was in the best position to act as liaison for us with Hal, he ought to be counterbalanced by someone who had an opposite point of view to his. You might call him the supportive angel and me the critical one—"

"That'd be the Exotic way," said Rourke, dryly.

Nonne turned on him.

"Actually, I find those not from Mara or Kultis often seem to tend to consider me rather atypical as an Exotic," she said. "However, that's a mistake on their part. My point of view represents one rather more common among our people than most of you realize. It's just one non-Exotics don't often see."

"You haven't explained this antagonism of yours," said Rukh, "only confirmed it."

"Very well," said Nonne. She looked back to Hal. "I'd have expected Hal to ask me about this, rather than one of you. But it doesn't matter. I'm not convinced you know what you're doing, Hal. You said essentially, the last time I questioned you about something, that you and Bleys were like master chess players, too skilled to make the wrong move, and only liable to the danger of making the right move either too early or too late."

"That's what I said." Hal nodded.

"Then I have to say I've seen no evidence of that level of competence, on your side at least, Hal. All I've seen is the Dorsai uprooted and brought en masse to fight for a world that doesn't even know they're coming; my own people—"

There was a momentary, almost unnoticeable catch in her voice.

"—stripped of everything they ever earned and accomplished and then abandoned, Earth turned into a walled fortress without being asked for its permission, and its people expected to commit themselves to a possibly-endless war with an enemy that has all the strength, all the wealth, all the matériel and all the advantage—when only a minority of those Earth people ever showed any understanding of the situation with the enemy, or a will to fight him in the first place—"

"You forget," Jason broke in, "how they've been educated, and their opinion changed, since Rukh and our other truth-speakers started telling their own personal stories of how it's been for us all on Harmony and Association. You forget how they've reacted down there, these last few days since news of her nearly being assassinated got out. I hear from our speakers daily. They're all being overwhelmed now with people who want to hear more of what they have to say. We've got a majority of opinion down below in favor of Hal's actions, now, not a minority!"

"Hardly in favor of Hal's actions," said Nonne. "They don't know about his actions. Emotionally, for Rukh and your people and mine, certainly—but that's a fire that can go out as quickly as it's been lit, the minute they find out their own lives and their own world have been thrown into the table stakes. Meanwhile, with all the population and resources of eight other worlds, Bleys goes on growing stronger daily; and I come to this suite now, only to hear Hal tell us he's seriously planning to split his energies even further by adding the Encyclopedia to his responsibilities."

She looked at Hal.

"Besides," she said, "it was none of the rest of you I've been waiting to hear some answers from. It's from Hal. Tell me, then, Hal. How do you justify adding something like the Encyclopedia to everything else you're supposed to be taking care of?"

"That's a question at a good time," said Hal, "because one of the things I was about to tell you was that my work with the Encyclopedia here is going to have to take priority over anything else, in the days and years to come. In other words, the defense of Earth is now set up. I'm going to be leaving it to the rest of you to handle."

Nonne stared at him.

"This is insane!" she said, finally.

"No," said Hal. He found himself feeling suddenly weary. "It's what's necessary. This battle between the Others and ourselves isn't going to be won with weapons at a shield-wall, or even on the face of any of the inhabited worlds. The only place it's ever going to be won is in the hearts and minds of men and women, on all the worlds; and the only source of the means to win that non-physical war lies here, in the potential of the Final Encyclopedia. This is where the meaningful battle is going to be fought, and won or lost; and this is where I'm going to have to do my real work."

Nonne still stared at him.

"Think," he said to her. "What else, or what thing different, could have been done to give us any chance at all before the inevitable growth of the Others to an overwhelming power that could threaten to make us prisoners of their philosophy? The only hope we ever had to resist them, and the worlds they owned, was for this planet and the other ones we still owned to combine their forces at one strongpoint. Because, unlike us, the only way the Others can win is to win utterly. And I explained to you once, I think, that the numbers of Earth's population and its existing physical resources made it the only reasonable choice for a citadel world, a world to garrison against the force that's going to be brought against us. How could we have asked in advance for Earth's permission to do this, making the possibility a matter of public debate for years, at least, without giving Bleys and his people the opportunity to move in while discussion was going on, and defeat us within at the same time as they were marshalling to take us over from without? As it was, Bleys saw the move we've just made, but moved to defend against it too late—the fault I explained to you earlier, Nonne. And so, we've stolen a march on him."

She opened her mouth as if to reply, but he went on without stopping.

"So tell me," he said, "given those imperatives, how could anything else have been done? Simply, from the beginning we've all been called upon to give whatever we had to give. The Dorsai, their strength; you Exotics, your wealth and information; Earth, its resources of people and matériel; and the Friendlies, their unyielding faith in an ultimate victory to hold all the rest of us together. Called upon that way, what could we have done differently? Give me the alternatives."

He paused again. But she had closed her mouth again and now sat silent.

"Your argument," he went on after a moment, more gently, "isn't with me, Nonne. It's with the forces of history—the movements of people that cause further movements; and so on, and on, until we finally have a situation like this that can only be dealt with in a single way. The choices have all now been either raised up and answered, or ignored. This is a final confrontation in the terms of our present moment; but every generation in its own time has had an equivalent confrontation, in its own terms. People have followed me in this, not because of what I say, or who I am, but because this is the only way things seem to have a chance of working out. There's no other path visible. Can you see one? If so, tell me what it is."

He stopped speaking.

She sat for a moment longer; and then when it became clear that he was not going to go on without an answer, she closed her eyes for a minute and sat blindly, tense and upright, in her chair for a long moment. Then she opened her eyes.

"You're right," she said. Her voice was brittle. "I've got no alternatives to offer. Go on, then—there's nothing more I can say, at this time."

"Thank you," said Hal in the following silence. He looked back around the gathering. "All right, we've already used most of our time before I'm to say my piece and introduce Rukh. I take it you understand the process by which the Dorsai are to be resettled here on Earth, with the help of the financial resources of the Encyclopedia and what we've been given by the Exotics? If not—if you want details—will you ask Rourke for them?"

He looked over at Rourke, who nodded at them all.

"We've no intention of announcing ourselves as coming here to be a defense force for Earth," Rourke said. "Our activity in that regard is only the subject of a private contract between our people and the Final Encyclopedia. We'll only fight for Earth if asked by the people of Earth, themselves; and with the Final Encyclopedia's permission, of course, which we take it won't be refused. So we'll wait until Earth asks us for help—if indeed that's what they want. All Rukh is going to say about us in her speech now—and she'll be the one to explain to Earth why we're here—is that we're refugees from the expansionism of the Others; and that the Exotics sacrificed all they owned to make sure we'd be refugees who'd be able to pay their own way and not be a burden on Earth—"

He broke off. The door annunciator had chimed.

"Forgive me, Hal," said the voice of Jeamus. "I've got some urgent messages for you."

"Bring them in," said Hal. "Go on, Rourke."

"That's all, actually," answered Rourke.

Hal turned back to the others.

"As I think I've said, I'm going to give the barest minimum of speeches," he said. Jeamus had entered and was circling the room to come up quietly at his shoulder. "I'll simply confirm the fact that Tam has given me a chance to take over the Directorship from him and I've agreed—thank you, Jeamus—"

Jeamus had slipped him a sealed envelope and a folded sheet of the single-molecule material used for hard copies in the Encyclopedia.

"The envelope's personal to you, brought by hand from the Dorsai," Jeamus whispered in his ear. "It's from an Amanda Morgan. The message is a picture-copy of a public letter Bleys had published on New Earth less than a standard day ago. It's even got his name signed to it. The Exotic Embassy on New Earth got hold of and sent it here by the new communication system. They also message they think that same letter's also being issued on those other worlds the Others control."

"Thanks," said Hal.

He slipped the letter from Amanda into his jacket's inner pocket and opened the folded sheet on his knee to read the message.

"Sorry again to bother you all," said Jeamus; and slipped out.

Chapter

> > **66** < <

As *the door* closed behind Jeamus, Hal was glancing over the sheet on his knee.

"I'll read this to all of you," he said. "It's a dispatch from an Exotic Embassy, which is still functioning in the city of Cathay on New Earth. Jeamus just got it over the new phase-communications system. It's a copy of a letter to the New Earth people published by Bleys, and, the Embassy thinks, to the peoples of the other worlds under Other control.

" *'To all who believe in the future for ourselves and our children:*

" *'I have been reluctant to speak out, since it has always been my firm belief that those like myself exist only to answer questions—once they have been asked, and if they are asked.*

" *'However, I have just now received information, from people fleeing Old Earth, which alarms me. It speaks, I think, of a danger to all those of good intent; and particularly to such of us on the new worlds. For some hundreds of years now, the power-center worlds of the Dorsai, with their lust for warlike aggression, the Exotics, with their avarice and cunning, and those the Friendly people have so aptly named the Forgotten of God—these, among the otherwise great people of the fourteen worlds, have striven to control and plunder the peaceful and law-abiding Cultures among us.*

" *'For some hundreds of years we have been aware that a loose conspiracy existed among these three groups; who have ended by arrogating the title of Splinter Cultures almost exclusively to themselves, when by rights it applies equally, as we all know, to hundreds of useful, productive, and unpredatory communities among the human race. We among you who have striven quietly to turn our talents to the good of all, we whom some call the Others but whom those of us who qualify for that name think of only as an association of like minds, thrown together by a common use of talents, have been particularly aware of this conspiracy over the past three hundred years. But we have not seen it as a threat to the race as a whole until this moment.*

" *'Now, however, we have learned of an unholy alliance, which threatens each one of us with eventual and literal slavery under the domination of that institution orbiting Earth under the name of the Final Encyclopedia. I and my friends have long known that the Final Encyclopedia was conceived for only one purpose, to which it has been devoted ever since its inception. That pur-*

pose has been the development of unimaginable and unnatural means of controlling the hearts and minds of normal people. In fact, its construction was initially financed by the Exotics for that purpose; as those who care to investigate the writings of Mark Torre, its first Director, will find.

" 'That aim, pursued in secrecy and isolation which required even that the Encyclopedia be placed in orbit above the surface of Earth, has been furthered by the Encyclopedia's practice of picking the brains of the best minds in each generation; by inviting them, ostensibly as visiting scholars, to visit that institution.

" 'Also, it has continued to be financed by the Exotics, who, records will show, have also had a hand in financing the Dorsai, who were from the first developed with the aim of becoming a military arm that could be used to police all other, subject worlds.

" 'Those conspirators have now been joined in their unholy work by the people of Old Earth themselves—a people whose early, bloody attempts to keep all the newly-settled worlds subject to themselves were only frustrated by the courageous resistance of the peoples on all those Younger Worlds. But it took a hundred years of continuous fighting, as you all know from the history books you studied as children.

" 'Now the people of Old Earth, under the leadership of the Final Encyclopedia, have finally thrown off all pretense of innocent purpose. They have withdrawn the unbelievable wealth accumulated by the Exotic Worlds by trade and intrigue from such people as ourselves, moving it to their treasury on Earth. They have also, openly, in one mass movement, evacuated the Dorsai from their world and brought them to Earth; to begin building the army that is intended to conquer our new worlds, one by one, and leave us enslaved forever under the steel rule of martial authority. And they have begun to ready for action those awesome weapons the Encyclopedia itself has been developing over three centuries.

" 'They are ready to attack us—we who have been so completely without suspicion of their arrogant intentions. We stand now, essentially unarmed, unprepared, facing the imminent threat of an inhuman and immoral attempt to enslave or destroy us. We will now begin to hear thrown at us, in grim earnest, the saying that has been quietly circulated among the worlds for centuries, in order to destroy our will to resist—the phrase that not even the massed armies of all the rest of mankind can defeat the Dorsai, if the Dorsai choose to confront those armies.

" 'But do not believe this—' "

Rourke snorted.

"He can say that again, right here and now," he said in an undertone, unfortunately a little too loudly not to interrupt Hal's reading, "and keep on repeating it until it penetrates a few thick skulls down on Old Earth!"

His eye caught Hal's.

"Sorry. It's just that we're all braced to hear a loud group down there, saying, *'but what do we need to do anything for? We've got the Dorsai; and they like to fight.'* "

He coughed.

"Sorry, again. Go on, Hal."

" *'. . . Do not believe this,'* " Hal continued, " *'It was never true, only a statement circulated by the Exotics and the Dorsai for their own advantage. As for massed armies, as you all know, we have none—'* "

"Not true," commented Amid. "Sorry. My turn to apologize, Hal. Go on."

" *'. . . we have none. But we can raise them. We can raise armies in numbers and strengths never dreamed of by the population of Old Earth. We are not the impoverished, young peoples that Old Earth, with Dow deCastries, tried to dominate unsuccessfully in the first century of our colonization. Now, on all the worlds our united numbers add up to nearly five billion. What can be done against the courage and resistance of such a people, even by the four million trained and battle-hardened warriors that Old Earth has just imported from the Dorsai—'* "

Rourke snorted again, as the number was mentioned, but this time contained himself and said nothing.

" *'. . . United, we of the Younger Worlds are invincible. We will arm, we will go to meet our enemy—and this time, with the help of God, we will crush this decadent, proud planet that has threatened us too long; and, to the extent it is necessary, we will so deal with the people of Old Earth as to make sure that such an attempt by them never again occurs to threaten our lives, our homes, and the lives and homes of those who come after us.*

" *'In this effort, I and my friends stand ready to do anything that will help. It has always been our nature never to seek the limelight; but in the shadow of this emergency I have personally asked all whom you call the Others, and they have agreed with me, to make themselves known to you, to make themselves available for any work or duty in which they can be useful in turning back this inconceivable threat.*

" *'The unholy peoples of Old Earth say they will come against us. Let them come, then, if they are that foolish. Let us lay this demon once and for all. How little they suspect it will be the beginning of the end, for them!*

" *'. . . Signed, Bleys Ahrens.'* No title, just the signature."

Hal handed the message over to Rukh, who was closest to him. She scanned it and passed it on around the circle of listeners.

"That business of four million battle-ready veterans!" Rourke said. "I tell you, I can see trouble coming from Earth about that. We'll have hell's own job to make them understand that we brought in families—families! If there's six hundred thousand battle-age and combat-fit adults among them, we're lucky; and at least two-thirds of those are going to have to be sleeping and eating, not to mention out sick or disabled, at any given time. Not to mention where the replacements are going to come from when we start taking losses. And they expect us to guard a perimeter considerably larger in area than the planet Earth, itself? Wait'll they discover they're going to end by putting more of their own people than our whole population into the firing line to defend an area that size."

"That's something the future'll have to take care of," said Hal. "Once they realize what's needed to survive, there'll be those who'll be ready to help. But my hope is that we can find another way to win, here in the Encyclopedia, itself, than by trying to match, one for one, the literally millions of soldiers he'll need to, and can, raise in order to put any iris we open in the shield-wall instantly under an attack that won't be halted until we close it again. But never mind that, too, for now. If you've all had a look at that message sheet—"

They had. Even Nonne had studied it.

"So there's another instance of what you meant by Bleys possibly making the mistake of moving too soon or too late!" Jason burst out. "He waited too long to come out with this letter, didn't he? If he'd brought it out even a month ago—certainly if he'd come out with the same sort of talk about a coalition against us, even if he hadn't been able to cite the Dorsai moving to Earth—he could have sown a lot of doubt down below and panicked a lot more of Earth's people into taking hard positions, that could have shut out the Dorsai before they could get here—"

He broke off. His eyes were bright on Hal.

"And that's why you were working so hard to set up the idea that the Dorsai were going to move to one of the Exotic Worlds!"

"It's true," said Rukh, "that this letter's going to be all it takes to solidify public opinion on Old Earth against the Others. It's what was really needed to make them realize down there what the Others are after. We probably could have managed without it; but now that it's here, it couldn't have come at a better time. Hal, I think I ought to read it as part of my speech."

"Yes," said Hal.

"He must have jumped the gun when he heard we were coming in here—" Rourke broke off, thoughtfully. "No, he wouldn't have had time to have found that out and still get this published so that we'd have a copy, now."

"Yes, he would," said Amid. "One way on Mara and Kultis we used to get information between the worlds in a hurry, faster than anyone thought it could be done, was to set up a chain of spaceships holding position between any two worlds at an easy single phase-shift apart. When there was a message to be sent, a ship would lift off one world with it, make one jump to rendezvous with the first ship in line, and pass the message on to it. The second ship'd make one jump and pass it on to a third jump—and so on. There'd be little search-to-contact time in the target area of each jump, since each one was so short; and the necessary calculation would already have been made by the ship ready to go; and because each pilot made only one jump, there'd be no problem with the psychic effects of enduring too many phase-shifts close together. The only requirement of the system was that you needed to be able to afford to tie up a lot of ships, standing idle in your message line and waiting. We could, then. Bleys can afford it, now."

"Hmm," said Rourke.

"Yes," said Amid, looking at him, "I understand Donal Graeme also came up with the same system, independently, in his later years after he had the ships to do it. At any rate, if Bleys had been keeping a watch like that on all worlds potentially hostile to him, he could've known within twenty-four hours, standard, when the first of the Dorsai transports lifted; and in the same amount of time when the first of them began to appear above Earth. And he'd have already known that none were appearing above Mara or Kultis."

"So he panicked and moved too soon," Jason said. "I thought that letter didn't sound like him."

"I wouldn't call it panic, with someone like Bleys," Hal said. "His plan would have been to beat the news of the Dorsai moving to Old Earth with his own announcement. He'll have gained that—it's just that he's lost in another area—and if he'd decided Old Earth was lost for now, in any case, he may have simply written off the effect his letter would have there—though he couldn't have expected Old Earth's people to read it so soon."

He paused.

"As for sounding like him," Hal went on, "there are sides to him that none of the worlds have seen, yet."

He had captured their attention. He went on.

"I've got one more thing to tell you," he said. "Bleys has also sent a message asking me to meet him secretly; and I told him I'd do it—inside the shield-wall. I've been interested in why he'd want to talk just now. This—"

He pointed toward the message sheet, which now lay on a table beside Rourke's chair.

"—tells me what he's after. He'll need to sound out the effect of the successful move of the Dorsai to Earth on my thinking. As soon as Jeamus lets me know he's here, I'll be going to meet him; and that could be at any time now."

"But if he had to get the message, then leave from New Earth—" Rourke interrupted himself and sat musing.

"He may not have been on New Earth," said Amid. "Even if he was, with Sirius at under nine light-years of distance from here, he could make the trip by crowding on the phase-shifts and using the old crutch of drugs, in two standard days."

"How would he know we knew about it yet?" demanded Rukh.

"I don't think there's much doubt he knows we have some newer, faster means of communicating," said Amid. "He just doesn't know how we do it, yet."

"It's almost time for us to talk," Rukh interrupted. "Hal, have you got your speech ready?"

"I don't have it written out, but I know what I want to say," Hal answered, as the others began to move their chairs and floats back out of picture range. He pressed a stud on the arm of his chair.

"Jeamus," he said. "Any time the transmission crew's ready, we'll get going on those speeches."

"We've been waiting outside in the corridor," Jeamus' voice answered from the door annunciator. "We'll come in now, then?"

"Come ahead," said Hal.

The technical crew entered.

"Are you going to wake up Ajela?" Rukh asked Hal. "If she's going to introduce you in a minute or two, she'll need a few seconds to come to."

"I suppose so," said Hal, reluctantly.

He got up, went over to Ajela and stroked her forehead. She slumbered on. He shook her shoulder gently. For a moment it seemed she would not respond even to that; but then her eyes opened suddenly and brightly.

"I haven't been sleeping," she said.

Her eyelids fluttered closed and she went back to breathing deeply.

"Jeamus can introduce me," said Hal. He picked up Ajela, carried her into one of the two bedrooms of his suite and laid her on the bed. She woke as he put her down.

"I'm not sleeping, I tell you!" she said crossly.

"Good," said Hal. "Just keep it up."

"I will!" She closed her eyes firmly, turned on her side and dropped off again.

Hal went out, closing the bedroom door behind him. He sat back down in his chair, and looked at the technical crew. "You alone first, Jeamus," said one of them, holding up one finger. "Ready . . . go!"

The small lights went on in the receptors aimed at Jeamus, who was standing beside Hal's chair.

"My name is Jeamus Walters," Jeamus said. "I'm Director of Theoretical Engineering at the Final Encyclopedia; and I'm honored today to introduce the new Director of the Encyclopedia, about whom you'll be reading in the information releases just authorized by the Encyclopedia.

"May I present to you, peoples of Earth, the Director of the Final Encyclopedia. Hal Mayne!"

The lights winked out. Jeamus stood back. The lights went on again. Hal looked into their small brilliant eyes, shining now on him.

"What I have to say today is going to be very brief," he said, "since we're particularly busy here at the moment at the Final Encyclopedia. There'll be details on what's keeping us occupied in the releases Jeamus Walters mentioned; and I believe Rukh Tamani, who'll be speaking to you in a moment, may also have something to say about it.

"I've been honored by being chosen by Tam Olyn, Director of the Encyclopedia for over eighty years, to follow him in that post. As you all know, the only Director before Tam Olyn was Mark Torre; the man who conceived of, planned and supervised the building of this great work from its earliest form, on the ground at the city of St. Louis in the northwestern quadrisphere of this world.

"Mark Torre's aim, as you know, was to create a tool for research into the frontiers of the human mind itself, by providing a storage place for all known information on everything that mind has produced or recognized since the dawn of intellectual consciousness. It was his belief and his hope that this storehouse of human knowledge and creativity would provide materials and, eventually, a means of exploring what has always been unknown and unseeable—in the same way that none of us, unaided, can see the back of his or her own head.

"To that search, Tam Olyn, like Mark Torre before him, dedicated himself. To that same faith that Mark Torre had shown, he adhered through his long tenure of duty here.

"I can make no stronger statement to you, today, than to say that I share the same faith and intent, the same dedication. But, more fortunate than the two men who dedicated their lives to the search before me, I may possess something in addition. I have, I believe, some reason to hope that the long years of work here have brought us close to our goal—that we are very near, at last now, to stepping over the threshold of that universe of the unknown which Mark Torre dreamed of entering and reaping the rewards of exploring—that inner exploration of the human race we have never ceased to yearn toward; unconsciously to begin with, but later consciously, from the beginning of time.

"When the moment comes that this threshold is crossed, the lives of none of us will ever be the same again. We stand at perhaps the greatest moment in the known history of humanity; and I, for one, have no doubt whatsoever that what we have sought for over millennia, we will find; not in centuries or decades from now, but within our lifetimes and possibly even in a time so close that if I could tell you certainly, as I now speak, how long it would be, the nearness of it would seem inconceivable to us all.

"But in any case, I give you my promise that while I am Director of the Final Encyclopedia, I will not allow work toward that future to be slowed or halted, by anything. There is no greater pledge I can offer you than that, and I offer it now, with all the strength that is in me.

"Having said this about myself and the Directory, I will now turn from that subject to introduce someone who, I think, means so much to so many of us, that this, too, would have seemed inconceivable a short year ago.

"Peoples of Earth, it's my pleasure and honor to introduce Rukh Tamani."

The lights went out before Hal and on before Rukh. He got to his feet and went quickly to stand beside the door to his suite, so that he would be easily and silently reachable from the corridor, during her talk. Standing with his shoulder blades against the wall, he found himself captured immediately by what she was saying. Whenever Rukh spoke in this fashion, everyone within hearing was caught and held; and he was no exception.

"I am sorry to have caused you grief," were her first words to the world below.

"I have been told that many of you believed me dead or at least badly hurt in recent days; and because you believed this you grieved. But you should not grieve for me, ever.

"Grieve instead for those things more important under Heaven. For any who may have shared their lives with you and now suffer or lack. For your angers which wound, your indifference which hurts or kills, more than any outright anger or cruelty does.

"Grieve that you live in yourself, walled and apart from your fellow women and men. Grieve for your failures in courage, in faith, in kindness to all.

"But, grieving, know that it is not necessary to grieve, for you need not have done or been that which causes you to grieve.

". . . For there is a great meaning to life, which each of you controls utterly for yourself; and which no one else can bar you from without your consent. . . ."

There was a touch on his shoulder.

"Hal—"

It was Jeamus, whispering beside him. Hal followed him out into the corridor and down it a little ways, away from the doorway they had just left.

"He's here," said Jeamus. "Standing off outside the shield-wall above us in a spacecraft. I didn't talk to him. Someone from his ship called in to tell me they were there and that he'd meet you as soon as you were ready."

Hal nodded. He had felt this moment coming close in time. All the instincts of his nature, all the calculations of intuitive logic had made it sure that he would not hear the end of what Rukh was now saying.

Jeamus was still talking.

". . . I told whoever it was I was speaking to that you'd said you'd be right along the moment you heard he was here. I also told him how Bleys was to find the iris in the shield-wall and how he should enter it and act after he was inside—I particularly warned him about the danger of touching the walls. The iris is open now, and we've run a floor the full length of it. You'll want someone to drive you to the meeting, won't you?"

"No," said Hal; and then changed his mind. "I'd like Simon Graeme to drive me. Would you find him?"

"Yes," said Jeamus. "Your craft's ready, with suits in it and everything else you need, in Number Three bay. Why don't you go directly there; and I'll have Simon along to you in a minute. I explained to the man I was talking to how he should park whatever small transportation he has well clear of the iris opening at their end; and how Bleys should enter it. . . ."

"Good," said Hal. "It sounds as if everything's set and fine. You get Simon for me. I'll go ahead."

The craft Jeamus had ready was a ten-passenger Space and Atmosphere vehicle. Hal had barely entered it and sat down in the Second Pilot's seat up front when Simon and Jeamus entered the craft.

Simon sat down at the controls without a word.

"Jeamus told you about this?" Hal asked him.

"On the way here." Simon nodded. He powered up and looked around at Jeamus; but Jeamus was still delaying his exit from the craft.

"You're sure you understand everything?" he asked Hal.

"Go over it again, if you like," said Hal, patiently.

"All right," said Jeamus, relieved. "The shield-wall is actually two walls—two phase-shift interfaces set at varying widths apart so there'll be room for protective personnel when we open irises under the attack conditions to let ships in or out. When we open an iris, we'll essentially make a tunnel varying in width up to anything we want and anywhere from fifty meters to several kilometers in length, depending on how far apart we want to set the two walls at that point—"

"Make it brief, if you can, Jeamus," said Hal.

"I will. I am. What I want to be sure you understand are conditions at the iris openings and inside that tunnel. The openings in this case will each have a non-physical, pressure airseal. You know those from experience. It'll be like any airseal; you just push your way through it. Inside, we'll have been able to build up a breathable atmosphere, not only for your sake and Bleys', but so we can supersaturate that atmosphere with moisture to reduce the chance of static charges to either one of you from the walls. A static link between you and the wall could be as bad as touching the wall of the tunnel physically. Stay in the middle of the tunnel at all times. Now the supersaturation will cause a lot of heavy mist. Follow the line of where the mist is thinnest, accordingly, and you'll be sure you're in the tunnel's center at all times. We've passed the same information to Bleys. We've also floated in that floor I mentioned for the two of you to walk on. It'll be gravity-charged."

"Good," said Hal. "Thank you, Jeamus. Simon, we'll go as soon as Jeamus closes the door—"

"You must—*must*—remember!" said Jeamus, backing to the door of the craft. "Any contact with the tunnel wall will be exactly like a contact with the shield-wall itself. You'll be instantly translated to universal position, with no hope of reassembly."

"I understand. Thanks, Jeamus. Thank you."

Jeamus stepped out of the vehicle and closed the door behind him. Simon lifted the craft and they floated out the bay entrance, which opened before them.

Chapter

> > **67** < <

As *they slid* through the pressure airseal of the entrance, Hal was already back up on his feet and putting on one of the vacuum suits. It turned out to be the one provided for Simon and therefore too small for Hal. He took it off and put on the other suit instead. Once donned, it was hardly noticeable, like transparent coveralls of thin material, except for the heavy, dark power belt around the waist. He left the rigid, but equally-transparent, bell of the helmet thrown back.

"There it is," said Simon as Hal came back to the front of the craft.

Hal looked in the front screen and saw what looked like a bright, opaque, circular hole in the grayness, perhaps ten meters in diameter. A thick, dark line cut a chord across its bottom curve—the end of the floor provided.

"Nicely illuminated," he said. In fact, the innumerable moisture droplets of the mist filling the tunnel opening seemed to cause its interior to glow as they individually reflected the lighting built into the upper and lower surfaces of the panel that was the floor.

"My directions from Jeamus were to park a good fifty meters off," said Simon. "I can run out a landing ramp for you right up to within half a meter of the iris opening—or would you rather use your power belt and jump?"

"I'll jump," said Hal. "If Jeamus wants you fifty meters off, poking a ramp in close to it might not be the brightest idea."

"There's no problem about my holding the craft steady," said Simon.

"I know you can do it," said Hal. "Still, let's play the odds. If I jump, I'll only have to be thinking about myself."

Simon parked. Hal closed his helmet and went out through the double doors of the vehicle, now on airlock cycle, and stepped toward the entrance to the iris, correcting his course as he approached with small bursts from the power belt.

At the doorway itself there was a little tension to be felt, like that of breaking through an invisible, and thin but tough membrane, as he penetrated the pressure airseal and let himself down, feet first on the mist-hidden floor. In fact, it was easy to imagine that he could feel the coolness of the white fog around him, even through the impermeable fabric of the vacuum suit. The suspended water droplets hid not only the walls of the tunnel and the floor beneath his feet, but floated about him in clouds of varying thickness.

He threw back his helmet and breathed in the moisture-laden atmosphere. It felt heavy as water itself in his lungs; and he knew that the feeling was not simply imagination, as the supersaturation under these abnormal conditions would be well above what Earth surface-pressure air could normally be induced to carry in the way of moisture.

He went forward.

After a hundred or so steps, he caught sight of a bobbing darkness through the mist ahead, which swiftly became the shape of a tall man, also suited, also with helmet thrown back, coming toward him.

Three more steps brought them face-to-face and they stopped. Through the transparency of Bleys' vacuum suit, he could see the other man was wearing his customary narrow tousers and jacket—but still, there seemed to be a difference about him.

For a moment the difference eluded Hal, and then he identified it. The tall man was as slim as ever, but in the vacuum suit he gave the appearance of being bulkier and more physical. His shoulders had always been as wide as Hal's but now they seemed heavier. His face was unchanged; but his body seemed more heavy-boned and powerful.

It was only a subjective alteration in appearance, but oddly important, here and now. And yet it was not as if the Other had put on weight. Eerily, it was as if he and Hal had grown more alike physically. Their eyes met. Bleys spoke, and his voice went out and was lost against the walls of the tunnel, its crispness blurred by the heavy air and the mist.

"Well," said Bleys, "you've got your Dorsai and everything you want from the Exotics locked up, here. I take it, then, you're determined to go through with this?"

"I told you," said Hal, "there was never any other way."

Bleys nodded, a trifle wearily.

"So now the gloves come off," he said.

"Yes," answered Hal. "Sooner or later they had to, I being what I am and you being what you are."

"And what are you?" Bleys smiled.

"You don't know, of course," said Hal.

"No," said Bleys. "I've known for some time you're not just a boy whose tutors I watched die on a certain occasion. How much more, I still don't know. But it'd be petty-minded of me to hide the fact that I've been astonished by the quality of your opposition to me. You're too intelligent to move worlds like this just for revenge on me because of your tutors' deaths. What you've done and are doing is too big for any personal cause. Tell me—what drives you to oppose me like this?"

"What drives me?" Hal found himself smiling a little sadly—almost a Bleys type of smile. "A million years of history and prehistory drive me— as they drive you. To be more specific, the last thousand years of history drive me. There's no other way for you and I to be, but opponents. But if it's any consolation to you, I've also been surprised by the quality of your opposition."

"You?" Bleys' face could not bring itself to express incredulity. "Why should you be surprised?"

"Because," said Hal, "I'm more than you could imagine—just as you've turned out to be something I couldn't imagine. But then when I was imagining this present time we live in I had no real appreciation of the true value of faith. It's something that goes far beyond blind worship. It's a type of understanding in those who've paid the price to win it. As you, yourself, know."

Bleys was watching him intently.

"As I know?"

"Yes," said Hal, "as you, of all people, know."

Bleys shook his head.

"I should have dealt with you when you were much younger," he said, almost to himself.

"You tried," said Hal. "You couldn't."

"I did?" said Bleys. "I see. You're using faith, again, to reach that conclusion?"

"Not for that. No, only observation and fact." Hal was still watching Bleys as closely as Bleys was watching him. "Primarily, the fact that I'm who I am, and know what I can do."

"You're mistaken if you think I couldn't have eliminated a sixteen-year-old boy if I'd wanted to."

"No, I'm not mistaken," Hal said. "As I say, you tried. But I wasn't a boy, even then when I thought I was. I was an experienced adult, who had reasons for staying alive. I told you I've learned faith, even if it took me three lives to do the learning. That's why I know I'm going to win, now. Just as I know my winning means your destruction, because you won't have it any other way."

"You seem to think you know a great deal about me." The smile was back on Bleys' face. It was a smile that hid all thoughts behind it.

"I do. I came to understand you better by learning to understand myself—though understanding myself was a job I started long before you came along." Hal paused for a fraction of a second as a surgeon might pause before the first cut of the scalpel. "If you'd been only what I thought you were the first time I saw you, the contest between us would already be over. More than that, I'd have found some way by this time to bring you to the side of things as they must be for the race to survive."

Bleys' smile widened. Ignoring it, Hal went on.

"But since that day at the Estate," he said, "I've learned about myself, as well as more about you, and I know I'll never be able to bring you to see what I see until you, yourself, choose to make the effort to do so. And without that effort, we're matched too evenly, you and I, by the forces of history, for any compromise to work."

"I'm not sure I understand you," said Bleys, "and that's unusual enough to be interesting."

"You don't understand me because I'm talking of things outside your experience," Hal said. "I came to talk to you here—as I'll always be willing to come to talk to you—because I've got to hang on to the hope you might be brought to consider things beyond the scope of what you look at now; and change your mind."

"You talk," said Bleys, now openly amused, "like a grandfather talking to a grandson."

"I don't mean to," said Hal. "But the hard fact is you've had only one lifetime from which to draw your conclusions. I've had three. It took me that long to become human; and because I've finally made it, I can see how you, yourself, fall short of being the full human being the race has to produce to survive the dangers it can't even imagine yet. Like it or not, that experience is there, and a difference between us."

"I told you you were an Other," said Bleys.

"Not exactly," said Hal. "If you remember, you left me to infer it. But I'm splitting hairs. In a sense you were right. In one sense I am an Other, being a blend of all that's new as well as all that's old in the race. But I'm not the kind of Other who's Everyman. Your kind, if it survives, are at best going to be a transient form of human. Mine, if it does, will be immortal."

"I'm sorry," said Bleys, gracefully, "I don't have a kind. I'm my own unique mixture."

"As are we all," said Hal. "But what matters is that on top of your own talents, you were raised on Association by a family that was pure Friendly, and it's that which dominates in you."

Bleys looked at him as if from an impossible distance.

"Where did you find records that told you that?"

"I know," said Hal, "that the official records of your birth and movements all show what your brother fixed them to say."

"Then what makes you say something like this?"

"The correct knowledge," said Hal. "An absolute knowledge that comes from joining together bits and pieces of general records that hadn't been tampered with—because there was no reason to tamper with them—at the Final Encyclopedia. I put them together only a year ago, and then made deductions from them using something I taught myself during my first trial of life. It's called intuitive logic."

Bleys frowned slightly. Then his frown cleared.

"Ah," he said; and was silent for a long moment, looking a little aside from Hal. When he spoke again, his voice was thoughtful and remote. "I believe what you're talking about may be what I've been calling interval thinking."

"The name hardly matters," said Hal.

"Of course not. So," Bleys' gaze came back to him, openly, "there's more to learn about you than I'd imagined. But tell me, why place so much emphasis on the fact that part of what I am by inheritance and upbringing may be Friendly?"

"For one reason, because it explains your ability of charisma, as well as that of those Others who have it to some extent or another," said Hal. "But I'd rather you called yourself Faith-holder than Friendly. Because, more than anyone on all the worlds suspects, it's a form of Faith-holding that rules you. You never were the bored crossbreed whose only concern was being comfortable during his own brief years of life. That was a facade, a false exterior set up in the first place to protect you from your older half-brother, Dahno—who would have been deathly afraid of you if he'd suspected you had a purpose of your own."

"He would, indeed," murmured Bleys. "Not that I'm agreeing with these fancies and good-nights of yours, of course."

"Your agreement isn't necessary," said Hal. "As I was saying, you used it first to protect yourself against Dahno, then to reassure the rest of the Others that you weren't just using them for your own private purposes. Finally, you're using it still to blind the peoples of the worlds you control to that personal goal that draws you now more strongly than ever. You're a Faith-holder, twisted to the worship of a false god—the same god under a different mask that Walter Blunt worshiped back in the twenty-first century. Your god is stasis. You want to enshrine the race as it is, make it stop and go no further. It's the end you've worked toward from the time you were old enough to conceive it."

"And if all this should be true," Bleys smiled again. "The end is still the end. It remains inevitable. You can think all this about me, but it isn't going to make any difference."

"Again, you, of all people, know that's not so," answered Hal. "The fact I understand this is going to make all the difference between us. You took over the relatively-harmless organization of the Others while letting them think that the power they gained was all their own doing. But now you'll understand that I'm aware it was mainly accomplished by converting to your own followers the people who were already in charge. Which you did largely through the use of Others who had a large Friendly component in their background, people with their own natural, culturally-developed, charismatic gift to some degree, who used it under your own personal spell and command, and Dahno's. Meanwhile, covered by the appearance of working for the Others, you've begun to spread your own personal faith in the inevitably-necessary cleansing of the race, followed by a freezing of it into an immobility of changelessness." Hal stopped, to give Bleys a chance to respond. But the Other man said nothing. "Unlike your servants and the Others who've been your dupes," Hal went on, "you're able to see the possibility of a final death resulting from that state of stasis, if you achieve it. But under the influence of the dark part of the racial unconsciousness whose laboratory experiment and chess piece you are—as I also am, on the other side—you see growth in the race as the source of all human evils, and you're willing to kill the patient, if necessary, to kill the cancer."

He stopped. This time there was a difference to the silence which succeeded his words and lay between the two of them.

"You realize," said Bleys at last, softly, "that now I have no choice at all but to destroy you?"

"You can't afford to destroy me," said Hal, "even if you could. Just as I can't afford to destroy you. This battle is now being fought for the adherence of the minds of all our fellow humans. What I have to do, to make the race understand which way they must go, is prove you wrong; and I need you alive for that. You have to prove me wrong if you want to win, and you need me alive for that. Force alone won't solve anything for either of us, in the long run. You know that as well as I do."

"But it will help." Bleys smiled. "Because you're right. I have to win. I will win. There's got to be an end to this madness you call growth but which is actually only expansion further and further into the perils of the physical universe until the lines that supply our lives will finally be snapped of their own weight. Only by putting it aside, can we start the growth within that's both safe and necessary."

"You're wrong," said Hal. "That way lies death. It's a dead-end road that assumes inner growth can only be had at the price of giving up what's made us what we are over that million years I mentioned. Chained and channelled organisms grow stunted and wrong, always. Free ones grow wrong sometimes, but right other times; because the price of life is a continual seeking to grow and explore. Lacking that freedom, all action, physical and mental, circles in on itself and ends up only wearing a deeper and deeper rut in which it goes around and around until it dies."

"No," said Bleys; and his face, his whole body seemed to shrug off Hal's words. "It leads to life for the race. It's the only way that can. There has to be an end to growth out into the physical universe, and a change over to growth within. That's all that can save us. Only by stopping now and turning back, only by stopping this endless attempt to enlarge and develop can we turn inward and find a way to be invulnerable in spite of anything the universe might hold."

"It's you who are wrong," said Bleys; and his face—his whole body—seemed to harden and take on a look of power that Hal had never seen it show before. "But you're self-deluded. Besotted with love for the shiny bauble of adventure and discovery. Out there—"

He stabbed one long finger back into the gray mist that obscured his end of the tunnel, at the upper side of the shield-wall.

"—out there are all things that can be. How can it be otherwise? And among all things have to be all things that must be unconquerable by us. How can it be otherwise? All they that take the sword shall perish by the sword—and this is a sword you keep reaching for, this so-called spirit of exploration and adventure—this leaping out into the physical universe. Is the spirit of mankind nothing more than a questing hound that always has to keep finding a new rabbit to run after? How many other races, in this infinity, in this eternity, do you think haven't already followed that glittering path? And how many of those do you suppose have become master of the universe, which is the only alternate ending to going down?"

His eyes burned on Hal's.

"What will be—" he went on, "what I'll see done will be a final reversal to that process. What you'll try to do to stop it is going to make no difference in that. You've made a fortress out of Old Earth. It makes no difference. What human minds can do by way of science and technology other human minds can undo. We'll find a way eventually through that shield-wall of yours. We'll retake Earth, and cleanse it of all those who'd continue this mad, sick, outward plunge of humankind. Then it'll be reseeded with those who see our race's way as it should be."

"And the Younger Worlds?" Hal said. "What about all the other settled planets? Have you forgotten them?"

"No," said Bleys. "They'll die. No one will kill them. But, little by little, with the outward-seeking sickness cured, and the attention of Earth, of real Earth, on itself as it should be—these others will wither and their populations dwindle. In the long run, they'll be empty worlds again; and humanity'll be back where it began, where it belongs and where it'll stay, on its own world. And here—as fate wills it—it'll learn how to love properly and exist to the natural end of its days—or die."

He stopped speaking. The force that had powered his voice fell away into silence. Hal stood, looking at him, with nothing to say. After a long moment, Bleys spoke again, quietly.

"Words are no use between us two, are they?" he said, at last. "I'm sorry, Hal. Believe what you want, but those who think the way you do can't win. Look how you and your kind have done nothing but lose to me and mine, so far."

"You're wrong," said Hal. "We haven't really contested you until now; and now that we're going to, we're the ones who can't lose."

Bleys reached out his hand and Hal took it. They did not grasp in the ordinary fashion of greeting, but only held for a moment. The Other's flesh and bones felt strange in Hal's hand as if he had taken the hand of a condemned man. Then they both turned and each went off his own way, in opposite directions into the mist.

Chapter

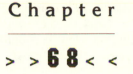

> > **68** < <

His mind was so full of the conversation just past, that he was hardly aware of reaching the end of the tunnel, making the jump into the airlock of the vehicle waiting, and being driven back to the Encyclopedia. Once parked back in the bay again, he thanked Simon absentmindedly and went off toward his own suite, brushing aside the people he encountered along the way who had matters they wanted to talk to him about.

He reached his suite, stepped in, and drew a breath of relief on finding it empty as far as he could see into it. He went through to the spare bedroom, saw Ajela was still asleep in the same position, and left her, going through his own bedroom to the small room beyond—the carrel in which his private work here at the Encyclopedia would be done.

He stepped into the carrel, closed the door behind him and sat down within the four walls that were all screen. He touched a stud on the control panel before him and suddenly, as far as the eye could tell, he hung floating in space—beyond the Earth, beyond the Encyclopedia and beyond the shield-wall.

The unchanging stars looked back at him.

Alone at last, he was free to remember the letter from Amanda; and with that all thought of Bleys and related matters was plucked from his mind. He reached into his inside jacket pocket and brought out the envelope waiting for him there.

For a moment, with the stars around him, he held it unopened. The sight of it had suddenly brought, on the intuitive wings of his mind, an unusual feeling of sorrow and apprehension. The Dorsai-made, thick, slightly grayish paper of the envelope reminded him of the mist in the iris tunnel.

He slipped his thumb under the sealed flap and tore the envelope open. Within it was a sheaf of pages, and the first one was dated five days, absolute, just past.

He read.

May 36, 208 Dorsai/2386 Absolute

My dearest:

I kept avoiding telling you when I'd be coming to Earth in the Exodus, because I had a decision to make. Forgive me.

But it's now made, and I will be standing by it.

We belong to our duties, you and I, for some little time yet. Yours is there, in the Encyclopedia; but mine isn't there with you, much as I'd give anything I have or may have—except you—to be where you are.

At Earth, I could be no help in the things that are going to need to be done, except to provide one more body to the ramparts. My real usefulness now is anywhere but there. At this moment, we're entering a time in which there'll be nothing in the large sense but two things, the citadel and the territory of the enemy outside it. My usefulness is also outside, in that enemy territory.

In the years that will be coming, as important as it'll be to hold the citadel against all attack, it's going to be equally important to make sure those who're now under the will of the Others don't forget what freedom is. The human spirit will never endure chains long, any more than it ever has; and there are going to be spontaneous uprisings against the rule of those like Bleys. And there will be those left on the Dorsai and on the Friendlies who'll hide out in the back country and other areas from which they will be difficult to dislodge; and they'll continue to fight, perhaps indefinitely.

From Earth, you'll be sending out people and supplies to help support groups like these on all the Younger Worlds. You'll also need people already out there who know how such fighting and surviving should be done; and whom you know are going to think the way you do, in terms of what has to be accomplished to prepare for the day when you can come back out of the citadel and take back what's been lost.

If you've thought at all about the needs to come, as I know you must, you've already recognized the need for people to go out now to advise and organize such groups and that the natural choice for such people would be from our ranks on the Dorsai. We faced that necessity ourselves early here, in making our general plans for the Exodus; and a number of us have already volunteered for this work, myself among them.

By the time you get this letter, I'll be between the stars; on my way, or already at, a destination that I've no way at this moment of knowing; and I'll have already begun my work, using contacts provided for me through Friendlies, Exotics and other people generally, who understand what needs to be done to help those who will still want to resist, outside Old Earth. But wherever I am when you read these words, you'll know at that moment, as always, I'll be carrying the thought of you and my love for you like a fireside warmth inside me, to warm me always, wherever I go and whatever I do.

If and when you find yourself in contact with those of us who are out there and can send a message to me, write and let me know that you understand what I've done and why I did it, in spite of all it would have meant to be there with you. I won't need to hear from you to know you understand, but it's going to strengthen me to read that you do, just the same.

And now, let me tell you how I love you. . . .

The page blurred before his eyes. Then it cleared, and he sat reading the letter, page by page, as if the words on them had the power to draw him down into them. At length, he reached the end of it; and sat gazing down at it with the eyes of the stars upon him.

The last five lines above her signature burned themselves into the patterns of his mind and soul.

You know I've loved you, and we've loved each other, longer than others would ever understand. You know as I know that nothing can part us. You know we are always together, no matter where our bodies may happen to be. Reach out at any time and find me. And I will do the same to you.

> All my love,
> Amanda

He reached.

Amanda . . . ?

It was as if one wave spoke to another, a call from the one washing the eastern shore of one continent reaching the one washing the western shore of another, half a world apart, but joined by the ocean to which both waves belonged.

Hal. . . .

Her response returned to him, and they touched across the vast space between them, touched and held. It was not in words that they spoke, but in surges of feeling and knowing.

After a time, they parted; and he felt her withdraw. But the warmth of her, like the fireside warmth she had spoken of early in her letter, stayed with him, strengthening him.

He looked at the stars and down at the control panel under his hands. His fingertips began to move and words lighted themselves into existence against the dark and stars' points before him.

"In morning's ruined chapel, the full knight
Woke from the coffin of his last night's bed. . . ."

The poem drew him into the work, and the work enlarged in him, taking him over at last completely. He grew to be part of it as it grew in him; and gradually, alone with the stars, he left behind all else except the warmth of the link to Amanda, and became fully occupied with what at last held and engrossed him, beyond all other things.